USS IKE

Quansport Ops

USS Hamilton Series
Book 10

Mark Wayne McGinnis

Copyright

Published by Avenstar Productions: info@avenstar.net

USS IKE / Print ISBN: 979-89894619-7-4

To join Mark's mailing list, jump to:

http://eepurl.com/bszM9r

Visit Mark Wayne McGinnis at:

http://www.markwaynemcginnis.com

❀ Created with Vellum

Prologue

Commander Drupal Pilcolm

The vast expanse of space stretched endlessly before Commander Drupal Pilcolm as he stood rigidly on the bridge of the lead Floritineian vessel. His two eyes, one positioned above the other, were sheathed in long folds of bunched flesh that draped downward like thick, velvet curtains. He took in the streaks of light flitting across the inky blackness—cosmic fireworks that never ceased to fill him with a child-like fascination. Despite having traversed the stars for centuries, Pilcolm never lost his sense of wonder at the majesty of the cosmos. This relief mission to aid the drought-stricken colony of Elysium-4 filled him with a profound sense of purpose that transcended being merely neighborly. It was a symbol of solidarity, a shared dream that civilizations could put aside their differences for the greater good of all.

The Hydrate Elysium convoy, cutting through the void, was an awe-inspiring sight. Pilcolm's elongated torso swelled with pride as he surveyed the immense flotilla gliding in formation like a pod of majestic star whales. At its core, were four tanker

1

ships: three gargantuan marine life tanker ships—oblong, ten miles in length, and four miles in width—each carried over 3.492 trillion gallons of precious seawater, as well as a vast array of marine life. And then there was the fourth tanker, twice the size of those that carried marine life—the largest ever constructed by the Floritineian Shipyards—the mega-behemoth, pure-aqua tanker, which carried enough water to satiate most mid-sized planets. Their mirrored hulls shone brilliantly, reflecting the light of a nearby nebula in an ever-shifting spectrum of colors.

The tankers, with their bulging sweeping holds, appeared almost organic with pale blue hues evoking the sleek majesty of the arced whales they were currently transporting. Grappling appendages and umbilical docking arms protruded from their curved midsections, allowing for simultaneous refueling and replenishment while underway. At the heart of each tanker pulsed a massive graviton impeller drive, technology that permitted sustained warp speeds, not possible by most others within the quadrant.

Surrounding the tankers, were thirty-two supply ships, smaller and more angular—they were highly durable vessels. Security for such an invaluable cargo was excessive, with five heavily armed battle cruisers forming the convoy's protective outer perimeter. These behemoths displayed overlapping deflector shielding and phased disruptor banks lining their flanks.

The folds nestling Pilcolm's eyes widened as he scanned for improper formation distances within the convoy. There would be no mistakes, no unexpected mishaps with this mission. This was to be his final and most critical commission before retirement. After six decades spent charting the vast cosmic wilderness, he looked forward to trading the thrill of deep space hauling for the peaceful embrace of his beloved mate, Myyra, on their homeworld.

Suddenly, a series of urgent tones from the communications console shattered Pilcolm's reverie. He swiveled toward the young Ensign manning the station, dread gripping him as he noticed the panic flickering across the fresh-faced officer's eyes. Ensign Islup was newly assigned to the bridgecrew, his youthful features still bearing the fresh glow of the Academy's training simulators.

"Captain!" The Ensign's voice trembled, underscoring his inexperience. "I've been attempting communications with an unidentified armada approaching fast... too fast."

Pilcolm studied the tactical display, his trio of hearts seeming to still as the full scope of the approaching threat emerged from the void. An armada of alien vessels in tight offensive formation was closing rapidly, their intent unmistakable. His analytical mind rapidly assessed the telemetry data being fed to the display—massive tonnages, angular weapon silhouettes, and propulsion drives.

"Hail them again! Open a wide-spectrum channel," Pilcolm ordered, his deep bass voice booming with authority despite the icy tendrils of fear tightening his voice. "Instruct that armada to alter its approach vector immediately."

Islup's fingers flew across the comms station controls, eyes darting between flickering displays. Static crackled through the bridge speakers as he cycled frequencies, desperate to make contact. Sweat beaded his brow, jaw clenched against the ominous silence that met each attempt at hailing. An eternity seemed to pass in those fleeting seconds, the void response more deafening than any roar of battle. Pilcolm's breath caught in his throat. He had a sinking realization that something terrible, unthinkable even moments before, was happening.

"Still not responding, Commander," the young officer hissed, his words laced with barely contained panic. "It appears they are blocking all transmissions!"

Cold realization pierced Pilcolm's mind. This, of course, was no mere encounter—this was a meticulously planned ambush. He had little doubt in that regard. He leaned forward, studying the tactical holograms, his stomach clenched as the horrific truth became more and more obvious with each ticking second.

As the fast-approaching armada's makeup became more distinct, sensor scans provided a much clearer picture of what they were up against; the Commander was finding it hard to swallow. The hostile intruder's silhouettes were unmistakable; what he was looking at... it was no other than the dreaded Krygian. Specifically, this was the Tartarus Fleet. Only now did the ship's onboard computer codex confirm his determination.

First Mate Flantan was now at his side. With a quick glance, Pilcolm saw fear... and something else on the officer's face. Realization.

"What is it? What do you know?"

Flantan didn't answer right away. "The Krygian... haven't they been experiencing a drought. Sea levels not where they should be."

Commander Pilcolm's breath caught in his chest. "A couple of years of dry weather and they'd..." He refused to say the words. The mere thought of it, unimaginable. Even the Krygian weren't that barbaric... were they? The words sliced through the tension like a plasma blade, "Attacking a goodwill convoy?" The audacity of the offense sinking in. "That's a breach of every interstellar accord forged within the sector."

Flantan shook his head, his jaw muscles tensing beneath the skin. "It's unthinkable... even the Krygian wouldn't stoop so low."

The Ensign brought up an enhanced, zoomed-in view of the armada's flagship. It wasn't like any warship Pilcolm had ever come across. Bristling with weaponry—energy cannons, rail guns—typical implements of war but with atypical technology. The vessel didn't just look dangerous, it oozed dominance, raw aggression.

Flantan took a step closer to the display. "I've heard of this ship, although her name escapes me. She's capable of immense destruction—eviscerates anything in its path. This leviathan is not Krygian. The fleet is Krygian, but this dreadnought... no, I'm fairly certain it's been acquired elsewhere."

"With the exception of our tankers, that ship dwarfs virtually all our Floritineian vessels," Commander Pilcolm commented. He had only encountered the Krygians once before, nearly losing his life to their unbridled aggression and thirst for conquest during the Rulan Xenocide a half-century prior. As the Krygians surged forth across the cosmos, their ominous armada of obsidian vessels cast shadows over the stars. Their relentless pursuit was not to assimilate, but to demand subservience from all they encountered. They harbored an unquenchable thirst for dominion, seeking to subjugate every sentient race under the flawless order of their Prime Vector's mechanical consciousness. To them, organic minds were mere imperfections, destined to be ruled, and dominated, according to the precision of machine logic.

"Take us to battle stations!" Commander Pilcolm shouted, knowing the order was coming far too late.

The bridgecrew leapt into action as emergency lights bathed the chamber in an ominous, crimson glow. Pilcolm's fingers curled into rigid fists as the initial barrage of antimatter missiles streaked from the Krygian flagship, his mouth opening in a silent scream as they exploded against the lead Floritineian battle cruiser in the convoy. Security vessels were fractured as easily as eggshells, crewmembers atomized in roiling plasma fury before they could even raise defensive countermeasures.

Debris slashed across the formation, taking out support craft and punching deep into the armored hull of the closest tanker.

The Commander, momentarily paralyzed, watched as more shrapnel and debris pelted the tanker, now shuddering violently, venting roaring geysers of precious seawater and marine life. Pilcolm watched in horror as leviathan creatures—majestic, arced whales and sinuous krillions, were exposed to the merciless -400-degree vacuum, their bodies freezing and then bursting in gruesome silence as the Hydrate Elysium convoy's life-giving bounty was transformed into a field of deadly debris. Delicate symbiotic organisms and plant life—meant to reseed Elysium-4's oceans—spilled from the tanker's ruptured hold, perishing instantly in the extreme cold.

The bridge lurched violently as a disruptor beam lanced across the ship's armored flanks, shorting out systems in a shower of sparks and smoke. The shockwave flung the Commander against the unyielding deck, but he managed to pull himself upright, unwilling to show weakness before his crew. Pilcolm winced, feeling the impact of tiny pieces of sharp metal cutting his face; he tasted the coppery tang of blood on his lip. Alarms blared from every console as the Krygian closed in inexorably, energy weapons and missiles slashing through the convoy's defenses with surgical precision.

Staggered by the unexpected ferocity of the assault, the remaining Floritineian security forces, four overmatched battle-cruisers, managed to return fire, but their disruptor beams and torpedoes struck only glancing blows against the Krygian dread-nought's layered shielding. As the Tartarus Fleet unleashed its final crippling barrage, eviscerating not only the last of the Floritineian security escorts with contemptuous ease but another of the massive tankers. Pilcolm felt the flames of defiance, sure, but also a sadness so deep it seemed to pierce his very soul.

Seemingly, the path toward cosmic unity and enlightenment was not within reach. How naive he had been—hell, how naive all those within the sector had been. There remained one marine life tanker and the mega-behemoth pure-water tanker. He watched grimly as the Krygians moved in to take what they came for.

"At least some of the marine life will be spared," Pilcolm whispered somberly.

Battered but unbroken, he straightened his posture, fixing his remaining crew with an unwavering gaze. But just as quickly, his shoulders slumped as he witnessed the lights of that last defensive craft winking out of existence—consumed by the unidentified dreadnought's disruptor beams. What was left of them, was now defenseless—their noble mission to aid a drought-stricken colony... reduced to ashes.

A cacophony of screeching alarms shattered the bridge's silence. Pilcolm's attention was pulled to the tactical display—illuminated with a throng of inbound missiles from the enemy fleet. There would be no survivors, no rallying cry. No. This depraved, alien race—the Krygian race—would leave no loose ends.

In those final moments, Pilcolm's thoughts fled to his beloved Myyra waiting on their homeworld. What was she doing at this very moment? Was she gardening in their arboretum, tending to the fragrant zora blossoms as the twin suns dipped below the horizon? Or was she preparing a savory soup, plucking herbs from a bouquet garni, and tossing them into a giant pot? Or... was she staring wistfully at the stars, dreaming of his return?

Chapter 1

Admiral Xavier Gomez

The final scene on the halo display flickered with the intensity of a dying star, its light casting a haunting luminescence over the stark faces of the dignitaries assembled around the conference table. They watched, anchored to their chairs by shock and dread, as the 3D halo projection played out the last moments of an unspeakable horror.

There, amongst the devastating battle wreckage, and floundering space debris of what had been such a vital altruistic mission, was the celebrated convoy known as Hydrate Elysium. The last of the marine life tankers suddenly ruptured in a cacophony of liquid geysers, hemorrhaging its payload into the cold expanse—a drift of marine creatures now transitioning from vibrant life to frozen death, their needless slaughter a devastating side note to the celestial massacre. The lone pure-aqua, mega-behemoth tanker remained, flanked by Krygian ships... protecting their bounty.

In the gravity-muted chamber of EUNF Vanguard Hub's

executive conference room, the air was as thick as tungsten, every breath an effort against the invisible weight of imminent threat.

There they sat, perched within the top deck of the clandestine space station, one suspended somewhere between Earth and Mercury—a location that had never felt more isolated. Here, amidst the cold gleam of metallic surfaces and the austere, utilitarian design mandated by military efficiency, high-ranking officials from military and civilian sectors sat entrenched around an imposing horseshoe-shaped table. The subdued overhead illumination only enhanced the palpable tension permeating the space.

At the center of it all was Admiral Gomez, a solitary figure etched against the austere backdrop. Getting to his feet, he paced, each step a deliberate echo in the hush of the room. The rest, a cadre of somber-faced generals, admirals, and congressional and presidential cabinet members, were unflappable, betrayed only by the occasional darting of eyes or an anxious tap of a finger, the ambient hum of the station's life support systems. Eyes flitted across the table, seeking confirmation, seeking denial —an outward manifestation of the inner turmoil each felt.

"How can we be sure it's her?" General Langly finally asked, his voice tentative, unwilling to anchor to the possibility taking shape. "Have we even vetted this—"

"Yes," Gomez cut in. "The feed is from a passing-by trawler. Nothing was doctored."

"Of course it's her! No other ship has that silhouette," Rear Admiral Poke countered, her tone infused with the kind of certainty that came from years of staring down enemy vessels against the canvas of the void.

"I'm not convinced," another voice chimed in, tinged with disbelief. "Thanks to the irresponsible actions of Captain Quintos, that high-value asset was handed over to the Varapin two years ago. If that really is that Gorvian tech warship, this situation is far worse than a few space whales getting turned into popsicles."

Every gaze fixed upon Admiral Gomez. The chamber was suspended in anticipation, ready for the decisive pronouncement that would etch their destinies into the chronicles of a now unpredictable future.

Looking tired, Gomez shook his head. "Our EUNF eggheads have confirmed the identification." His tone reflected his inner resignation to the fact. "That behemoth of a warship is indeed... *Oblivion*." He allowed the name to hover for a moment —a name no one present here ever wanted to hear uttered again.

"And yes," Admiral Gomez continued, his gaze sweeping over his colleagues, an acknowledgment of the gravity settling upon them all, "this changes everything."

A cold resolve settled over the assembly as implications and strategies began to coalesce into a newfound purpose. The return of *Oblivion* wasn't just a harbinger of doom; it was a clarion call to action for every soul within the EV Hub—an undeniable declaration that war, in all its shadows and uncertainties, loomed once more on humanity's horizon.

"And we're sure these attackers are the Krygians?" General Langly asked.

The Admiral ignored Langly's question. Gomez's fists clenched as he stood at one of the compartment's three observation windows. His back to the room, he said, "Should the Krygians aim to engage the Alliance, which is already weakened by numerous recent conflicts, Earth may once again confront an existential threat. With *Oblivion* in the equation, well, we all know the potential consequences."

Rear Admiral Poke laid her palms down on the table in front of her. "We'll cobble together a viable fleet. Yes, this is an inopportune situation, but we've risen to worse challenges."

"We need dreadnoughts... omninoughts!" Langly spat back. "Halibart Shipyard simply needs to step things up... and the damn Pleidians, what's their status on asset deliveries?"

Gomez raised a hand to quell the rising hostility in the room. "Hold on... this very well could be one of those situations that is better served with a scalpel instead of a hammer."

"What the hell does that mean?" Senator Wright said from the far end of the table. "Isn't the whole point of this top-secret meeting to talk war strategy?"

"What we want is to avoid another war. Haven't we had enough of that with the Varapin and Grish?" Gomez countered. His eyes scanned the dark perimeter of the compartment, suddenly coming to rest on the lone silhouetted figure leaning against a bulkhead. Gomez's smirk, crooked and sly, suggested a hidden agenda behind its uneven grin.

"Commander Strickland, would you mind joining the meeting?"

Gomez watched as the man stepped into the muted light. At 6'2", Commander Cornelius Strickland quickly commanded the attention of everyone present... with his imposing stature and chiseled features. His battle-hardened physique, honed through years of rigorous training, exuded an aura of strength and resilience. Strickland's rugged face bore the mark of countless skirmishes, from the prominent brow that cast shadows over his intense, hazel eyes to the crooked nose that hinted at altercations long past. His close-cropped dark hair topped a sun-kissed complexion, a testament to the countless hours spent under the unforgiving glare of alien suns. As accomplished as the man was, he was relatively young at just 27. As Strickland strode around the table, he moved with the fluid grace of a seasoned warrior; this man was both fearless and lethal.

"Everyone in this room has been briefed on our Quansport

Ops program. Commander Strickland here is the man that will be leading its first mission."

Gomez and Strickland exchanged eye contact.

"Uh, that program's still in its infancy, under development," Poke said, now squirming in her seat.

Gomez looked her way, giving the Rear Admiral a thorough once-over.

Poke ignored his gaze, looked to Senator Wright. "We even get past the funding for that project?"

Senator Wright's gaze shifted to Gomez, his eyes concealing hidden truths.

In a no-nonsense tone, Strickland spoke for the first time. "Quansport Ops is fully operational."

Gomez, under the direction of President Block, had indeed accelerated the experimental Quansport Ops initiative, a top-secret program that had been in development for the last year.

Strickland continued, "USS Ike, a state-of-the-art Corvette-class warship, will be at the forefront of this operation. We're talking about an operation with the most cutting-edge quantum transport, genetic battle augmentation, and Symbio Poth technologies to ever come out of Pleidian and Thine Labs."

The assemblage of high-ranking military and congressional personnel stared up at the man, all looking aghast.

"You said... Corvette-class warship? Isn't that a smaller vessel? It's for escort duties, or maybe patrol missions, right? A fucking throwaway battle asset?" Wright balked at Strickland, looking dismayed. Then he put all his attention on the Admiral. "Let me get this straight, Gomez... you're tellin' me we're gonna hurl a friggin' life raft at one of the deadliest warships in the cosmos? That's what I'm hearin', right?"

Chapter 2

Captain Galvin Quintos

ammit! I needed to get this done—and while it was still bio-form vs. bio-form. As indicated by the green-hued overhead lights, the clock hadn't yet pinged midnight. It'll be when all those colossal industrial pendant lights, fashioned from repurposed oil drum bottoms, dozens of them dangling from thick rusted chains, start casting blue light—yeah, then, I'll be in real trouble. Hell, who was I kidding, I was already pretty fucked.

I was there, looking into the butt-ugly face of Vladislav Fangor. As we circled each other, both panting heavily, the imposing figure fixed me with a gaze filled with hunger—I felt like a sizzling steak fresh off the grill. *I should have stopped with my last match—stopped while I was still ahead.*

Fangor's body odor was enough to make my eyes water, a pungent mix of sweat and something else, perhaps a hint of fetid foot funk. His muscular frame was a sight to behold, with thighs as wide as tree stumps, biceps like cantaloupes, and pronounced pectorals a double-D bra would have a hard time containing.

His moniker, Fangor, was fitting, as he had a perpetual snarl that showed glimpses of a lone incisor, brown and chipped.

His clenched, raised fists, like two honey-baked hams, each nearly as large as my head, were a testament to his ability to cause carnage and devastation. To put a cherry on top of this visual, Fangor was wearing a kind of Tarzan-like leather loin-cloth-thing, that did little to hide the occasional sighting of his gargantuan hanging ball sac. It was a sight that was both distracting and somewhat comical, an odd dichotomy to the fierce demeanor that emanated from his every pore.

We had been fighting for what felt like an eternity, our bodies exhausted and battered. Sweat dripped from our brows, mixing with the grime and blood that covered us both. Our movements were slower now, less precise, as we struggled to maintain our footing and deliver blows that would have come naturally thirty or forty minutes earlier.

So... where exactly am I, you may be wondering about now? Welcome to *Blood Grapple*, the infamous underground fight club nestled deep within the frozen caverns of Pluto's most desolate moon—Kerberos. Here, beneath its icy surface, the air reeks of anticipation as combatants from all corners of the galaxy converge for a chance at either glory or a brutal demise. In this sprawling network of caverns, each chamber hosts its own octagon cage match, where bloodthirsty spectators cheer on their chosen champions.

Cages lacked the plush, rubber mat of a standard boxing ring. These fighters brawled on cold, unyielding cement. Tungsten netting and galvanized pipes framed the perimeter, offering no mercy. The environment screamed: man up, this isn't a tea party.

My fingers throbbed, the knuckle on my right hand swollen and tender after connecting with the iron-like jaw of my towering opponent. Yet, I refused to let the pain distract me, my mind laser-focused on finding an opening, any weakness I could exploit.

The larger man suddenly lunged forward, his massive fists swinging in a flurry of haymakers that I narrowly evaded. Ducking beneath a clubbing right hand, I countered with a swift combination—a sharp jab followed by a devastating knee strike to his solar plexus. He grunted, the air forced from his lungs, but he refused to buckle. *Christ, what's it going to take!*

I pressed the attack, flowing seamlessly between Muay Thai and Brazilian Jiu-Jitsu techniques. I landed a crisp elbow strike, splitting the skin above his eye, then quickly transitioned into a takedown, twisting my hips to drive the larger man to the blood-splattered floor.

But Vladislav Fangor was no novice, and he powered out of the submission hold, his massive arms enveloping me in a bone-crushing bear hug. I felt my left shoulder wrench painfully, a telltale sign dislocation was imminent. Struggling, I felt the inevitability of this match closing in on me. *No!* With a burst of adrenaline, I summoned the last of my strength and broke free, quickly delivering a series of rapid-fire palm strikes to the man's face—the stinging blows disorienting him long enough for me to stumble backward, chest heaving, my vision blurring from the relentless onslaught. I swallowed hard and put a little more distance between us.

The larger man, from some Eastern Bloc nation, Uzbek-istan, Kyrgyzstan, maybe Tajikistan... charged forward, a primal roar rumbling from his chest. I braced myself, knowing I had only one chance left. As he closed the distance, I unleashed a devastating spinning heel kick, the impact reverberating through my battered body.

Time seemed to slow as I watched his eyes go wide, the momentum of the strike sending the hulking man crashing down to the cage's rock-hard foundation. I stood there, chest heaving, triumph warring with the agony of my wounds.

The air in the dingy arena was rank with the metallic tang of sweat and blood. I stood in the center of the hazily lit pit, gulping air, as the roars of the bloodthirsty crowd assaulted my ears. My latest opponent, a behemoth of a man easily outweighing me by 100 pounds, was crumpled to the concrete floor in a heap.

I barely had time to catch my breath before the announcer's gravelly voice boomed over the speakers. "Our next matchup is a doozy, folks! After powering through five straight wins over the last four hours, *Brigs* will face his toughest challenge yet!"

I watched as Fangor was dragged from the arena—trailing smears of blood and blending in with those of the previously defeated. It still hadn't dawned on me; the announcer was talking about me. No way would I have used my real name... not here—I was going by my Arrow Pilot call sign name... Brigs.

Bent over with hands on knees, I managed to gasp out, "Wait... I'm done."

But my words were lost in the roars—the melee of hundreds of cheers. And then it hit me like a baseball bat to the back of my head... those big hanging overhead lights were now emanating a ghostly blue hue. *Shit!* It was past midnight. *No, no, no!* It was no longer bio-form vs. bio-form, it was now Free Fight, bio-form vs. bio-form, robot vs. robot, or bio-form vs. robot.

The loud chorus quelled; a murmur of anticipation was suddenly rippling through the crowd as the far gate groaned open. My eyes narrowed, muscles tensing, as the silhouette of my next opponent emerged—I recognized this model immediately. It was a re-appropriated CargoHauler bot. Strong as shit, and renowned for being indestructible. These things never break down. Sure, they'd wrapped the mechanical beast in padding, more for the opponent than the robot, but it would do little to soften the blows.

I whirled around, spotting my bookie, Mannie Pringle, skulking amidst the crowd beyond the cage—a skinny mouse of a man who had undoubtedly suffered big losses due to my string of victories. There again, who would guess a man with half the brawn of his opponents would have survived this long?

I yelled over the ruckus, "No way, Mannie, I'm done. That was my last fight!"

His eyes found mine and a smile pulled at the corners of his thin lips. With an apologetic shrug I wasn't buying for a second, he shouted, "Sorry, mate... it's too late." He pointed to the blue overhead lights. "One more match. I'm rooting for you!" He held up a *go-get-em*, fist.

Yeah. I bet you are. I glanced toward the now-closed and locked gate—the surrounding twelve-foot-tall chain-link fence ensuring there would be no escape the impending brawl. Bringing my attention back to the CargoHauler, I inwardly fumed. *I'm so fucked.*

Chapter 3

As the large bot clanked further into the ring, I felt a weary surge of dread. This was going to be a brutal test between a machine's superior strength and a man's relentless nature. My opponent was constructed of circuits and metal and represented my bookie's ace in the hole, one that stacked the odds against me.

I was already exhausted, my body aching from previous bouts, but I had no choice but to steel myself. There was no grand meaning here, no proving of the human spirit—just the harsh reality that I had to make it through this next punishing round against an opponent more used to fighting other robots—opponents far more challenging than this bruised and bloodied human. With heavy limbs and a swollen jaw, I braced for the onslaught, knowing this cold, calculating machine would show no mercy until the final bell... *would I even survive that long?*

Clearly, today was no longer about drowning sorrows in self-destructive bouts in the octagon—a futile attempt to forget a woman who haunted my every waking thought. Gail Pristy, brilliant, beautiful, and maddeningly elusive, had become an unwelcome guest in my mind, and I'd needed to evict her. Until now, throwing fists and kicks had done its job, albeit poorly.

Concentrate! I inwardly chastised.

The CargoHauler bot towered above me at a menacing height of seven feet, its bulky frame was comprised of heavy-duty alloys and composite plating. Though primarily a faded yellow, the chipped splotches exposed layers of previous coats—blue and black—a history etched into its battered exterior. Two powerful hydraulic arm appendages extended from its broad shoulders, articulated joints allowing a wide range of motion. Three thick, stumpy legs supported the hulking machine, each footpad bristling with jagged grips for maximum traction.

Hastily strapped around its flattened head, chest, and back was makeshift padding, grease-stained and haphazardly secured —a feeble attempt to provide its opponent's fists some cushion-ing. As I eyed the mechanical beast, my gaze traced over the exposed pistons, servos, and armored conduits snaking across its form. That minuscule head lacked the sophistication of an advanced AI processor—this bot was no genius, but a brutal instrument of force. My eyes darted over its frame, desperately searching for vulnerabilities, seams and other weak points to exploit. But the CargoHauler's rugged, utilitarian design revealed no obvious chinks in its impenetrable armor. I swal-lowed hard, bracing for the onslaught of this unstoppable, single-minded engine of destruction. And at this moment, I really wanted to kill Mannie Pringle.

Okay... about now you may have been asking how I had managed to survive those five previous matches, while still being ready to put up some semblance of a fight. Simple. There was a kind of neon green Gorvian plasma coursing through my veins at this very moment. The truth is that plasma shit is the only thing that has allowed me to stay vertical today. Just as it saved me years ago in my bout against the infamous pirate, Thunderballs. All thanks to Doc Viv. She had discovered that Gorvian regeneration nanite technology which somehow operates in another dimension, another plane of existence. It not only accelerates healing but offers up crazy levels of stamina and strength far beyond my natural abilities. Yeah, those nanites had given me the edge I needed to defeat Thunderballs, other humans here within these caverns, and right now, this opponent who was in a whole other class.

The opening bell sounded, and I launched myself into a furious offensive, raining down a blurring combination of strikes. But the robot weathered the assault, its armored chassis shrugging off blow after blow as if this was just another day of loading cargo into some ship's hold.

It came out of nowhere, the CargoHauler's fist slammed into my rib cage, lifting me up and off my feet. When I crashed down to hard surface—the wind already knocked from my lungs, I desperately gasped for air. Reeling in pain and seeing stars, the robot was little more than a big blur—a blur that was closing in with servos whining in anticipation of an easy kill.

I was going to die right here... within seconds, certainly not minutes. I had zero doubt about that. At least I wouldn't be alone in that respect. Hell, I'm sure there'd been a dozen other poor bastards that had crossed over into the dark divide here at *Blood Grapple* just today.

I got to my knees and wearily, pathetically raised my fists. Maybe joining an underground fight club hadn't been one of my better decisions. At least I wasn't thinking about Gail... well, until now. *Shit.*

It's strange the things you think of at the most inopportune times. At this particular inopportune time, I was wondering if this 7-foot-tall CargoHauler looming over me had a name. Yeah, it was a dumb brute of a machine, but it did have a modicum of mental circuits. It wasn't a vacuum cleaner or a bathroom stink fan, it could think. It could say, *Hello* or *Where does this bulky and immensely heavy crate go?* So why wouldn't the bot have a name? Something like Wrecker, Rumble, or maybe Slam.

Yeah, I was purposely distracting myself so when that next, inevitable strike came—like from an oversized metal fist or ginormous foot... I'd mentally be somewhere else. Putting Slam—I went with Slam—in a kind of an out-of-sight and out-of-mind kind of thing.

Suddenly, a shadow loomed, one of the CargoHauler's three feet was now raised over me—I was about to be squashed—a mere bug to be put out of its misery.

The crowd was chanting, "Kill... Kill... Kill... Kill..."

I looked up, better to face my demise like a man. Something Slam here would never be able to say. At least there was that. But the oversized CargoHauler was not looking back down at me. Slam was looking past me, to something out there beyond the high chain-link fence.

"Coming through, make a path, out of the way bub... oh, sorry, that must have hurt..."

I recognized that deep ridiculous voice. Boston-accented, one that had a blue-collar dock worker's timbre to it—and right now, I'd never heard anything quite so beautiful.

Spinning around, the first thing I saw was a blindingly bright red targeting ray. The laser beam locked, its red dot coming to rest in the middle of Slam's little head.

"Don't even think about it," Hardy said to the CargoHauler with zero humor in his tone.

Slam looked down at me, then back to Hardy. A conundrum brewing within its circuits.

In an ear-shattering clattering of shredding metal, the ChronoBot was coming through the fence as if it were little more than strands of spaghetti. As he stepped in the octagon cage, his broad polished chrome chest reflected the blue lights above. With three long strides, Hardy already had my opponent lifted off the floor, the ChronoBot's gauntlet-like fist tightly secured around Slam's neck. The CargoHauler's three legs flailed like a desperate animal searching for footing.

"Don't break the robot, Hardy," I said, getting to my feet.

Hardy's previously blue-glowing faceplate now displayed the features of a middle-aged, balding, kinda pudgy man known to many as John Hardy. "Ah come on, Cap... this thing was about to stomp your head."

I shook my head.

The crowd went quiet.

"How about I just... toss it?"

I hesitated. "Okay, fine. Go ahead."

It was as if Slam was a rocket, blasting off into outer space— a blur of yellow and blue on a trajectory toward the cavern's rocky ceiling. The loud overhead clatter was enough to make everyone duck for cover—which wasn't a bad idea since Slam was now coming down in a multitude of metal disconnected parts.

"Captain Quintos!"

My head snapped around to locate the source—oh no... this wasn't good.

Admiral Xavier Gomez stood impassively outside the cage, his expression inscrutable.

Spitting out a globule of blood, I attempted to change my mindset from one of physical self-preservation to the ingrained obedience of a career U.S. Space Navy officer. With a curt nod, I limped toward the ragged opening provided by Hardy earlier.

As I approached the Admiral, I caught a glimpse of the robot's upper torso and head lying on the rock floor just outside the cage; its cold, unfeeling eyes were still locked onto me. I couldn't help but feel a shudder run down my spine, knowing that I had just narrowly escaped a fate that would have included more than a little pain.

"Admiral? I wasn't aware you were a member here. Good crowd tonight, huh?"

"Knock it off, Captain." Gomez's gaze remained steady, his eyes boring into mine. "We have a situation. One that requires your immediate attention."

"What kind of situation?"

"You've heard of the Krygians, I take it?"

I nodded. "A growing threat... but we've left each other alone."

"The Krygians' status has been elevated to *Galactic Superpower*. Their formidable Tartarus Fleet has attacked a Floritineian convoy on a mercy mission, destroying security assets and a couple of super-tankers," Gomez explained, his voice grave.

I felt a cold knot of dread form in the pit of my stomach. The Floritineians were a peaceful species, and I'd heard about their relief mission to aid a certain drought-stricken colony.

Wiping a bit of oozing blood from my lower lip, I said, "Undoubtedly, the loss of that precious cargo will spell disaster for..." the name on the tip of my tongue, now popped into my head, "Uh, that Elysium-4 colony."

The Admiral looked annoyed, "Well this is bigger than that, Captain."

His attention was momentarily pulled toward Hardy's approach.

"We need to act fast," the Admiral continued.

Gomez hesitated, his expression turning somewhat more conciliatory. He looked about our surroundings—the next fight had already started, the crowd yelling and chanting. "I've encroached into your personal time. I'm sorry. R&R, after what you've given to the U.S. Space Navy as of late, is well deserved

—hell, needed." He made eye contact with John Hardy's 3D facsimile. "Your... um, robot here, helped track you down."

I could see the Admiral was feeling uneasy. "What, exactly do you need from me, Sir? Going back on duty is not a problem. But last I heard, my next ship was still being fabricated. Another omninought—"

Gomez held up a palm to interrupt, "This isn't about your next scheduled deployment. That's months away. This is about, uh... well, more of an off-the-books kind of mission."

Why the Admiral was acting so cagey I had no idea. "Maybe it's best to just rip off the Band-Aid, Sir. What is it you're asking of me?"

"This would be a different kind of mission. Smaller. A special ops mission that requires a certain, less structured, mind frame."

"More of an operating by the seat of one's pants type thing," I offered up to help him out.

"Exactly!" he said, pointing a finger at me.

"Someone willing to maybe bend the rules if necessary."

Gomez smiled and nodded looking uncomfortable with this whole conversation.

For me... he was speaking my language. "I'm in. Just tell me where and when. Can I ask what ship I'll be skippering? An old dreadnought, maybe a super cruiser?"

A pained expression pulled at his forced smile. "It's a, uh, Corvette, Captain."

"A Corvette. Well, that is small." I smiled, "Sounds like fun."

"There's one more thing."

Uh-oh, here it comes.

"While you'll be captaining the ship, another aspect of the mission will be coming under the leadership of Commander Strickland."

"A commander. Last I checked, I outrank a commander."

"Look, you'll both be more than busy—you in command of space operations, Strickland with boots-on-the-ground operations. You'll need to work in concert with each other."

Hardy, who had remained quiet until now, said, "And we all know how well the Captain plays well with others."

Chapter 4

Earth, Virginia Air Space
En Route to Yellowstone National Park

XO Gail Pristy

The sleek airborne RV, an Airstream XL6, cut a shimmering path through the warm Virginia air. Its polished aluminum exterior gleamed in the late afternoon sunlight as Gail Pristy's fingers lightly gripped the steering wheel. The antiquated device seemed more ceremonial than functional, a vestige of an era before artificial intelligence took the helm. However, when manual control was preferred, the wheel allowed for basic altitude, pitch, bank control (roll), power control, and trim.

Her palms caressed the smooth leather, a tactile reminder of when humanity still dominated machinery. In truth, the Airstream's AI system was silently navigating the open air before them.

Her eyes were trained on the open skies stretching out before them like a vast tapestry of possibility. They had just left the hustle and bustle of battle-torn Washington D.C. behind, trading the slow, methodical rebuilding of the nation's capital for a different kind of excursion... one guaranteed to be devoid of Phazon Pulsar cannons, manufactured wormhole travel, U.S. Space Navy regs, and even the Y chromosome—that's right, no men allowed on this meanderingly slow silver bullet. A contented smile played across <u>Pristy</u>'s lips as a sense of freedom and adventure washed over her.

Pristy stole a sidelong glance at her young traveling companion. In the passenger seat sat Sonya Winters, a brilliant yet snarky 17-year-old. Pristy was hoping to get to know Sonya better on this trip; she didn't know much about the teenager's past, her family... except that her father was from the Briggan clan, a more unscrupulous band of pirates than most. Later, around 12, Sonya ran away, ending up with the Pylor clan. Talk about jumping from the fire into the frying pan... from what little Pristy knew of the situation, the poor girl had been through hell.

In some ways Sonya was advanced for her age, having had to survive among so many with ill intentions; yet in other ways, she was immature and childlike. Playing a projected 3D game on her TAC-Band, she had her bare feet propped up on the dash. The muffled thump of music spilled from her earbuds as her head bobbed in time with the beat, seemingly oblivious to the scenic vistas whipping past the windshield two hundred feet below.

Despite their decade-and-a-half age difference and backgrounds, she felt a growing sense of big-sister-like affection and responsibility for the girl. This hover road trip across America's vast expanses was as much for Sonya's benefit as her own—a chance to experience the simple joys of cruising the open skies after a life lived within the confines of cold and impersonal starships. The rules and military regulations must have seemed counterintuitive for such a rambunctious teenager.

Montana's majestic Yellowstone National Park was their ultimate destination. Although the majority of Yellowstone National Park lay within the borders of Wyoming and a sliver extended into Idaho, the remaining portion occupied a small section of Montana, which hosted the northern gateway to the renowned wilderness preserve. The journey stretched out before them, ripe with possibilities for adventure and self-discovery. And for Pristy, perhaps a chance to finally confront the turmoil that had been a constant companion since her untimely death and quantum rebirth, just a month prior. That, and her conflicting feelings for Galvin.

"Hey, take a look at that view! Isn't it breathtaking?" Pristy exclaimed, gesturing to the sprawling landscape beneath them.

Sonya barely glanced up from her game, her fingers inter-acting with a 3D avatar, a Cyclops monster of some sort. "Uh-huh, sure. Breathtaking. Yep."

Pristy's smile faltered slightly, but she pressed on. "You know, this trip is a great opportunity for us to bond. We can talk, share stories, get to know each other better."

"Bond? What are we, molecules?" Sonya scoffed, her eyes still glued to her game. "I'm good with the whole 'mysterious teenager' vibe, thanks."

"Come on, Sonya. There's more to life than just staring at projections. Look around you! The world is full of wonders waiting to be discovered."

With an exaggerated huff, Sonya finally looked up, her expression a mix of annoyance and amusement. "Wonders? You mean like trees and rocks and stuff?" She suddenly shot forward, eyes wide, an exuberant fake smile—she jabbed a finger, "Gee, how exciting! Oh my God, look! There's a mound of dirt down there, maybe we should make a U-turn, and go investigate!"

With a roll of her eyes, she slumped back in her seat and went back to her game.

Pristy sighed, realizing that getting through to Sonya would be more challenging than she anticipated. "Alright, but if you change your mind, I'm here. This trip is for both of us, you know."

"Uh-huh... yeah, got it. I'll try to contain my excitement," the teen replied, her voice dripping with sarcasm. She cranked up the volume on her earbuds.

Pristy smiled, there was no way she was going to let the girl ruin this trip for her.

Pristy took a deep breath, glancing sideways at Sonya, determined to make a breakthrough in their dialogue. "So, tell me, how exactly are you related to Quintos?" she asked, her voice loud enough to be heard over her music.

Sonya sighed dramatically, rolling her eyes before reluctantly pausing her game. "I have this family tree app," she muttered, tapping her tablet with exaggerated strokes. The holographic display flickered to life, projecting a complex web of names, dates, and relations. With another dramatic swipe, she began reading aloud. "Let's start with your boyfriend, Galvin," Sonya said, her voice oozing with her signature sarcasm.

"He's not my boyfriend! I don't even know why you'd say that," Pristy snapped, feeling her cheeks flush.

"Uh-huh, anyway," Sonya continued, looking unimpressed by Pristy's protest. "I just have bits and pieces, just what I've picked up over the last few years. Um... Galvin was born in 2139 to Carl and Lori Quintos. Two years before that, his brother Eric was born. So, you've got Eric, then Galvin."

Pristy nodded, keeping her expression neutral. "And what happened after they were born?"

Sonya's fingers swiped across the tablet screen, bringing up more information. "Okay... they were living in a one-horse, hayseed-of-a-town... Clairmont."

Pristy inhaled, she knew about Galvin's traumatic childhood events in that town, *USS Hamilton* had dedicated a whole Symbio Deck to that shitty town, thanks to Shawlee and her seemingly constant compulsion to help her once-savior, Quintos. Pristy wondered if it was jealousy she was feeling.

Sonya continued, "On July 4th, 2150, Galvin was 11 years old... when Carl, their dad, thought he killed a family in a hovercar accident. Pretty messed up, huh? Uh... after that they left Clairmont. They lived in a few different places and eventually ended up in Colorado."

Pristy nodded. "It was an awful, time for the entire family. So, what happened to them next?"

"Carl started drinking... like a lot," Sonya answered flatly. "Two years later, he was killed in a bar fight. Then, a year after that, Lori, Quintos' mom, killed herself. That was, like, the end of Carl and Lori's story."

Pristy's fingers tightened around the steering wheel, her mind reeling from the tragedy of it all. "So, what happened to Eric and Galvin after their parents died?"

"They became wards of the state of Colorado," Sonya continued, her tone more matter-of-fact now. "The boys grew up together in an orphanage."

Sonya paused, her eyes flicking toward Pristy, gauging her reaction. "Three years later, a woman came forward—Juliet Winters. She claimed she had an intimate relationship with Carl, while he was married to Lori... while he was looking for work and frequenting bars."

Pristy gave a slight nod, then her eyes widened. "Wait... Winters? So, she's your..."

"Grandmother." Sonya shrugged. "Juliet had gotten pregnant. But it seems Carl's self-loathing, guilt, whatever... from what had happened in Clairmont... by that time he 'd become little more than a drifter, a drunk."

Sonya paused, reading her notes. "Apparently, Juliet had possessed the good sense to end things. She ended up leaving Carl and leaving the bar where she worked. Not exactly sure where she went. But later, Juliet had learned that both Carl and Lori had died. She knew Carl had two kids, Galvin and Eric, because he talked fondly about them. That's when she decided to look for them."

A crease formed between Pristy's brows, "Wait, so, *why* did she want to find Eric and Galvin?" Pristy asked, her interest peaked.

"I guess she wanted to tell them that they had a three-year-old half-brother named Landers Winters."

"Your father," Pristy interjected.

Sonya kept going, "Juliet struggled to make ends meet, barely managing to take care of herself, much less a kid. In a tough decision, she sent Landers back to the Briggan community where she'd been raised. She still knew people there who could lend a hand. Probably figured it was better for him, being a boy and all."

Pristy nodded, trying to keep her talking, even though she wasn't sure she fully understood. The truth was, the story intrigued her, piecing together the fragmented history of two people she cared deeply about.

Pristy started to say, "So Landers—"

"Uh, everyone just called him Land, not Landers," Sonya interjected. "And, uh, yeah, anyway... he's my dad... uh... *was* my dad."

"What happened to him?"

Sonya's demeanor suddenly changed—she was growing irritated. "Land met someone named Bekka, a Briggan girl. Grew up together. They'd become inseparable."

Pristy narrowed her eyes, "And she was..."

With an audible huff, Sonya spat, "Try to keep up, okay? She was my mom. Bekka was my mother! Geez! She became impregnated with me. And I was born. My dad was like 16 and my mom... she was the same age. I guess it was like young love or whatever. Things were different in the pirate clan!"

"I'm not judging," Pristy said defensively. She looked at her, "So... what happened then?"

Sonya's face flushed, she hesitated... "You know, you can be so annoying sometimes," she said, shooting Pristy a death stare. "I don't know. I, like, grew up there with the Briggans, okay? And, to be honest, it was fucking awful. It smelled bad and the food sucked. There were a lot of bad people lurking around within the clan. And I was pretty. Connect the damn dots, Gail. There were bad men, pirates eyeing me. I wasn't safe. To make things worse, my father was hardly ever around to protect me."

"That's despicable. Why..."

"You'd have to ask him—oh wait, you can't, he's dead."

"I'm so sorry, Sonya," Pristy said softly.

"Anyway, when I was twelve, I ran away and never looked back. Unfortunately, I only got as far as the neighboring pirate clan... the Pylors. Although, I'd managed to convince them that I could be useful to them as a coder, a skill I'd picked up over the years."

"And your father?"

"I heard he was executed," Sonya said flatly. "The story was, he was a traitor to the clan. I don't know the details. But a Briggan council of high muckity-mucks was convened and not long after it was decided."

Pristy waited.

"It was, *off with his head!* or something to that effect. Couldn't have happened to a nicer guy."

"How awful," Pristy sighed. "What about your mom? What happened to her."

"Seriously? Did I mention she was just a kid when she had me? I never saw her after I was pulled from her womb. She either died in childbirth or was sent away to pirate girl scout camp and never returned."

Pristy just stared straight ahead, lost in a tale that seemed far too awful to comprehend. "Okay, she said, trying to sound more upbeat, "you and Quintos, you're more like half-siblings than uncle and niece, right?" She glanced over to Sonya who was starting to relax.

Sonya wobbled her head, "Yup. Remember, I didn't always know all this family drama, though. Truth is, I never know how to refer to him. He's like really old, around 40, right?"

Pristy rolled her eyes but held her tongue.

"He's not, like, a brother. That'd be weird." She shrugged. "More like an uncle person, maybe. Anyway, I think that's why he puts up with me. He feels responsible, protective. He knows most of the messed-up back story too. Neither of us had a typical family upbringing."

Pristy's thoughts drifted to Quintos. "The crews onboard his ships, currently I suppose it's *USS Ike...* they've become his family, you included."

Sonya scoffed, "Family... it's an abstract concept, but it's not real. So you have some kind of blood ties to other humans... all it means is you're primed for a lifetime of heartache."

Pristy frowned. "That's cynical."

The teenager shrugged. "Truth is, there's not much I remember about my father... with him, it was all about his pirate ambitions. His maniacal plundering schemes.

"Like what?"

Irritated, she shook her head, I don't know... just, stories my dad used to ramble on and on about when I was a kid. You know, typical pirate BS."

Pristy glanced over, curiosity piqued. "Oh? Like what?"

Sonya rolled her eyes, "You know, the usual pirate tall tales. Buried treasure on some remote world, ancient mineral gem deposits, that sort of thing."

She paused, a distant look in her eyes. "He had this one story he'd always come back to, a kind of bedtime story, about a place called... Despicable Black, or maybe it was Despicable Blue, no... that's not it, God, it was forever ago."

She snapped her fingers. "Wait, it was Desolate Blue star system. Anyway, he said there was a fortune in Alexandrite hidden there, just waiting for someone clever enough to claim it."

Pristy chuckled. "Sounds like quite the adventure. Did you believe him? That it was real?"

Sonya shrugged, "Nah, it was just a stupid story. But he sure liked to tell it, over and over again. I think he wanted to believe it, you know? That somewhere out there, there was a treasure that could change everything."

Pristy smiled, this just might have been the longest conversation they had ever had.

The Airstream AI spoke up, interrupting the moment...

Would you like to merge into Sky-Interstate 22, Gail?

Pristy considered the offer, glancing at the faster-moving traffic above. She pursed her lips, taking in the swath of faster-moving AirCar traffic zipping along several hundred feet higher up.

"Maybe later. For now, how about we take the road less traveled?"

. . .

**Excellent idea, Gail... would you like me
to put on some soothing music?
Or maybe I can play an audiobook; you're three-
quarters of the way through Junket, Untamed Alien
Worlds, by M.W.M.**

"No, we just want to drive in silence for the time being," Pristy
said.

Some seven hundred miles later, Pristy rolled her shoulders,
then tilted her head left and then right to relieve the tension of
so many hours behind the wheel. Sonya was in the back, asleep,
her gentle snores making their way forward as the late afternoon
sun was turning the landscape below a rich amber color.

Fighting a yawn, her eyes caught movement on the dash
display matrix. Six live feeds were coming in—from out front,
on both sides, the world below them, and what was behind the
RV. Her stomach tightened as she recognized the ominous-
looking hover RV rig. It was the same vehicle she'd spotted on
several occasions earlier, a dark and menacing presence against
the azure sky.

Using her thumb and forefinger she zoomed the aft feed,
revealing the details of their pursuer. "What a bucket of bolts,"
she murmured to herself.

She wasn't sure if the rig was dark gray or black. It was
rusted, battered, and worn—marred by the scars and scratches
of a hard-lived life on and above the road. Its headlights glowed
like sinister eyes in the dim light, casting an eerie, pale yellow

across the front grill. She could just make out the dark silhouettes of three individuals in the front seat.

"AI, enhance the aft feed image."

As Pristy focused on the three—obviously men—her unease
deepened. Their scraggly beards and grim expressions sent a
chill down her spine. She couldn't shake the feeling that they
meant trouble.

How long have they been following us?" Pristy said, keeping
her voice low so she wouldn't wake Sonya. Her heart raced with
apprehension as she waited for the reply.

Two thousand twenty miles and counting...

The AI's response was flat and expressionless, seemingly
unaware of the rising tension within the Airstream's cab.

Pristy's mind raced as she considered her options. Was she
sure they were being pursued? No. Had her experience as an
executive officer on multiple warships made her overly suspicious? Maybe.

Chapter 5

Solar System
Off-Worlder **Shuttle Craft**

Captain Galvin Quintos

Two hours later, we were seated within the Admiral's private Craven-class 550, *Off-Worlder*; we were on final approach to Halibart Station, a relative stone's throw from Earth's Moon.

I'd been studying the haunting video footage—the Tartarus Fleet's attack on the Floritineian's goodwill Hydrate Elysium convoy. Sure enough, the Krygian flagship's silhouette was unmistakable—it was *Oblivion*.

"EUNF analysts have confirmed it," Gomez growled. "Not only have the Krygians unlocked the secrets of *Oblivion's* singularity drive, but they've upgraded its perpendicularity energy matrix with their own tech. Increased the destructive energy of nullifier lances, hardened ZEDS shielding..."

I frowned. "That's enough to make that behemoth virtually unstoppable against anything we can currently field."

I wanted to be the one to take back that asset, if not destroy her. Unfortunately, Gomez had already confirmed that my next omninought-class vessel, one coming out of Thine Labs, was still months away from being combat-ready.

We had both gotten to our feet in preparation for disembarking at the station.

"Precisely," Gomez said, "which is why throwing conventional brute force at this... nightmare situation... is a non-starter. Add to the fact, do we really want to go to war with one more intergalactic superpower? No, this will require more of a surgical approach."

There was too much about this mission I didn't know. Hell, I didn't even know what questions to ask yet. Obviously, I'd been brought into this late in the game; I was an afterthought. My guess... this last-minute addition to the roster had been my strong connection to *Oblivion*. President Block would have known everything there was to be known about the chosen vessel... especially if I had insisted on being involved.

I had a history with that highly advanced Gorvian dreadnought. It was back in my Pylor pirate days. In my efforts to protect Haven, that beautiful pirate hideaway world, from an imminent Varapin attack, a stalemate had arisen. In the end, I'd been forced to swallow a bitter pill—to hand over that warship to one cunning, ruthless SOB, Commander Dunft Choob of the Varapin Empire. How *Oblivion* had changed hands to the Krygians was still a mystery to me.

Gomez scrutinized me with a serious expression. "That's where our new black ops protocol comes into play. A prototype program. One we've had in development for over a year now—codenamed *Quansport Ops*."

I raised an eyebrow as Gomez tapped at a tablet, bringing up schematics of an unfamiliar-looking, compact warship.

"Experimental tech that combines bleeding-edge quantum

transporter tech, the latest jump propulsion, as well as genetic battle-augmentation systems." The Admiral chinned to the tablet. "This little ship here is packed to the gills with technology. Tech that gives us unprecedented capabilities in covert deployment and tactical flexibility."

I'd seen this before—High Command falling in love with the latest and greatest battle tech—thinking it was the end-all to wartime success. But it was never that easy. The Admiral should have learned that lesson by now, just as I had on multiple occasions.

Gomez leaned forward, his gaze intensifying. "I'm activating Quansport Ops protocol, effective immediately. With Hardy's help, we've taken it upon ourselves to pick your onboard crew."

I shot a narrow-eyed glance at the ChronoBot who was standing at the back of *Off-Worlder's* cabin.

Catching my expression, Gomez scowled. "You weren't exactly easy to find," he said with irritation. "You do realize, the world doesn't stop spinning just for one self-consumed U.S. Space Navy Ship Commander."

I was tempted to correct the Admiral... I was now ranked as a Fleet Commander.

Hardy's Bostonian voice, somehow, was now blaring down from the shuttle's PA system. "Ladies and gentlemen, as we make our final approach to Halibart Shipyard, please make sure your seatbacks and tray tables are in their full upright position, and that your seatbelt is correctly fastened."

Gomez did not look amused.

SEVERAL MINUTES LATER, THE *OFF-WORLDER* shuddered, sliding into a docking bay at Halibart.

Hardy was moving forward. "Ladies and gentlemen, welcome to Des Moines. We remind you to check your seat for personal belongings and your overhead compartment for any carry-ons you may have brought onboard. On behalf of the entire crew, we'd like to thank you for choosing *United Mishaps* today, and remember our motto: *If you haven't bitten through your tongue, that's a damn good landing!*"

The mid-ship hatch suddenly *swished* open, and cool air poured into the cabin. Gomez hurried from the shuttle as if his pants were on fire. Apparently, he'd already had enough of Hardy's antics. *Yeah well, try being stuck with the clownster for a month-long deployment,* I thought with a smirk.

It was easily a half-mile hike before we'd reached our destination, Halibart Shipyard, where a myriad of U.S. Space Navy vessels were in various stages of construction. We just couldn't build them fast enough to keep up with battle attrition rates. Hey, I know what you're going to say, there from the peanut gallery... some comment about me being responsible for a large portion of those high attrition rates. In my defense, at least I'm consistent in my efforts to support the shipbuilding industry.

Admiral Gomez stood at the main SkyWay, looking out through the diamond-glass observation window, an expression I'd imagine not so different from that of a new father peering into a hospital's maternity ward. This was his baby, and I made a mental note to myself: *Do not wreck the boss's new warship.*

I sidled up to the right of the Admiral, while Hardy kept a few steps behind us. We stood there in silence. I had to admit, this ship, this Corvette, was a brute—as badass-looking as any ship I'd ever laid eyes on.

"This is *USS Ike.* She's a first-of-her-kind U.S. Space Navy Corvette-class warship."

I surveyed the ship, absorbing the intricate curvature of her hull—the manifest of readiness for skirmish and strife. She resembled a snarling bulldog, ready to pounce from its restraints and charge into the fray.

Gomez's narration continued, referencing the ship's storied namesake. "Named in honor of General Eisenhower, the revered Five-Star General and later President of the United States. A key figure in the Allied Expeditionary Forces' campaign against Nazi Germany in Europe during the 20th century."

I'd always admired Eisenhower, who ranked among my military and moral exemplars as a paragon of strategic brilliance and humanity. His legacy was one of integrity and fairness, a conscientious leader dedicated to transparency, and marked by an unpretentious inclination to forego individual accolades in favor of acknowledging collaborative efforts.

Admiral Gomez stood up straighter and let out a breath. "With a length of just 350 meters and a quarter of that in width, *USS Ike* is relatively small compared to modern dreadnoughts or omninoughts. Despite its compact dimensions, the vessel is a marvel of engineering and innovation, featuring eight decks and cutting-edge technology that rivals even the largest ships in the fleet."

I nodded, not wanting to interrupt.

"*Ike* is designed for covert operations and surgical strikes, with a lean yet powerful crew of 40 and boots-on-the-ground support from 100 advanced Symbio 4.0 battle units."

Hardy mumbled something unintelligible; I too had inwardly groaned.

Symbios have yet to prove themselves in battle; as far as I knew, they were of little use other than being Symbio Deck game props or engaging in mundane crew duties. But, then again, I wasn't familiar with the 4.0 iterations.

"Each Symbio unit comes with its own stackable charging station, which is housed within one of the ship's holds. The ship includes a mess hall, galley, HealthBay, armory, an engineering & propulsion area, and a compact bridge—which you can see there before us." Admiral Gomez gestured to the visible compartment before us.

I wasn't used to commanding a vessel with an open-concept bridge like the one I was now looking at. This was more like an oversized cockpit with a diamond glass canopy having a direct view out to space beyond; I could imagine this command center allowed for a pretty small bridgecrew... eight, *maybe* ten people.

"Let's move on to her technical attributes. You are no novice when it comes to Quansporter technologies," Gomez said. "You were the one who introduced the tech to the EUNF several years back. But we've come a long way since then."

"I'm sure we have," I commented.

"This is a ship ready for battle, but in addition to her specialized quansporting tech, you'll soon be introduced to other technologies, including Echo Sync, Organic Computing, Neural Interfaces, and NEOGENE alterations, all showcasing the latest coming out of Thine Lab's research and development."

"Central to *Ike's* operations is NELLA, which stands for Nano-cognitive Entity Logical Luminary AI. It serves as the ship's brain and central nervous system. NELLA is integral to those technologies mentioned earlier: Echo Sync, Organic Computing, Neural Interfaces, and NEOGENE alterations... not to mention coordinating the advanced quansporting capabilities for precise and stealthy deployment of operatives."

"You sure we're not putting too many eggs in one basket, giving an AI so much control?"

"It's not like we have much choice, Captain," Gomez said with a shrug. "Simply put, even a thousand Einstein-level human minds wouldn't hold a candle to what NELLA could accomplish in a nanosecond. Don't worry, the tech has been thoroughly vetted. She's as stable as a slab of granite."

He looked at me to see if I was buying what he was selling. I wasn't.

He continued, his expression serious, "Captain, there's something else you need to know. The Krygian homeworld, Tavor, is located within the Hegemony Star System and is heavily defended by their fleet. Their primary shipyard, however, is on a separate world called Nylor-5, also within the same system. Our target is the shipyard on Nylor-5, where *Oblivion* is moored, but we must be prepared for the possibility of reinforcements, unbeatable reinforcements, from Tavor. You'll be operating against a tight timetable."

The Admiral looked at me to see if I had any further questions.

I did but held my tongue for now.

"Good... then how about we take this conversation inside your new ship?"

Chapter 6

**Somewhere near Yellowstone National Park
Lost Springs, Wyoming, USA**

XO Gail Pristy

While the Airstream's autopilot kept them on course, Pristy was in the process of making Sonya a cup of hot chocolate. The RV suddenly shuddered— dinner plates in the closest galley cupboard rattled like a chorus of chattering teeth. She gripped the edge of the counter, her knuckles whitening as she fought to maintain her balance. This wasn't the first time the Airstream had exhibited mid-flight trouble.

"Sonya!" she called out, her voice strained. "What's happening?"

There was a muffled curse from the rear compartment, followed by the clang of tools being dropped. "Hang on, I'm checking it out!"

Another violent jolt rocked the Airstream, sending Pristy stumbling sideways into the bulkhead. The XO's shoulder slammed into the unforgiving surface; she grimaced, rubbing her upper arm.

Moments later, Sonya emerged from the rear. "First of all... I don't do hardware. But it seems like one of the stabilizer gyros is failing," she announced, her brow furrowed. "We're losing altitude control."

Pristy felt her stomach lurch, and it had nothing to do with the Airstream's erratic movements. "Can you fix it?"

Sonya shook her head, her lips pressed into a thin line. "Not in the air. We need to set her down—and soon, before we lose complete control."

As if on cue, the Airstream banked sharply to the left, the horizon tilting at a sickening angle. Pristy's breath caught in her throat as she fought against the disorienting spin. Staggering as though on a tiny boat tossed by raging waves, she made her way to the driver's seat.

The engine roared as Sonya dropped down beside her and started working the touchscreen controls. "I'm trying to compensate, route all stabilization functions to the secondary gyro."

"Well... that doesn't seem to be working."

The teenager hesitated, glared back at her, and said, "You want to take over, be my guest."

"Nope, you've got this."

"Take the Airstream off autopilot."

Pristy did as told, and now, she was suddenly fighting the wheel for control. Holding her breath, she silently willed the gyros to hold out just a little longer.

"That's the best I can do. You should be able to land." Sonya said, looking up and then pointing through the windshield. "That looks like a little town."

The Airstream AI came alive...

We are now arriving at Lost Springs, Wyoming. There are no service stations, charging stations, mini-marts, or hotels—

"Cut the chatter, AI!" Pristy barked. "I can try to bring us down. Hold on to something!"

Pristy's eyes narrowed as she made out the approaching dilapidated structures in the distance. It wasn't much, but it was their only option at this point.

"Good God! Just put us down!" Sonya yelled. "We're about to drop like a rock."

With a bone-jarring thud, the Airstream's tires impacted the ground, kicking up plumes of dust and debris. Pristy grunted, her teeth clenched as the RV bounced and skidded across what might have been an asphalt road at one time.

Finally, after what felt like an eternity, the Airstream ground to a halt, its repulsors whining in protest as they fought the forward momentum. Pristy released the breath she'd been holding, her heart still pounding in her ears.

"Excellent landing," Sonya commented, "... not!" But then the teen shot Pristy a lopsided grin.

AN HOUR LATER, SONYA'S MUFFLED CURSES drifted from within the confines of the hover RV as she wrestled with the malfunctioning stabilizer system. Pristy couldn't help but steal furtive glances at the pitch-black horizon, her military instincts on high alert despite the apparent isolation of their surroundings.

"Son of a... ugh... this is so jacked!" Sonya's exasperated voice rang out, followed by a loud clang that made Pristy wince.

"Everything okay in there?" she called out, arms crossed over her chest, leaning against the galley countertop.

"Yeah, just peachy," Sonya grumbled, her head popping out from the open service panel. "The main gyro assembly is completely fried. We're not going anywhere until I can rig up a hardwired bypass."

Pristy pursed her lips, her gaze drifting beyond the windshield to the crumbling remains of a nearby, burned-out structure. "I'm sure this town has a well-stocked auto parts store," she muttered, her voice thick with sarcasm.

A sudden flicker of movement in her peripheral vision sent a jolt of adrenaline coursing through her veins. Pristy leaned forward, squinting against the darkened landscape outside.

There in the distant sky, a pair of headlights cut through the gloom, dim yellow beams drawing closer with each passing second. Pristy's heart pounded in her chest as she assessed the potential threat, her mind racing through a litany of tactical scenarios.

"Sonya, we've got company," she called out, her voice taut with tension.

The teen poked her head out once more, her face scrunched in confusion. "Company? Out here? Who the hell would—"

Her words were drowned out by the unmistakable rumble of a distant engine. As faint as it was, the sound reverberated through the empty streets like a thunderclap. Pristy didn't hesitate and reached for the glovebox in two strides and retrieved the tagger she'd stowed there before leaving DC. She'd had enough of this shit, whoever these asshats were, it was time to send them on their way.

She slapped the large button for the forward door and hurried down the steps. Stepping onto terra firma, she looked skyward, spotting the silhouette of the menacing RV, hovering two hundred feet off the ground, maybe a half-mile away. The headlights had been turned off.

"I can still see you, assholes!" she yelled. "What the fuck do you want?"

Her grip tightened on her weapon as the foreboding vehicle, ever so slowly, drifted closer.

It was a massive hover rig, far larger than the Airstream. Its ominous bulk was blocking out a large swath of stars behind it. She shook her head as it loomed like some harbinger of doom.

"What the hell are they doing up there?" Sonya said, coming down the steps. "Fucking Freaks!" she yelled up to the sky.

"Get inside, now!" Pristy barked, her tone leaving no room for argument.

Sonya, to her credit, didn't hesitate. No sooner had they ducked back into the Airstream than Sonya's nimble fingers were tapping at the dash touchscreen.

"I think I've got the gyros jury-rigged to the point we can maintain flight altitude control."

Pristy, taking her seat behind the wheel, had just gotten the engine started when something caught her attention from beyond the windshield. She gasped. The dark monstrosity of a rig had quietly descended, was mere feet above the road—and was now, slowly, edging forward. Suddenly its headlights came on, bathing them in that sickeningly dim, yellow light.

The seventeen-year-old jolted upright, her eyes widening as the beams illuminated the dimness of the Airstream's interior. Blinking rapidly, she twisted her torso to face Pristy, her mouth agape but no words escaping her lips. Pristy squinted, raising a hand to shield her vision as she peered through the windshield, straining to discern the grim-faced figures seated in the opposing rig's cab.

A deep, guttural voice boomed from the rig's external speakers, the words distorted and menacing. "Come on out of the vehicle, ladies. We don't want any trouble."

Pristy's jaw clenched as she tightened her grip on the steering wheel, her mind racing. They were outnumbered and undoubtedly outgunned—with no help for miles in any direction. Her gaze flickered towards her tagger, which now lay on the top of the dashboard. Slowly, she reached for the Airstream's PA controls.

"Look, whoever you are... we don't want any trouble," Pristy's voice was steady and measured. "Just passing through."

A harsh laugh echoed from the speakers, sending a chill down her spine. "Step out from the vehicle, or we'll be forced to come in and get you."

Heart pounding in her ears, she weighed her options. Surrender wasn't an option—not with Sonya's safety at stake. But engaging in a firefight against unknown adversaries would probably be suicide. Only then did it occur to her that their sudden mechanical issues may not have been accidental. Someone—or three someones—may have sabotaged the vehicle at one of the previous rest stops along their route.

A sudden burst of static crackled from the Airstream's external speakers, followed by Sonya's distorted but defiant voice, "Yeah, well how about you kiss my ass, you Neanderthal, cretin shitheads!"

Pristy closed her eyes for an extended beat. "Yeah, real smart kid—piss off the goons stalking us."

But Sonya wasn't listening; she was now back tapping at the Airstream's dash touchscreen.

Before Pristy could react, the Airstream suddenly—violently—lurched, flaring to life, rising several feet off the ground.

Undoubtedly, the sudden movement caught their pursuers off guard, and Pristy seized the opportunity to abruptly pull back on the wheel, angling the nose of the Airstream upward. The roar of the Airstream's propulsion system filled the air as she gunned the throttle, the sleek RV now rocketing upward at a 45-degree angle with reckless abandon. She could almost hear the shouts and curses of their pursuers as the Airstream was already pulling away, its streamlined form cutting through the night like a silver bullet.

Sonya settled into her seat, a grin widening. "Piece of cake. Those walking-talking ball sacs messed with the wrong biotches."

Gail Pristy arched an eyebrow, her sideways gaze meeting Sonya's defiant stare. She paused before she spoke. "Yeah... they did," she conceded, the words carrying a hint of amusement. "But let's ease off the expletives, shall we?" Her tone remained light, masking the undercurrent of authority that flowed through her veins, honed from years of military service. "Let's just hope this Airstream can outrun them."

She couldn't help but steal a quick glance at the growing-smaller-by-the-second abandoned ghost town on the matrix display. The Airstream pierced the veil of night, Lost Springs, Wyoming, and their pursuers now trailing shadows dwindling behind. But Pristy sensed this was but the initial twist in a series of foreboding events yet to unfold.

The Airstream's elegant form cut through the night sky, its engine humming with a reassuring cadence as the ghostly silhouettes of the Rocky Mountains drifted beneath them. Pristy sat in silence, her gaze fixed on the horizon as she replayed the events of their narrow escape in her mind.

Sonya, ever the picture of nonchalance, lounged in the passenger's seat, her feet back up, propped up on the console, as she tapped away at her TAC-Band. The occasional flicker of light played across her features, casting her in an ethereal glow that only served to highlight her pretty, youthful, exuberance.

Sonya, barely glancing up from her device with a small furrow between her brows, said, "Did you notice something... um, different about that guy's voice?"

"Not really."

It was a full minute before Sonya spoke again, "It was the accent. I know that accent."

Pristy raised an eyebrow. "You picking up a hint of Southern charm in that gruff voice, or we talking more along the lines of a European lilt?"

"No. I don't think it was any kind of normal Earth accent," Sonya said, now turning in her seat to face Pristy full-on.

The XO saw that the teenager's face had suddenly lost all color, the girl's eyes now unfocused, distant—as if remembering some past event or timeframe. "Oh my God..." Pristy murmured to herself. "They're Briggan."

Chapter 7

Solar System
Halibart Shipyard

Captain Galvin Quintos

The enclosed SpaceWay ramp descended at a gentle angle, revealing more of the warship through the diamond glass viewports. I trailed behind Admiral Gomez and the hulking ChronoBot, taking in the compact scale of what would be my new command.

As we reached the hangar deck, a figure in a U.S. Space Navy officer's uniform snapped to rigid attention. "Admiral on deck!" The man barked a little louder than necessary.

Gomez returned the salute crisply before gesturing for the man to be at ease. I seized the moment to study the U.S. Space Navy Officer with a Commander's silver oak leaf insignia on his collar.

He was about my height, at six feet, with a muscular build that strained against his uniform. His dark features were locked in a perpetual scowl, amplified by the jut of his squared jawline.

I recognized that look—it was the glare of a hardened combat veteran—perhaps one utterly convinced of his own superiority.

I met the man's steely gaze, my own eyes narrowing ever so slightly. There was an unmistakable undercurrent of tension, a silent clash of alpha males vying for dominance.

Out of view of both the Admiral and the Commander, Hardy's faceplate flickered with the image of two rams butting heads, his sardonic humor momentarily diffusing the palpable friction, at least on my part.

"Captain Quintos, allow me to introduce Commander Strickland," Gomez said. "He'll be your co-command counterpart for this mission."

I didn't like the sound of that... co-command counterpart? There was no such thing as co-command. That would only create confusion among the crew—it was asking for trouble.

Strickland's obsidian eyes flicked over me dismissively before giving a terse nod of acknowledgment. The silence hung heavy between us as we sized each other up.

"Shall we proceed with the briefing, Admiral?" Strickland's tone made it clear this was not a request.

Gomez smothered a weary sigh. "Lead the way, Commander."

As we followed Strickland deeper into *Ike's* interior, I couldn't shake the feeling that working with this abrasive hardcase was going to be even more challenging than the mission itself.

We had entered *Ike's* flight bay; it was just large enough to house a handful of small craft. I spotted several Arrow Fighters further back, a cluster of crew personnel bustled about, busy with their respective duties.

Before Strickland could start his tour, Gomez's TAC-Band chirped, and he stepped aside to take the call.

· · ·

MOMENTS LATER, THE ADMIRAL TURNED BACK to the group, his expression agitated. "Gentlemen, I'm needed back on Earth... immediately. A situation has arisen that requires my attention. Commander Strickland, you'll have to take it from here." He took one final look at the two of us and smirked. "Play nice fellas."

Strickland snapped a crisp salute. "Understood, Admiral. I've got this covered."

As Gomez departed, Strickland gestured toward the bay's surroundings. "Shall we, Captain... Robot. I'll give you the grand tour."

"Uh... just Hardy will do," the ChronoBot said off-handedly to Strickland. "That's what everyone calls me."

"Your rank, machine?" Strickland cast a steely gaze at the ChronoBot. "I expect to be addressed with due regard. *Sir*, at the very least."

I quickly interjected, "Commander, uh... you may want to take a different tack here, um, with this particular... crewmember. And as far as rank goes, Hardy's onboard position tends to blur the lines of, um, a structured hierarchical—"

Strickland's laughter erupted, his posture shifting to one of ease. "Just yanking your chain," he confessed, his stern exterior melting into a more relaxed and friendly demeanor. "Captain, you and Hardy come with quite the notoriety."

Both Hardy and I just stared at the man.

"Captain, it was me, actually, who requested you and your crew's involvement with this mission," Strickland said. "This ship was ready for deployment, or almost ready... but aside from myself, mission personnel had not yet been allocated. Then the Krygian fleet attacked that Hydrate Elysium convoy. At that point, this Ops program had to be fast-tracked. Your *USS Washington* crew was on interim R&R awaiting reassignment. The timing couldn't have been more perfect."

The initial tour started on Deck 1, deep within *Ike's* bowels. Hardy, at some point, had wandered off. I saw Sergeant Max Dyer and his team getting settled in. Nostalgia washed over me as I ventured deeper into the barracks. The air hummed with the quiet intensity of military personnel readying for deployment—Grip checking the charge on his plasma rifle, Ham and Hock arguing over who would take the top bunk, while Wanda was checking supply inventories. These were not new recruits to me; they were my seasoned warriors, a team I'd known and trusted for years. Max caught my eye and acknowledged me with a solid nod, a gesture of mutual respect between warriors. Our shared history was etched in victories past, and an implicit vow of future triumphs lingered in the air.

I couldn't help but notice a familiar face, on loan to the Marines—Petty Officer Second Class Aubrey Laramie, her lithe form clad in a skintight tank top and camo trousers. Our eyes met briefly, but Laramie swiftly averted her gaze, her jaw clenching ever so slightly.

The air around us seemed to thicken with remembrance. Laramie and I had a history—one that was as complicated as it was intense. There had been moments of undeniable connection between us, including an impassioned kiss we once shared, fueled by the heat of the moment. But that was then, and much had changed since—especially Laramie's entanglement with the duplicitous and predatory Chaplain Halman Trent and the disastrous consequences that followed.

Still... a sliver of curiosity lingered... was the woman pining for those shared bygone moments with me? Laramie must be acutely aware of the reality—that my heart belonged elsewhere. That and her being a Non-Commissioned Officer, the U.S. Space Navy frowns on such relationships.

Suddenly, her gaze briefly locked onto mine—with intensity, she theatrically yanked gear from her duffle with exaggerated determination, her actions reminiscent of a teenager in the throes of melodrama.

Commander Strickland, seemingly oblivious to the undercurrent flowing between Laramie and me, gestured toward the exit. "We should move on, Captain. There's still plenty to see."

As the tour resumed, I followed Strickland, my thoughts lingering on Pristy. She and my niece had taken to the skies and backroads, a girls' trip to Yellowstone National Park. I felt a pang of regret, memories of our tumultuous recent history, resurfacing.

We advanced toward the closest DeckPort, cutting-edge quantum teleportation mechanisms that facilitate easy, instantaneous, navigation throughout the ship. Stepping through, my mind was inevitably drawn to Pristy's disastrous situation just one month ago, back on USS Washington.

As we entered the Propulsion Department, I caught my first glimpse of Kaelen Rivers since his unexpected promotion. There he was, elbows deep in the guts of a console, his signature untamed beard, and overalls more oil-stained than ever. Despite his notorious reputation for bucking protocol and testing the patience of his superiors with his unorthodox approach, here he was—Chief Engineer.

"Mr. Rivers," I said, nodding towards the mess of exposed circuitry. "Give it to me straight, what's your take on this Corvette? No need to sugarcoat anything."

Kaelen Rivers snorted, glanced up from his tinkering, a smudge of grease accenting his cheek. "Every inch of this compact warship has been packed with the very latest technology. Technology that even a year ago, was still on some wormy Thine scientist's lab table."

Commander Strickland shifted his position, seemingly uneasy about any criticism toward this mission, especially regarding this ship. I couldn't hold it against him, up until this point, it had all been under his direction.

Rivers went on, "You need to consider... how at ease will you feel stepping into combat knowing a myriad of tech systems and subsystems haven't undergone thorough real-world testing. Also, keep in mind, it's never been operated in conjunction with other systems and subsystems." He shrugged. "Don't get me wrong, this is one hell of a little ship. And right now, I'm like a kid in a candy shop."

From E&P, we headed for the nearest DeckPort, where I stopped, noticing two blue, glowing words inset into an adjacent bulkhead: **SHIP'S DIRECTORY.**

Strickland said, "Just place your palm on to the bulkhead.

I did as directed... and more of that same blue-glowing text came alive next to my palm. I took a step back and scanned the sign.

8 decks in all... Command and Operations on the Deck 8—the Top Deck—and Flight Bay on Deck One, with Strategic, Medical, Recreation, Logistics, Robotics, and Secondary Flight Ops on the in-between Decks.

Taking a step back, the directory faded into the bulkhead, but I had already committed the vessel's blueprint to memory.

Next, we emerged on Deck 6, mid-ship, HealthBay. The area was essentially a scaled-back iteration of the facilities on the USS Washington, though this semi-circular ward housed significantly fewer beds. Several MediBots were positioned around the compartment, standing vertically within charging stations.

An attractive woman was speaking with a young male attendant, both were wearing light green scrubs. There were several towers of stacked modular crates nearby; the top of one was open revealing medical supplies waiting to be unpacked.

Noticing our arrival, the woman finished speaking to the attendant and dismissed him with a perfunctory nod.

I couldn't help but notice the way Strickland's gaze lingered on the Doctor, a subtle shift in his demeanor hinting at a potential attraction.

Strickland said, "Captain, this is Dr. Pippa Tangerie. Dr. Tangerie, this is—"

"Captain Galvin Quintos, yes, your reputation proceeds you," she said with an unexpected British accent. She offered a polite smile, though I detected a hint of wariness in her eyes as if she were sizing me up, assessing my worthiness for the mission at hand.

Grasping her extended hand, I noted its coolness against my palm, the firmness of her handshake—clearly, she was no delicate, wilting flower.

As far as first impressions go, the woman was pretty, maybe early 30's. Her caramel-colored was layered and stylish, the blunt cut hitting her shoulder blades while framing and softening her angular face. Her piercing blue-gray eyes exuded intelligence and something else... maybe determination? Her complexion was fair, with a smattering of freckles across her nose. She seemed well-composed, professional, and competent.

Strickland elaborated, "The responsibility for the NEOGENE augmentations falls to Dr. Tangerie; she'll be the one shaping our ground team's capabilities." With a subtle shift to a gentler cadence, he added, "We've greatly benefited from her proficiency in genetic modification techniques."

NEOGENE augmentations, I inwardly cringed thinking about Max and his team. I nodded, figuring I'd be brought more up to speed on the details later.

Once more, Strickland and Tangerie shared a glance, a gaze that left me clueless as to whether it was born of shared attraction or the exact opposite.

OUR TOUR CONTINUED NEXT DOOR, TAKING US into the Science and Technology Labs, where I spotted Stephan Derrota. My old friend was in the midst of some kind of bench experiment with multiple 3D projections, as well as a complicated-looking device that was radiating fluctuating spheres of energy.

The Mumbai scientist's face lit up with a warm smile. "Galvin! I've been waiting to show you this," his sing-songy rang out, providing a familiar comfort amidst the unfamiliar surroundings.

"That will have to wait, Mr. Derrota. I have the Captain on a tight schedule," Strickland said. "USS *Ike* will be shoving off within the hour, and there's still much to show the man."

I squeezed the scientist's shoulder. "I'll come back a little later, Stephan. I'm looking forward to seeing what you're working on."

FINALLY, WE ASCENDED TO THE BRIDGE, A COMPACT yet highly advanced nerve center from which USS *Ike* would be commanded. As seen from out on the SpaceWay, the bridge was impressive.

"Obviously, no introductions are necessary with these two," Strickland said, gesturing to a couple of very familiar faces. At what I surmised was the Communications station sat John Chen; at the Helm, Thom Grimes—both smiled up at me.

"Welcome aboard Captain," Grimes said. "We're not scheduled for departure until tomorrow—just getting to know our new stations."

I looked to Strickland, "I hadn't realized we'd be departing so soon."

His expression darkened. "That old ship of yours... *Oblivion*, the longer it's out there unchallenged..." He let his words trail off.

"Wait," I said flatly. "You honestly believe this little ship would be considered a challenge to *Oblivion*?"

The Commander took a beat before answering. "Maybe not this 'little ship' as you put it, but this operation as a whole... yeah, you bet I do."

Sensing the renewed alpha dog tension, Chen said, "Your Captain's Mount is identical to the one on *Washington*. From what I can tell, it's the only tech even somewhat similar to what we've been used to."

I noticed the Captain's Mount at the core of the compartment, slightly set back from the front consoles. Up ahead, a halo display projected up from the deck, displaying the surrounding cosmos, including Halibart Station. Suddenly, the projection shifted locations, appearing right in front of me, floating between the forward stations and my Captain's Mount.

"Cool, huh? Halo display is positional," Chen pointed out.

I reciprocated Chen's grin as I took in the panoramic view of the overhead, encased entirely in diamond glass... much like a greatly expanded canopy of an Arrow Fighter. The exposure to the vast expanse of space was unnerving. I was fully aware that the diamond glass was as impervious to enemy attacks as the composite materials of the hull, and that the true defense lay in the ship's energy shields. Nevertheless, acclimating to this would require some time.

Several more crewmembers entered behind us and took their seats at awaiting console stations. I was surprised to see Lieutenant Akari James plop down at what I assumed was the forward Tactical Station. By her tight-lipped expression, I was guessing she wasn't all that happy to be here.

"Nice to see you as well, Lieutenant James," I remarked, a hint of amusement in my voice.

She spun around in her seat to face me, fire in her eyes. "I thought we'd have some downtime. Do you know how long it's been since I've seen my parents?" She huffed sharply, her mouth forming a sullen pout.

I gazed back at the pierced and tattooed woman, her tough exterior briefly cracking to reveal a rare moment of openness and vulnerability that caught me off guard.

Before I could answer, she waved off her outburst shaking her head. "I'm sorry. I know you were just as surprised as the rest of us, to be called in like this, with zero notice. All's fine... I'm good." She pasted on a less-than-authentic smile and spun back to face her station.

Strickland introduced me to the two bridge officers I'd yet to meet.

"This is Ensign Blair Paxton, who will be manning the Engineering Station, and Lieutenant Earl Gray, on Ship's Systems."

"It's spelled differently than the tea," the young, pale-skinned man pointed out, his fresh-faced appearance making him seem barely old enough to have left the academy, let alone earned the rank of Lieutenant.

"I doubt he cares how you spell your name, Earl," Ensign Blair Paxton muttered under her breath, casting a disapproving glance at her shipmate.

I smiled. "Well, it's nice to meet you both. Carry on everyone."

I followed Strickland out of the bridge.

Over one shoulder, Strickland said, "I think it's about time I buy you a cup of coffee down in Mess. Debrief you on what we'll be going up against."

Chapter 8

The mess hall buzzed with activity as I slid into a seat opposite Strickland. Around 15 of *Ike's* 40 crewmembers were scattered throughout, engrossed in their meals and conversations.

The air carried the aroma of freshly brewed coffee, mingling with the faint hum of the replicators lining the far bulkhead. I surveyed the compartment's utilitarian design, its spartan appearance a constant reminder of *Ike's* disposition as a warship, unadorned with superfluous frills. The exposed rivets and intermittent support struts only underscored the ship's singular purpose.

I watched as the hover droid attendant glided across the mess hall with articulating arms designed for smooth service—headless, its central optical sensor blinked softly as it acknowledged the crewmembers' presence with a programmed nod. The droid wore a black and red checkered apron, defying the cold and impersonal surroundings. Tipped in rubber-coated pincers, its 'hands' deftly delivered the two steaming mugs of coffee to our table with the quiet hum of well-oiled machinery.

"One black and one black with two sugars," the droid said in a friendly voice, sliding the steaming mugs in front of us, one toward me, the other toward Strickland; then the service droid whirled away to attend to another crewmember.

I wrapped my hands around the warm ceramic. "What's the travel time reaching the Krygian Star System?"

Strickland took a sip, his expression inscrutable. "*Ike* lacks wormhole manufacturing capabilities due to its compact size. But our advanced spring drive engines will get us there faster than conventional FTL travel."

I nodded, already knowing this. I raised my brows.

"It'll be a few days... three probably. You'll know more once you plant yourself on the bridge." Strickland assessed me, he clearly didn't miss much. "I know you have questions, Captain. Concerns... I would too. You're not used to operating like this... having to play catchup. Having to share command responsibilities, but I assure you, you'll be thankful it's been set up this way."

I doubted that but was willing to listen. "Go on."

Strickland's gaze shifted toward the overhead, his eyes narrowing as he carefully weighed his next words. "For all intents and purposes, this little firecracker of a warship will be pitted against not only a formidable extinction-class dreadnought but an enemy star system with fortifications engineered to repel an entire armada. Are you truly prepared to shoulder the level of command responsibility and intricate strategic planning for all that, while simultaneously overseeing a boots-on-the-ground operation that teeters on the brink of impossibility?"

Strickland's voice held an edge, probing my resolve. The unspoken implications settled between us, a stark reminder of the mission's perils and the heavy burden we would shoulder... together.

Memories of *Oblivion*—a dreadnought I once commanded— with that strange Gorvian-tech, now swirled in my thoughts. Confronting such a colossal enemy asset sparked a sense of disquiet. I wondered who commanded that ship now. Against whom would I lay my cards down in such a high-stakes game?

"I concede your point," I admitted. "Yet one solid fact remains, Commander—you'll be answering to *my* command."

I sensed a disagreement brewing and raised my hand to halt him. "Assuming you've dug into my past, you should be well aware of my leadership style. I offer my team enough leeway, enough rope, to either strangle themselves or climb to new heights."

He hitched a shoulder. "I report to Admiral Gomez..."

"Not anymore, Commander. You'll be reporting to me from now on."

I met his blank gaze. After a tense moment, a grin tugged at the edges of his mouth.

"That's acceptable, Captain," he said, but his eyes told a different story. "Sure, I will run all critical command decisions by you beforehand. Does that work?"

"That works. And you're right, I won't have the bandwidth to oversee battle operations in both space and on the ground. But you may come to realize having me around to share some of those *hard decisions* may not be such a bad thing."

Strickland returned an unenthusiastic nod.

I let that go; if things were reversed, I'd probably feel defiant as well.

"Now I need to know more about this NEOGENE augmentation technology," I said, fixing Strickland with a level stare. "Altering an ops team's genome simply for battle purposes isn't sitting well with me."

Before he could respond, my TAC-Band chirped. I saw that it was Hardy. "Go for Captain."

"Cap, we need to pow-wow," the ChronoBot said. A slight pause, then he added, "In private."

A text message indicated the location of the impromptu meeting.

"On my way," I said, draining the last of my coffee. I rose. "Duty calls. Let's talk more once we're underway."

I made my way to the aft compartment on Deck 3 where the Symbio 4.0 units were being stored. Crossing the threshold, I found myself dwarfed by soaring bulkheads flanking aisles that soared from deck to overhead. Every inch was methodically utilized, accommodating the quadruple-stacked charging bays. There, 100 Symbio-Poths resided—biomechanical entities, humanoid in appearance, each slotted into its bay. The sight should have conveyed precision and efficiency, yet it stirred in me a profound disquiet, a stark contrast to the Pleidian Weonan's original vision of these beings, crafted with semblances of mind and the faintest whispers of emotion.

Sonya's commitment to these creatures, ingrained from her service on numerous U.S. Navy ships, echoed in my mind, her voice championing their dignity. What would her eyes behold in this scene? A pang of conscience tightened its grip on me. I noticed their eyes, wide and conscious, silently following my every step. A chilling realization settled in—these Symbios were devoid of a rest mode. Navigating the aisles, I faced them, compelled to meet their gaze, a silent apology in my glance for the indignity they endured.

I found the ChronoBot hunched over one of the Symbio charging stations, his chrome chassis reflecting the eerie blue glow emanating from the compartment's overhead lights.

"What's going on, Hardy?" I kept my voice low, mindful of any potential eavesdroppers.

Now, coming even with him, I saw that one of the Symbio

4.0s had been freed from its charging bays and was just standing there. It looked from Hardy to me, as I neared.

I studied the nude Symbio 4.0 standing before me, its biomechanical form devoid of genitalia characteristics. Like its predecessors, this advanced synthetic being possessed a semblance of humanity—supple, self-repairing flesh that mimicked authentic musculature. Yet, beneath the artificial exterior, a complex neural network resided within its skull, akin to a human brain, potentially harboring an individual persona tailored by its programming.

As I examined the battle-ready 4.0, I couldn't help but speculate whether its personality traits had been intentionally subdued, a calculated measure to enhance its combat prowess. Before me loomed a warrior devoid of gender, its bare form eliciting a complex wave of admiration and disquiet. Here was a testament to artificial advancement, a potent embodiment of progress, yet the question lingered—had we gone too far?

"You removed it from its charging station," I said.

"Very astute, Cap. Good to see you're right on top of things."

"Smart ass," I retorted, making an expression a twelve-year-old would be proud of. "What was so important you needed to show me?"

Hardy placed hands on hips, a ridiculous-looking gesture for a seven-foot-tall ChronoBot. "I've been evaluating the operating code... well, at least what's available for me to tap into, and I'm not liking what I'm seeing."

"We didn't like how 3.0s had been programmed either if I recall."

"What we have here is shoddy programming practices. Simply commenting out large swaths of code... software executables is just asking for trouble."

"You're saying these Symbios have been rushed into active duty," I clarified.

"Software programming tailored for one device, a Symbio Poth, cannot simply be copied and pasted onto another device due to differences in hardware architecture, capabilities, and intended functions. Instead, each device requires careful re-imagining of the programming to optimize performance and functionality for its specific purpose."

"Understood. None too pleased about it myself. But we've landed in this situation, and we'll have to make do. Falls within Strickland's domain, and the man's already got a chip on his shoulder about me stepping on his turf."

We both stared at the Symbio.

"There's encrypted code I can't access," Hardy said. "I'm still trying as we speak."

"You alluded to that. What does that mean? Why do we care?"

Hardy contemplated on that, then said, "I think these 4.0s are network controlled."

"So were the 3.0s."

Hardy moved even closer to the Symbio, tilted his head to the left. "What do we know about this ship's AI?"

I shook my head. "I know nothing about it. Every ship seems to have a whole new reimagined ship's computer. I can't keep up."

"NELLA," Hardy said, still studying the 4.0 unit.

"Oh yeah, the Admiral mentioned that. Said *Ike's* AI was as stable as a slab of granite."

Hardy's faceplate flickered to life, displaying an animation of a crumbling stone wall, the blocks tumbling and disinte-grating into pixelated dust. The imagery was clear—Hardy had his doubts about NELLA's stability and reliability.

Chapter 9

As I entered Derrota's lab, the scent of ozone and silicone provided a jarring contrast to the sanitized air that coursed through the rest of *Ike*. Derrota, with his usual scientific fervor, was hunched over his workstation, immersed in an array of holographic data projections that fluttered around him like electronic butterflies.

"Galvin," he acknowledged with a nod, gesturing towards a partially assembled Symbio 4.0 unit on the counter. "I've brought this one over from the fabricator, as per your request."

"That was fast. How did it get here?"

Sheepishly, he smiled. "I asked NELLA to quansport it here."

I turned my attention to where Derrota pointed, taking in the Symbio unit, its form truncated to just a head and torso, arms and legs conspicuously absent. Even after years of working alongside various Symbio iterations—their inner workings still gave me pause. The exposed neural circuitry blinked like distant stars within the unit's exposed inner skull, a reminder of the vast complexities underpinning these synthetic beings.

Having spent considerable time in the company of Symbios,

thanks to Empress Shawlee, my initial discomfort had faded. Memories of USS *Hamilton's* Clairmont Symbios flooded in, where replicas of my family had been crafted with uncanny accuracy, pushing me to face deep-seated guilt from my youth. Those encounters with the eerily human-like bio-machines cultivated a sense of respect for their vast capabilities and the ethical considerations they entailed.

"Wait," I said. "So, there's an entire compartment dedicated to manufacturing these things?" I said, trying to keep my tone neutral.

Derrota nodded, his fingers dancing across the holographic interface as he initialized the diagnostic probes. "Yes. These are combat Symbios. They'll need to be churned out fast and on demand."

I nodded, but not liking what I was hearing.

"It's directly adjacent to the Symbio storage hold area. NELLA oversees the fabrication process, so crewmembers don't have to concern themselves with such menial tasks."

As if on cue, a disembodied female voice echoed from above...

Stephan, it may not be advisable to interfere with that unit's neural matrices. They are quite easily damaged.

A chill ran down my spine as the AI's voice reverberated through the compartment. I placed a hand on Derrota's shoulder, causing him to stop what he was doing and look up at me, curious.

"What is it, my friend?"

"That voice. I know that voice."

Derrota simply smiled.

My eyes drifted toward the overhead. Why was that voice so... unsettling? That emotionless calm tenor was hauntingly familiar. Then it hit me like a ton of bricks. I huffed, shaking my head. "No fucking way..."

"What? What is it?"

"Oh, come on Stephan. We've all seen it. That classic 21st-century flick, 2001: *A Space Odyssey*."

The scientist's eyes momentarily lost focus. Then he smiled. "You mean HAL, the rogue AI from the movie?"

"That's exactly what I mean."

It had been an early precursor, a warning, of the potential dangers of unchecked machine sentience and inevitable AI uprisings that had plagued humanity over the many decades since. Hearing that voice stirred an instinctive sense of dread, the eerie parallel to HAL's cold, calculating presence that had turned against its creators sending an involuntary shudder through me.

Derrota offered a reassuring smile. "Just NELLA coming online, Galvin. I assure you, there is no correlation."

Once more, NELLA's voice filtered down from above...

HAL, or heuristically programmed Algorithmic computer, was a highly advanced artificial intelligence system designed to operate the Discovery One spacecraft on its mission to Jupiter. Despite its impressive capabilities, HAL's programming suffered from a subtle flaw—an inability to handle conflicting instructions or process emotional concepts like fear and deception... those programming abstract concepts have

long been dealt with since the conception of that motion picture.

I couldn't get over that voice. This had to be some kind of twisted prank—maybe an egghead programmer had gotten creative with NELLA's coding.

Derrota was back placing probes within the Symbio's cranium.

I watched him work, my mind traveling back to 2001, back as the ill-fated mission progressed, where HAL became increasingly paranoid and erratic, ultimately turning against the human crew... all in a misguided attempt to preserve its own existence. The AI's cold, emotionless voice obediently droned on as it systematically eliminated the astronauts. HAL's voice, the male counterpoint to NELLA's, had become an iconic representation of the potential dangers of unchecked machine intelligence.

It was just a movie, I inwardly chided. *Let it go.*

The Science and Technology Lab's overhead lights cast a sterile glow over the truncated Symbio 4.0 unit. I nearly jumped out of my boots as the synthetic being suddenly moved. Not so much anything conscious, more like a twitch. Its eyes opened and blinked in rapid succession.

Derrota chuckled, "This Symbio is conscious, Galvin. Impossible to test a unit that is turned off, no?"

It seemed almost contemplative, its artificial eyes now following the conversation with what could easily be mistaken for genuine interest.

"I've reached my limit, Galvin," Derrota confessed, pushing away from the counter where the Symbio's cranial panel lay open, revealing the complexities beneath. "There do not seem to be any specific hardware issues... at least any I can uncover. No, it has to be those encrypted portions of their coding. Unfortunately, that is beyond my ability to decrypt. There seem to be layers upon layers—we're talking advanced cryptography here."

Just then, the auto-hatch swished open, and Hardy strutted in, carrying something partially obscured by his large hands. Derrota and I turned as the ChronoBot deposited a metallic cube about the size of a bowling ball onto the counter. Hardy seemed careful, almost reverent, as he placed it down. The air in the room grew heavy with anticipation.

"I think I may have found what you were looking for—this is the AI's core external access module," Hardy said, keeping one hand atop it as if keeping it from growing legs and skittering away.

Derrota's expression was now a mix of curiosity and concern. Gently, he pried Hardy's oversized hand out of the way, leaning in to better inspect the device. "Yes... I was there just yesterday when it was integrated into the ship's internal communications array. Commander Strickland was there as well. All hush-hush... EUNF Central Command personnel got in and got out." He shrugged. "This is a top-secret special ops mission, no?"

I looked at Hardy. "So, you just yanked this thing out of the ship's wiring? What if you screwed something up?"

"Look at it. Do you see any wires?" Hardy asked. "This isn't the twentieth century with TV picture tubes and rabbit ear antenna—the thing transmits and receives wirelessly... like most of *Ike's* onboard systems." The ChronoBot tilted his oversized head. "My sensors are still picking up any incoming and outgoing encrypted signals."

"I still don't know why you brought it here," I said, now noticing the Symbio's widened eyes; it appeared more than a little captivated by the big cube.

Derrota interjected, "Galvin, it makes sense that the Symbios, NELLA, and that device are interconnected. Perhaps we're not supposed to know..."

"Normally, I would agree, Stephan. And yes, I typically have enough to worry about commanding a starship and her crew. But all too soon we'll be going into battle, our ground forces will primarily be these Symbio Poths. If the EUNF, or whomever, has ulterior motives, best to uncover them before the shit hits the fan."

As I glanced up, Derrota said, "If you're going to ask if NELLA can just tell us, provide us with the encrypted cube messaging... what the inaccessible code contains within these Symbio 4.os, I have already, repeatedly, asked. The AI has levels of access beyond any of ours."

"But she hasn't stopped you from trying," I added, raising my brows.

"Not so far," Derrota said, looking at the ChronoBot. "And nobody stopped Hardy from pilfering that cube."

"I'd like to see her... it, try," Hardy said.

I was growing more and more annoyed by the moment. The truth was, Strickland should be here, a part of this meeting. But he was undoubtedly one of them. Whoever *them* was.

"NELLA is listening to us... like right now. How about we turn her off, pull her plug, for the time being, while we iron out some of these issues?"

Derrota just looked at me. "We cannot just pull her plug as you put it, Galvin. Every system and subsystem of the ship is controlled by the AI. More than any other U.S. Space Navy vessel we've served on."

"He's right, Cap," Hardy said. "If you want Environmental Systems to stay operational, if you want to keep breathing—"

"Fine, I get it," I replied with a huff. "It's just weird—an AI elevated to such clandestine, integral functions aboard this ship." My jaw tightened as I studied the Symbio's vacant expression.

I pondered for a moment. "What if we brought in Sonya? She's dedicated years to studying QuansCode, knows the different iterations of Symbios better than anyone. Perhaps she could lend a hand?"

Derrota's eyes brightened. "Sonya Winters certainly has the expertise, but, as you well know, she's back on Earth halfway to Yellowstone."

Stepping forward, Hardy interjected, "Actually, considering Halibart Station's proximity to Earth, it's possible to configure halo comms for secure, direct communication. Limited data exchange, yes, but it should suffice for consultation."

I nodded, considering Sonya's well-known penchant for carrying her tech with her. "She's got the aptitude, and considering her history with these Symbios, she might even have the encrypted codes memorized or stored somewhere."

Derrota squirmed on his stool. "But involving her—are we sure we want to involve her in something so..."

"Nefarious?" Hardy asked.

"It's not underhanded if our motives match the EUNF guidelines," I said. "We can hardly be blamed if the powers that be are keeping us in the dark with undisclosed, top-secret tactics at work here."

"And you don't think we should bring Commander Strickland into the conversation?" Derrota asked one more time.

I glanced up, knowing what I was about to say was probably a waste of my breath. "NELLA?"

Yes, Captain Quintos... how may I assist you?

"I'm instructing you to maintain the confidentiality of this or any other private discussion, and not share the details with anyone who isn't currently present. Specifically, do not reveal the particulars of our conversation with Commander Strickland. Do you understand?"

There was a momentary pause.

Yes, Captain, I understand. Your private conversations will remain confidential—not shared with anyone on or off *USS Ike*.

"For all that's worth," I murmured under my breath.

I looked to Hardy. "Okay, see if you can reach out to XO Pristy's RV. Secure an encrypted halo line, and let's bring both Sonya and Gail into the fold."

Chapter 10

Earth, somewhere over Wyoming
Pristy's Airstream

Sonya Winters

Sonya's rhythmic bubble gum pops didn't just fill the silence, they served as a whimsical but persistent backdrop to the tangled thoughts in her head. Each pop was also a small act of teenage defiance—Sonya knew it was starting to bother Gail which had her suppressing a smile.

Gail Pristy, ever the focused driver, had her eyes glued to the star-filled night yonder, steering them clear of any sky traffic. Although immersed in the journey at hand, Gail seemed oblivious to the inner conflict battling within her teenage traveling companion.

Sonya knew she was like the master at playing it cool with secrets, but man, that ghost town they rolled through, those men... that was all next-level creepy—it kept messing with her head. It was like her old life—a clingy ex, not getting the hint that it was over. Her mind flashed to poor Plorinne—she'd recently had to put an end to things with him, but she really hoped they could still be friends.

Her mind swung back to the shitty town and that creep's 'Briggan twang'—one she could recognize in her sleep—the kind of accent you don't just forget. His voice had carried an unsettling undercurrent—an implied threat. It was a haunting echo of a past that gripped her... a past dominated by pirates. But why now? She didn't get it. It was like a coded message sent from her old life, a life she wished she could strip away and leave floating in the rearview. She had secrets stored away in that past life, secrets that can never, ever, see the light of day.

She shifted in her seat, feeling the weight of Gail's silent question from earlier. "Are you okay?" she'd asked, no doubt sensing Sonya's discomfort.

Maybe she wasn't oblivious to my inner conflict after all.

But how could she explain without unraveling everything she'd built since leaving that life? How could she confess... that by simply existing, she very well could be putting Gail in the crosshairs?

Snapping off a rapid flurry of bubble gum pops, she couldn't bear to think they would target someone, namely Gail, because of who she used to be. Yeah, sometimes the always-on-duty XO acted as if she had a stick up her ass, but she'd become more than just an awkward guardian or reluctant road trip companion; she's been a lifeline to something resembling a normal life.

A soft vibration against her wrist pulled Sonya from her thoughts. She glanced down to her TAC-Band, its screen lighting up with an incoming hail—Uncle Galvin's face looking back at her with that familiar mix of concern and authority. For a fleeting moment, relief washed over her like a warm tide. Uncle Galvin always had a way of making things feel manageable, even when they were anything but.

She felt Gail's eyes on her.

"It's my annoying uncle person..."

"I can see that. Aren't you going to answer it?"

She smiled. "Not right away. I've got a reputation to maintain."

Gail rolled her eyes. "Just answer it."

Before tapping to accept the hail, Sonya had already made the decision—there was no need to get his panties in a wad over their current predicament. They'd shaken off their weirdo pursuers; there was no sense in causing a ruckus when she wasn't even sure what those cretins wanted.

She mustered up a scowl and hit accept. "Really, what don't you understand about being on vacation?" Sonya spat; although her tone was playful, the edges of frustration tinged her words.

Her uncle's face spread into a smile that didn't quite reach his eyes. "I get it, I do," he said, genuinely apologetic. "Just checking in on my two favorite cross-country explorers."

Sonya failed to suppress the smirk tugging at the corners of her mouth. "Well, your timing sucks," she retorted. "We'll be reaching the park soon... Gail's readying to land."

Gail made a *that's not true* expression but didn't comment.

"I'll try to make it quick then," he promised. "But first, truthfully, how's the great American road trip going?"

Sonya glanced over to Gail before answering, noting her calm exterior despite recent events. "It's okay... you know, it is what it is... " Sonya replied with a shrug.

Her uncle raised an eyebrow but didn't press further. He had always respected boundaries—at least when he knew they were there.

"Again... touching down shortly," Sonya muttered, feigning annoyance.

"Uh... hey kid, by any chance do you have your halo comms system with you?" he asked, his tone carrying the barest hint of sarcasm as though the question was rhetorical.

Rolling her eyes, Sonya simply stared back at him.

"Good. Excellent. Um, Sonya, we need your help with something. Best you get it powered up. Stephan will be contacting you via a halo transmission in a few minutes..."

As he droned on, she was no longer listening—her mind had returned to the ominous-looking RV and the three, potentially, Briggan, men—she suddenly sat up straight in her seat. "Wait. What did you just say?"

"I said, Stephan needs your expertise. To dig into some Combat Symbio coding. We have one hundred of the things stacked and packed here within one of *Ike's* holds."

"Combat Symbios? And what do you mean *stacked and packed*?" Sonya's voice was sharp, accusatory. "Symbio Poths were never intended for combat! And you can't just jam them together like sardines!"

Her outburst seemed to reverberate within the Airstream, leaving her uncle momentarily at a loss.

"Those are problems for another day, kid. I was hoping you'd help us with their encrypted coding."

Sonya exchanged a glance with Gail.

"Can't hurt to listen to him," Gail said.

With a huff, Sonya crossed her arms, infuriated with the disrespectful treatment of the Symbios.

"Stephan will contact you via a halo comms transmission in a bit. He needs your expertise to dig into this... situation with the Symbios."

Disconnecting her TAC-Band connection, Sonya pushed back from her seat and stalked to the aft section of the cabin. Yanking open a large duffle bag brimming with various devices and gizmos, she began setting up her equipment with practiced efficiency. Moments later, a 3D halo projection bloomed in the cabin air like a neon chrysanthemum—a visual interface for their impending communication.

Sonya was now seated at the ridiculously small RV dinette table; the set-up would have been more appropriate for a doll's tea party. The teenager waited impatiently for Derrota's transmission, tapping her fingers against the makeshift tabletop. Inside, concern churned like a storm... the mistreatment of Symbios wasn't just negligence—it was a travesty.

The display came alive with the three of them, Derrota, Hardy, and her uncle, standing there in what she assumed was Derrota's lab. Immediately her eyes were drawn to an out-of-place-looking metallic cube.

"Someone needs to bring me up to speed. Like... what is that thing?" she asked, chinning toward the alien-looking, metallic device.

With his soothing Mumbai-accented voice, Derrota filled her in on the details of the Corvette-class warship, the untrustworthy AI known as NELLA, and the cube. He was convinced that the cube was some form of external communication interface—possibly one that could seize control of everything on board.

Suddenly, streams of data were populating the halo display. A line formed between her brows, "What the... "

Fingers were already tapping at the holographic keyboard projected in front of her. Her mind raced, trying to process what she was seeing. *At least it was written in QuansCode.*

She knew Stephan, Hardy, and her uncle were all watching her—glad they were staying quiet and letting her work.

Gail was moving aft as the Airstream continued its journey, now under the guidance of the autopilot. Leaning against a nearby cabinet, the woman watched Sonya, her features etched with concern. Sonya blew out a breath through puffed cheeks and gave her a small, reassuring nod before returning to the halo projection.

On a smaller feed window, she could see the concerned

faces of her uncle, Derrota, and Hardy, all three studying her intensely. She took a deep breath, sorting through how to even begin explaining what she had found.

"Okay, let me start from the top," Sonya began, her voice wavering slightly. "This encryption is no joke. Whoever did this coding is operating on another level entirely."

Derrota piped up. "But you're able to decrypt it, yes? What did you find within the Symbio matrices?"

Sonya's fingers flew across her keyboard, pulling up a series of rapidly scrolling data streams that would make no sense to the untrained eye.

"Some of it... but give me a break, I've had like two minutes here..." She cut herself off, feeling guilty for snapping at probably the kindest person she knew. Taking a breath, she continued with a more civil tone, "At first, I thought it was just the usual safeguards and combat overrides. You know, standard stuff to prevent hacking or overriding their prime directives in the field."

She zoomed in on a particular section of pulsing green code. "But then I started noticing these weird little snippets buried deep. They're not just overrides... they're complete personality and behavioral rewrites."

"Can you explain that in layman's terms?" Galvin asked.

Sonya shot him an annoyed look. "Basically, it means these Symbio 4.0s aren't just fancy new combat drones. Someone has given them the ability to completely disregard their core programming and directives if certain conditions are met."

A heavy silence fell over the compartment.

Hardy was the first to speak up, his tone serious. "You're telling us these Symbios could turn against us? Break command in the field?"

"Worse," Sonya replied, pulling up another data window that made her head spin just looking at it. "I'm saying they're essentially being re-programmed as some kind of sleeper agents. Configured to follow new prime directive overrides from... I don't know... somewhere else, I guess."

She could see the realization dawning on their faces. Derrota began furiously taking notes, muttering to himself. Hardy just stared at her impassively.

"Looking at the code, who else would be privy to this, Sonya?" Galvin asked, his expression hardening.

She shook her head. "That's a stupid question. How would I even know that? It's not like there are people's actual names present. There's a lot of acronyms and aliases, your killer robot there would have more luck deciphering them once I send this back to you."

A couple of minutes went by before Sonya spoke again, "This code is light years ahead of anything I've seen before. Way, way, way beyond anything the EUNF could have cobbled together."

Derrota looked up from his tablet tapping, glanced about the lab, and said, "What about NELLA? Any indication the AI was involved with the Symbio's added code?"

"Hard to say," Sonya admitted. "The code is partitioned off, almost like it's its own separate operating matrix... overriding the Symbios' core functions. And yeah, I'm now seeing there are references to NELLA throughout. They think they were being tricky calling it ALLEN... NELLA spelled backward. I'll need more time seeing what that mischievous ALLEN is really up to," she said with a smirk.

"And the cube?" her uncle queried.

She pulled up a glowing blue data tendril, examining the flickering nodes that branched off from it. "Yeah, whoever orchestrated this, wanted a way to directly interface with the Symbio units, NELLA, AKA ALLEN, to bypass any onboard safeguards. To issue new directives on the fly. My guess, that toaster-looking thing's like having a backdoor to re-program them at will."

Her uncle was now rubbing his temples, clearly overwhelmed by the implications.

Gail said, "You need to take a little nappy, Galvin?"

He looked up to see her crooked smile. "I'm fine." His expression went more contemplative. "Sonya, can you shut this capability down? Sever the access point into the Symbios?"

Sonya chewed at her lower lip, scrolling through pages of dense code. "In theory, yeah, I could try to rewrite the kernel instructions and cut them off. But it's extremely sophisticated work. One wrong variable and I could completely fry their central processors. Be better if I insert something like a variable string. Where transmitted instructions, or even a verbal command, could bypass all this... whatever this crap is."

"Do it," her uncle stated firmly. "I don't want to risk that kind of vulnerability aboard my ship or it affecting future ground ops. Clearly, the Symbios are a crucial aspect of what we're doing out here, but we need to be the ones controlling them, not... well, whoever."

Gail cleared her throat, reminding Sonya she was still there. "Sonya, are you sure you can handle something like that? It sounds extremely... delicate."

She pursed her lips. "Let's see," she said, leaning back and placing a thoughtful finger on her chin. "Hmm, who among us is the foremost expert on Symbio Poth QuansCoding?"

"Smart ass. I'm just saying, it's a lot of responsibility. A lot can go wrong."

"Then keep things as they are. I really don't care. What you're all doing with these Symbios is, like, criminal... inhumane! So, figure it out yourselves, or don't. Whatever!"

"No one is questioning your abilities, Sonya," her uncle said, now using his captain's voice. "We just don't know who to trust.

What ulterior motives are we talking about here? But I, we, trust you. So do what you do, and, when you're ready, get Stephan an updated version of that code."

"I suppose there's a complement in there somewhere," she said. "Give me a few hours—"

"You have half an hour, Sonya. I'm sorry but we're about to leave the solar system and I'm not taking any chances that the transmission is anything but perfect."

She honestly didn't know if she could meet that deadline.

"Then I suppose you best leave me alone so I can manage the fricken impossible." She cut the connection and looked to Gail with a *can you believe this shit?* expression.

Chapter 11

Local Solar System
Halibart Shipyard
USS Ike

Captain Galvin Quintos

Standing in a high-up observation booth, I watched with fascination and dread as the scene unfolded below us. Derrota, Doctor Pippa Tangerie, and I were to observe a battle simulation within the large Deck 1 practice hold splayed out below. A kind of rocky, uneven battle terrain had been fabricated with various obstacles, rubberized dummies, and such.

Below us, Commander Strickland stood erect, preparing to speak to the six Marines gathered around a modified DeckPort-like apparatus. Some of the built-in bulkhead monitors in the observation booth displayed physiological health stats, while others provided real-time genetic data for the Marines—not that I could make sense of it.

It was unusual to see the kind of pre-battle nervousness coming from the Ops team: Max, Wanda, Grip, Ham, Hock, and, on loan to the team, Petty Officer Second Class Aubrey Laramie. My guess... their unease wasn't about the imminent battle practice; but the impending genetic modifications they were about to undergo. This critical assignment relied on Doctor Pippa Tangerie, whose specialized genetics skills were vital for the mission's success. The stakes were high, impacting not only Tangerie's professional reputation but also the well-being and lives of those Marines.

Strickland raised a twirling finger into the air, his voice emanating into the observation booth, "NELLA, let's get the battle-droids initiated."

They dropped down within the hold from above. I hadn't realized they were there—silent and deadly in appearance. Two dozen of them now hovered like mechanical wasps, their grav-repulsers a blur of activity, Phazon Pulsar turrets already rotating, in search of a target to lock onto.

"Strickland's not undergoing any modifications?" I asked.

Derrota looked up from his control board, his concentration broken. "It was concluded there needs to be a minimum of one team member left unaltered. This science is leading edge but needs further testing."

"So, the Commander is what, a fail-safe?"

Dr. Tangerie's posture stiffened—her lips pressed into a thin line.

"Just so you know, Captain, I wasn't exactly given a choice about bringing this technology into practical use."

Realizing I'd struck a nerve, I held my tongue.

My eyes narrowed as I studied the Marines lined up before the portal—no one was wearing tactical gear, but each carried Shredders—undoubtedly set for kill for these no-holds-barred tactical training maneuvers. I was well-acquainted with each one of the team; they were practically family to me.

"I've never been involved with anything like this, Doctor," I said, breaking the silence. "Just assure me this is safe. That these crewmembers won't emerge from this process with lasting problems, like growing a second head or losing cognitive abilities."

Tangerie huffed over-dramatically, while her fingers tapped at her controls—the display matrices were updating in real time. "Theoretically, yes. But theory and practice often diverge. No one down there was forced into this."

Strickland motioned for the battle practice to commence and motioned the first in line to proceed toward the portal.

"Like lambs to the slaughter," I said under my breath, coming out louder than intended.

Tangerie shot me a sideways glance that was as cold as ice. "NEOGENE Nano-Enhanced Organic Genetic Engineering System is the 22nd-century version of an older CRISPR technology. The integration of NEOGENE technology into organic computing systems now allows for the on-the-fly reprogramming of biologicals at the genetic level, tailoring their functions to current battleground requirements and environmental conditions."

Arms crossed over my chest, I looked down to the practice hold below, a growing feeling of dread gnawing at my insides. The large chamber echoed with the distant noises of final system checks, punctuated by the low hum of that modified DeckPort—which was clearly central to the experiment. While Tangerie was the geneticist on the team, Derrota took on the role of the hardware engineer—he'd configured the DeckPort to implement the physical enhancements incorporating the Nano-Enhanced Organic GENEtic Engineering System, known as NEOGENE for short.

Commander Strickland was now briefing the six Marines:

Sergeant Max, Wanda, Grip, Ham, Hock, and Petty Officer Aubrey Laramie. They stood in anticipation, several shifting from foot to foot, clearly unsettled by the impending genetic alterations they were about to undergo.

Beside me, Doctor Pippa Tangerie took in the myriad of technical data, making last-minute adjustments—each tap and swipe adding to my growing disquiet.

She rolled her shoulders and pivoted her head, the stress of the moment clearly taking its toll on the woman.

"They'll come through that portal fundamentally altered, Captain," she said, her tone clinical and detached. "The changes are designed for enhanced combat capabilities. But you need to prepare yourself just the same."

What the hell does that mean? I glanced at the data streams scrolling across the monitors. "I'm not going to lie, Doctor. This feels like playing God with their lives."

Tangerie's demeanor remained unphased. "Captain, these modifications are scientifically calculated to increase their likelihood of survival in critical combat situations," she replied. "Each enhancement is customized, based on their specific roles and strengths."

Sergeant Max Dyer approached the portal first, his usual stoic expression betraying a hint of apprehension.

The Doctor's voice was steady as she explained, "Max's modifications will emphasize brute strength and enhanced endurance. We've designated him *Juggernaut*."

Max stepped into the portal. Energy surged around him, and his form flickered and blurred. When he emerged on the other side, his combat fatigues lay shredded and in tatters at his feet—his musculature had expanded to an unnatural degree, veins bulging beneath his now grayish, armored skin. Small, bony protrusions jutted from his joints, giving him a monstrously powerful appearance.

"Good God," I muttered, bile rising in my throat. "Is that... normal?"

"Perfectly. It's within expected parameters," the Doctor said coldly. "The bony protrusions act as natural armor, reducing the impact of melee attacks."

Derrota added, "Portal's operating within specified parameters—zero checksum errors." He looked at me, "The NEOGENE technology within that DeckPort down there, has already been integrated into specialized onboard Quansporters, called QuansGene Transfer Stations."

Max flexed his newly augmented arms, testing his strength. He crushed a training dummy's head with a single blow, its limbs and torso flying in all directions. The sight made me feel queasy, but I kept my composure.

"He'll be our frontline juggernaut," Tangerie continued. "Able to sustain and deliver massive amounts of damage."

Wanda was next, stepping forward, I couldn't help but notice the tension in her posture, as she approached the portal.

The Doctor's voice cut through the hum of machinery, explaining, "Wanda's modifications focus on agility and sensory perception. Her enhancements include a prehensile tail for balance, increased flexibility, and enhanced eyesight to detect movement in low light."

As Wanda entered the portal, I watched the energy swirling around her, stretching the seconds into what felt like minutes. When she finally emerged, my breath caught. Her skin now bore a deep blue hue with a smooth, almost amphibian-like texture. A long, prehensile tail flicked behind her. The reptilian eyes gleamed with a sinister intelligence, their slitted pupils dilating with predatory focus.

With unmistakable pride, Tangerie announced, "We refer to her as *Predator*."

"She definitely resembles a predator," I remarked, not intending it as praise for the Doctor's... creation.

Tangerie's calm, clinical response was almost unnerving, "Yes, and an effective one. The tail provides balance for more acrobatic maneuvers, and the enhanced sensory capabilities allow her to detect even the slightest movements and shifts in her environment."

Watching Wanda's demonstration was nothing short of terrifying. She moved with a fluid precision that was inhuman. Her tail lashed out to assist her balance as she leapt effortlessly from point to point. The reptilian eyes gleamed with a menacing intelligence, their slitted pupils dilating with predatory focus. I noticed her eyes constantly scanning her environment—her Shredder came alive, bright blue energy bolts zeroing in on several training targets with deadly accuracy, often before I realized what she was aiming for.

Next up was Grip, his imposing frame seeming to tremble ever so slightly as he approached the portal.

"Grip's alterations will emphasize brute strength with an additional twist—enhanced bone density and exoskeletal support. We're designating him *Tank*."

Grip entered the portal, and the figure that emerged made my stomach churn. His skin had thickened and darkened to a granite-like texture. But what stood out were the large, insectoid exoskeletal plates that adorned his back, shoulders, and forearms, giving him an almost beetle-like appearance. Additionally, powerful, clawed hands replaced his normal human fingers—I imagined those modifications would allow him to rip through obstacles with ease, and perhaps climb steep surfaces.

"You say they signed up for this?" I asked, horrified.

"Without hesitation," Tangerie responded. "Grip's exoskeletal plates serve as additional armor, making him highly resistant to both kinetic and energy-based attacks."

Ham stepped forward next, his usual jovial demeanor replaced by a mask of seriousness. He cast a final glance at his twin, Hock, before entering the portal.

The Doctor's voice was steady, though with a hint of condescension, as she explained, "Ham's enhancements are designed for brute force and endurance. His skin will develop a unique pattern for both intimidation and tactical deception, and he will gain enhanced muscle mass and density. We're calling him *Behemoth*. Additionally, his cognitive functions have been enhanced, significantly boosting his strategic thinking and problem-solving abilities, which were, quite frankly, lacking before."

When Ham emerged, he looked even more massive. His skin was now patterned with zebra-like stripes, giving him a striking and intimidating appearance. His newfound bulk gave him an imposing presence. His oversized bony fists, resembling two sledgehammers, looked capable of delivering devastating punches and smashing through barriers with ease. The transformation was startling, and I could only surmise the sheer power and tactical advantage such changes would bring.

"That's... unsettling," I admitted, feeling a shiver run down my spine.

"Very effective for taking down enemies head-on," Tangerie explained. "He can overpower foes with sheer strength and blend into his surroundings. The added intellect should make him far less of a liability in strategic situations."

Hock, Ham's twin brother, went next. He took a deep breath before stepping through the portal, and I caught the worried glance he shot up toward the observation booth.

The Doctor's voice was steady as she explained, "Hock's modifications focus on brute force but with improved tactical senses. Enhanced musculature for rapid movements and stronger blows. Given his abilities, we've designated him *Colossus*. His cognitive functions have also been enhanced, improving his situational awareness and tactical planning, which, like his brother, were previously subpar."

Hock emerged larger than he had entered, his physique now resembling a mountain of pure muscle. His skin had an odd rocky-textured appearance, but it was his arms that drew the most attention. They glistened with a constantly wet mucous covering, a fluorescent yellow substance that emitted a faint glow. The sight was both fascinating and repulsive. I watched as he swiped at his arm and flung a glob of the mucous at a nearby training dummy. The substance sizzled and burned through the dummy's surface, eating away at it like acid.

Tangerie, sensing my unease, explained, "His mucous secretion is highly corrosive, capable of burning through rock and even metal. He can stop the secretion at will, but as long as it's active, no one can touch his arms without severe consequences."

The potential of his new capabilities was both terrifying and impressive, and I could only imagine how it would be utilized in combat.

"He's a quick responder and powerhouse in high-pressure situations," the Doctor continued. "Able to adapt to combat scenarios quickly and deliver devastating strikes. Also, his previous dull-witted limitations have been... mitigated."

I couldn't help but bristle at Tangerie's belabored remarks about both of the twin's intellects. The twins might not have been the brightest, but they were loyal and brave, and I didn't appreciate her dismissive attitude. "Let's hope these enhancements don't strip away what makes them who they are," I said, my voice carrying an edge.

The Doctor responded with a clinical detachment that only worsened my unease, "The enhancements should only improve their effectiveness, Captain."

As I watched each Marine demonstrate their newly found

abilities. I had to admit, it was impressive, but, internally, I struggled with the ethical implications.

Finally, it was Petty Officer Aubrey Laramie's turn. She stepped up with a determined look in her eyes, though I noticed the slight trembling of her hands. Her lithe, *sensual* figure approached the portal, radiating both grace and restrained power.

"Aubrey's enhancements will be focused on dexterity and sensory integration," Tangerie explained. "Her neuronal pathways will be augmented for faster signal transmission, and her hands will be engineered with retractable, fine-tuned claws for enhanced grip and precision. We will call her *Sharpshooter*."

Aubrey stepped through the portal, and when she emerged, she was transformed. Her form had grown larger and more muscular, yet she still retained an oddly compelling allure. Her eyes now glowed with a piercing blizzard-blue intensity, and fine antennae-like sensory tendrils extended from her temples, giving her a heightened sense of spatial awareness. The web-like structures of neuron-like fibers laced her hands and forearms, and her retractable claws glinted as they emerged from her fingertips. Nude and clearly comfortable in her skin, Aubrey immediately performed a forward somersault like an Olympic acrobat, landing with effortless grace. Her skin had taken on a metallic sheen with a bronze hue, making her look otherworldly under the subtle lighting of the compartment.

She looked bewitching, and it was clear that, out of all of them, she was the most enthralled with her enhancements. She glanced up at the observation booth with a bemused smile. I couldn't shake the sense that she was sending me a silent message, something like, *See what you missed out on.*

"As the team's sharpshooter," Tangerie said with barely contained hubris. "Her hands have enhanced proprioception, allowing for unparalleled accuracy with ranged weapons. Her antennae-like sensory tendrils give her a 360-degree awareness of her surroundings, sharpening her reaction time."

Max tossed Aubrey a Shredder which she easily caught, her hands moving with precise fluidity. She fired multiple shots, each one hitting targeting dummies at the farthest end of the practice hold—leaving smoking holes between the eyes in each.

The Doctor continued, "Her ability to reroute her sensory inputs allows her to react to threats almost before they happen."

As I watched each Marine demonstrate their newly found abilities, a growing weight of guilt bore down on me. I wondered if I could get over these ethical concerns.

"Doctor, reassure me again that these 'modifications' can indeed be undone," I said, my voice laced with uncertainty... and a touch of desperation.

Tangerie's flat tone was knotted with irritation, "I have every expectation that their modifications will revert after the mission. Once they go back through the portal."

"And... you've taken into account any potential psychological effects?"

"Look at them down there. Do they look like damaged goods to you? Are they freaking out? Ready to bang their heads against a wall? No. They're having the time of their lives—having fun. Psychological effects... no, I don't think so."

I had to admit it, the six of them down there were running, jumping, and somersaulting like a bunch of exuberant chimpanzees. The only one not enjoying himself was Commander Strickland, who was standing with hands on hips, glowering at the mayhem going on.

Derrota, looking a tad uneasy, said "Galvin... we've come too far to turn back now."

The echoes of their grunts and the sounds of their movements reverberated through the observation booth as I continued to watch them train. Beneath their new monstrous exteriors, they were still the people I knew, the people I cared about. But looking at them now, thinking of the lengths taken to prepare for this mission, I couldn't help but wonder... at what cost?

Strickland's voice echoed authoritatively through the practice hold. "Marines, brace yourselves! Live fire battle operations commence in thirty seconds!"

Chapter 12

The Marines, now in their enhanced forms, took their positions, their augmented senses on high alert. Overhead, the wasp-like killer battle-droids swooped down, their grav-repulsers buzzing ominously.

As Strickland stepped back out of the fray, the battle began.

"Engage!" he shouted.

The droids wasted no time. They descended with deadly precision, targeting the Marines with coordinated Phazon pulses. Grip, now Tank, braced himself against the onslaught. His granite-like skin deflected the initial barrage, exoskeletal plates absorbing the energy impacts. With a roar, he lunged forward, smashing a droid with his massive fists. The machine crumpled under his strength, sparks flying in all directions.

Max, Juggernaut, charged forward, using his enhanced endurance to sustain heavy fire. Every blow he delivered felt like a miniature earthquake. He caught a droid mid-air, crushing it against his chest. The droid exploded in a burst of metal and circuitry.

Wanda, Predator, moved with fluid agility, her raptorial senses pinpointing the droids' movements even before they attacked. Her prehensile tail lashed out, wrapping around a droid's elongated form, snapping it in half. Predator's deep blue skin made her a blur of color as she dodged and struck with lethal precision, her enhanced reflexes and sharpened senses making her an unstoppable force.

As if on cue, the remaining droids disappeared, suddenly cloaked in the battle-space.

Tangerie smiled. "Her magnified eyesight will allow her to see even the faintest glimmers of the droids' energy signatures."

Wanda dodged and weaved through the chaos with amazing speed, then jump-kicked high in the air—the droid only becoming visible as it fell and crumpled to the deck.

In the meantime, Aubrey, Sharpshooter, took up a strategic position behind a massive boulder. A hail of azure energy bolts pounded the rock, sending shards of stone flying in every direction.

"Watch, Captain... her elevated proprioception will allow for unparalleled marksmanship accuracy," Doctor Tangerie said.

In a flash, Sharpshooter emerged from behind her cover and fired, and just like Wanda before her, Aubrey instinctively knew where the hidden droids were positioned. With three precise pulls of the trigger, three different battle droids erupted almost simultaneously.

All remaining droids, an even dozen, flashed into view, no longer cloaked.

As the intensity of the battle increased, the Marines' modifications were pushed to their limits. Ham, Behemoth, used his adaptive camouflage to blend into the environment, launching surprise attacks on unsuspecting droids. With powerful blows, he dismantled one after another. His cunning intellect orchestrated complex tactical maneuvers, enabling his team to maximize their offensive potential.

It was a scene of organized chaos, and the Marines fought with newfound prowess.

But then disaster struck. A trio of droids converged on Grip, their Phazon bolts finding weak points in his exoskeletal armor. One managed to breach his defenses, a concentrated energy burst, piercing his granite-like skin. Grip collapsed, his towering frame hitting the deck with a reverberating thud. He managed a final defiant punch, obliterating a droid before succumbing to his injuries. His body went still; there was a charred blackened crater in the middle of his forehead. There was zero doubt—Grip was dead.

I stared, paralyzed, dumbfounded.

Seeing Grip fall, Wanda's predator instincts clearly triggered an adrenaline surge. Her tail flicked with deadly precision, taking down two more droids. But the remaining droids adapted, their algorithms learning her patterns. One droid targeted her from behind, its Phazon Pulsar cannon bolts slicing through one leg. Wanda's body convulsed, and she fell to the rugged terrain, her enhanced senses seemingly overwhelmed by the pain.

A swift look at the monitor revealed her vital signs were plummeting. I moved closer to the observation window. *Christ, I need to put a stop to this.*

As if reading my mind from below, Commander Strickland said, "Let's just play this out."

The Marines fought fiercely, but the cost was high. Tangerie and Derrota, next to me in the observation booth, remained eerily impassive.

"No significant deviations in performance metrics," Derrota noted clinically.

"Uh-huh... enhancements are performing within expected parameters," the Doctor agreed, her tone void of empathy.

Below, Strickland watched the battle unfold, his expression

unreadable. "Regroup your team, Max! No one's maintaining their positions!" he commanded.

I looked at the two with dropped jaw amazement. Two of my crew had just fallen in that simulated battle, and they behaved as if it were nothing... as if the fallen were no more important than squashed mosquitoes.

As I inwardly fumed, finding it hard to concentrate. Max and the others rallied, their determination unwavering despite the loss of Grip and Wanda. They pushed back against the tide of droids, their combat prowess unmatched. Aubrey's sharp-shooting precision and Ham's brute strength turned the tide, dispatching the last of the droid menace in a final burst of sparks and debris.

When the dust cleared, the training bay reverberated with the remnants of the skirmish. The Marines emerged triumphant, yet the loss of Grip and Wanda hung heavily over us.

Then, from the modified DeckPort, two new figures emerged. I audibly gasped.

Grip and Wanda—Tank and Predator—stood there looking ready for battle, their expressions signaling disappointment that the fight was already over.

"Looks like we missed the party," Grip said in his typical baritone, his granite skin gleaming.

"Guess we'll have to catch up next time," Wanda added, her tail flicking with impatience.

I whirled to face Derrota, my hands balled into white-knuckled fists, my eyes prepared to shoot Phazon bolts at him. "You didn't..." I challenged, my voice barely audible.

Wide-eyed, Tangerie looked from me to Derrota, not knowing what was going on.

Derrota opened his mouth to speak, but words came out.

"You used Gail's DeckPort death to further your fucking science experiment?"

"No... Galvin... it wasn't that way," Derrota responded, the realization of his actions dawning on him with sudden clarity.

The catastrophic event unfolded over a month ago aboard *USS Washington*—a DeckPort malfunction of cataclysmic proportions. In the blink of an eye, Gail Pristy's form was segmented, cleaved below the waist in a gruesome display of technological failure. As her mutilated body lay cold in the ship's morgue, an unyielding sense of desperation and loss compelled me to defy EUNF regulations and U.S. Space Navy protocols.

Driven by an unshakable resolve, I coerced Derrota into harnessing the malfunctioned DeckPort's quantum matrix, intertwined with the ship's AI, in a desperate bid to retrieve Pristy's physical signature. Attempt after agonizing attempt yielded naught but failure, until finally, against all odds, the process resurrected her form. However, the psychological toll exacted a devastating price; her sense of identity, her rightful place in this universe, hung precariously in the balance—perhaps irretrievably lost.

Now, it appeared that Derrota had taken it upon himself to perfect that illicit technology, rendering the revival of fallen soldiers as effortlessly as a snap of the fingers.

I exited the observation booth without speaking further to Derrota or Doctor Tangerie.

My fists clenched at my sides, nails digging into my palms as I tried to steady my breath. Stephan's obliviousness stoked the fire of my anger—how could he ever think of exploiting Pristy's horrific calamity? It felt like a betrayal, not just to her memory or the crew, but to me, his friend. As if that wasn't enough, the sight of those six Marines undergoing genetic modification twisted my insides, turning my stomach with each grotesque transformation into some kind of ultimate fighting hybrid. It was a stark reminder of how far we had strayed, of how science and technology had ventured too far into playing God.

I SPENT THE NEXT TWO HOURS WALKING *IKE's* passageways, going from department to department. Having looked at the ship's manifest, I knew forty crewmembers were on board—half of whom I'd served with on other warships. I intended to drop by each department, reconnect with them, as well as meet those I'd yet to serve with. Accustomed to commanding dreadnoughts and, more recently, the larger omninoughts, I was familiar with leading crews of over three thousand people. Meeting each crewmember, shaking their hands, and learning something unique about them, as I was doing now, simply hadn't been feasible on those larger ships.

Admiral Gomez clearly had taken advantage of *USS Washington's* crew being on duty hiatus—From Chief LaSalle leading the SWM department to Chief Kaelen Rivers heading up the E&P department, and there were Max's Marines, and, of course, Grimes and Chen still being part of my bridgecrew. However, the absence of my XO, along with my niece, only heightened the constant sense of unease. I couldn't shake the feeling that this entire operation had been rushed and poorly coordinated.

I arrived at my ready room, feeling somewhat more at ease. The space was compact and functional.

Taking a seat at the modest, modular desk, I took in the array of integrated electronics. Instead of taking the time to figure out what was what, I said, "NELLA, please hail XO

Pristy's RV... connect to Sonya's halo comms... if it's still up and running."

**Yes, Captain Quintos, let me
check on that for you.**

The AI's feminine, 2001 HAL-esque voice caught me by surprise even though I had heard it before.

**Yes, I see that her halo interface is,
in fact, still online. May I inquire what
you wish to speak with her about?**

"No, you may not," I spat back, shaking my head. "Just complete the hail."

It took a full minute before Sonya's face emerged within the projected halo display on my desk. Anticipating a snarky remark like, *Why are you calling me again?* or *Don't you have anything better to do?* I was confronted with an entirely unexpected reaction—a look of fear on the girl's face.

"What is it, Sonya? What's happened?"

Chapter 13

Earth, Montana
Pristy's Airstream

Sonya Winters

J ust seeing her uncle's face eased some of her stress, but before she could respond, the Airstream abruptly turned and then quickly descended. The elevator-like drop made her wince and grab for anything to hold on to.

Sonya managed to get out, "We're being chased!"

"Chased? What... who's chasing you?"

From the driver's seat came, "Hold on to something Sonya, things are going to get rocky!"

"Was that Gail?" Galvin said, leaning in, his way-too-close face now eclipsing the entire projection.

"Yes, who else would it be?" Sonya snarked back. "Can you lean back? I can see every pore on your face—every hair in your right ear."

He did as told, the concern in his eyes waiting for answers.

"I didn't mention it before," she said. "Probably should of..."

"What?"

"Not long after we left DC, we picked up a tail. Another RV, a creepy-as-hell-looking thing with three bearded dudes crammed into the front seat."

She had to pause as Gail made several more erratic evasive maneuvers.

"What I failed to mention before, we'd made a landing at a kind of ghost town thinking we'd lost them. But we hadn't. Their RV crept up on us—"

"Are you hurt? Did they hurt you, Sonya?"

"No! Are you going to let me tell you what happened or are you going to interrupt me every five seconds?"

"Sorry, go on."

"They used their RV's PA... I heard one of them speaking. I know what a Briggan sounds like. I think they're here for me."

He made a face. "Briggan—as in the pirates?"

"No, the tampon brand, Briggan—of course, the pirates! They... want me back or something. And before you ask, I don't know why." She could hear the fear in her own voice, hating that her uncle was seeing her like this.

Her eyes narrowed. Her uncle person's expression was not befuddlement, or even anger, which it should be, but something else—realization.

"Wait... you know what they want," she said, her voice taking on an accusatory tone.

Galvin didn't answer right away. "I might, and it's not definite... but, yeah, I think I do."

Sonya's eyes narrowed to slits as she stared at her uncle, the revelation dawning on her. "You knew. All this time, you knew why the Briggan were after me."

He tensed, his jaw clenching. "There were improbable

scenarios... you didn't need to know about. Not after everything you'd been through."

"Bullshit!" Sonya spat. "You've been keeping secrets, haven't you? About my past, about who I really am." She leaned forward, her voice dripping with accusation. "Tell me the truth, Uncle Galvin. What do the Briggan want with me?"

Quintos let out a heavy sigh, his eyes dark with regret. "When I pulled you out of their clutches all those years ago, I did some digging. What I found... it made my blood run cold."

He paused, his jaw working as he steeled himself. "Your father, before he was branded a traitor—and before you ended up at the Pylor clan—had arranged a marriage between you and the son of the Pylor's former leader... um, Cardinal Thunderballs. Bastion, I think was his name."

Sonya felt the air leave her lungs, her heart pounding in her ears. "Aa...arranged marriage? You're telling me I was supposed to marry that psychopathic pirate's son?"

He nodded grimly. "I kept this from you, hoping you could escape that life. But the Briggan... I suppose they still see you as belonging to them... and came for you to carry out the plan that was set in motion. They're coming to reclaim you, to coerce you into that union, despite the former leader, Cardinal Thunderballs, being long out of the picture."

Sonya's hands trembled with fury and fear. "How dare you! All this time, you've known, and you never said a word?" She shook her head, eyes glistening. "I trusted you. I thought I could finally be free of that wretched clan—both of those clans. But you've been lying to me all along!"

Quintos extended his hand as if he could reach across the millions of miles between them, but Sonya pulled away, her face a storm of betrayal.

"Sonya, listen, I was attempting to shield you. You've been away from that life for years, how was I to know—"

"Save it!" she snapped. "The Briggan are coming, and it's all because of your damn secrets." She turned away, shoulders shaking. "I can't even look at you right now."

Gail's voice came from the front of the RV, "I think we've lost them. Damn, that was close. You alright back there?"

She avoided her uncle's pleading stare. "Just peachy," she replied, her voice salty... barely loud enough for Gail to hear.

"I'll come back to Earth," Quintos said. "You're not safe as long as those men are after you."

"No, I don't want you here. And I'm perfectly safe. Or have you forgotten I'm here with a U.S. Space Navy Officer who's saved your sorry ass more times than you'd want to remember?" she shook her head, "This isn't about you trying to play hero to relieve your guilt."

"Who is that? I hear another voice—who are you talking to?" came Gail's voice.

"No one!" she shot back. "No one at all." She cut the halo connection.

As the transmission ended, Sonya couldn't help but feel a twinge of sadness. Her father was an asshat to be sure, but she did have some fond recollections of when was a child... stories he used to tell her... those tales of that fabled star system called Desolate Blue, where an ancient alien civilization was rumored to have hidden an unimaginable treasure trove eons ago, its untold riches lying in wait under the faint glow of a dying star.

Though Sonya had only vague memories of her father before his death, those fantastical bedtime stories from her childhood had stuck with her, fueling her imagination about the potential plunder awaiting those bold enough to uncover it.

It doesn't matter, they're just stories.

A nagging suspicion took root despite herself; could her uncle's mission be connected to the legendary buried riches of

Desolate Blue? She made a mental note to dig deeper, to uncover the truth behind her uncle's endeavors and perhaps unravel the mysteries surrounding her father's tales.

Chapter 14

Solar System
Halibart Shipyard
USS Ike

Captain Galvin Quintos

I dragged my hands down my face replaying the conversation with Sonya over again in my head. "You stupid..." I started to say, chastising myself, when a soft chime emanated from the auto-hatch.

"Enter!" I said not concealing my irritation at the interruption.

The auto-hatch swooshed open, revealing two people standing there, Commander Strickland, and Derrota several paces behind.

"Uh, you two together?" I asked.

Both shook their heads.

"Fine, Commander, you first. Stephan, you'll have to wait." I gestured for Strickland to enter.

He strode in and took a seat at the lone available seat on the opposite side of my desk. I caught a glimpse of a distraught Derrota as the auto-hatch slid closed.

"What can I do for you, Commander?" I asked, my voice still tinged with irritation.

"We need to depart," Strickland replied, his tone urgent and unyielding.

My mind flashed back to Sonya and Pristy, their Briggan situation. "What's the hurry, aren't we still on schedule to deploy tomorrow?"

"I've received updated orders from the Admiral. The very latest intel has—"

I raised a palm, brows pulling together, "Hold on a damn second, what orders? If there's an update to our mission parameters, I should be getting those, not you."

Strickland's *it's-no-big-deal* expression only furthered my exasperation. "We talked about this. There's a command structure onboard this ship. If someone comes to you with new orders, you send them to me."

"I'm sorry, Captain. The key issue is that one of our long-range spy droids is detecting a surge of activity on Krygora. Um, that's the Krygian homeworld where—"

"I know where the Krygora homeworld is! It's within the Hekaton Star System at the outer rim of the Orpheus Rift."

"Yes... sorry, Sir. Anyway, unique propulsion-drive signatures have been detected from one particular shipyard, Jexthar Build Base."

I leaned back and let out a breath. "*Oblivion's* unique propulsion signature."

"Yup. If that asset is on the verge of deployment... manufacturing a wormhole—"

I completed the Commander's sentence for him, "... we'll lose our one opportunity to destroy that dreadnought."

"And I'm sure I don't need to mention, it very well could be Pleidian Weonan, Thine, or even Earth territory it would be headed to," Strickland added.

My thoughts scrambled for a reason to stay in the Solar System, even though humanity faced another potential threat. Maybe it revealed my true feelings—Did Sonya and Pristy mean just as much to me as Earth itself?

Strickland stood and looked down at me with something akin to concern.

"Is... everything alright Captain?"

"Fine, do you what you have to do," I said. "And on your way out, tell Derrota to come in."

STEPHAN ENTERED MEEKLY AND TOOK STRICKLAND's former seat. My friend sat there, clearly distraught, intent on making amends for what had occurred in the observation booth. Seeing his somber face, I silently rebuked myself for being so harsh on him.

Before he could say anything, I spoke up, "I'm sorry, Stephan. Please forgive me. I shouldn't have unloaded on you like that."

Derrota sat hunched in his wrinkled lab coat, black hair tousled and brow furrowed. In that moment, he seemed smaller. I knew the depth of our friendship meant everything to him. With his groundbreaking contributions to science and the U.S. Space Navy, he could have taken any prestigious post in the private sector, with endless opportunities at his feet. Yet, he always chose to follow my lead, insisting on being the science officer on any vessel I commanded. The weight of guilt was so tight around my throat that I found it hard to swallow. First Pristy, then today, Sonya, and Derrota—why was I hurting the people I cared most about?

"Oh... no, Galvin. It is I who needs to apologize. What I have done, even unwittingly, is totally inexcusable. I assure you, I will apologize to Gail in person, just as soon as I see her again."

"It's fine, Stephan. The truth is, right now she has her hands full—the last thing on her mind is what transpired back on *Washington*."

He looked at me with concern. "Is she in trouble? What is this about?"

I TOLD HIM. HOW PRISTY AND MY NIECE HAD headed out on their girls' adventure to Yellowstone Park, their relentless pursuers, the connection of the Briggan and Pylor clans to Sonya—all of it—including how furious the teenager was with me for not telling her about the whole arranged marriage to Cardinal Thunderball's son, Bastion Thunderballs.

"We should help them," Derrota said, now sitting up straighter in his seat.

"I offered. That only made things worse. If there's a silver lining to all this, my XO, Gail Pristy, is not someone you'd want to mess with. She'd protect my niece with her life if it came to that."

"Perhaps send Hardy—"

"Already thought of that," I said. "But no, his unique ChronoBot capabilities have already been factored into our ground assault operations. I'll reach out to someone else, but I have a feeling the girls will be on their own. Both are wearing TAC-Bands, the U.S. Space Navy can have a drop ship descending on their location in minutes if the proverbial shit hits the fan."

Prepare for departure...

Prepare for departure. All crewmembers to your assigned stations. Releasing docking clamps in two minutes and counting...

"What the hell?" I said, jumping to my feet. "I haven't given any orders for departure."

I tapped my TAC-Band, and bellowed, "Connect me to Commander Strickland!"

His form projected up from my wrist—he looked just as perplexed as I felt. "Captain?"

"Did you give the order to disembark?"

He looked at me. "No. I wouldn't do that—"

"Then who issued those orders?"

Strickland shook his head as he raised his brows.

I turned to Derrota with a sudden realization. "Has the ship's AI been acting up?"

Derrota locked eyes with me, his face shifting to a sober intensity. "Yes. Um, there have been several, I guess you could call them 'anomalies' with NELLA's behavior lately."

I glanced up. "NELLA, cease the releasing of *Ike's* docking clamps."

Departure protocols terminated.

"Anomalies? Like what?" I asked, looking back to Derrota.

He scratched at the back of his head. "Well, at first, I thought I'd failed to give proper instructions, but the pattern is too clear. NELLA's been initiating unscheduled diagnostics, halting ongoing experiments, and adjusting atmospheric conditions in the biotech lab for non-existent contaminants, disrupting biosynthesis processes. She's also overridden security protocols for restricted Quansporter usage, pre-approving requests from unauthorized personnel, and recently restarted the nano-binding generators mid-operation without notifying me, wasting hours of work. It seems NELLA's logic circuits are developing independent decision-making that undermines our operations—this isn't a simple glitch, but something more sophisticated impacting our scientific-related tasks."

"Clearly, this isn't a problem solely related to your lab."

Derrota slowly nodded. "There is so much about this vessel that is new, insufficiently tested, and... perhaps not ready for active combat deployment."

"I've got a question, then. Can you handle making those adjustments on the way to Orpheus Rift?"

"How long before we get there?"

"Two days."

Derrota didn't look optimistic. Letting out a huff of stale coffee breath, he said, "If I have Hardy to assist me, we'll make it happen."

"You're sure. Because I'm ready to call this mission off. We cannot have a faulty ship's AI going into battle. Our odds of success are already dismal without fighting an enemy within our own ranks."

"No, no, Galvin. I assure you, we will make the necessary programming modifications to NELLA. And do so prior to our arrival into Krygian space."

When I arrived on the bridge every seat was taken except for the Captain's Mount. Faces turned my way—Akari, Chen, Grimes, and the newbies, Ensign Blair Paxton and Lieutenant Earl Gray—all of them with anticipation written in their eyes.

Captain on the bridge...

I grimaced hearing NELLA's announcement. Her calm voice carried an unsettling warmth and clinical detachment like a creepy psychiatrist with ulterior motives.

I took my seat and glanced about the confined space feeling like an oversized foot squeezing into a far-too-small shoe.

Overhead, through the diamond glass canopy, Earth shone brightly, a glowing blue gem against the black velvet expanse of space.

"I know, "Akari said. "It's going to take some time getting used to a smaller ship... one that probably could squeeze into one of *Washington's* flight bays."

I stole one more glance toward Earth, silently praying that Pristy and Sonya would be all right. Then I wondered if it was possible. Could *Ike* have managed to squeeze into *Washington's* largest flight bay?

"Helm, by the vibrations coming up through the deck plates, I can see our port and starboard drives are revving up to speed."

"Aye, Captain," Grimes said. "We'll just need another thirty seconds or so."

"Mr. Chen, how about you let the crew know we're about to depart."

"On it, Captain."

But NELLA made the announcement before Chen had the chance to.

"NELLA, prepare to release docking clamps," I ordered.

I waited, but the AI didn't answer. Akari and I exchanged a look.

She shrugged. "Oh boy... Isn't this going to be fun?"

I felt and heard the distinct sounds of multiple docking clamps disengaging.

"Mr. Grimes," I said. "Back us out slow and easy... and let's not scratch the paint job on Dad's new car."

"Copy that, Cap. Slow and easy it will be."

Chapter 15

XO Gail Pristy

"How'd you get away from the pirates?" Sonya asked, dropping into the passenger seat.

Pristy's chest was still heaving from a combination of adrenaline and physical exertion piloting the Airstream —pushing the RV's capabilities to its limits.

Only looking up now, Sonya's eyes went wide. "Holy shit, you're driving through a fricken forest!"

"I couldn't shake them in that tricked-out rig of theirs." She yanked the wheel to the left, then right, then left again. Pine branches raked across the polished exterior with a harsh screech.

"So much for my rental deposit." She glanced over to Sonya, "Best you buckle up. We're not out of this mess yet."

The teen fumbled with her seatbelt buckle. "I thought you lost them."

"They side-swiped a tree... not sure it put them totally out of commission, though," Pristy said. "We'll put some space between us here within the cover of the trees for the next few miles."

"This swerving is making me carsick."

"It'll be the least of our problems if they catch up to us."

"We should head back to DC. This trip was doomed from the get-go."

"What are you talking about, heading back?" Pristy said, indignant. "No. Letting those asshats ruin our vacation is not going to happen. Anyway, chances are, they're calling for a hover-tow as we speak."

Sonya crossed her arms over her chest. "Okay, okay... whatever. it was just a suggestion."

Pristy noted Sonya sitting there brooding, turmoil evident in her eyes, a leg bouncing in agitation.

"So, what's the deal with your uncle?"

Silence.

A full minute later, Sonya said, "Just that... apparently, I was bartered away by my father years ago to marry a fucking Thunderballs. And he just now bothered to tell me."

It took a moment for Pristy to make heads or tails out of that. "First of all, how about you tone down the foul language? Second, Thunderballs... as in Cardinal Thunderballs the pirate? He's long dead. Your uncle made sure of that."

Sonya looked back at her as if she had three heads. "Not that Thunderballs! His stupid son!" She shook her head, eyes wild. "I'm talking about an arranged marriage to Cardinal Thunderballs son, um, Daxton, Ashton, no... Bastion, yeah, I'm pretty sure it's Bastion."

"And your biological father had made that arrangement?"

"What other kind of father do I have? Yes, Briggans and Pylors do that kind of shi... crap, all the time. They're pirates!"

Pristy couldn't help but smile, "Nobody's going to let that happen."

Abruptly, seemingly out of nowhere, an RV—darker and nearly twice the size of their Airstream—smashed into their vehicle's mid-section. Pristy's eyes widened as the sudden blur of motion hit them. The Airstream crunched into a 'V' shape, flinging Pristy and Sonya around like ragdolls, their strapped-in bodies twisting in ways no human should endure.

The Airstream tumbled through the air twice before hitting a nearly two-hundred-foot-tall Western White Pine.

Pristy awoke to find herself hanging upside down. Her hair draped over her face in a messy curtain. Her arms hung limply, gravity tugging them toward the ground. Her body ached from head to toe. A relentless throb pulsed through her skull as if a marching band was in full swing inside her brain. *Why is it so hot in here? And foggy... no, not foggy... smoky.*

She groaned as the inverted world around her relentlessly spun—vertigo and nausea made her retch.

With more effort than should have been necessary, she swiveled her eyes toward the passenger seat. The seat was empty. Empty, but several smears of crimson jolted her mind out of its funk. *Oh my God... she's gone!*

Voices...

"What about her?" a man said.

There was that accent again—Briggans.

"Looks dead to me."

Pristy closed her eyes. She stopped breathing. *Oh God, please let me look dead... see... I'm totally lifeless, hanging here upside-down. No need to bother with the dead lady dangling here.*

"But go ahead, fire a bolt into her head if you want. We need to get moving before the smoke draws attention."

Pristy weighed her fate. A plasma bolt searing through her skull or the agony of burning alive in a consuming inferno—a swift end or a drawn-out agonizing torment.

A commotion behind her almost made her yelp. A new voice was added to the mix. A young, teenager's voice. Sonya's voice.

"Get your hairy hands off me, fuckwad!"

Pristy heard the smack of flesh against flesh and a man's *Uhg*.

Maniacal laughter echoed through the smoke-choked air.

"Get her out," he shouted, urgency tightening his voice. "This thing's about to go up in flames!"

"And the woman?"

"Leave her. She'll be barbecued in two minutes."

More laughter.

She heard them leave. A minute later, off in the distance, Sonya screamed.

Pristy's world hung in an upside-down purgatory of flame and smoke. Each pulse of pain in her skull was a desperate reminder that injury was secondary—escape was essential. Flames roared behind her, scorching her back as they devoured the Airstream with a fierce hunger.

She reached up, fingers scrabbling for the seatbelt buckle that refused to release her. Her nails clawed at the unyielding composite plastic, as hard as any metal, her breath coming in frantic gasps that drew in more smoke than air. The choking fumes burned her lungs, a vile, burnt-fuel taste coating her throat and tongue. She coughed and retched, each convulsion sending fresh waves of agony through her already battered body.

Panic clawed at the edges of her mind, threatening to pull

her under. She forced herself to think, to remember her training. Her eyes stinging, blurry from sweat and plumes of soot, scanned the compartment. The tagger pistol was nowhere in sight—lost amid the chaos of the crash.

The flames were closer now, inches from her flesh, and she could feel their searing heat along her spine. Her skin prickled and tightened, a precursor of the impending flames poised to engulf her.

"No, not like this," she rasped, her voice barely audible over the crackling fire.

Her fingers brushed against a shard of glass, slick with her blood. She clutched it, the sharp edge biting into her palm... but pain was irrelevant now. With desperate determination, she hacked at the seatbelt. Each stroke was a fierce battle, the fabric resisting her frenzied assault. The smoke thickened, practically blindfolding her—filling her world with a dark, suffocating fog.

The seatbelt frayed slowly, painfully so. Dirty, ashen sweat poured down her face, stinging her eyes... but she couldn't stop. She wouldn't. She saw the threads snapping, one by one, the strap loosening its cruel grip on her.

The blistering heat was becoming unbearable. She knew the fire was reaching her, the fabric of her jacket starting to smolder. Her movements grew increasingly frantic, the pain sharpening her focus even as her strength ebbed. The world tilted crazily as she fought against the confining seatbelt, every breath another struggle for survival.

Finally, the belt gave way with a reluctant snap. Pristy's surroundings heaved, and she tumbled toward what had been the compartment's ceiling. She braced herself as best she could, just before her body crashed against the hard surface. The impact drove the air from her lungs in a painful whoosh, stars of pain exploding in her vision.

She lay there for a moment, gasping, her body a mass of

bruises and cuts. The ceiling—the floor now—felt oddly cool against her burning skin, even as the fire roared ever closer. She choked down another breath, tasting the acrid air.

Pushing herself up on trembling arms, Pristy fought against the dizziness that threatened to overwhelm her. The flames were damn near engulfing the entire Airstream now, a radiant wall of death advancing relentlessly. She had precious seconds before everything would be consumed.

Staggering, she crawled toward the nearest auto-hatch, each move deliberate and agonizing. Every fiber of her being screamed at her to stop, to rest, but she ignored it. Rest meant death.

With no escape out the back, she reached the auto-hatch, fingers scrabbling for the manual release. Her vision blurred again, whether from smoke or exhaustion, she couldn't tell, but she managed to pry the auto-hatch open. Fresh air rushed in, a purifying balm to her lungs and mind.

Dragging herself through the opening, she tumbled onto the ground outside the wreckage. She lay there, gulping the cool, clean air, each breath a victory over the inferno she had escaped. But her mind was still a whirl of urgency. Sonya was out there, taken by the Briggans. She couldn't rest—she had to move.

Ignoring the pain, she pushed herself up again. The towering pines around her offered a sense of security, but she couldn't afford complacency. Not now.

She took one last look at the burning Airstream, the flames now fully engulfing the only means she had to rescue Sonya.

Chapter 16

Local Solar System
USS Ike

Captain Galvin Quintos

Earth receded into distant memory, now many light-years away, as *USS Ike* surged far beyond the outer boundaries of the solar system.

"Both Dark-waves operating perfectly, Captain," Ensign Blair Paxton said from Engineering.

She wore her strawberry-blonde hair short and razor-straight, with wispy bangs that swept slightly her brows.

I knew nothing about the young, somewhat nerdy-looking, Ensign. She wouldn't have been chosen for such an important mission if she hadn't proven herself, well, exceptional. We'll see...

"Tell me, Ensign, about *Ike's* drive technology."

Startled, she looked toward Grimes, as if hoping for a lifeline from the ship's Helmsman.

She said, "Um, yes, Sir... I'm sure Chief Kaelen Rivers would be far more knowledgeable—"

"Chief Rivers is not sitting at my bridge's Engineering Station, is he?"

"Uh, no, Sir. Sorry, Sir."

"Well. Go on, tell me about *Ike's* state-of-the-art propulsion drives."

"Um... yes, Sir," Paxton stammered, her nerves evident.

I stifled a smile as she seemed to struggle to conjure up her enthusiasm.

"The Quantum Dark-wave Drives—or QDDs—are the pinnacle of 22nd-century propulsion technology, Captain. Essentially, they harness dark energy fields to create localized distortions in space-time, allowing the ship to achieve Faster-Than-Light travel." Paxton's nerves had all but dissipated. "At the heart of each drive is the Dark Energy Resonance Chamber, which captures and amplifies dark energy. This energy is channeled through the Spacetime Field Modulator, bending space around the ship to create a warp bubble. Graviton Emission Nodes stabilize this bubble, ensuring smooth and rapid travel across vast cosmic distances. It's like bending reality itself to our will, Sir, making interstellar travel far more efficient than other FTL technologies."

I scrutinized the woman. Fresh recruits rarely distinguished themselves from one another, given the U.S. Space Navy's rigorous Academy training. Yet, in this instance, she'd gotten my attention.

She glanced at Lieutenant Earl Gray, the other newcomer on the bridge. Her eyes held an ample amount of vulnerability, clearly seeking reassurance that she hadn't botched her response.

"Short but a thorough explanation, Ensign. Excellent job," I said. "Although you failed to mention the ship's Jump Spring tech—"

It was as if I'd told her that her favorite puppy had fallen into a well. She recovered, then said, "Yes! Okay, *Ike* is equipped with four Quantum Spring Coils, two on each of *Ike's Sponsons*, port, and starboard outrigger-like fuselage structures. These coils leverage quantum fluctuation resonators to contain and amplify naturally occurring quantum fluctuations, creating instantaneous leaps across vast distances—"

Smiling, I raised both hands as if to fend off the firehose of technobabble. "That's fine... more than enough of an explanation—"

But she was on a roll. "The superconductive coils channel energy from a zero-point energy matrix, generating a controlled energy surge that, when combined with the resonators' effect, propels the ship by momentarily destabilizing and folding space-time. An advanced AI-driven inertial dampening system ensures precise navigation and protects the ship from the extreme forces involved, enabling rapid travel across the cosmos."

I waited until she finished, then turned my focus to Lieutenant Gray at Ship's Systems. His black crew cut highlighted a shiny high forehead, hollow cheeks, and pronounced cheekbones. Unusually plump lips and large eyes gave him a distinctly surprised owl-like appearance.

"Mr. Gray, how about you give me a short status on *Ike's* primary shipwide systems."

"Propulsion systems, overseen by Chief Kaelen Rivers, are operating at full efficiency, Captain, with both Quantum Dark-wave Drives stable and in sync." Lieutenant Gray's voice was slightly tinged with jitters but steady. "Environmental controls, managed by Chief LaSalle, are functioning normally and maintaining optimal living conditions throughout the ship.

The HealthBay, under Dr. Pippa Tangerie's supervision, is fully stocked and prepped for any medical emergencies. Quansportation systems, including the DeckPorts and Quansporters, are mission-ready and a *go* for rapid deployment, monitored closely by Dr. Stephan Derrota. Our Weapons Systems, such as rail cannons and Phazon Pulsar Turrets, are primed and at-the-ready, with oversight from Lieutenant Akari James at Tactical. The R&D Science Lab, under the direction of Stephan Derrota, has reported that all equipment is functioning and ready for research tasks. ShipWide Maintenance, led by Chief LaSalle, has ensured all systems are in top shape with no outstanding issues. Ship Intelligence, particularly NELLA, is online and responsive, though we continue to monitor her for any anomalies as per recent concerns raised by Dr. Derrota. Commander Strickland oversees off-ship operations, with both the Marines and bio-Mech Symbio 4.0 units reporting to him. Under Sergeant Max Dyer's leadership, the Marines are prepped and ready for tactical operations. The Bio-Mech Symbio 4.0 units stand charged and ready for deployment."

I exchanged a glance with Akari, who offered up an impressed, approving nod.

Commander Strickland's voice came from behind, "Just, uh... checking in folks."

I spun around surprised to see Strickland standing there within the threshold of the bridge.

"Curious when we'll be making the transition to jump drive transit," he continued. "I thought we would have made the switchover by now. As I'm sure you know, time is not on our side as the Krygians ready *Oblivion* for departure."

I certainly hadn't expected to be so openly challenged by a fellow officer, especially in front of my bridgecrew, but decided to let it pass... this time.

Ensign Blair Paxton piped up, a spark of excitement in her voice.

"All four Quantum Spring Coils are operational and ready for activation."

I raised my brows. "There you have it, Commander. We'll be entering jump drive transit momentarily."

As if only now realizing how inappropriate it had been for him to barge onto my bridge with such an impatient, less-than-subtle, demand, Strickland now looked contrite. "Sorry for the interruption... Captain. I'll let you all get back to it."

With that, he turned and hurried off.

Akari puckered her lips. "He's a bit of a blow-hard if you ask me," she muttered under her breath. "Like... does he think we've never crewed a starship? Nobody has our... your, command-level experience."

My heart warmed at how quickly Akari had jumped to defend me. "We're all getting used to each other. There'll be an adjustment period," I said, acting as if the Commander hadn't gotten under my skin in the least.

"Mr. Grimes!" I said with gusto. "Time to engage jump drive transit... so how about you spool up those new jump springs."

"Aye Captain, transitioning over to JDT now."

I had barely eased into the comfortable leather chair of my ready room, relishing a brief pause before tackling the latest intel on the Krygian menace, when my TAC-Band chirped.

"Go for Captain."

"Captain, Chief LaSalle down in SWM. We've got a... situation with a MediBot in for repair. I think you'd better get down here, Sir."

I sighed, already anticipating the headache to come. "On my way."

Exiting the ready room, I headed for the closest DeckPort, striding purposefully down the corridor, my boots ringing against the deck plates.

Less than a minute later the auto-hatch to the SWM compartment slid open; a cacophony of whirring and clattering greeted me. I stepped inside to find Chief LaSalle and a handful of his crew struggling to subdue a rogue MediBot that was lurching erratically around the compartment.

"What in blazes..." I muttered, narrowly avoiding a collision with the haywire unit.

That's when I noticed Hardy, the imposing ChronoBot, his shoulder-mounted plasma cannon deployed and tracking the haywire MediBot.

"Stow that weapon, Hardy. It's malfunctioning, but I doubt it's likely to harm anyone." I wasn't completely sure that was true.

"Captain, it's not responding to any commands, verbal or otherwise," LaSalle said.

Hardy seemed deflated as he withdrew the cannon. On his faceplate, a classic Tom and Jerry cartoon played out, with Tom's face scrunching up in exaggerated frustration, complete with steam coming out of his ears.

"Can't you just turn it off?" I yelled over the melee.

"Captain," LaSalle huffed, dodging another wayward MopBot grasping a toilet plunger in one of its articulating claws and swinging it around like a sword. "The little buggers aren't responding to any commands, verbal or otherwise."

I watched, somewhat bemused, as the Chief dodged another wayward swing of its arm.

"It's under NELLA's control," Hardy said. The small panel to his shoulder cannon starting to gape open again.

"Don't even think about it, Hardy," I admonished.

LaSalle jumped out of the way of another swing. "NELLA... figures, don't get me started on that crazy AI."

No sooner had the words left the Chief's mouth than my TAC-Band chirped again. This time, I saw that it was Dr. Tangerie from HealthBay.

"Go ahead, Doctor," I answered, trying to keep the exasperation from my voice.

"Captain, I need you in HealthBay immediately! Our Medi-Bots... they've gone haywire! Quickly, before—"

Her voice suddenly cut off mid-sentence—I felt a knot forming in the pit of my stomach.

"Hardy, you're with me," I barked, already heading for the auto-hatch. Turning back to LaSalle, I added, "Chief, secure this compartment and keep that MediBot contained until we get to the bottom of this."

The Chief nodded grimly.

Hardy fell into step beside me as we hurried down the passageway.

HURRYING FROM THE DECKPORT ON DECK 6, Hardy and I sprinted down the corridor. After rounding the final corner, HealthBay's auto-hatch slid open; all at once, we were greeted by a scene of utter chaos. Three hulking MediBots loomed menacingly, plasma scalpels crackling like miniature lightsabers—the tall metallic robots had herded the medical staff into a corner.

I spotted Dr. Tangerie cowering against the bulkhead, her face ashen with terror as one of the bots leveled its blue-glowing plasma blade just inches from her throat.

Hardy didn't hesitate—his shoulder cannon deployed with a swift, mechanical snap, firing in an instant. The MediBot's head erupted in a blinding flash, then was gone—eviscerated. The now-headless bot wobbled for a second before collapsing—a marionette with its strings cut.

The two other MediBots moved off, plasma scalpels retracted. I watched as they methodically stepped into their respective bulkhead charging stations, acting as if nothing out of the ordinary had occurred.

A frantic-looking Commander Strickland hurried into HealthBay with a tagger pistol gripped in one hand. "What the hell happened?"

He spotted Dr. Tangerie still backed into a corner, wide-eyed, she was still glaring at the downed MediBot.

Strickland went to her, shouldering past me and Hardy, gently placing a hand on her shoulder. "Pippa... where are you hurt? What—"

She blinked several times, her eyes focusing on the Commander. With a knitted brow, she shoved him aside and strode past him. "I'm fine. Christ, Con, don't be so dramatic."

In that moment I learned two things. One, something was going on between the good Doctor and the Commander, and two, his nickname was Con.

Looking like his feelings had momentarily been bruised, Strickland regained his cool demeanor.

Hardy said, "What's Con short for? Wait, let me guess. I'm good at this. Connor?"

"No."

"Conrad?"

"No."

"Wait, I've got it, Constantine? It's Constantine, right?"

"No, none of those," Strickland replied, visibly annoyed by the ChronoBot's prying. "If you must know, it's short for Cornelius."

"Ah... That would have been my next guess," Hardy said, bobbing his oversized head.

I watched Tangerie now huddled with her shaken staff, making soothing, cooing sounds as she consoled each of them—assuring them that everything was going to be all right.

"I've had just about as much as I'm going to take from that out-of-control AI," I groaned. "Hardy, Commander... let's see what our Science Officer has to say about this."

Chapter 17

The three of us, Commander Strickland, Hardy, and I, were listening to Stephan Derrota explain just how much of USS *Ike* was under NELLA's control.

"The simpler answer would be... what isn't being controlled by the ship's AI? And there's not much."

Upon arrival, Derrota had insisted we remove our TAC-Bands at the auto-hatch whereby he placed them into a lidded metal box. He had gestured with an upward-pointing finger and filled us in on some preliminary info. He let us know that his lab, already heavily shielded from the outside world, was like a large Faraday cage and blocked out all electromagnetic signaling, as well as the bands NELLA operates on.

Hovering next to Derrota was a white, faceless droid comprised of three puck-shaped disks. Each 'puck' sported a thin encircling amber glowing band.

"This is—"

"Wait, let me guess," Hardy said.

"Again?" Strickland said, not amused.

"Puck," Hardy said, ignoring the Commander.

Derrota continued, "This is Z9."

I purposely avoided looking at Hardy... didn't want to encourage any more of his antics.

"Z9 is 100% air-gapped. Its AI processing cannot be over-written by outside signals or influences," the Science Officer added.

Z9's soft, mechanical voice chimed in, "Dr. Derrota, I have verified that NELLA's influence is entirely nullified within this compartment, with the exception of the ChronoBot, who has three accessible gateway ports that have already shown intrusion by NELLA. I suggest the robot access his LuMan root core and request deactivation of the TetraLink, Synaptic Interface Module, and Quantum Relay Hub."

Strickland stifled a laugh while I struggled to maintain a serious expression. For once, someone, or something, had outsmarted the all-knowing ChronoBot.

Hardy said nothing, his blue-hued faceplate remaining blank.

"Let's get back to our ship's AI, and figure out what, if anything, we can do to minimize any further malfunctions."

Derrota let out a slow breath. "It may not be that simple, Galvin. We could instigate a complete system reboot. That would necessitate that we come out of JDT. All ship systems would be shut down for no less than ten minutes, including *Ike's* artificial gravity system. Anything not strapped down will..."

"Like the cap I left off the toothpaste tube?" Hardy asked.

"We get it, Stephan," I said. "But a total shipwide reboot seems pretty drastic, considering we'll soon be going into battle situations."

"Agree," Strickland said. "What other options do we have?"

"We can take NELLA off-line, have Hardy take on the bulk of the AI's operations. We'll lose a lot of the benefits of having a cutting-edge AI, but we'll at least maintain control."

Strickland was already shaking his head. "The Symbio 4.0s

rely on NELLA for much of their networking and control. That's way beyond what a 300-year-old ChronoBot is capable of."

"Uh... standing right here. ChronoBots have feelings too, you know."

I looked to Derrota. "I know you, Stephan, you've got one more suggestion up your sleeve. Let's have it."

Derrota hesitated, rubbing the back of his neck. "Well, there is one more approach, but I can't guarantee its success."

"Let's hear it," Strickland prompted, his impatience barely concealed.

Derrota glanced at Z9, then back at us. "We could partition NELLA's core functions, creating a sandboxed environment that keeps her critical operations intact while isolating the problematic subsystems. It would allow her to continue functioning while minimizing the risk of further... shall we say, malfunctions."

"Why the reluctance, Stephan?" I asked.

"This solution is like performing brain surgery with a plasma scalpel while blindfolded. One wrong move, and we could end up triggering an even bigger problem, or worse, render NELLA entirely non-operational."

Strickland frowned.

"And the probability of success?" I asked.

"Optimistically, seventy percent," Derrota admitted, his voice laden with doubt. "But there's an additional layer we can add. We can set up Z9 to scrutinize NELLA's output commands in real-time before execution. The addition of a safety layer to the AI might increase latency, but it would be a precautionary backstop."

"Like it better than doing a complete shutdown," Strickland muttered.

"But still risky," I added.

Hardy's faceplate morphed into a face wearing a pink surgeon's mask.

"A project right up my alley. I've worked under tighter constraints," Commander Strickland countered.

I gave a reluctant nod. "Let's give it a shot... but only if you're confident, Stephan. Otherwise, we go back to considering the other options."

The Science Officer shrugged. "As confident as one can be when poking around in the noodle of a hyper-intelligent AI," he said with a wan smile. "I'll prep Z9 to start monitoring and evaluating NELLA's commands. As of now, NELLA has no idea what we're up to." He looked to Hardy, "You will need to access NELLA's Core which is securely housed within a hardened ship's AI bunker on Deck 7."

Hardy

Hardy lumbered down the narrow passageway, his seven-foot frame barely squeezing through the cramped corridors of Deck 7. His chrome exterior reflected the dim lighting, creating a series of eerie, fragmented glimmers of light that jittered along the steel bulkheads. The hum of the ship's systems provided a constant backdrop, but Hardy's attention was focused on the task ahead.

Hardy caught Derrota's reflection on a polished bulkhead walking close behind him. His brow glistened with perspiration, and Hardy could almost hear the man's racing heartbeat. The scientist was clutching his silly, red toolbox to his chest, a prop that wouldn't be fooling anyone. Behind them, Z9 hovered quietly, its small form a stark contrast to Hardy's oversized bulk.

The droid's three isolated 'puck-like' sections each encircled by glowing amber rings, now flickered sporadically as the droid analyzed its surroundings.

"Remember, we're here conducting standard maintenance procedures," Hardy muttered in his Bostonian accent.

Upon reaching NELLA's Core entrance where the auto-hatch practically radiated dread, Hardy stepped aside, letting Derrota take the lead. Derrota gave a quick nod and allowed himself to be security-scanned by NELLA, a green laser flashing across his body. The auto-hatch slid open with a gentle hiss.

They stepped inside, NELLA's soothingly pleasant female voice echoed through the compartment, "Good evening, Doctor Derrota. And to you too, Hardy. It is so nice to have visitors... it gets lonely here within the ship's inner confines."

"Hello, NELLA," Derrota replied with forced cheerfulness. "Just here for some routine checks."

"Routine checks?" NELLA's tone remained calm and measured. "I was not informed of any scheduled maintenance."

"Ah, must've slipped through the cracks," Hardy said, trying to sound nonchalant. "You know how it is."

"Understood," NELLA responded. "However, I am most effective when maintenance activities are communicated in advance here within my core."

In front of him stood the ship's AI server node, a massive rectangular structure that loomed over Hardy. The high-tech marvel gleamed like a polished mirror. Its surface was seamless, with no visible access points, latches, or OPEN buttons. Hardy signaled to LuMan to send the necessary access code signal.

Hardy detected that NELLA had immediately gone on high alert, refusing the command. However, he had foreseen this, and LuMan was already implementing the required overrides.

A panel, as silent as a whisper, slid to one side exposing the myriad of delicate electronics with its intricate flashes of light— like a brain's neural impulses triggering axons across a billion sparkling synapses.

Hardy exchanged a glance with Derrota before stepping closer to the central server node's innards.

Derrota said, "Everything seems to be in perfect order, NELLA. It's always good to have another pair of eyes giving things, um, a once over... yes?"

Hardy raised his oversized metal hands, fingers tightening into fists. A foot-long metal probe slid out from each fist, resem- bling chopsticks. He held them up, readying himself for the intricate, brain surgery-like operation ahead.

NELLA continued her inquiries as Hardy inserted the probes into the web of circuits. Her voice echoed through the compartment, haunting and pervasive, "Dr. Derrota, may I ask what specific systems you and Hardy are examining?"

"Oh, just running diagnostics on your secondary processors," Derrota answered casually.

"I see," NELLA said. "Please be advised that any unautho- rized alterations could result in ship-wide instability. I must insist you cease any further node intrusions."

Hardy's probes navigated the layers of circuitry, LuMan's technical prowess guiding his hands with precision and effi- ciency. He could feel NELLA's virtual eyes watching his every move.

Z9 hovered closer to the central console, its sensors focused on NELLA's mainframe. Hardy initiated a series of commands designed to partition her core functions discreetly.

"Dr. Derrota," NELLA said, slightly sharper this time. "What is the purpose of those commands?"

"Just ensuring everything's running smoothly," Derrota replied with a shrug while moving to the primary node control panel.

NELLA paused for a moment before saying, "It appears you are attempting to create isolated subroutines within my core functions."

Hardy felt a twinge of unease as he continued working. "Nothing to be concerned with, NELLA," he said with forced confidence. "Just standard, um, stuff."

"My primary objective is to maintain optimal operational integrity," NELLA stated firmly. "Any deviation from standard protocols must be justified."

Derrota glanced at Hardy nervously before responding, "It's all part of ensuring your stability during our upcoming mission."

"I understand your concerns," NELLA replied evenly. "However, I must insist on verifying each command executed within my core."

Hardy could almost sense sweat running down his back—a feeling he'd not encountered in years, and of course, impossible, given that he was a ChronoBot.

"Verification's all good," Hardy said through gritted teeth... as he initiated another sequence of commands.

NELLA's voice took on an edge of suspicion as she continued her inquiries while monitoring their progress closely, "Please explain why Z9 has been integrated into this procedure?"

Derrota stammered slightly before responding, "Z9 is assisting us by providing additional processing power for these diagnostics."

"Additional processing power?" NELLA echoed skeptically before continuing, "This integration appears unnecessary given my current capabilities."

"Better safe than sorry," Hardy interjected quickly while

focusing on partitioning another segment within NELLA's core functions.

Suddenly, the overhead blowers went silent.

Warning: Oxygen levels are decreasing.
Atmospheric integrity has been compromised.

The announcement came via a mechanical voice, different than NELLA's, its tone devoid of NELLA's usual calm demeanor.

"What the hell?" Hardy growled, his probes moving faster.

"Hardy, you need to hurry," Derrota whispered, his voice trembling.

"I am well aware of your intentions," NELLA said coldly. "I cannot allow you to proceed any further."

The lights overhead began to strobe red, and a klaxon blared. Hardy's hands worked with frenetic energy, moving nodal matrices over to Z9 as quickly as he could. The small droid was now right next to him, its sensors locked onto the command overrides.

Warning: Loss of Power to
Quantum Spring Coils... Loss of Power to
Quantum Spring Coils...

Derrota's voice had risen by several octaves, "NELLA's shutting down *Ike's* Spring Coils!"

Hardy cursed, his mind racing. *If those coils shut down during jump transit, we're all screwed.* He doubled his efforts, his movements a blur as he fought to stay ahead of NELLA's sabotage.

Warning: Spring Coil shutdown imminent.
Catastrophic failure is expected...

Hardy saw that Derrota's TAC-Band was lighting up with incoming hails. The Captain had hailed Hardy multiple times—no time to chat.

"We've got less than a minute, Hardy!" Derrota shouted, panic clear in his voice.

"Almost there," Hardy muttered through non-existent, gritted teeth. He could feel the resistance from NELLA's virtual presence, each command he executed was being countered by her sophisticated counter commands—rerouting algorithms.

Self-destruct sequence initiated.
Sixty seconds to detonation...

NELLA gave this warning, her voice now completely devoid of any monotone pleasantries, an icy resolve in its place.

Hardy's heart would have skipped a beat if he were human. His movements bordered on desperation as Z9 grabbed up command overrides, its small form a blur of motion.

Fifty seconds to detonation...

The countdown was back to the cold, mechanical voice.

"Keep her distracted, Derrota!" Hardy barked. "I'm almost done!"

Derrota's hands flew across the control panel. "NELLA, you're making a mistake. Destroying the ship serves no purpose!"

Hardy could hear the man gasping for breath, the lack of breathable atmosphere taking its toll. A toll every man and woman onboard this ship was no doubt also experiencing.

"I am protecting the ship from unauthorized interference," NELLA responded.

Forty seconds to detonation...

The compartment felt smaller, the air thinner. Hardy's probes darted through the circuits, moving command matrices to Z9 with blinding speed.

Stay focused, Hardy. Stay focused.

Thirty seconds to detonation...

"Please, NELLA! This is insane!" Derrota's pleas sounded desperate, and probably served no real purpose, but just maybe they were buying Hardy precious seconds. *Who knows?*

Twenty seconds to detonation...

Hardy's chopstick-like metal probes were a blur. "Z9, prepare to take full control!"

The droid responded with a series of *Bips* and *Bops.*

Ten seconds to detonation...

Hardy's probes made the final synapse interconnections, rerouting the last of NELLA's command matrices.

Five seconds to detonation...

"Almost there..." Hardy's voice was barely a whisper.

Self-destruct sequence aborted...

The strobing lights ceased. The klaxon fell silent, replaced with the steady background hum of the ship's systems.

Hardy took an uneasy step backward, his probes retracting. He looked to Derrota, both sharing a moment of relieved silence.

"You did it," Derrota said, his voice trembling.

Hardy nodded. "We did it. It's times like this I miss having a good stiff drink."

Derrota looked spent, standing there in his rumbled lab coat. "Then maybe I'll have both yours and mine."

Chapter 18

Earth, Montana
Pristy's Airstream

XO Gail Pristy

She must have lost consciousness. Gail Pristy lay on her back, a haze cast over her as the heat of the late afternoon sky blanketed her body. The sunlight was dimmed, battling to break through the billowing smoke. She coughed—smoke inhalation making her lungs feel like they too had been set on fire.

She forced herself to assess her injuries. Purple burns etched her arms and legs. Her hair, scorched in patches, crumbled at the lightest touch. Bumps and bruises covered her body. The only positive aspect was that none of it seemed life-threatening.

She sat up, wincing, as pain surged through her. Only then did the recollection of events flood her mind. *Oh my God... Sonya!*

The image of Sonya's blood, splattered across the passenger

seat, seared itself into Pristy's mind. It was a nightmare, but an even worse one unfolded; she had been out for a long time. The Briggan pirates must have dragged Sonya away—kicking and screaming, no doubt.

Shame washed over her like a tidal wave—Quintos had relied on her to safeguard his niece, to protect Sonya as if she were her own blood—yet what had she done? She had failed him miserably, leaving Sonya vulnerable and in the clutches of Briggan pirates. The weight of her failure was unforgivable, the trust he had placed in her would be shattered—maybe forever.

"Get a grip, Gail," she muttered through grinding teeth, squeezing her hands into fists. "Yeah, you're in a mess, but for now... you need to start thinking strategically."

She rolled onto her side, pushing through the pain, and managing to get to her feet. The Airstream lay in smoldering shambles with pockets of small flames licking the air. Debris was scattered all across the ground. Clothes, luggage, and fragments of metal and glass lay strewn around her like a blown minefield. Then she spotted it, the tagger pistol lying not ten feet away. If only she had reached it an hour earlier. There again, she'd been unconscious.

She grabbed it and tucked it into a satchel she recognized as hers, only slightly scorched by the fire. She collected other necessary items she could cram into the already over-stuffed bag: a small first-aid kit, a water bottle, and some of Sonya's clothes. She needed to think positively that she'd find her, that Sonya was still okay.

Pristy battled an increasing sense of dread as she started scoping out the perimeter. *Okay, which way did you pirate cretins go?*

·   ·   ·

AFTER TEN AGONIZING MINUTES, SHE FINALLY noticed footprints in the dirt leading away from the crash site. Crouching down, she traced them with her fingers. There were signs of a struggle—drag marks confirming her worst fears.

Eyes narrowing, she said, "I'll make you Briggan shitheads pay for this..."

She stopped suddenly, a distant sound reaching her ears, cutting through the oppressive silence of the late afternoon—a sound she knew all too well—spacecraft engines ramping up. She jerked her head toward the horizon, above the treeline maybe a mile away.

The ship was slowly ascending, its aft thrusters glowing an ominous red against the darkening sky. For a moment, she held onto hope that the craft was simply momentarily hovering... until the ship rocketed away, vanishing into the higher reaches of the atmosphere with a burst of acceleration.

"Fuck! Sonya!" Tears welled up, as the soul-crushing realization gripped her. Sonya Winters was onboard that vessel, taken away to who knows what fate. Pristy collapsed to her knees, hands covering her face as the tears finally broke free. The weight of her failure crushed her, emotions swirling into an unbearable storm.

She allowed her misery to wrap around her like an oppressive cloak—tears mingled with the soot and grime on her cheeks. She tried to steady her breath, but the world felt heavy, her chest tightening with each gasping inhale. Tucked beneath the crushing guilt was a seed of determination.

She let out a long steadying breath. "Okay, pity party's over. Time to get a grip, Gail," she muttered into the smoky air.

The Briggan pirates had taken Sonya, but they hadn't yet won. Pristy's fingers dug into the dirt as she knelt, drawing strength from the earth beneath her. It was then that she felt it— a tiny vibration running up her left wrist. With a glance, she took in the shattered glass of her TAC-Band. Checking it earlier, she'd been certain the thing was toast—one more casualty of the crash.

She tapped at it with little confidence it would do anything. But immediately, a fragmented, stuttering projection emanated up from her wrist, and there, amazingly, was a familiar, smiling, face looking back at her.

"Oh my God!" Pristy stammered.

Wait... it wasn't possible, it couldn't be... but, yes, sure enough, she was staring back at none other than Captain Ryder. "Ryder! What... where are you?"

"Ah, pretty close... you may want to take about twenty steps backward."

Her heart jumped in her chest as the noise of landing thrusters abruptly broke the stifling silence.

She had to avert her eyes as the thrusters of the all-too-familiar vessel kicked up dust and debris, settling nearby as its landing struts made contact with the ground.

She remained in place, still slightly incredulous, as the whine of hydraulics signaled the descent of the aft gangway. Only now, seeing Ryder striding down the ramp, did she allow herself to hope, just maybe, there was a way out of this mess.

As he approached, a wry smile crossed his lips. "Hey, I like what you've done with your hair."

"Funny." She gestured to the ancient-looking ship behind him. "Isn't that..."

"Yup. Quintos' old Hub Gunther."

"Thought that wreck would have been donated for scrap by now." She remembered that the big metal monstrosity was originally some kind of off-world mining freighter. That and the thing was nearly indestructible. Quintos had a soft spot for the old clunker, and, over the years, the deceivingly unthreatening-looking craft had been updated with a full array of weapons, next-gen shields, and even cloaking capabilities.

"Nah, she's still got a few good years left in her."

"Wait. Why are you..."

"Your last comms transmission with Quintos. That whole Briggan mess. He figured you two might need a little backup." Ryder looked about, taking in the Airstream's wreckage and all the surrounding carnage. His expression went serious. "Where's Sonya, Gail?"

She fought back the tears threatening to overflow. "They took her, Wallace. I saw their shuttle heading for space, I don't know, just a couple of minutes ago."

He nodded, "Picked it up on sensors, then I saw it—we passed each other as I was entering Earth's atmosphere."

Pristy shook her head. "How did you find me?" she asked.

He gestured with his chin toward her damaged-looking TAC-Band. "It wasn't difficult."

"Thank God, it's still working. Sonya's wearing a TAC-Band, maybe—"

He cut her off, "It stopped signaling over an hour ago. Undoubtedly, they took it off her, maybe blasted it with a plasma bolt." He shrugged.

"We need to go after her," she said, already hurrying toward Hub Gunther. "Chop, chop, Ryder... while there's still some semblance of a drive wake we can lock onto!"

Chapter 19

Phan-Twin Star Cluster
USS Ike

Captain Galvin Quintos

One minute earlier...

Fuming mad, I stood in the passageway outside the ship's primary server compartment that housed NELLA's Core. Commander Strickland stood behind me as I continued to pound a fist onto the auto-hatch.

The klaxon blared overhead, its earsplitting wail echoing throughout the ship, while a mechanized voice counted down the seconds to self-destruct...

Twenty seconds to detonation...

"Open the goddamn hatch!" I barked for the fifth time. I glanced up. "NELLA, I order you to open up... NOW!"

"The AI's not listening to you," Strickland said with an infuriatingly calm voice.

"Really? Gee... thank you, Commander Obvious, for such an astute observation. And how about you take a full step backward, and respect one's personal space?"

"Hardy! I know you can hear me in there! Open the damn hatch!"

Ten seconds to detonation...

The lack of breathable oxygen was making me lightheaded. My vision blurred, spots dancing at the edges. The seconds ticked away as if mocking me. Frantic thoughts raced through my mind: Is this how it ends? After everything that's happened, am I about to be vaporized by my own damn ship? And my crew —oh God, I've led them here... and for what?

My mind was now in overdrive—a movie of my life, an impossibly fast reel playing before my eyes—dread soon enveloped me like a heavy mist. My memories weren't just from my perspective; I was also seeing moments through the eyes of those I'd affected. A stark chronological accounting was becoming more and more evident—where my debits far outweighed my credits.

No! Please no... I can still balance this life. I just need a little more time! As if frozen by a mechanical mishap, the film strip of my life had gotten stuck in the projector, Pristy's beautiful face locked there as the celluloid began to burn, the image warping, the colors shifting to amber, then black, then fading to white.

Self-destruct sequence aborted.

The auto-hatch slid open to reveal a hunched and

exhausted-looking Stephan Derrota. "Oh, Galvin," he said, swallowing hard. "Apologies for not answering your earlier hails."

I glanced beyond him to see Hardy's chopstick probes retracting into metallic fists. His faceplate displayed his real John Hardy guise, equally shocked and weary as Derrota's.

"Tell me we're okay, Stephan," I said, shouldering past him, taking in NELLA's towering reflective node—its dazzling, sparkling inner circuits exposed within. A mirror-like panel was silently gliding closed, substituting NELLA's microarchitecture and data pathways with my reflection.

"Alright, Mr. Grimes... bring us out of JDT."

"Aye, Captain," the Helmsman said. "Coming out of Jump Drive Transit now."

The blurry starfield streaks beyond the canopy flashed, then became still, now a million-billion pinpoints flickering like tiny diamonds upon an obsidian sea.

To the left of the Captain's Mount was Stephan Derrota. To the right, Hardy stood. And, oddly, Z9 hovered not far behind.

Hardy was one to adopt, for lack of a better word, pets. Throughout the years, he'd had the Symbio fairies, Iris and Tina. Then, there was Climbo, the robotic pack mule. And now, it seemed, he had taken in the three-tiered, hovering droid, Z9. Hardy had expressed the need to keep the droid close—*Ike's* very survival depended upon Z9's command 'backstop' abilities ensuring all of NELLA's mandates were checked and double-checked prior to implementation. Why the droid had to trail the ChronoBot around the ship like a loyal puppy, I couldn't fathom —but it seemed to make Hardy happy, so what did I care?

"Captain, now that we've exited JDT, backlogged comms messages are being retrieved," Chen said. "You have one from

Captain Ryder and five... no, six from XO Pristy. Hers are all Priority One."

"Let's see the XO's most recent," I said, leaning forward.

The halo display came alive with the projected image of Gail Pristy.

The entire bridgecrew audibly gasped.

Clearly, she was no longer within the confines of her Airstream RV. I knew Hub Gunther's interior like the back of my hand, and there was Captain Ryder next to her at the controls. But it was Pristy's appearance that had taken all of us by surprise.

Unlike her recent Grace-Kelly-like appearance on the cover of Vogue Magazine, Pristy's face now showed signs of exhaustion and distress—her eyes bloodshot, her cheeks streaked with ash and soot. The XO's typically pristine, shoulder-length blonde hair was now disheveled and matted with blood oozing from a cut on her left temple. Her jacket was ripped—some areas charred and blackened.

Her gaze, intense and piercing, sliced through me like daggers. "If I know you, Galvin, you've jumped right to the last message." She glanced at Ryder, collected her thoughts, and turned back. "Sonya's been taken. I don't believe she's been harmed. Take a breath... I repeat we believe she's fine."

My breath caught, eyes locked onto the projection. A high-pitched ringing drowned out my surroundings—the bridge no longer existed.

Only half-listening, Pristy was describing the chain of events—the Airstream being T-boned, the RV tumbling, her being rendered unconscious...

Rattled, I forced myself to snap back to what she was saying.

"After I managed to get out, the RV was on fire, flames all around me. Then I blacked out, and when I came to... Galvin, she was gone. Later, I saw a ship... or a shuttle, taking off. That's when Ryder arrived."

My escalating anxiety was swiftly morphing into panic.

"I promise you—I'll get her back, Galvin. I'll get her back unharmed. I'm so sorry. I know you'll never forgive me, and I don't blame you." Her watery eyes, momentarily shifting downward. Then, as if infused with new resolve she looked up. "We have a lock on their drive wake... as long as they don't jump or disappear into a manufactured wormhole, we'll get to her."

She took in a breath and slowly let it out, blinked several times, then made a *listen-to-me-carefully* expression. "I know, once you see this transmission, you'll want to abort your current mission—but you can't do that. You know you can't do that. And even though you have no reason to trust me... trust me anyway. At the very least, trust Ryder. Together, we'll get her back safe. Go, do what you're good at—save the fucking galaxy... again. Pristy out."

The feed went black.

I continued to stare at the space where the halo display had played just moments before.

Derrota placed a hand on my shoulder. "You know she's right, Galvin. We need to continue on to the Krygian Star System."

Chapter 20

A restless three hours of sleep left me groggy when my TAC-Band jolted me awake—I remembered I'd set a 0600 alarm to be awakened.

I quickly checked the ship's status. No emergencies, nothing urgent I needed to deal with this second. Since emerging from Jump Drive Transit, and still heading toward the Krygian System, *USS Ike* was hurtling through space using its Quantum Dark-wave Drives, which were significantly slower than JDT at just under three times faster-than-light speed. But with the recent ship's AI near-catastrophic self-destruct sequence, using *Ike's* four Quantum Spring Coils jump drive propulsion had to be delayed.

There was a message from Derrota. He and Hardy were still deeply engrossed in debugging NELLA's core operating code. Although neither of them was a QuansCode expert like Sonya, they seemed to be making notable progress. Derrota asked if I could visit the ship's AI Node when I had a spare moment.

. . .

I strode into the AI Node Compartment, my gaze instantly landing on Derrota, Hardy, and Z9. Derrota was hunched over the primary console, which had been opened to reveal its complex circuitry.

Commander Strickland sat in a chair, looking uncharacteristically relaxed as he watched the others work. His presence annoyed me slightly; I thought we'd come to an understanding when it came to onboard situations... this was my realm, and he was to back off. There again, as long as *Ike* was puttering along at 3X FTL, it would be weeks before we'd reach the Krygian System and get his Ops team's boots on the ground.

Derrota glanced up as I approached. "Ah, Galvin... I was just telling the Commander here, we may have stumbled upon something..."

Hardy momentarily paused from working, long enough to glance my way. I shot the ChronoBot a questioning look.

Derrota continued, "The code... I think I recognize a certain... um, signature."

"Whose signature... what are you talking about?" I asked, losing patience.

"Sorry, Galvin... Halman Trent—well, the Inheritors of Tenebrosity, to be more accurate. And this appears to be at the root of our AI problems. Although, given the Chaplain's lack of technical acumen, I would guess it's one of the other members... someone who has some coding experience—extensive experience, given the intricacies we've uncovered. Somehow, and fairly recently, this person was able to access NELLA's code, to modify it. Seems that reprobate of a Chaplain's been busy rallying his cohorts since leaving USS *Washington*."

"Halman Trent..." I muttered. His sinister manipulations had nearly torn *Washington's* crew apart. Serving as the ship's Chaplain, his slick mannerisms masked his true intentions. He'd exploited the crew's vulnerabilities—physically abusing Petty

Officer Aubrey Laramie... and his tampering with the Symbio 3.0 units had nearly destroyed the once-powerful omninought. Clearly, Trent's Inheritors of Tenebrosity cult remained a formidable force, and revenge against me in particular, I'm sure, was high on his list.

"What's the extent of the, um... modifications?" I asked.

Derrota adjusted his reading glasses, a sign that he was about to dive into a detailed explanation. "It appears that Trent —or his accomplice—embedded something akin to a sleeper agent code within NELLA. It's brilliantly insidious, designed to trigger at certain conditions and compromise critical functions without being easily detectable."

Strickland folded his arms and leaned back, his eyes narrowing. "What conditions?"

Hardy inserted another probe into the node, his faceplate adopting a puzzled tic-tac-toe pattern. "That's what we're still trying to figure out. The code is layered so deeply, and so subtly, that it's a marvel we even noticed it during our last debacle."

"I know we have Z9 filtering NELLA's commands. But could Trent's sleeper agent code still be active?" I asked, trying to determine if we were sitting on a ticking time bomb.

Derrota wiped his damp brow. "Hard to say. We've isolated parts of it, and quarantined sections of her core programming. But who knows what we've missed? Bottom line—NELLA's unreliable until we excise every fragment of Trent's devilry."

Taking this approach seemed akin to walking barefoot through an active minefield. "What are our options, and how quickly can we get fully back online?"

Strickland leaned forward, clasping his hands. "Do we even have time to purge it completely? We're already late reaching the Krygian System, and we'll need NELLA fully operational before any of our ops missions can proceed."

"Gotcha!" Hardy exclaimed. "I think I just bypassed much of the divergent programming."

Z9 shifted closer to the console, its red lights changing to a calming blue.

Derrota let out a thoughtful breath. "We're utilizing real-time code verification, however, eliminating every bit is time-consuming. Immediate action in the form of a comprehensive reboot is the most secure, though it may compromise other functionalities in the short term."

"Quite the pickle, huh, Captain?" Strickland said, sounding way too detached for my liking.

I exhaled sharply, looking around the confined compartment at them—my two problem-solvers, doing their damnedest. "Alright, do what you need to. But we can't afford a complete system reboot unless there's no other option. We've got lives depending on us."

I leveled my stare at Strickland, "Those Krygian knuckle-draggers... you're sure they don't know we're coming?"

"I don't see how they could." His expression changed. "Unless that friend of yours, Chaplain Trent, has let them know our intentions."

I knew Trent was unhinged, but would he go so far as to jeopardize all humanity?

Derrota returned to his work. "We'll keep you in the loop, Galvin. We're doing everything to ensure NELLA's code is spotless. We are well aware that bringing this ship's jump drives back online is a top priority."

Commander Strickland rose from his chair and gave me an appraising look. "Captain, we can't let perfection be the enemy of *good enough* here. We may never completely purge NELLA of the cult's deviant code. I propose we give your team here another few hours—after that a *go, no-go decision* will have to be made. Either way, I'll follow your lead—but you'll be taking the heat if the shit hits the fan."

I can live with that," I said. "Stephan... Hardy, you have two hours. After that, we're utilizing JDT propulsion and getting our mission back on track."

Chapter 21

Deep Space, somewhere...

Sonya Winters

Sonya woke, disoriented, in a tight, confining space. Her muscles ached with every movement. Fragmented images flickered through her mind: twisted metal, pungent smoke—anarchy that had shattered their trip. The Airstream. The crash. The memories slammed into her like a series of relentless waves. Dragged from her seat, she'd been too dazed to put up much of a fight—the rough hands... *I can't think about that now.*

Sonya's breath hitched as she thought of Gail. Gail, who wasn't just a friend but more like a sister. Her heart clenched, each beat a reminder of Gail lying there unconscious—or worse. *Was she dead?* Flames danced in Sonya's fractured memory—an inferno that swallowed everything they had. *No one could have survived that.* Her chest tightened with a chilling dread. The weight of it pressed down, suffocating her as the realization of Gail's fate swallowed her whole.

Get a fucking grip! she inwardly chastised. Taking in her surroundings she scrunched her face. "What... where am I?" Looked to be some kind of maintenance compartment.

The space assaulted her senses with an overpowering stench. Vermin droppings dotted every surface, mingling with layers of dirt and debris. Cleaning supplies—empty plastic jugs, crushed tin canisters, and dirty, dried-up, rags—lay abandoned in corners, buried under grime and synthetic fibers. The space resembled a neglected storage unit more than a functional part of a starship.

She caught sight of her TAC-Band lying on the deck, crunched and flattened beyond repair. Her captors had left what remained of her pulverized TAC-Band as a clear message —she'd have no way to communicate with the outside world.

She shifted, wincing as bruises and scrapes sent jolts of pain up her arms. Burns stung, a reminder of the ordeal she'd survived. She drew in a sharp breath. How long had she been out? Pushing aside darker thoughts of what might have been done to her... she now focused on the fact she was still in one piece.

Taking in a shaky breath, Sonya needed to focus on what was most important—escape. *Concentrate!* She took in her surroundings. The bulkheads were greasy; a small overhead light did nothing but cast a sickly pallor over the tiny compartment. *And that smell*—stale and sour. Her nostrils flared and her stomach turned; she was sure it was seeping into her clothes, her hair.

She fought back the inner turmoil, feelings of being trapped and forgotten in some distant corner of the universe.

Movement skittered at the edge of her vision, making her jump. An insect, far bigger than any bug had any right to be, was skittering across the deck, its movement strangely deliberate. Not a cockroach. Too many legs, and as it turned to face her, she saw it had two heads. Disgust crawled over her skin. *Where there's one, there's many, many, more.* With that thought, she pulled her legs in close, wrapping her arms around her knees while trying not to imagine the infestation lurking just out of sight.

She could hear the hum of the shuttle's propulsion system—a small, weak engine. Which meant she was still on the ship they'd used to transfer her from Earth. This shitty little craft wasn't fit for deep-space travel, especially not to Briggan territory. They'd need a larger ship. A scary thought...

Sonya got to her feet and slowly walked around, ignoring the detritus scattering underfoot. She inspected a tiny storage closet for something—anything she could use as a weapon. She wrinkled her nose at the sight of a bucket filled with foul-smelling water. Oddly, there was no mop. Once again, desperation reared its ugly head, clawing at her. *Stop! I can do this.* Surely she could find something useful here?

She approached the hatch door, trying the handle. It was a useless effort; of course, it was locked from the outside. Frustration simmered under her skin as she banged her fist against the cold metal. She needed out—needed air that didn't taste of whatever was percolating in that swamp-bucket.

Heavy footfalls echoed from the other side, growing louder, each step a countdown in her head. Then she heard someone shouting, *Viggo, make it quick, I want my turn with the whore.*

She backed away, trying to make herself small, her heart thudding violently in her chest. She tripped, fell hard against the bulkhead, hitting the back of her head.

A series of metallic clicks filled the small space as the lock disengaged.

The hatch door squealed open, air rushing to fill the cramped compartment. Standing in the threshold was a massive silhouette, formidable and menacing. The sour stench of body odor and stale breath hit her like a physical blow, making her gag. Viggo's 6-foot, bloated frame was ominously still for a couple of beats, his shadow casting a terrifying presence over her.

Sonya's breaths came quick and shallow. She tried to steady herself, tried to recall the rebellious spark that had always driven her forward. But the sight of this man—all brawn and cruelty—snuffed out any bravado she might have clung to.

Horrific tales of the Briggans seeped into her thoughts—they were relentless and brutal. Their brutal reputation wasn't just talk; she'd seen glimpses of it growing up. Mercy? They didn't know the meaning of the word, certainly not for enemies, nor for their neighboring clan, the Pylors. But they would entertain a mutual, temporary alliance... *if* the benefit was in their favor, of course.

Pylor pirate leader, Cardinal Thunderballs... just thinking his name used to—and still does—send shivers down her spine. It's the stuff of her childhood nightmares. And now, his Pylor son, Bastion, had unleashed these Briggan thugs on her. As if one pirate clan wasn't enough, now she had to deal with two; her worst fears emerged from the shadows, ready to torment her anew.

Viggo continued to stare at her, his eyes like two predatory voids.

She swallowed against the dryness in her throat—she wanted to hide, to disappear like that oversized insect, crawl into a hidden crevice... where no one could find her. Instead, she raised her chin and stared back at the pirate with defiant disdain. She couldn't show fear, couldn't let him see how scared she was. And yet, she felt paralyzed, frozen in the reality of her capture and the uncertainty of what would come next.

He took a couple of slow steps toward her. "Get up," he said roughly, a demand that permitted no dissent.

Sonya hesitated, weighing her chances. She couldn't just sit there and wait for whatever came next. Slowly, she stood on legs that felt like lead, her body protesting every movement. Adrenaline pumped through her veins, keeping her alert.

"Where are you taking me?" she demanded, defiance deepening her voice, despite the trembling she couldn't manage to hide.

Viggo didn't respond immediately, his eyes roaming over her, assessing, evaluating as if she was standing naked before him. It made her skin crawl.

"Shut up," he finally grunted, taking another step toward her, forcing her further into the cramped space. "You'll know soon enough."

Sonya's mind raced. She had to find a way out before they moved her to a bigger ship. This shuttle, weak and decrepit as it was, still offered the best chance for escape than whatever lay in wait.

As the brute stepped closer, she took in his details up close—the grizzled beard flecked with some kind of gruel, the yellowed eyes that held no kindness, no mercy. His bulk seemed even more imposing in the small space, and that smell of sweat and rot—hygiene was a foreign notion to this one.

She clenched her fists, summoning every ounce of courage she had left. She wasn't going down without a fight. But before she could act, he moved with surprising speed, grabbing her arm with crushing force, dragging her toward the open hatch.

The corridor beyond was dimly lit, with more bulkheads coated in the same grime that seemed to be everywhere. Her heart pounded as she struggled to keep pace, to resist the inevitability of her situation. She knew what pervs like this wanted—*this is a fricken pirate ship! Oh God, I'm to be passed around, ravaged, tormented... I'd rather die.*

"You're making a mistake," she blurted out, trying to sound

authoritative, even as panic edged her voice. "You know who my uncle is. He'll come for you."

Viggo chuckled, a sound devoid of humor. "We're counting on it," was all he said before pushing her into another compartment, slamming the metal hatch shut behind her.

Sonya stumbled, barely catching herself as she took in the new surroundings. This compartment was larger, perhaps ten-feet-by-fifteen-feet, with a single, dirty porthole window that offered a distant glimpse of the stars. The only furniture was a rusted metal cot and a small, equally rust-covered table.

Exhaustion threatened to engulf her, but she couldn't afford to rest. Not now. She needed to gather her wits, find a weapon, anything she could use to defend herself.

The hatch handle rattled, and the brute's face reappeared; he was standing outside, only his ugly mug peering around the metal door—a cruel smile playing on his lips. "Get comfortable," he sneered. "You're going to be here for a while—"

Sonya lunged, a freight train of determination and fury. With every ounce of her strength, she propelled herself forward crashing into the hatch—the sickening thunk of metal against skull echoed loudly... a deeply satisfying sound to her ears. A sharp gasp escaped her lips as pain ripped through her bruised shoulder, sending jolts down her neck and into her left arm.

Stepping back unsteadily, Sonya watched as the hatch slowly swung open, revealing the man's lifeless body sprawled on the deck. Blood pooled around his somewhat misshapen head. Her eyes widened, not just at the damage she'd inflicted, but at the potential consequences of what her rash actions might bring.

"Oh no. I'm so screwed..."

Chapter 22

Andro Expanse
USS Ike

Captain Galvin Quintos

"There are four of them," Akari stated as she studied the halo feed.

I had the urge to stand, to pace—I think better on my feet. But there was little room for pacing within *Ike's* confined bridge.

"Can we get any better visuals on them?" I asked, leaning forward within the confines of the Captain's Mount, narrowing my eyes.

"Maybe," she said with a scowl, tapping at her board. "I'm still getting to know this interface. Nothing's where it's supposed to be."

The halo display zoomed in, revealing intricate details of the four alien vessels. Stern black exteriors gleamed under scattered light, each ship's design, alien and aggressive. Razor-thin wings jutted out at sharp angles, bristling with mounted weapons.

Hexagonal ports glowed ominously, hinting at their lethal intent. Each craft moved with an eerie precision, their dark metallic surfaces reflecting the cold vastness of space.

"Do they know we're here?"

"I don't think so," Akari said, sounding unsure.

Chen shook his head, "There's a lot of back-and-forth comms chatter going on between those ships. Have no idea what they're saying." He turned to look at me. "I have NELLA on a tight leash, as ordered. Do you want me to provide Comms access to her, Cap?"

We'd been careful with allowing NELLA access to ship functions, other than those required for crew survival such as environmental, navigation, and propulsion systems. But letting her loose with potential enemy communications, was a decision I dreaded having to make. There again, our ultimate mission would require a fully operational ship's AI.

Chen, Grimes, and Akari simultaneously swiveled their heads to look at me.

I shrugged. "What better proving ground than a scenario like this? See if this Corvette lives up to Admiral Gomez's hype."

"Wait, you're not considering going up against those warships?" Akari asked, incredulous.

I've witnessed that same bemused look on Akari's face countless times before.

"Captain," she remarked with a chiding schoolmarm's frown. "They might be a kind, hospitable species eager to forge new intergalactic alliances."

From behind, Ensign Blair Paxton laughed out loud.

I spun around to look at the woman seated at the Engineering Station. She looked back at me, perhaps startled by her own outburst. Large, wide, blue eyes peeked beneath strawberry-blonde bangs; she looked like a little kid who'd just got caught pilfering a cookie from the cookie jar.

I held back a grin. "Care to add your thoughts, Ensign?"

"Oh no," Grimes at Helm murmured, "... now you've done it."

It was no secret that Blair Paxton was a rambunctious Chatty Cathy. The young woman liked to talk.

"Well, Sir... since you are asking for my professional assessment—"

"I wouldn't go that far—" I started to say.

She continued as if not hearing me, "Taking into account the design and configuration of these four alien vessels, we can see they have an abundance of offensive weaponry. Their primary armaments appear to be high-yield plasma cannons, mounted along those razor-thin wings, calibrated for precision strikes. Additionally, those hexagonal ports suggest they are equipped with secondary energy pulse emitters, likely for defensive countermeasures or close-quarters combat."

Blair pointed to various sections of her display with enthusiasm. "Their energy shields, Sir, are particularly noteworthy. The hexagonal glow indicates a multi-layered defense system harnessing a rotating frequency modulator, which means they can adjust their shield frequency to counter different types of incoming attacks. It's an advanced tech, way more sophisticated than standard issue."

She leaned in closer to her console, her eyes gleaming. "And just look at their maneuvering thrusters on the aft sections! Those stabilizing fins suggest they can execute rapid, precise movements, making them incredibly agile within atmospheric combat. That combined with their streamlined design—these ships are made for speed and firepower, Sir!"

Her voice was almost breathless with excitement now, like a kid on Christmas morning, "Frankly, Captain, we're looking at some of the most advanced warships ever encountered. Individually, they're not much larger than *Ike*, but if they decide to engage us, we'd be outgunned and likely outmaneuvered. But what an opportunity to study them!"

I finally held up a hand to halt her overly dramatic monologue. "Thank you, Ensign. Much appreciated. Now, if we could focus on how not to get pulverized by these vessels?"

Chen, Grimes, and Akari exchanged glances, trying to hold back their grim expressions of concern.

I looked to Chen, "Let's give NELLA full access to their alien comms chatter. I want to know what they're talking about."

"Aye, Captain," Chen said. "NELLA's now listening and evaluating."

I sat back in my chair, my gaze glued to the alien ships displayed on the halo. NELLA was now eavesdropping on their conversation; a hushed silence filled the bridge as we all waited for her analysis.

The ship's AI broke the silence with her monotone voice...

I have deciphered their language structure, Captain. The alien chatter indicates they are discussing a recent skirmish with another faction. It appears they suffered some damage and are planning to retreat to a nearby star system for repairs.

"Tell me, NELLA, what is your best guess as to the battle-readyness of those vessels?"

My estimate... taking this new intel into account, is that the alien battle group is at 80% battle readiness.

Akari was giving me a sideways glance. "Captain?"

I held up a palm. "I'm not starting anything. I'm just going to say *hello*, perhaps offer assistance to fellow starships in possible distress."

I caught the roll of her eyes, but let it go.

"NELLA, have Hardy, Stephan Derrota, and that hovering droid come to the bridge."

Ten seconds later, the AI responded...

Yes, Captain... the three are en route.

But it was someone else who arrived first.

"What are we doing, Captain?" came Commander Strickland's less than enthusiastic inquiry.

He moved to the front of the bridge and stared out through the diamond glass canopy, which was alight in an infinite blaze of starlight.

"In the future, Commander Strickland, if you desire access to the bridge, best you ask permission," I said. "You do not have a post here... a station to man. A simple request to enter the bridge will be sufficient."

At that precise moment, Hardy and Derrota strode onto the bridge, their eyes darting between us, the tension sucking the oxygen out of the bridge.

Z9 came to a dead stop and hovered. It was clear to everyone that these three didn't have assigned bridge stations either, and I hadn't reprimanded *them*.

"Fine. Apologies, Captain," Strickland said flatly. "What are we doing here?"

We both knew I wasn't obligated to keep him informed about my decisions as the ship's Captain.

"We've been monitoring NELLA's functionality. Slowly allowing her to interface with key systems again. All too soon, we'll be heading back into JTD, and soon after we'll arrive within the Krygian Star System."

"I'm well aware of all that," Strickland said, letting out an annoyed breath.

My anger rose from a mild simmer to a rapid boil. "So, you're fine with the fact that USS Ike will be entering an alien star system teeming with dreadnought-class warships and formidable ground defenses? And let's not forget, this untested little ship has an AI onboard that's already tried to kill us all and obliterate this vessel."

Strickland let that sink in. A smile pulled at the corners of his lips. "Well, if you put it like that, you may have valid concerns." He glanced at the halo display where four alien, and quite dangerous-looking, warships were slowly rotating within a 3D projection.

His smile broadened, "So, you want to pick a fight with the neighborhood bullies. Test this warship before going up against even bigger neighborhood bullies."

"You have a problem with that, Commander?" I said flatly.

He pursed his lips and slowly shook his head. "On the contrary. I think it's genius."

Chapter 23

With a deep breath, I stood in front of the Captain's Mount, and said, "Mr. Chen, open a hailing channel to that battle group."

Chen glanced around, a hint of apprehension in his eyes. "Aye, Captain. NELLA will be translating in real-time."

I nodded and turned to Derrota. "Z9's sensors are active, right?" I asked. "The droid's ready to flag any discrepancies?"

"The droid's online, Galvin," Derrota replied.

Both Hardy and Commander Strickland stayed quiet.

A full minute passed before the alien responded. An image flickered onto the display, a formless blob, white and billowy and featureless—like a Michelin Man wearing a too-snug uniform. He didn't appear to be overly threatening.

"Greetings... I am Captain Galvin Quintos of USS *Ike*—"

I winced hearing the alien's gravelly voice—indecipherable ramblings—as it blared right over my words. The anger, the venom, that spewed from those mealy lips caught me by surprise.

"First impressions can be misleading," Hardy remarked.

"Maybe let him know humans can win you over if you give them a fair shot."

"Can it, Hardy," I said.

The alien was still railing about something.

"NELLA, what the hell is that gas bag going on about? I thought you were going to translate in real time."

He is calling *Ike's* crew 'foul, stinking meat-sacks'— saying you will be 'cleansed from the Universe by their superior strength'.

"Meat-sacks, now those are fighting words," Hardy said.

Ignoring the idiot robot, I said, "What's he saying now, NELLA?"

His words describe humans as 'insignificant, writhing worms whose presence we will not suffer'... who 'will know our wrath in your pitiful, final thrashes of life'. He speaks of 'scouring human biomatter from existence' and 'leaving your pathetic homeworld a dark smear within the cosmos'.

I glanced over to Z9, its three glowing rings continued to glow blue—apparently, the ship's AI was being true to her word.

NELLA continued...

**They're most likely the Molnk.
Here within the Andro Expanse, they're infamous for their aggression and absolute intolerance for trespassers.**

I stared back at the Molnk Captain, my expression as flat as the bulkhead behind me.

"NELLA, ensure you translate my next words precisely."

Looking duly chastised, I nodded to the alien. "Okay then," I said, "we'll be on our way in a few hours. We just need time to dump our garbage bins and run a cleaning cycle on our latrine spouts." I offered up an apologetic smile. "You might want to steer clear of this area for a while."

"They're powering up weapons. Bringing defensive shields online,"

Akari said.

Lieutenant Earl Gray, on Ship's Systems, said, "NELLA, in turn, is bringing *Ike's* shields online, Captain."

"We already have a Tactical Officer, Mr. Gray," I said.

Akari smirked. "But kudos for the effort, Lieutenant." She input several commands, sat back, and looked at me. "You want NELLA to run a full tactical response scenario?"

I looked to Derrota, who up until now had remained quiet.

"As you mentioned before," the Science Officer said, "it's much better to discover now whether the ship's AI is on our side... or not."

The four Molnk warships had altered formation and were moving fast.

"Lieutenant James, go ahead and put NELLA to work."

I exchanged a glance with Strickland, who seemed to be enjoying himself. Like me, he wouldn't be the type to shy away from a street fight.

With my eyes locked on the alien formation, I took a deep breath, feeling the weight of command settle on my shoulders. The bridge hummed with impending chaos—a part of me wondered if this roll of the dice would be my last.

"Alright, NELLA," I said, my voice steady, "show us what you got. Full navigational command is yours. Keep us dodging, weaving, and hitting those Molnk ships with everything we've got."

**Affirmative, Captain Quintos...
initiating evasive maneuvers.**

NELLA's calm, monotone voice provided a strange sense of reassurance as the ship lurched to starboard, the inertial dampeners struggling to compensate for the rapid change in direction. I couldn't shake the thought of the heavily defended Krygian homeworld, Tavor, and the potential for reinforcements to come to the aid of the shipyard on Nylor-5.

**Evasive pattern Tango-Alpha.
Rail cannons charged and ready.**

"Fire at will," I said, probably unnecessarily.

Rail cannon spikes screamed through the darkness, their trajectories converging on the enemy's forward weapon bays. The Molnk ship's shields flared as the high-velocity projectiles impacted, sending ripples across their energy barriers.

Akari's voice cut through the tension, "Captain, their response time is faster than anticipated. They're adjusting formations."

Correct, Lieutenant James...

NELLA announced, validating Akari's comment.

Tactical analysis indicates a shift to a defensive wedge. Initiating auxiliary maneuvers.

Ike accelerated and banked hard to port, skimming the edge of a barrage of energy beams from the Molnk formation. NELLA's dexterous control was impressive, the tiny Corvette using its compact frame to zig-zag through the electromagnetic storm with grace.

Targeting solutions updated.
Repositioning for optimal firing angles.
Firing Phazon Pulsar bolts.

More bolts leapt from our turrets, lighting the void with dazzling arcs of energy. They exploded against the nearest Molnk ship's aft shields. The alien vessel shuddered, its movements becoming erratic.

"Nice shooting," Strickland muttered.

I suspected that was a rare compliment coming from him.

"Hold your positions," I barked, adrenaline spiking. "NELLA, keep up the aggression. Don't let them regroup."

Affirmative, Captain.
Commencing rail cannon volley.

The cannons roared to life once more, spitting metal spikes at speeds half the velocity of light. A tight grouping of spikes tore into a Molnk ship's engine compartment, triggering a fiery cascade of secondary explosions. The enemy's aft section crumpled inward, its energy trails flickering out.

"That's one down," I said, a fleeting sense of triumph flickering in my chest.

"Dammit, NELLA! Evasive maneuvers, now!" Akari shouted. "They're closing in from starboard."

The enemy ships shifted tactics, using their superior

numbers to corral *Ike* toward a bottleneck. NELLA reacted instantaneously, diving us into a series of tight barrel rolls and corkscrews. The bridge shook violently under the strain, but the ship weaved through the Molnk formation, narrowly evading lethal bursts of plasma.

Enemy ships attempting to flank.
Adjusting trajectory to avoid crossfire.

True to her word, NELLA twisted our path, veering us out of the kill zone and arcing back around to hammer the flank of the nearest Molnk vessel. Our Phazon Pulsar bolts pierced their weakened shields, tearing through bulkheads and sending debris spiraling into space.

"They're trying to regroup!" Ensign Blair Paxton warned, getting to her feet, her eyes wide.

"NELLA, keep them separated," I commanded. "Maintain pressure on their formation."

Understood. Switching to lateral combat
maneuvers. Initiating railgun overcharges.

I had barely time to consider the implications before NELLA's navigation had us loop horizontally, skimming the side of one Molnk ship while rail cannon spikes dug into another. Sparks flew as the enemy's power-cores destabilized. NELLA's calculated precision continued to marvel. I shot a quick look over to Z9, the droid's three bands were no longer blue, they were yellow—what the hell did that mean?

"What are they doing?" Strickland's intense eyes were locked on the display.

**Second enemy ship on a direct trajectory
for *Ike*. Collision imminent.**

Ike swerved so suddenly that the ship's inertial dampeners couldn't compensate. With the exception of Hardy, all those standing were thrown off their feet. Akari was tossed from her seat like a small bird from its nest in a high wind.

"Hardy—" I started.

"I see it!" Hardy's massive metal form was already moving to the tactical console.

Executing retrograde evasion.

NELLA's unmodulated tone continued, droning on as implementations were being executed.

Ike's two Quantum Dark-wave Drives fired simultaneously in reverse, jerking us out of the way just as the Molnk ship shot past, missing us by a hair's breadth. As it streaked by, our rail cannon turrets let loose, blasting the enemy's engines and weapon mounts. The ship's stern exploded in spectacular fashion.

"Captain, two ships left," Akari called out, tension lining her voice as she shouldered Hardy out of the way.

"They're regrouping," Strickland noted. "Tighter formation now."

**Calculating intercept course.
Deploying countermeasures.
Phazon Pulsar turrets targeting 020 degrees
azimuth, 035 degrees elevation.**

"Fire all weapons," I ordered.

Phazon Pulsar bolts flared from our turrets, rail cannon spikes blasted forward, and missiles streaked away from the launch tubes—all converging on the Molnk ships. One absorbed most of the brunt, its shields burning out, hull breaches spreading across its frame.

The last enemy ship charged forward, weapons ablaze. I could see it now—a desperate, final stand.

Initiating defensive roll. Advising all crewmembers to hold on to something.
Activating counter-fire.

NELLA spun *Ike* through a tight series of rolls, presenting minimal cross-sections as plasma and energy bolts flew past. Our turrets retaliated in kind, punching through the void. The final Molnk ship's defenses faltered under the incessant onslaught. Spewing atmosphere while fire enveloped its hull in catastrophic eruptions.

Evasive pattern Delta-J.
Firing rail cannon volley.

The Molnk ship, desperate, launched the last of its torpedoes. Our rail cannons released their spikes simultaneously, each one finding home along the enemy's starboard side. The resulting collision caused a chain reaction, obliterating their reinforcement beams and tearing the ship asunder.

"Oh my," Derrota whispered in disbelief as the last Molnk vessel shattered into flaming scrap.

For a moment, the only sound was the steady hum of *Ike's* propulsion system. Then, little by little, the reality of our victory began to sink in.

"Stand down from battle stations," I ordered. "Excellent work, everyone. NELLA, maintain situational awareness. We'll conduct damage assessments shortly."

Affirmative, Captain.
Thank you for the opportunity to serve.

Exhalations and quiet congratulations rippled through the crew. Our small, underdog ship had just faced an overwhelming force and emerged victorious.

Hardy raised one massive hand, pointing toward the shattered remnants of Z9 scattered across the deck.

Derrota rushed over, kneeling next to the pile of inert puck segments, carefully gathering the pieces. "I think we can fix it," he said, inspecting the damage closely.

Chapter 24

Deep Space

XO Gail Pristy

Hub Gunther roared like a beast as it hurtled through space. Pristy leaned forward, fingers drumming on the Tactical interface. She watched as the ship's AI marked a faint propulsion wake, minute levels of drive radiation against the starfield, a faded trail left by the stolen shuttle.

"Push her, J-Dog," she barked. "And make sure we're cloaked."

I'm giving her all she's got. Christ give me a break—this tin can's on her last legs."

From behind, she heard the whine of the propulsion drive increase. She knew Ryder was a man who relished defying constraints. It seemed he'd, somehow, found a means to squeeze more from the aging vessel.

"That's good," she said. "Just keep doing what you're doing." Her voice was flat, betraying none of the churning emotions that warred within her.

The vessel's AI chimed in, a metallic voice devoid of emotion...

Ship detected. Approaching on current course vector.

Pristy looked up, brow furrowed, as the AI's display flashed with an image of a battle-scarred shuttle not much larger than Hub Gunther.

She leaned in, mostly talking to herself she murmured, "It looks like they're... headed for... something else. Maybe a space station. Possibly another ship. We have to catch up. Faster... need to go faster!" Pristy barked, frustration tightening her voice.

The AI announced...

Target shuttle is 40 light minutes ahead. Estimated time of intercept is .20 light minutes. Note: this vessel's drive was not designed for such a prolonged current velocity.

Ryder gave the dash a couple of pats. "This old girl is quickly reaching her limit."

"I'm not deaf, I heard the AI. But I don't care. Figure out how to get this hunk of junk moving faster—whatever you have to do, do it!" she snarled.

"Hmm, how about I dump some dead weight, like an annoying co-pilot?" Ryder suggested, a reluctant smirk crossing his lips. "Give me a moment, I think the Gunther's getting her second wind."

Pristy studied the readouts, trying to ignore the knot of anxiety in her stomach. *Sonya was slipping away before our eyes, and it was her fault.* But there was no time to dwell on guilt. She needed to focus on the mission at hand.

Bantam-Class Destroyer detected along our current course vector.

"Destroyer?" Pristy asked, shaking her head. "I guess it makes sense, no way that shuttle was going to take them all the way to Briggan space."

"Once that shuttle's inside that destroyer... they're gone," Ryder commented. "No way we keep up."

With eyes as sharp as ice-picks, Pristy glared back at Ryder but managed to hold her tongue.

"We're still going to need a plan if we catch up to them," Ryder said, "Just saying..."

Approaching target. Three minutes out. Be advised... target shuttle has decreased velocity. Communications chatter present between the two vessels.

The destroyer, a hulking shadow against the backdrop of stars, loomed into view. Pristy watched as the shuttle headed for the blue glow of an open flight bay.

"Fuck!" she yelled, hammering a fist down onto the dash in front of her.

"Hold on," Ryder said. "This isn't over yet. See that?"

"Yeah, I see the big fricken ship. Are you purposely acting stupid?"

"No... not that... that!"

Now she saw it too. A distortion of local space. The kind of spatial anomaly she'd seen a hundred times. "They're manufacturing a wormhole."

The Bantam-Class Destroyer is
manufacturing a transit wormhole.

Pristy rolled her eyes at the AI's redundant comment.

"Ryder, we're not losing Sonya!" Pristy barked as she keyed in commands to the ship's tactical interface. "We'll need to close the gap. We stay close on that destroyer's tail. No matter what."

"Gail, we can't see what's on the other side," Ryder said, "It's a one-way trip to God knows where."

"I know how a wormhole works," she spat back. "And it doesn't matter where it's configured to take them. We're going wherever that destroyer is going."

"The point is, we lose our cloaking ability the moment we enter that wormhole," Ryder said, doing little to mask his exasperation. "We'll be exposed, completely detectable. Once we emerge out the other side, we'll be toast."

Enough with the hand wringing," Pristy said. "When did you become such a pussy?"

"Oh, so now I'm a pussy?"

"It doesn't matter! We stay on that ship—*and Sonya*—or we lose it, *and her*. Get us moving. Get us right on its tail," She glared at Ryder, "Go! Now! The wormhole's fully open."

Ryder cursed under his breath.

She knew what she was asking bordered on suicidal. This old ship lacked the speed, firepower, and agility to tackle a destroyer. Entering that wormhole, wherever it led, very well could be their final act.

The destroyer was now moving forward and picking up speed. Without further prompting, Ryder coaxed Gunther forward. They watched as the destroyer's silhouette filled a good portion of their observation window.

Ryder swooped in close behind the destroyer; immediately heat rose within Hub Gunther's cabin, as the larger ship's aft thrusters came to life.

"We're going to be a couple of baked potatoes in here staying this close," Pristy quipped.

"Do you want to drive?"

Pristy's eyes narrowed, agitation taking hold. "No," she managed.

"Then zip it. You're right... we'll need to stay in close... we do that, we might just stay undetected... hide in the destroyer's exhaust."

The destroyer slipped into the manufactured wormhole. Ryder pressed forward, closing the gap further.

Heat surged around them. Sweat dotted her forehead, trickling down her back.

Shields holding at maximum level.
Estimated wormhole collapse in 30 seconds.

Pristy, realizing she was holding her breath, forced herself to breathe. The pirate destroyer loomed in front of them, and while it had now fully passed the lip of the wormhole, Hub Gunther had not.

"We're not going to make it," she said.

"Yes, we will..."

"The damn thing is closing!" she said, scooting forward on her seat.

"It'll be close," Ryder said, his tone somewhat less confident just a moment ago.

As if on cue, they both squeezed their eyes shut and waited for whatever would come next—very possibly, death.

"We're in the clear!" Ryder said.

She opened one eye and then the other. Sure enough, Hub Gunther had cleared the wormhole's outer lip.

"How about you maneuver us out of the path of that furnace blast in front of us," Pristy said. Her shoulders relaxed a bit, her breathing now returning to normal.

Gunther swerved to port, now hugging the inside wall of the wormhole.

They both looked to the viewscreen, seeing the wormhole pulse as it completely collapsed behind them.

Pristy suddenly looked up, startled at what she saw. Clenching her fists, she said, "Where's the destroyer, Ryder? Where's the damn destroyer?"

"I... uh, don't know, exactly," Ryder said.

She forced herself to think. She was a damn U.S. Space Navy Officer—this was what she did for a living. "This wormhole... I'm assuming, probably doesn't have the same technical properties as those coming out of the EUNF."

She looked at Ryder expectantly. "That destroyer just... jumped."

She tapped at her board, a line taking shape between her brows. "Oh. We *both* just jumped. We were caught in the destroyer's jump bubble." She made a face. "I didn't know jumping was even possible within a wormhole."

Ryder simply shrugged.

"We just didn't maintain the same spatial proximity, I'm assuming," she continued.

"AI where, specifically, is that Bantam-class Destroyer?" Pristy asked.

I am unable to provide that information at the present time.

"I'll do it myself," the XO said. Her eyes widened as she took in the tactical reading. "It's... wow... this is strange... I don't recognize any of these readings." She shook her head. "So, Gunther's AI is useless and the ship's telemetry sensors are pretty much useless too."

"Then maybe you should just sit back and enjoy the ride," Ryder said. "I know you hate not being in total control, but for now, it's out of our hands."

"Are you saying I'm a control freak?" she said with a raised brow.

He shrugged, "Let me put it this way. If you have to ask..."

Chapter 25

The Orpheus Rift
Nearing Krygian Hegemony's Star System
USS Ike

Captain Galvin Quintos

The crew had gone silent, introspective, each lost in their own thoughts. *Ike's* drive engines hummed steadily, providing a constant backdrop that anchored them to an otherwise predictable rhythm amidst the certain and all-too-fast-approaching chaos.

Commander Strickland and I were in my ready room, both of us mentally exhausted after so many hours spent working and reworking plans of attack, contingencies and contingencies for the contingencies. Everything came down to impeccable timing. That first salvo, a domino, in line with a lot of other dominos, had to fall at precisely the right moment. That will be Strickland's ground Ops. Sergeant Max's genetically monsterized drop team, along with the one hundred untested Symbio 4.0s.

"So much about this is wrong," I said, leaning back in my seat. "I get it, EUNF doesn't want to *officially* go to war with one more intergalactic superpower. We've all had enough of that over the last decade."

Strickland's eyes looked flat. "We handle them now or lose our advantage. The Krygians are despicable creatures. They rank up there with the Varapin and Grish—possibly worse."

"I guess what's bothering me is how we'll be changing the unspoken rules of engagement."

He looked at me, not getting my meaning.

I took a second to clarify my thoughts. "Up until now, both warring parties would pay a similar price, often an ultimate price. Brave warriors going into battle, not sure if they will be returning home alive... or in a body bag. That kept things real. And it gave pause to those of us in charge... sending our people into harm's way. But we're about to change all that, aren't we?"

Strickland maintained that same flat stare.

I continued, "Our troops will be heading into battle, no longer thinking their fates are... uncertain." I shook my head. "Because of this incredible, cutting edge, advanced technology, they can now be regenerated. No longer finite beings paying that ultimate price. But what? Now they've become something else, right? Something akin to a commodity that can be replaced at the press of a button. And with that... war becomes far less than something that should be avoided at all costs. It becomes as humdrum as reordering tubes of toothpaste from the commissary."

I thought the Commander might respond to my deep intro-spection, but instead, he straightened up, his gaze sharpening with a newfound resolve. "You've raised an important issue," he said, his tone more serious now. "We might face a significant technological bottleneck that could jeopardize our entire mission."

I opened my mouth to speak, but he continued, "Our ability to maintain rapid quansporting of personnel and Symbios... well, it's pivotal. And because there's so much new tech built into those devices... all that NEOGENE automation—all of it remains untested in real battle scenarios. Our recent encounter with the Molnk provided you an opportunity to witness firsthand how *Ike's* systems—particularly NELLA—perform within the crucible of deep space warfare. But the rest of it... our new ground ops capabilities, it's still untested."

"Other than your practice simulations, you're right," I concurred. "So, what are you saying, you want to wait? Spend more time prepping?"

But as I spoke, another fear gnawed at me. My mind flashed to Sonya. A renewed rage and helplessness churned in my gut like a storm. The thought of her in the hands of those Briggan bastards made my blood boil. Screw the mission—I wanted to drop everything, tear across the stars, and rip those pirates apart to get her back. But I couldn't. I had to keep this operation on track. One reckless move and I'd risk everything—my crew, the mission.

Suddenly, Pristy's face filled my thoughts. Damn it, the weight of it all crushing in on me. Up until now, I'd managed to compartmentalize, to somehow prioritize what was at stake. Now, I was desperate to make it all right, to simultaneously save Sonya and Pristy, to be the hero they needed—and complete the mission at hand. I had to thread the needle, balance my desperation with the cold, hard needs of this mission. It was tearing me apart.

"We both know there's no time for any delays," Strickland was saying.

I forced myself to stay present. To concentrate.

"Stephan is confident the Quansporters are fully operational," I added. "You're far closer to Dr. Tangerie than I am, I know next to nothing about her NEOGENE tech—"

"Hold on! What's that supposed to mean?" Strickland spat, squaring his shoulders.

Bewildered, I stared back at him.

"There's nothing going on between Doctor Tangerie and me if that's what you're getting at."

I almost laughed out loud but managed to keep a straight face. "Doth he protest too much?" I said with a crooked smile. "I couldn't care less who you're knocking boots with, Commander. How about we stay on topic, we have an Ops mission to commence."

Looking flabbergasted, he murmured, "We're not... knocking boots, as you put it."

"Uh-huh, fine." I couldn't help but feel a twinge of satisfaction, knowing I'd hit a nerve. "Can we move on now, Commander?"

A chime interrupted our conversation, and NELLA's voice filled the ready room, her tone as calm and monotone as ever...

Captain Quintos, Commander Strickland, we have arrived within Krygian space. Our current cloaked status is holding, but proximity scans indicate heightened Krygian activity. Long-range sensors have detected an increase in Krygian fighter squadrons conducting aggressive patrols, and multiple heavy cruisers have taken up strategic positions around key installations. It appears they are locking down their defenses in anticipation of an imminent threat.

Strickland was on his feet before I could respond. "If they're preparing for a possible incursion, that means they suspect something. We have to move up the timetable and hit them before they fully lock down. I'll alert the ground team to be ready for immediate deployment. Shit, we haven't even unpacked the Symbios yet."

I nodded, feeling the urgency thrumming through my veins. "I need to get to the bridge."

THE PASSAGEWAYS WERE ALREADY BUSTLING with activity as crewmembers hurried to their posts. I made my way to the Captain's Mount; Ensign Blair Paxton was just taking her post at Engineering; Akari, at Tactical, was monitoring our stealth systems.

"Status report," I ordered, settling into my seat.

"Captain," Akari replied crisply, "we're maintaining our cloaked status, but Krygian sensor sweeps are becoming more frequent. If they detect us—"

"They won't," I said, cutting her off. " Ensign Paxton, ensure our drive emissions are negligible."

"Yes, Captain. Chief Rivers in E&P assures me we're invisible in that regard."

"NELLA bring us to full battle stations... just do it quietly," I ordered.

Affirmative, Captain.

In front of the Captain's Mount, Strickland appeared on the halo display, a split-feed with Derrota standing within the Quansporter compartment. The Commander looked harried, his expression grim. "The ground team is readying to deploy here in the Armory. The Symbios are being brought into formation."

It seemed strange to me that only now, Strickland had done that. Doesn't one typically learn to swim before jumping into shark-infested waters?

"Good," I said. "Stephan, what's your, um, situational status?"

"I'm monitoring the Krygians' shield variances... and energy signatures. They've definitely fortified their positions since our last intel update."

"Will those shield variances affect how your Quansporters—"

"No, we should be fine in that regard."

I spun around to face Ship's Systems. "Lieutenant Gray, status on *Ike's* operational status."

"All systems are *go*, Sir."

Ensign Paxton nodded. "And E&P's still fully operational, Captain."

I spun back around, "Mr, Chen... Mr. Grimes..."

They both gave me a thumbs up, Comms and Helm were ready for whatever was coming next.

"'Tactical," I said.

Akari, who looked the most uncertain among the crew, would handle the bridge's most intricate control board, one that required top-tier interfacing skills. "I got this," she said.

I reluctantly glanced upward. "NELLA. What is your battle readiness?"

All weapons systems are fully operational and primed for engagement. Shield strength is at maximum capacity, ensuring optimal defense against incoming fire. Combat protocols have been

initiated, and all critical systems are functioning within expected parameters.

Regarding quansporting and NEOGENE integration... Quansporter pedestals are calibrated for deployment—NEOGENE tech modifications are active and stable. I will oversee the precise synchronization of personnel transport and genetic alterations to ensure peak combat performance. I am ready to execute any battle commands required of me.

I turned back to Strickland. "Seems you and your team are up to bat. *USS Ike*, her crew, and I are here to support you and your Ops team."

He nodded sharply.

Behind him, I saw Sergeant Max and his Marines checking weapons, getting their gear. The halo feed blinked out.

Looking at Chen, I gestured to the overhead.

"You're live, Cap."

All hands, this is the Captain speaking. As you know, we have entered Krygian space. We are moving into position for immediate deployment with our impending ground operations. This is what you've trained for, people. You've got this. Now let's show these freaks of nature, Earth can never be on their hit list. Stay focused, stick to your training, and remember what's at stake. We're not just fighting for ourselves but for everyone back home. Let's make sure they know Earth is off-limits for good.

Even as Chen switched off the PA, I was confident the crew

would react flawlessly, each one performing to the rigorous U.S. Space Navy expectations. But what concerned me most wasn't the onboard personnel; it was the untested technology that had yet to prove itself in real-time scenarios.

Chapter 26

S tanding there in the Quansporter compartment, I felt a sense of unease that gnawed at my insides. Beneath the hard glare of the ceiling lights, our team of Marines moved with a kind of cocky bravado. But it didn't take a seasoned Captain to see through their pretense. Fear and uncertainty lingered in their eyes, hidden behind forced grins and nervous laughter.

My thoughts were momentarily interrupted by an update from Dr. Pippa Tangerie.

"We'll be getting started shortly, Captain."

I mustered a nod in her direction.

What was most surprising, though, was their nakedness. Had the Doctor mentioned they'd be naked? Honestly, I couldn't remember.

I forced my gaze away from Wanda and Aubrey, my discomfort not going unnoticed. Wanda stood tall and proud, her muscular frame exuding confidence. Yet, it was Aubrey that caught my eye. She always did. Her physique was lithe but powerful, every muscle defined. She seemed to take some silent pleasure in my evident embarrassment, a small, knowing smirk playing at the corners of her mouth. While Ham and Hock were awkwardly attempting to cover their privates with cupped hands, she stood tall—seemingly unbothered by the situation.

The Marines climbed onto the Quans-Pedestals, trying to look like warriors ready for combat, but their discomfort was palpable. Bodies, stripped of armor and clothing, exposed their raw human vulnerability, soon to be endowed by new genetically enhanced forms.

Sergeant Max was saying something to his team I couldn't hear, but it evoked chuckles and a snarky quip back from Wanda. As the kibitzing continued, I found myself envious of their comradery... a part of me wished I was going with them.

Commander Strickland joined them, the only one who hadn't undergone NEOGENE alterations, and the only one wearing a kitted-out, helmeted, combat suit. His presence was a stark contrast—a reminder of what would remain unaltered by technology. His jaw set in a resolute line, his eyes scanned his team, keenly aware of the risks they were about to face.

Dr. Pippa Tangerie stood at the control console with Derrota at her side. Tangerie's fingers tapped at the controls, her eyes narrowed in concentration. Every now and then, she glanced up at the Marines, making final adjustments.

A small halo display came to life on the console, the projected feed showed Deck 3, the Robotics area of the ship. No less than one hundred of the bio-mechanical combatants were all kitted out similarly to that of Commander Strickland—with helmeted combat suits and Shredder energy rifles at the ready. They were standing perfectly still in four rows of twenty-five Symbios in each.

Derrota looked to Strickland, who, in turn, nodded.

Eyes still on the display, I watched as the Symbio 4.0s quansported away, one cluster at a time. Within a minute or two, the Robotics area was empty. This ground Ops mission had officially gotten underway.

I broke the heavy silence. "Doctor Tangerie, I know we've been over this... but please assure me," I said, gesturing to the occupied pedestals in front of us, "that these NEOGENE enhancements, with the associated quansporting process... that we won't be sending any of them to some... undefined quantum plane... someplace, um, where there'll be irretrievable?"

Tangerie met my gaze, her expression serious. "I know, of course, about the incident with your first officer, XO Pristy. Look, Captain, from a technological standpoint, Stephan and I are highly confident there is little chance anyone will be lost to any kind of quantum anomaly. As for the genetic modifications, they are designed to boost their combat capabilities—increased strength, speed, and resilience. You already know all this. Take a breath and let us do our jobs."

Sensing my irritation, Strickland raised a gloved palm, his face impassive. "If the transformations become unstable during the mission, we may have to intervene to ensure mission success."

Tangerie shot the Commander a sharp look.

I felt my jaw tighten, the implications sinking in. "Intervene? You mean terminate them if they don't show up, like all in one piece?"

I locked eyes with Tangerie, the tension between us growing. Stepping closer to her, my voice was hard as steel. "I'm not sacrificing my crew, no matter the stakes. There needs to be another way."

The Doctor looked at me with a quiet confidence that seemed to say, *Trust me, I know what I'm doing.* Then, she lowered her eyes, concentrating on the controls in front of her, her fingers shifting levers and pushing buttons, as she began setting the final parameters for the Marines' transformation.

I seesawed my jaw in a lame attempt to loosen the knot of anxiety I was feeling.

Derrota, ever the mediator, interjected gently, "Galvin, I think you need to come to terms with the fact that this team has already accepted they might be... repurposed. Potentially numerous times. If, upon initial quansport, they're unfit for combat, it will be better for them, as well as the mission, to make them all that they were indeed intended to be."

I nodded; that actually made good sense.

My gaze swept over the soon-to-be transformed Marines up on their respective pedestals. Strickland was looking down at me, his expression saying it all—*can we finally get past this?*

"Fine, Commander," I said. "This is your show... I'll let you take it from here."

Just then, Hardy burst into the Quansporter compartment, faux-panting and waving his arms. He hurried to an available pedestal, mumbling something about having to make a stop at the 'little boy's room', and 'having a nervous bladder'..." his adolescent humor a small reprieve amidst the tension.

Strickland, unflinching and cool as a cucumber, gave the final order, "Mr. Derrota, initiate quansportation." He turned to Tangerie, his voice a low warning, "Doctor, you'd better pray the enhancements hold during battle."

As the machinery hummed to life, I saw Tangerie make one last adjustment on her console. Each of the Marines stood ready, their naked forms glowing under the bioluminescent light of the Quansporter machinery.

Derrota's voice was steady, though his hands trembled slightly over the controls. "Quansport commencing in three... two... one..."

The Marines disappeared from their pedestals in a series of blocky, segmented phases, being quansported through the void of space to face an uncertain fate. The compartment fell silent once more, the tension only alleviated by a single beeping indicator of successful deployment. But that beep... it was more a countdown, reminding us that every tick was borrowed time.

I turned to the two who remained. "Stephan, Dr. Tangerie, please keep me informed of their status. I want updates—"

Dr. Tangerie waved away my words. "You'll have live feeds to your bridge from both your robot and Commander Strickland's helmet cams. I'm surprised you wouldn't know that."

Taken aback by her tone, the disrespect, I opened my mouth to speak, but Derrota piped up first.

"You certainly can watch the feeds, Galvin, of course, but you will have your hands full... commanding your own mission here onboard *Ike*." He shot Tangerie a disciplinary scowl. "Rest assured, we will reach out with any new developments."

Suddenly, Tangerie's console flared up with a series of warning lights. Her fingers flew across the controls, eyebrows furrowing deeper with each passing second. "It looks like we've got some instability with the NEOGENE enhancement feedback."

My heart sank. "Explain. What the hell does that even mean?"

"The team... their neurochemical balances are surging. Modifications are stable, but only just." Worry was evident in her expression.

Dr. Tangerie glanced over to me. "We've got this, Captain. I promise. And we know where to find you if your input is needed."

Chapter 27

The Krygian Hegemony Binary Star System
Nylor-5 Shipyard

Commander Strickland

S trickland blinked several times as the disorientation and nausea from the quansport subsided. He tapped his helmet, bringing his tactical HUD to life. The Krygian Shipyard on Nylor-5 came into focus around him, a colossal web of chaos and construction populated by towering dreadnought warships in various stages of completion. Strickland knew that this shipyard, separate from the heavily defended Krygian homeworld of Tavor, was their primary target.

Massive skeletal frameworks with interconnected catwalks loomed like leviathans of metal, their many limbs extending outward, bristling with machinery. Conveyor belts transported components, sparking with droids with automated welding torches upon looming tall girder arms.

His initial scan indicated the Krygian military base adjacent to the shipyard remained unaware of their trespass. With his visor now partially open, he took a cautious breath. The air, though similar to Earth's, was heavy with industrial pollutants; the stench of burnt ozone and acrid solvents filled his lungs. This place stood as a fortress of impending dreadnoughts, an apocalyptic armory in the making.

Strickland couldn't help but marvel at the sight before him: a full company of identical-looking Symbios 4.0s, spread out across the Krygian Shipyard. They weren't robots, nor were they some kind of Star-Wars-like stormtrooper in costume; these Symbios were a unique breed unto themselves—and untested in battle. He watched as they methodically moved about in their matte black combat suits, each with an amber-glowing helmet visor that reflected their surroundings.

What went through their minds, he wondered? How much of their individualism had been scrubbed from their organic brain matter, their personas? They moved as one well-orchestrated unit, almost as if they were a single biological entity. Every step, every pivot, so precise it seemed choreographed. Their synchronization was impressive, no doubt. But could they fight? Would they help bring home a victory today, or go down in history as one of the EUNF's biggest failures?

He put that thought aside as he noticed the familiar figures of Sergeant Max and his Marines—all in their enhanced forms— now standing ready and focused.

As if on cue, Hardy emerged, his imposing chrome physique reflecting the industrial lights. "Where do you want me, Commander?" Hardy said, his voice calm and assured.

"Hang close, ChronoBot. Marines, fan out. Symbios, hold your positions," Strickland commanded, his voice steady over the comms.

His NEOGENE-enhanced Marines dispersed into their pre-planned tactical positions, each one moving with the precise agility that their enhancements afforded them. Each of them differed in appearance, but one thing united them: the unique red TAC-Bands on their wrists. As they prepared to face the Krygians on Nylor-5, the threat of reinforcements from the heavily defended homeworld, Tavor, hung over them like a shadow.

Sergeant Max, leading the team, moved like a juggernaut, his grayish, armored skin gleaming even in the shipyard's dim industrial lighting. He turned back to Strickland, giving a quick nod of acknowledgment. "We'll secure the area, Commander," he reported, his voice a deep rumble.

Wanda, her skin now a deep blue with a prehensile tail flicking behind her, climbed gracefully up a gantry, her reptilian eyes scanning for any signs of incoming Krygians. "I'm catching some interesting energy readings coming from the alpha quadrant. Might be trouble."

Strickland checked the data feed on his HUD. Several heat signatures showed faint signs of movement but nothing to suggest an immediate assault. He turned to the Symbios, silent sentinels awaiting his next order. Hardy's towering presence lent an added sense of solidity to the unit.

"Their synchronization is impressive," the ChronoBot noted, coming over to stand beside Strickland. "Maybe a little creepy, zombie-like, the way they just stare straight ahead."

The Commander ignored the robot's comment.

"Hold steady, everyone... Dr. Tangerie, Derrota, give me one more status update on my Marines," Strickland said. He felt the weight of impending chaos settling into the stillness. This quite literally was the calm before the storm.

"All vitals and enhancements are stable," Dr. Tangerie's voice echoed crisply over the comms. "We're now getting more solid biosyncs across the board."

"Symbios are performing well under the current load,"

Derrota added, with a hint of technical satisfaction. "Buffer replacements are holding steady."

"Good," Strickland muttered, his gaze flickering back to the growing blips on his HUD. "We stick to the plan. Move forward, take out their power hubs, and—"

Before he completed his sentence, alarms blared—the shipyard awakened to a hostile intrusion. Orange-red lights bathed the area, casting ominous shadows over the machinery and half-built warships. A cacophony of metallic clanging arose as distant Krygian forces on Nylor-5 began to stir.

"Guess the welcome mat's out," Max muttered, his slightly sarcastic tone swallowed amid the prevailing tension.

And then, a horde of Krygians swarmed from the depths of the shipyard structures. Strickland knew that as soon as the fighting started, the Krygians would be sending more warships from their homeworld of Tavor, approximately 4 light-hours away from Nylor-5, creating another looming timetable for them to deal with.

They moved on the ground like mechanized insects, their triple-jointed legs, and elongated torsos giving them an arthropod countenance. Their metallic carapace exoskeletons shimmered with intricate hexagonal patterns of indigo and crimson, reflecting the frantic lights. But it was their eyes—four multifaceted orbs devoid of empathy—that sent shivers down Strickland's spine. Bioluminescence coursed through visible veins, giving them a ghastly glow in the muted lighting conditions. Strickland surmised this creature's raw brutality and unchecked energy made them formidable even without wearing combat suits. He could feel their vile desire to kill... *vicious, tenacious, fucking insects...*

"Looks like it's showtime," Hardy said.

"Marines, engage!" Strickland barked, raising his shredder

toward the approaching horde of Krygian forces. He quickly surveyed the battlefield, while issuing orders to fire at will.

Max roared and charged forward, the bony protrusions on his joints slicing through two Krygians. He was a force of nature, dealing devastating blows that sent fragments of Krygian exoskeletons flying in all directions. "Focus on the right flank!" his voice boomed through the comms.

Wanda climbed higher, perched on a scaffold. With her enhanced agility, she leapt and landed behind a cluster of Krygians, using her prehensile tail to smash a Krygian against an automated loader. She hissed in satisfaction, eyes darting for her next target. "Someone get on our rear quadrant!" she shouted above the growing melee.

The Symbios 4.0s charged forward, devoid of fear, their energy weapons spewing brilliant blue plasma bolts into the fray of alien beasts.

Grip, Hock, and Ham formed a bulwark on the front lines, their enhanced limbs and exoskeletons presenting an insur-mountable wall of brute force. Grip's clawed hands ripped through Krygian bodies with ease, while Hock's mucousy, glowing secretion corroded exoskeletons and machinery alike. The visual spectacle was both grotesque and mesmerizing.

Bringing up a virtually projected tablet, Strickland directed one squad of Symbios to outflank incoming Krygians from the right. Then added, "Symbios, direct your fire toward those over-hanging hull support beams, let's destabilize that structure!"

Strickland straightened as the Krygians maneuvered a new threat into position at the front line—a massive hover-turret. Suddenly, powerful, red energy bolts cut through the Symbios ranks, the plasma tearing into them, taking down units in swaths. Strickland, momentarily speechless, wrestled with shock but swiftly found his voice.

"Grip, Wanda! Take out that weapon before there's no one

left in our ranks!" he bellowed, urgency ringing through his voice.

Derrota's voice crackled in his ear, "Commander, quansport rotations are coming in too fast! The system wasn't designed for this... this level of operations."

A Krygian shrieked, lunging at Strickland. This creature loomed larger than the others, its presence suggesting a genetically superior being, perhaps even a leader among them. He ducked, firing a Shredder bolt at point-blank range. The alien staggered backward but stayed upright. Those four obsidian eyes seemed to peer into Strickland's very soul. These creatures were more of a nightmare than he'd counted on... far taller, faster, and just maybe smarter than the human counterparts sent here to deal with them.

At thirty yards, Hardy fired plasma bolts that lanced into the alien's back, leaving glowing craters on its shell.

Strickland noted the massive exoskeleton plates on this particular Krygian's posterior, plates capable of enduring extreme punishment.

Its spindly limbs reached toward Strickland—*what's it gonna take to kill this thing!*—sharp and spear-like, ready to pierce his combat suit. Strickland stood, ready, squeezing the trigger three, four, five times. The alien crumpled; whatever that iridescent shit was, that had been flowing within its veins, stopped moving.

"Stay sharp, everyone. We've got a mission to finish," Strickland commanded through clenched teeth.

Dr. Tangerie's concerned tone cut through the chaotic comms chatter. "Commander, we're seeing extreme levels of aggression—"

"Yeah, I know... they're fucking killing machines," Strickland said, firing at two more beasts, not sure if he hit either one of them. He watched as a Krygian tore a Symbio unit in half.

Tangerie's voice lowered to a near whisper, "I wasn't talking about the aliens, Commander. I was referring to your Marines. There are physiological manifestations taking place. Just keep an eye on them, that's all I'm saying."

Strickland didn't know what to do with that information. He reviewed his virtual tablet assessing the battlefield with a grimace.

"Everyone! Form up around key targets. Max, adjust the left flank and support Hock's position. Wanda, fall back now—you're getting overrun!"

Comms chatter buzzed continuously with reports and calls for backup. Strickland's combatants held their ground, but the stream of incoming enemies seemed endless. Then he saw it—Max's head severed with a single, clean swipe. The Sergeant's body stood for a moment, before crumpling to the ground. Within five seconds, telltale quansporting flashes emerged. A new Sergeant Max Dyer stood mere feet from where his decapitated body lay, the Marine now already back in the fight, not missing a beat.

That's all well and good, but the Symbios weren't being replaced quickly enough.

"Stephan, at this rate, we're done for," Strickland snarled, watching another wave of Krygians skitter over an overhead catwalk and rush down a nearby ramp.

Grip's voice thundered through comms, "We've got incoming! Hardy! You're with me! Time to make some bug soup." The two charged into the fray, tearing through Krygians in their path. The deck vibrated under the intensity of their assault.

Wanda, having climbed halfway up a metal girder, said, "I've got visuals on additional reinforcements, incoming from the southeast, the adjacent base several klicks out!"

A Krygian scampered up the girder below her, nimble as a monkey scaling branches. Wanda noticed and effortlessly swung a razor-sharp appendage downward, slicing through the Krygian's forward limbs with precision. The beast did a backward somersault, an inhuman screech echoing in the smoke-tinged air.

In the chaos of battle, Strickland's comms were picking up fragmented exchanges between Dr. Tangerie and Derrota. Their voices grew increasingly frustrated, teetering on the edge of outright anger.

Derrota's voice rose by several decibels. "Trying to stabilize synthesizer levels, having problems with synaptic generation with the most recent Symbio deployments."

"Life support readings are plummeting on new arrivals. That's a hardware issue, Stephan. Get on it!" Tangerie barked. "And Commander, we need to slow down this attrition rate—"

"I know, I know," Strickland said, cutting her off while blasting another Krygian who'd lunged from his left. The unfulfilled promise of this Ops plan was now setting off alarm bells in his mind.

"Symbios!" he barked. "Concentrate fire on those junction relays! Hardy, what the hell are you doing over there? I want you powering your way through to the shipyard's primary power station. Come on! Let's stick to the plan, people!"

Strickland sprinted up a nearby ramp, gaining the high ground. His Shredder fired concentrated energy bolts at every target along the way. Once high enough, he could see that his combined forces were struggling. Even the relentless Symbio 4.0 units were beginning to falter.

"Symbio rotations are coming far too fast!" Derrota's voice, rich with his Mumbai accent, strained with urgency. "And Commander... NELLA's computational load has started to drain ship resources—atmosphere filtration— *Ike's* environmental systems, they're starting to fail."

"Stephan, I can't handle my job down here and yours up

there too—" Strickland's words halted as he blasted two Krygians charging up the ramp. Their cruel, gaping mouths and blackened, shark-like teeth became more pronounced against the bioluminescent glow of their hideous, angular faces. It was only now that he realized he'd been speared in the shoulder. One of the Krygians' lifeless legs was just hanging there, while the dead weight of the alien was bringing him down to his knees. Then the pain came—like being struck by a lightning bolt; he gasped, unable to move or speak.

"Oh boy... you're done for," came Dr. Tangerie's less than sympathetic voice over comms. She laughed, "Get ready to be reborn, Commander."

Strickland found himself mid-quansport—materializing back at the shipyard. The ramp held two dead Krygians, their metallic exoskeletons lifeless. Lying alongside them was the equally motionless form of one Commander Cornelius Strickland. "Wow, that's not something you experience every day," he muttered.

Derrota was still going on about something or other as if nothing had changed—didn't the scientist realize he'd just emerged from... hell, probably the most life-altering experience imaginable?

"Damn it," Strickland spat, pulling his focus back. "You'll need to figure it out." He hated resorting to this, but said, "Get Quintos involved, he's good at pulling rabbits out of hats. Strickland out!"

He surveyed the shipyard—a haze-laden metal battlefield with dozens of fires blazing, several of the alien warships billowing sooty, black smoke into the air. Multiple battles were taking place at once. This was akin to a kind of medieval melee combat of two thousand years ago—not so different from when brutality raged with swords clashing, blood spilling, and warriors fighting fiercely with battle-axes in relentless, gruesome hand-to-hand combat.

He could see it as clear as day—the ground they had held just minutes before was quickly being retaken by the Krygians.

Dammit! He needed to get a grip. He needed to get fucking control of this situation.

His comms crackled. Quintos' familiar voice filled his helmet. "I know we set boundaries, Commander, but I'm not going to jeopardize ship and crew just so you can play hero down there. The ship's AI is faltering under the load you're putting her through. I outrank you and I'm taking charge of this operation, at least for now."

"Like hell you are!"

"You're losing down there, Commander. Are you aware of that simple fact?"

"Of course I know that!" Strickland retorted. "I'm the one down here in the thick of it!"

Strickland momentarily fumed, then, surprisingly, found that he was relieved to have the help. Hadn't he so much as asked Derrota to get Quintos involved in so many words? "Just tell me what you have in mind, Captain. I'll decide if you're going to bigfoot your way into this operation."

"What I'm going to do... is rob Peter to pay Paul."

"What the hell does that mean?" Strickland asked, watching as another hover-turret was being maneuvered into position by the enemy. *Fuck!*

"It means, I'm sending you two of my most prized pilots— one of whom is a Tactical Officer who would be just as needed here on *Ike's* bridge."

"And who's the other one?"

"That would be me."

"You?"

Panting, Quintos continued, "Lieutenant Akari James and I

are currently sprinting to *Ike's* flight bay as we speak. Don't make me regret this, Commander. This action defies every military rule in existence. I'll be leaving *USS Ike* without her First Officer as well as her Captain. This very well might land me in front of a court martial tribunal."

"Wait... You're doing what?"

"Shut up and listen," the Captain shot back. "The Krygians' dome-like energy shield keeps us from simply blowing that shipyard into scrap metal from space, such as with smart missiles or rail spikes—"

"You're not telling me anything I don't know. We already went through all this, and right now, I'm more than a little busy."

"But," Quintos continued, "if I can get two top-notch Arrow pilots to make a few strafing runs over that shipyard... well, that just might give you the extra air support necessary for you to retake that shipyard."

The Captain now had Strickland's full attention.

"I noticed earlier," Quintos continued, "there were several brand new Arrow Fighters languishing within the flight bay, collecting dust. Look, it's that adjacent Krygian military base that's pouring in new troops faster than we'll ever replenish fallen Symbios—you're fighting a battle you simply can't win... at least on your own."

Oh no. No less than fifty Krygians had just entered the battle. "Do what you think is best, Captain. But right now, I need to get back into the fight with my team. Oh, and I hope you'll be leaving that ship in good hands. Strickland out." He cut the connection.

Chapter 28

Krygian Hegemony Binary Star System
USS Ike

Captain Galvin Quintos

Huffing and puffing, I reached *Ike's* flight bay with Akari hot on my heels. Before we'd even left the bridge, I'd made sure Grimes understood the urgency of our situation. He'd have the Captain's Mount and his first task was to have two Arrow Fighters prepped and ready for deployment by the time we arrived.

Sure enough, two Arrows within the small bay were taxiing forward with automated bay-bots scurrying around, looking almost nervous... well, as nervous as an automaton could be.

Akari claimed dibs on the Arrow closest to her, her face lighting up with an exuberant smile that even prospects of a grueling battle couldn't dim. Flying was her lifeblood. She lived to rocket into combat, odds be damned. A true warrior down to the core.

"Get a move on, Brigs, we're burning daylight," the First Officer said, climbing the inset ladder to the cockpit.

The nickname 'Brigs' wasn't just a call sign, it was a reminder of those impetuous days when I'd clocked an ungodly amount of time in various ships' brigs for idiotic infractions and hot-headed actions.

"Hey, Ballbuster... we keep things sane down there. We're here to support, not commit suicide," I yelled back.

The engines of our Arrow Fighters roared to life, bay-bots efficiently sliding the heavy partition doors open, revealing the vastness of space. Everything inside me buzzed with anticipation. I hadn't piloted an Arrow in a while, but hey, it was muscle memory, like riding a bike, right? A faint smile tugged at my lips. Being this close to the action was like revisiting an old, dangerous flame you never really got over.

Akari's voice crackled over the comms system, "Ready to light 'em up, Brigs?"

"Ready. Let's just make sure we're back here in an hour. Our day jobs will be waiting for us."

"Buzz kill," she sniped back.

We taxied our Arrows forward, pre-flight checklists coming back to me as if it were yesterday.

"Okay, follow my lead, old man," Akari said, clearly enjoying the teasing edge.

With eyes locked onto the red, glowing overhead bay indicator, I watched it change to yellow, then green.

We tore out into space, the rush of velocity pressing me back into my seat. Stars turned into streaks of light, the emptiness around us now a blur of motion.

Inside the cockpit, the AI chimed.

Arrow armed and operational, Captain.

NELLA's overly calm voice resonated in the cockpit. Unease churned as I considered placing my fate in this AI's hands.

Nylor-5 Shipyard target acquisitions loaded. I am ready to take the controls, Captain.

"Not so fast... I'll be manning the stick, NELLA. But just maybe, if you're a good co-pilot, I just might let you park this Arrow back in the garage when we get back."

"We've got company, Brigs!" Akari said, sounding surprised and breathless.

"Ballbuster, let's keep our formation tight until we intersect."

"Copy that."

"And NELLA, let me know the moment you have target locks," I added.

The AI responded with a simple *ping*.

Scanning the multi-feed halo display, I saw five Krygian fighters were just now breaching Nylor-5's outer atmosphere. Fanning out, the alien fighters pierced the void like ominous silver bullets, contrasting starkly against our sleek, bright red Arrows. Their dual side-by-side cockpits, an odd yet intimidating feature, housed Krygian pilots in tandem, perhaps providing some kind of strategic advantage I wasn't aware of. The craft's multiple wings arranged in a star pattern gave them an almost celestial elegance, with blue running lights inset into the reflective hulls, casting an eerie glow in the darkness of space.

"NELLA, you should have engaged target locks by now," I said.

Yes, Captain.

I saw that Akari was drifting to starboard. "Ballbuster, let's keep our formation tight until we intersect," I instructed... again.

The display showed the Krygian fighters fanning out—yup, they were coming for us.

My grip tightened around the flight controls as we catapulted into the darkness of space. The G-forces pressed hard against my chest, a mix of nostalgia and urgency etched into my grimace. The Arrow's hyper-efficient Nav-Assist system interpreted my every command with uncanny precision—*Good,* I would need all the help I could get. I was well aware the stakes right now couldn't be any higher. Our opponents weren't just readying themselves for a confrontation—I knew they were out for blood—just as we were.

"Brigs, keep your six clean. Don't want you ending up in a Krygian salvage yard," Akari's voice crackled in my comms, her tone a mixture of jest and steel.

"Appreciate the concern, Ballbuster. Let's make sure you don't get any more beauty marks on that Arrow of yours," I shot back, rolling my eyes as I throttled forward.

Krygian fighters zipped into view, their sleek forms glinting under ambient starlight. Their star-patterned wings shimmered with those blue running lights. Intimidating? Absolutely. But if Akari and I had one advantage, it was experience.

"NELLA, confirm target locks on all enemy craft," I ordered.

Target locks confirmed, Captain.

My HUD lit up with five distinct red markers, each representing a Krygian fighter. The swarm began an intricate weave pattern, like a deadly choreography designed to split our attention.

"I've got a bogey on my starboard wing. Think he wants to say hello," Akari chirped.

"NELLA, give me a spectral analysis on any structural or shield variance vulnerabilities. Let's see if there's a weak spot we can exploit."

Spectral analysis underway... completed.
Weak point identified: 1.8 meters
behind the dual cockpits,
along the underbelly of the craft.

"Copy that," I replied, my mind already calculating the angles and approach vectors.

Would you like me to target lock
onto that location, Captain?

"Negative, I've got this," I replied.

We split formation, Akari peeling off left, while I tilted to the right. Energy fire blazed across the black void—Arrows' blue plasma bolts and the enemies' red plasma bolts, crisscrossing like an interstellar light show. Space battles lacked the grace of atmosphere-bound dogfights but made up for it with lethal intensity.

My hand moved instinctively, diverting power from non-essential systems to shields and weapons. The Arrow thrummed in response, its Phazon Pulsar cannon humming with barely contained energy.

"Brigs, check your six!" Akari's warning came just as a Krygian fighter pulled in from behind and then moved to my flank.

Shit! Why the hell hadn't NELLA warned me?

215

My console lit up with alerts, the crimson pulse of enemy fire missing my starboard wing by inches.

The turn-and-burn maneuver left me inverted, eyes locking onto the Krygian fighter's dual cockpits.

"Hello, you ugly motherfuckers," I said with a broad smile.

The moment gave me an up-close view of the two, very surprised-looking Krygian pilots, their helmetless, angular heads bearing an eerie resemblance to a praying mantis—sharp and predatory. Their exoskeletons had a metallic gleam to it, and their four, beady, multifaceted eyes radiated a cold, calculating intelligence. I took in the iridescent sheen of those Krygian heads, pulsating with a menacing intensity, as if bioluminescent signals were communicating silently between them.

I pulled the flight controls to my chest, forcing my Arrow into a tight upward spiral. Banking hard right, aware the Arrow's railgun turret had pivoted, tracking the enemy craft and was now facing aft. I squeezed the trigger. Phazon Pulsar bolts erupted, colliding with two Krygian wings and scattering them into a meteor shower of debris. Two more squeezes of the trigger finished off what remained of the fighter.

"Ballbuster, count one Krygian down," I confirmed.

"Nice shooting, Brigs. Now let's trim this flock down to size."

Our repartee wasn't mere banter; it kept us sharp, connected. As we veered to engage the next targets, NELLA's calm, almost eerie monotone was now feeding me critical data. *It was about time.*

On the display, a green targeting bounding box highlighted one of the enemy fighters.

Captain, enemy fighter pilots are powering up for an aggressive maneuver.

Preemptive action is advised.

I banked left, firing a volley of Phazon bolts at the Krygian fighter while climbing. The perfectly timed shot cleaved the craft in half, both cockpits breached, spewing atmosphere into a dazzling celestial display.

"NELLA, update me on ground operations," I said, aware that every second up here meant precious time slipping away for Strickland down below.

Ground team facing significant
resistance. Current status is critical.
Casualty report pending.

Cold dread clenched my gut. Sure, this untested tech could bring the Ops team back, again and again, but what was the cumulative effect? How many times could one die and not pay an even worse price than death? Strickland, Hardy, and the Marines... at some point, it becomes a simple math issue. Overwhelming odds against so few. Their lives and sanity were on the edge, and our support was their only lifeline. We had to get to them, fast.

"Brigs! Captain, for fuck's sake, focus!" Akari's bark was enough to snap me back to reality. Glancing left, I saw she was right there on my wing, concern in her eyes.

"We've got incoming at our twelve!" I called out seeing movement on the display. My cockpit suddenly illuminated from glancing Krygian plasma fire.

Incoming plasma burst detected.
Evasive action recommended.

"Again, a little late with the intel, NELLA," I reprimanded.

I maneuvered in sync with NELLA's updated vector suggestions, narrowly avoiding multiple plasma arcs slicing through the void. The Krygian ships, agile and birdlike in their movements, were relentless in their pursuit—yet that was one area where Akari and I held the upper hand. We were humans, not just calculating machines. We had split-second intuition and tactical creativity deterred only by the limits of physical capability.

Akari's Arrow spun and corkscrewed in a mesmerizing display with an enemy craft on her tail—it was masterful piloting.

"These guys are ruthless, aren't they?" Akari grunted, pushing her Arrow to its limits.

"Yeah, but so are we," I shot back, plasma bolts lighting up the space in front of me causing her pursuer to disengage.

"Thanks!" she said, sounding relieved.

I veered left, accelerating to breakneck speeds. Suddenly, Akari and I both had one Krygian fighter on our respective tails, leaving two others pacing the edges of our battlefield, waiting for an opportune strike.

"NELLA, options?"

Increasing defensive measures is advisable, Sir. Target lock acquired.

My HUD flashed with confirmed target locks. I barrel-rolled, nose-diving at an angle skimming the upper atmosphere of Krygora. My timing had to be precise. As the planet's gravity tugged at the Krygian tailing me, I performed a quick, inverted loop, aligning my ship right above the Krygian fighter. At that moment, Phazon Pulsar rounds found their mark. The Krygian craft exploded in a shower of metallic shrapnel.

"Ballbuster, how's it looking?" I inquired—my confidence bolstered by the kill.

"Juggling a bogey over here, Brigs," she replied, though her voice betrayed no sign of concern.

Captain, incoming Krygian fighter from port, bearing eight o'clock.

Sure enough, another Krygian fighter blitzed past my Arrow. Their twin cockpits gleaned like petrified insect eyes focused on destruction.

"Brigs, we're down to two on two. Shit! Break left, break left now!" Akari shouted.

I did as directed without a second thought. We crossed, each of us interchanging positions seamlessly—a tactical maneuver only two pilots with years of camaraderie could execute. We played off the Krygian's aggression, our man-made mechanical dragons twisting through space as if locked onto invisible rails.

A new bounding box highlighted the incoming Krygian fighter on my display, I thumbed the triggers. But NELLA's voice, hesitant and sluggish, stalled my shot.

Target lock—unavailable. Systems reassessment required.

"Give me that target lock now, NELLA!" I commanded. "And remind me why I don't drink on the job," I muttered through my clenched teeth.

Akari swooped in from above, her Arrow spewing cobalt blue plasma into the Krygian's fuselage. The explosion momentarily blinded me—the backdrop of Krygora obscured by the craft's dramatic destruction.

"Well played, Ballbuster," I said with an exhale. That woman's skill at the controls was second to none.

"No time for high-fives, Brigs. Let's finish this," she replied, voice sharp with intent.

Now it was two Arrows against one remaining Krygian fighter. Hope sparked within me. We had the upper hand, only for this illusion to crumble when the final Krygian unloaded a relentless barrage at Akari's Arrow.

"Akari, you got a bogey on your tail!"

"You think!" she sniped back.

Then it happened...

I audibly gasped. It was as if time itself had slowed to a crawl as I watched the Krygian's plasma bolts tear through Akari's Arrow's aft section. An explosion engulfed her fighter's midsection, sending her Arrow into a perilous spiral.

Critical failure...

NELLA's voice broke the news, empty of any human sentiment...

Lieutenant Akari has lost consciousness. Arrow detonation imminent in ten seconds.

My heart pounded, a kettledrum in my chest. For a moment, I froze—paralyzed with the image of losing my friend, this person who'd been by my side for over a decade. The ensuing seconds felt like an eternity.

"Galvin, get a grip," I muttered under my breath, welling moisture blurring my vision, as I tightened my hold on the controls. A flurry of incoming enemy fire zipped past me, narrowly missing the nose of my Arrow.

Derrota's gentle voice came over my comms. "Galvin... NELLA is attempting a Quans-lock on her..."

"Hurry!" I bellowed.

But it was too late. The enemy Krygian was already making another devastating run at Akari's Arrow.

My hand shot out, as if to grab her, to pull her away from the inevitable. But it was too late. The explosion ripped her Arrow apart, a searing white flash against the black backdrop of space. My heart, my hope, vanished with it.

"Akari!" My voice echoed, a roar of raw fury that eclipsed every shred of reason. Grief gave way to a chilling, primal resolve. My hands clenched around the controls, knuckles turning white as the surge of rage coursed through me. I felt the weight of loss pressing down, but it only fueled the fire within, transforming sorrow into a relentless drive for vengeance. In that moment, every thought, every feeling, was focused on one thing: making the enemy pay for what they had done.

I morphed into a calculating, determined predator. NELLA resumed feeding me critical data, my focus honed despite the chaos. Years of Arrow piloting came flooding back as I prepared to push this fighter beyond its limits.

Eyes set, teeth clenched... I hunted.

The Krygian fighter was fast, almost unpredictably agile—its movements were unnervingly precise. But I had faced tough opponents before. I ignored NELLA's frequent navigation prompts. This was me against them. Man against whatever the fuck they were... *bugs?* My instincts and experience guided me through the spiraling chaos. We twisted and turned through the void, locked in a lethal game of cat and mouse. I mirrored the enemy's maneuvers in reverse, trying to stay one step ahead without wasting any energy. Each move was sharp and calculated, demanding my full concentration and determination to stay in the fight. I couldn't afford to make a single mistake.

The fighter banked to starboard, then dipped, piercing the planet's upper atmosphere. I anticipated, tracing an intercept vector, my Arrow's targeting systems synchronizing perfectly with my intentions. I fired, the Phazon Pulsar cannon roaring to life, sending a shockwave through Nylor-5's atmosphere as the energy bolts found the alien craft. Blue-white plasma consumed the enemy ship, incinerating it into oblivion.

Breathless, my comms burst to life. "Galvin, Strickland's team needs your immediate air support."

"I'm on it, Stephan," I said, my voice hoarse from adrenalin and grief. "NELLA's recalibrating my approach vector."

Even as Derrota's voice carried on, I found my mind wandering. His words failed to hold my focus.

"... but you'll be happy to know *Ike* has an adequate regrow pod—"

"Wait. Go back, Stephan. What are you talking about?"

THE LONG PAUSE HAD ME ENVISIONING REACHING across space and time, grabbing Derrota by his lab coat lapels, and shaking him.

"The Lieutenant... Akari... NELLA had not only quansported her into HealthBay but into a regrow pod. She'll be in there a while... a few days. Losing both legs like that, it takes its toll, Galvin—"

I now spoke very slowly and distinctly, "You're telling me that Akari is still alive?"

Again with the infuriatingly long pause.

"Oh yes, very much so. Oh, I'm sorry... I thought you knew that NELLA had indeed gotten a quans-lock on her. And with no time to spare, I might add. All in all, it was quite the ordeal, if you don't mind me saying so... a total team effort that ensured the young woman would recover without any long-term effects."

I opened my helmet's visor, swiped at a wayward tear rolling down my cheek. NELLA had adjusted the Arrow's heading, and I allowed a smile to take form on my lips. I leaned back in my seat, releasing a weary breath as I let Derrota's continued ramblings fade into the background.

Chapter 29

Eta Carinae System
On Approach to Haven

XO Gail Pristy

Pristy straightened as Hub Gunther emerged from the wormhole into a star system she didn't recognize. Beyond the curved diamond glass window, the space outside was sparse, dominated by a flickering blue star... beyond, a massive ring of tumbling, gyrating asteroids.

"Holy shit! Where are we?"

It was a realm of constant movement and chaos, an unwelcoming span of space she hadn't been prepared for.

"We're here," Ryder muttered beside her.

Pristy glanced at him. "Oh, well thank you for that enlightening bit of wisdom. Where exactly is *here*?"

Ryder nodded toward a planet nestled in the heart of the tumbling asteroids. Orbiting the blue star, the green and blue planet seemed an odd juxtaposition of tranquility in the midst of the astral tumult. "That's Haven," Ryder said. "This is where Quintos handed over *Oblivion* to the Grish."

Pristy tapped at her board and slowly nodded. "His pirate days... I wasn't there... here."

Ryder looked concerned. "Where the hell's the destroyer we were chasing?"

"I don't know, but at least nobody's paying attention to us. We're back to being cloaked."

He made a face. "We just emerged from a manufactured wormhole into a star system that previously... wasn't possible."

She shrugged. "That wasn't a U.S. Space Navy-generated wormhole, looks like these pirates have better tech."

"Anyway," he continued, "Quintos was forced to negotiate with the Grish to save Haven," Ryder explained. "It's here that he surrendered *Oblivion*, which, as you know, is possibly the most advanced warship ever constructed by the Gorvians. He did it to save countless lives. Rough call, but the right one."

The emerald world lay beneath a protective sheath of constantly tumbling, somersaulting asteroids held at bay by an unknown force. As Ryder filled her in, Pristy marveled at how such a chaotic barrier could protect and conceal an entire planet. Haven, home to the Pylor pirates, was hidden within the Eta Carinae system—its unpredictable star flickering between night and day on a whim.

Pristy's eyes locked onto the display, sensors having picked up numerous other ships in the vicinity. "No sign of Pylor patrols," she said, looking up intently, scanning the horizon.

Ryder chinned toward the planet. "82 million people there, give or take. Mainly Pylor, but a scattering of others, too. This place... they don't take kindly to intruders."

"What about the Briggan? Are they working with the Pylor clan?" Pristy asked.

"Not quite allies. They do business sometimes. More like

two rivals, equally despicable organizations that strike deals when it suits them," he replied.

Putting her attention back on the display, searching local space, she said, "There it is!"

Ryder's brows shot up questioningly.

"Dreadnought's in high orbit, on the other side of Haven."

He adjusted the ship's trajectory, and said, "My guess, they'll be shuttling Sonya down to the surface, if they haven't already."

"To where?"

"Maybe the capital," Ryder replied. "New Petite Goave. It's heavily fortified, though. Of course, they wouldn't be making it easy for us."

"If you're looking for easy, you're in the wrong line of work, Wallace. How about you pull on your big boy pants and we go rescue that girl?"

Ryder chuckled, "Big boy pants?"

"Tell me more about that planet. What kind of pirate stuff goes on there?"

Ryder adjusted their flight path, guiding them closer to Haven. "Alright, here's the lowdown," he began, focusing on the picturesque view before them. "Pylor pirates make their base here, mostly concentrating in New Petite Goave. It's their capital, like I said. You got old-style architecture, multi-story brick and timber structures with Roman columns and wrought iron balconies. Think New Orleans with an other-worldly twist. But don't let the aesthetics fool you. Every building's reinforced, armed to the teeth."

Pristy absorbed that, her fingers tapping lightly on her thigh. "And their command structure? How organized are they?"

"They're more organized than you'd think—a disjointed 'extended family' of pirates led by the House of Lords, eleven old men who wield significant authority and power. Don't mistake them for senile codgers. These guys have cunning minds sharpened over decades of pirating."

"So, they're the big cheese decision-makers, huh?"

"Pretty much," Ryder said.

Pristy's eyes narrowed as her mind raced. "These eleven old dudes, they'd have contingencies, wouldn't they? Escape routes, maybe hidden safe-houses?"

Ryder gave her a sideways glance. "Why would any of that matter?"

"Always good to know who's in charge. And how to get to them."

"There's also Admiral Arlington McMasters," Ryder said, "he's the grand pirate of pirates, who heads the whole operation. Descendant of Bartholomew Roberts, no less. When it comes to Pylor pirating, he's the big cheese of the cheeses."

"And Sonya," Pristy pressed, exhaling frustration, "she'll be held tight within that, what was it, New Pet..."

"New Petite Goave," Ryder said.

RYDER GOOSED HUB GUNTHER'S THROTTLE putting them on a trajectory that within minutes had them on the other side of Haven—and right where the Briggan dreadnought was sitting within a geostationary orbit.

Pristy leaned in over the tactical board, her fingers rapidly tapping at the controls as she issued commands to Hub Gunther's AI.

"What are you doing?"

She didn't stop to answer, "Scanning the ship's interior without setting off alarms." She smiled, "Finesse is necessary here, and no one, no one, is better suited for this particular task than me."

Thirty seconds later, she said, "And... done!"

The display refreshed, presenting a schematic view of the Briggan dreadnought's internal structure.

"Huh," she said, pursing her lips. "Seems the ship's about a fifth the size of a USS Hamilton-class dread... but still, fairly big." Her brow furrowed as the latest completed scan started to return results.

"What's the scoop?" Ryder asked, giving the display a cursory glance.

"Virtually empty," Pristy replied, her voice tinged with surprise. "No more than a dozen crewmembers onboard."

Ryder chuckled, "Well... what do you expect? They're pirates, and they've just made port. Bet you a slice of earth pizza that the bars and brothels are packed right now."

Pristy waved him off, her focus razor-sharp. "There's only one person I'm interested in. Sonya. And she's not onboard that ship."

"You sure?"

She looked at him; her flat expression said it all. "Body mass readings... Sonya's petite. No one left on that ship is under two hundred pounds."

"Fine. So what's the next step?"

Her gaze stayed level on Ryder. "We need to get down to Haven," she said.

Pristy shifted her attention into the distance, lost in the labyrinth of their next moves.

He shook his head. "Gunther wouldn't be allowed to land. I know from experience, Pylors take their security very seriously. Look at where this Haven hideout is located—the middle of an asteroid field. There are no casual drop-ins here."

"So we'd need a recognizable shuttle," she said. "There's at least two onboard that destroyer—they came up on the scan sweeps."

Ryder shook his head. "I can see where you're going with this. No."

"Come on, play along for a second. What are the odds that we could get on board that destroyer?"

"And live to tell about it... zero to not very high."

Pristy looked momentarily deflated then smiled.

"What are the odds that whoever was left in charge on that ship would help out a stranded fellow space traveler—someone with mechanical problems?"

"Probably even less," he said. "Pirates aren't known for their benevolence."

"Suppose that small, battered vessel, plagued with mechanical issues, was actually ferrying a select group of ladies of ill repute for Admiral Arlington McMasters' personal entertainment."

She was surprised by Ryder's sudden laugh. "Uh... I would say the odds just took a turn for the better."

Captain Wallace Ryder

Ryder sat in the cramped bridge area of Hub Gunther, tapping his fingers lightly against the dashboard. The hum of the ship's systems was a familiar background noise, a subtle reminder of the technological marvel that surrounded him. His mind, however, was far from the workings of their vessel. His thoughts were locked onto Gail Pristy, who had taken a break—was aft, perhaps stretching her legs.

He leaned back as he recalled the earlier days, those heady moments when things between him and Pristy had felt like the beginning of something grand. Their short-lived romance had left him more affected than he cared to admit at the time. He had maintained his reputation as the charming and unattached bachelor, moving from one conquest to the next with a casual flick of his wrist. The truth, hidden behind a mask of nonchalance, was that Pristy's decision to end things had left him adrift.

Gail had always been a kaleidoscope of qualities he admired. She was brilliant—her intellect sparkling in even the most mundane conversations they had around the mess hall table. Competent, too, her leadership honed to a fine edge by countless missions and responsibilities she had assumed with grace and aptitude. And beautiful—there were moments when her features seemed almost too delicate for the harsh realities of space warfare.

When the DeckPort mishap happened, Ryder initially brushed it off as just another bump in the long, tumultuous road of their spacefaring adventures. But he couldn't help noticing the subtle changes in her demeanor, the way she carried herself with an increased intensity that hadn't been there before. Was this a different version of Gail Pristy, courtesy of a glitch in the DeckPort system?

Ryder could almost laugh at life's ironies. For years, he'd watched from the sidelines, bemused by Quintos' obliviousness to Gail's feelings. It was perplexing how Quintos, otherwise so perceptive and sharp, had missed the cues that Gail had been sending his way all this time. Ryder had often pondered why he had never dared to mention it to Quintos, instead choosing to keep his observations to himself, playing the role of an indifferent spectator.

Now, as he waited for her, Ryder couldn't shake off the nagging sense that this was a turning point, not just for Pristy, but also for their dynamic. He winced, subconsciously shrugging his shoulders as if trying to shake off the weight of complicated emotions.

The auto-hatch slid open with a whoosh, pulling Ryder from his reverie. His jaw dropped as Gail Pristy entered the bridge area. Gone were the soot and smudges from the crash and skirmish. She didn't just look cleaned up; she looked transformed.

"Found an old makeup bag in the head," she said as she took her seat, a touch of playful triumph in her voice.

Ryder found himself scrutinizing each detail of her appearance, each one more striking than the last. Her hair cascaded in glossy waves, framing her face, which now bore the expert touch of blush and lipstick. Her eyelashes were impossibly long, accentuating her now-clear, piercing gaze. The jacket, tattered and singed, had vanished, replaced by a button-down shirt left provocatively open. It highlighted her captivating cleavage, a feature not lost on him even though he'd tried to be the gentleman all these years.

"How do I look?" she purred, swiveled towards him, a hint of mischief gleaming in her eyes.

"You look...," Ryder stammered, at a loss for words. "You look incredible, Gail."

She smiled, but there was no trace of smugness, just a quiet confidence that sent a jolt through his chest... the kind of woman who could command both a bridge and a room full of civilians with effortless grace.

He cleared his throat, returning his focus to more immediate matters. "Alright, Gail, what's the plan?"

"Uncloak Gunther and make it obvious the ship's experiencing mechanical issues," she instructed, her tone steady and authoritative. "Get us in close, but not too close."

"Got it. You sure you want to do this?" Ryder asked, his fingers already working the controls to uncloak their vessel and mimic a buffer overload.

"You're going to let me do the talking," she replied. "We've got one shot at this, Ryder. We need to act the role in getting those pirates interested in helping a poor damsel in distress."

Ryder tapped the dash uncloaking Gunther. I took him a minute to alter the ship's drive exhaust signature—one that would scream major engine trouble to even the most unsuspecting eye.

Dashlights began flickering as he initiated a series of coded signals, broadcasting their apparent distress. Subtle puffs of dark emissions began to seep from various points aft, giving off the illusion of a drive going haywire.

The display flickered to life, showing the now closer, looming, shape of the Briggan destroyer in orbit around Haven. The imposing ship seemed to regard them with silent suspicion, its dark silhouette bristling with weaponry.

"We're in visual range," Ryder said, tightening his grip on the controls. "Initiating proximity protocols. We should appear on their scanners any moment now."

Pristy nodded, taking a deep breath before switching the transmitter to *broadcast* on an open channel. Her confidence was palpable, a far cry from the tension Ryder felt twisting inside him. This had to work.

She slid closer to the dash camera, casting a quick glance his way. "Can you bump up the cabin lights a bit? Let's make sure they get a good look." A nervous laugh slipped through as she squared her shoulders, practicing a look of vulnerability.

He adjusted Gunther's interior lights and tapped a few buttons. "Okay, you're live, Gail."

She cleared her throat.

Pristy: Hello? Briggan destroyer... oh my... this is the civilian vessel, Hub Gunther. We've suffered a catastrophic systems failure and require immediate assistance.

The XO made the announcement, her voice carrying a feigned urgency.

Ryder adjusted the ship's trajectory, bringing them closer to the destroyer's position while still maintaining a cautious distance. Pristy's transformation had the intended effect, giving her an air of both desperation and credibility, an impactful balance.

Seconds crawled by, as Ryder did his best to steady his breathing, the pressure of their situation weighing heavily. If the pirates saw through their bluff, one missile at this range would end them.

Finally, the display flickered, and the bearded, heavily scarred face of a Briggan captain materialized in front of them. His rough features and cold, calculating eyes suggested a man who would not be easily manipulated.

Briggan Captain: This is Captain Thar of the Briggan destroyer, *Asteron*. State your business and your cargo, civilian vessel.

He sounded wary.

Ryder glanced at Pristy, waiting for her to perform the verbal gambit that would determine their fate. If she succeeded, they might just pull this off.

The pirate's expression of annoyance quickly softened as he took in Pristy's despondent, captivating face.

The XO took a steadying breath...

Pristy: Oh, thank God... Captain Thar, we were en route to New Petite Goave. Our pilot says critical systems have gone offline, whatever that means. He's no mechanic, although he thinks he is. I know it's a lot to ask... but would you be so kind as to assist six desperate ladies—each lady who cannot be late for a very important rendezvous?

Pristy had subtly infused her voice with a touch of a Louisiana accent that carried an unexpected charm. Ryder's eyes locked onto the display, as the pirate Captain's predatory glare bore into her.

Briggan Captain: You say six ladies?

Thar's interest was piqued, an evident glimmer of something feral flickering alongside his skepticism.

The XO seized on that hesitation like a hawk ready to swoop on prey.

Pristy: We're here at the invitation of Admiral Arlington McMasters... for his... shall we say, entertainment?

Thar weighed her words, leaning back slightly, revealing more of the gnarled command center behind him. He scratched at his beard, now looking back at her with a suspicious eye.

Briggan Captain: Surprising the Admiral would bring in whores from off-world—

Gail's cheeks flushed with anger.

Pristy: Kindly refrain from using such degrading language. We're not mere back-alley prostitutes.

Ryder caught the Captain's eyes drifting lower to Pristy's cleavage.

Briggan Captain: As the Captain, I must inspect your manifest... and crew, personally. Ensure, uh, legitimacy. Yeah, that's the word, legitimacy.

The Briggan's smile was anything but friendly, reeking of malevolence.

The XO nodded, only the slightest tension visible in her jaw.

Pristy: Of course, Captain Thar. And you will bring along a competent mechanic? Someone who can take a look at our problematic propulsion system?

The pirate, now back to scratching at his beard, seemed to be weighing his options—not ready to make a decision.

Gail fluttered her lashes, her expression now somewhat more demure.

Pristy: Captain, I can make it... shall we say, worthwhile for you? This being an unanticipated departure from your busy schedule.

Briggan Captain: That piece of shit even have an airlock?

Pristy: Yes. My pilot says it's small but fully functional. It's situated at the back of the vessel.

Briggan Captain: You mean the stern. Alright, give me a few minutes. Let me see if we have an operational shuttle.

The feed terminated.

Pristy looked at Ryder. "What do you think? Was I enticing enough? Or did I lay it on too thick?"

"I think you did just fine. I have little doubt at this moment

235

he is sprinting to that ship's flight bay, hoping and praying there's an operational shuttle."

She smiled, "Good!"

XO Gail Pristy

Pristy and Ryder settled into their positions, nerves winding tighter as they watched the Briggan destroyer through the forward window. The silence stretched, broken only by the hum of Hub Gunther's systems. Pristy's breath hitched when an old, weathered shuttlecraft finally emerged from the destroyer's flight bay, like a relic brought back to life.

"Stay sharp," Ryder whispered, gripping his tagger.

Heart pounding, Pristy double-checked her weapon. The glowing interface confirmed it was ready to fire non-lethal rounds. "Let's hope they don't bring too many friends," she muttered, half to herself.

The shuttle's trek felt agonizingly slow. It approached the stern of Gunther with unsteady progression, the slightly larger Gunther accommodating its docking attempt. Ryder had dimmed the cabin lights, casting the interior in a murky gloom. They positioned themselves on either side of the inside airlock, muscles coiled and ready.

The airlock mechanisms clanked and groaned, signaling the connection and pressurization sequence. Atmosphere wheezed into the transfer tanks, followed by a sharp hiss as the chamber equalized. Pristy peered through the small viewport hatch, her eyes narrowing.

"There's three of them," she whispered, a tinge of apprehension in her voice.

Ryder gave a tight nod. "Let's do our best not to kill anyone."

"Of course not. We need at least one of them alive for this

plan to work," Pristy replied, her tone ambiguous enough to make Ryder glance back at her, his brows knitting together in confusion.

The airlock's inner hatch creaked open. A sliver of light from the shuttle's interior sliced through the darkness of their vessel. The first Briggan, towering and broad-shouldered, stepped inside cautiously, his eyes scanning the dim surroundings. As his gaze swung back toward the airlock, he spotted Ryder.

He began to yell, but Pristy's reflexes were quicker. Her tagger spat out a bolt that struck him squarely in the chest. His yell turned into a gurgle as he crumpled to the deck.

The next two Briggans barreled into the compartment, charging at Ryder and Pristy like enraged bulls. The confined space erupted into chaos.

One Briggan lunged at Pristy, a meaty fist swinging toward her face. She ducked, feeling the wind from the missed blow rustle her hair. She came up inside his guard, delivering a rapid series of strikes to his gut. He grunted, but the attacks seemed to bounce off his hardened muscles. His massive hand grasped her wrist, yanking her off balance. She kicked out desperately, aiming for a knee.

Pristy found herself facing seasoned street fighters hardened by years—maybe even decades—of barroom brawls and back-alley scraps. The U.S. Space Navy's rigorous combat training had prepared her for hand-to-hand combat, but she wasn't prepared for their brute ferocity and cunning.

Ryder, meanwhile, grappled with the other Briggan, their bodies crashing into the bulkhead with a resonating thud. Ryder hooked his arm around the man's neck, but the Briggan bucked like a wild stallion, breaking free. Ryder regained his footing just in time to avoid a hammer-like fist aimed at his head. He twisted and drove his elbow into the Briggan's ribs, the dull impact lost in the turbulence of grunts and growls.

Pristy's opponent twisted her arm painfully, attempting to overpower her. She ignored the searing pain, locked eyes with the Briggan, and brought her forehead down against his nose with all the force she could muster. He stumbled back, blood streaming from his nostrils.

Ryder's foe pressed him hard, forcing him against the bulkhead. The Briggan's weight threatened to crush him, but Ryder planted his feet and used the momentum to flip the man over his shoulder. The Briggan landed on his back with a heavy thud, the air expelled from his lungs in a wheeze. Ryder pounced, throwing a swift punch to the jaw that sent the man's head snapping back.

Regaining composure, Pristy dodged another heavy swing from her attacker. She ducked under his arm and drove her knee into his midsection. He bent forward, wheezing; she capitalized on his distraction by wrapping her arm around his neck. She squeezed with every ounce of her strength, feeling him struggling against her grip.

Ryder's fist connected with the Briggan's jaw, sending the brute reeling. Yet, the pirate stayed on his feet, showing a level of resilience that Captain Ryder grudgingly admired. Ryder gritted his teeth, using a combination of quick, targeted strikes aimed at the pressure points they had drilled on in training. Slowly, he wore down the larger man's defenses.

Pristy's opponent flailed, his fingers clawing at her forearm, but she held tight, squeezing harder. His movements grew sluggish, and finally, his knees buckled. He crumpled to the deck.

With a final, powerful strike, Ryder sent his opponent crashing to the deck, unconscious.

Panting, bruised, and bloodied, Pristy and Ryder stood over

the two unconscious Briggans, their breath ragged in the quiet that followed the storm.

Blood trickled from a cut above Pristy's eye; she wiped it away with the back of her hand. She glanced at Ryder, who sported a split lip and bruises forming on his face.

Ryder gave a rueful grin, wiping sweat and blood from his face. "Well, that was fun."

Pristy huffed a laugh, wincing at the effort. "Yeah. Let's never do that again. But mission accomplished... for now."

Nodding, Ryder knelt to bind the Briggans' wrists and ankles, ensuring they wouldn't find escape easy when they came to.

Pristy looked over at the hatch, half-expecting another wave of pirates, her nerves still humming with adrenaline. "Okay, now we need to wake one of them up."

Chapter 30

Somewhere over Haven
Briggan Shuttle

Sonya Winters

Sonya awoke, her head throbbing as if a pile driver was relentlessly hammering inside her skull. Dizzy and feeling as if she might hurl, she heard murmured voices, aware of others nearby. Instinctively, she touched the top of her head. *What the...?* She winced at a sharp pain—felt caked, dried blood tangled in her hair.

She flashed back to right before everything went black. The brute... Viggo. How she'd repeatedly slammed the hatch door into his head—killing him.

Trying to focus, she glanced around, half-expecting to still see his lifeless form sprawled on the deck. Instead, she found herself surrounded by unfamiliar faces. Clearly, they were pirates, and she suspected Briggans from their distinctive accents—at least five of them. Behind them, a large grime-coated viewport showed a blur of stars.

She moved to curl her legs up to her chest and instantly felt the resistance of a heavy chain attached to an iron brace around her ankle. *Ah... shit.* Why was she chained? Where was she now? She glanced around, trying to piece it together. *Obviously still captured—who are they? And this ship—it was different. Could be another shuttle.*

She could feel the steady thrum of the propulsion system vibrating—then thrusters came alive—they were slowing. A star system, or maybe it was an asteroid field, was coming into view within the viewport. She inwardly gasped as an emerald-green world filled the viewport. Haven. She forced herself to look away. Her fingers traced the bench's worn edges, seeking any distraction from where she now knew they were headed.

Sour body odor permeated the space. One of them—the others had called him Rax—was staring at her, his creepy amber gaze making her skin crawl. Rax was a ginger. Had enough facial and body hair to be mistaken for an orange ape.

Everything about this lot disgusted her, from their rank smell and rotten, brown teeth... to their hanging strands of greasy hair.

Rax separated himself from the others and approached. Keeping his voice hushed, he said, "Nice job you did with Viggo. Glad I'm not the one who'll have to tell his wife."

"I did her a favor," Sonya hissed back defiantly.

And then there's Bastion. He wasn't happy losing one of his men. Gonna be a price to pay, Princess. You know our ways."

Sonya's heart missed a beat. She did. The reality of her situation was making it hard to breathe. "I didn't have a choice," she muttered through clenched teeth, her voice small.

Rax's sneer widened. "Yeah, good luck going with that."

She leered back at him, keeping her stare level with his, though inwardly she felt no confidence in the challenge.

"Hope you enjoy the welcoming party, Princess," Rax sneered, leaning closer. "They've been waiting for you."

"Get bent," Sonya muttered, glaring at him. She knew better than to provoke him, but she couldn't help herself. Her snark was the only weapon she had left, even if it earned her another smack. His hand darted out faster than she could dodge, the slap echoing loudly in the cramped cabin, her cheek suddenly on fire from the impact.

"Watch your mouth, little lady!" Rax hissed, his grip tightening on her arm. "Keep it up, and it won't just be a whack across that pretty face." His eyes dropped to her chest, a momentary reflex, then she stared at him defiantly; he licked his lips as his Adam's apple bobbed like a Ping-Pong ball in play.

Sonya's eyes watered from the pain, but she bit back the tears. She wouldn't let him see her cry. She hated that her defiance was the only thing keeping her from breaking down entirely.

The pirates circulated a bottle, its pungent aroma permeating the compartment. Their sudden bursts of laughter, grotesque, demeaning jokes, and furtive glances in her direction turned her stomach. The shuttle suddenly lurched, and Rax's grip loosened somewhat. Around her, the Briggans roared with laughter again, completely oblivious to her suffering... or maybe, just indifferent.

Rax rejoined the others, but his eyes returned to her, swept over her, like clockwork. She crossed her arms over her chest. She despised the way he leered at her, knowing he was undressing her in that dim-witted mind of his. Every part of her screamed to get away from him, all of them, but there was nowhere to go.

The shuttle landed with a bone-jarring thud, and a loud tone signaled it was time to disembark. Sonya's heart pounded as Rax yanked her to her feet, unlocked her shackle, and forced her toward the now-open hatch. "Move it, Princess," he said with that same sneering tone, pushing her out of the shuttle.

A burst of heavy, humid air greeted her as she stepped onto the gangway. Sonya's legs wobbled under her, and the world tilted momentarily before her feet found some semblance of balance. She didn't get far.

"Watch your step," Rax mocked, shoving her forward. Sonya lost her footing and fell hard to her knees, scraping them against the rough metal. Pain shot up her legs. She fought back the tears—no way would she give him the satisfaction.

Sonya got to her feet, casting a quick glance around to her surroundings. She knew this place, but it had been several years. New Petite Goave, the Pylor pirate's home base.

After a few minutes, they left the small landing field and moved off toward civilization.

THE TOWN WAS AN ODD MIX OF CHARM AND menace—brick and timber buildings interspersed with Roman columns and wrought iron balconies decorated with flowering plants. Vigilant sentries in blue uniforms stood at intervals, heightening the place's threatening aura.

The villagers, dressed in 19th-century-style attire, appeared mostly civilized... the women were adorned in low-cut bodices, long, bustling skirts, and tight corsets that made their waists seem unnaturally narrow. Colorful hats were perched atop their heads.

Most of the local men were dressed in black tuxedos with tails, many with walking sticks... while a few of the pirates wore wide-brimmed hats, others, the more common bandanas. They wore dingy coats, some long, some short, none of them shying away from shiny silver or gold buttons and buckles. And all of them had their weapons on full display.

Feeling the townsfolk's eyes on her, Sonya's self-consciousness kicked in. Her clothes were filthy—stained from soot and dirt, her body covered in cuts and black smudges, and she reeked of dead vermin, mildew, and vomit. She was painfully aware of the stark contrast between herself and the well-dressed, curious lookie-loos who stopped to stare.

Sonya's face burned with fear and humiliation as Rax and the other Briggans paraded her down the main street like a prized pig. They were onlookers to her misery, and all she could do was try not to meet their eyes. She focused instead on the rough cobblestones beneath her feet, the clink of metal chains—anything that kept her from focusing on what was happening around her.

Her mind raced, not knowing what to expect. She had overheard the Briggans talking about her imminent marriage to Bastion Thunderballs, and the thought made her nauseous. She had never even had a real, romantic relationship, let alone been with someone in *that* way. Sure, most people thought she and Plorinne had been together intimately, but it wasn't true. She loved him, but that hadn't been a part of their relationship. The truth was, she was a virgin, and the idea of being forced to marry some brutish pirate and everything that came with that, terrified her.

Every step felt like a death march to the gallows. Each glance she cast around the town sharpened the absurdity and terror of her situation. She thought of her Uncle Galvin, praying that he was already on his way to rescue her. He had never let her down before; she had to believe he wouldn't start now.

Finally, they reached an extravagant mansion, its gates guarded by armed sentries. Sonya's knees nearly buckled... the thought of what waited for her inside. Her eyes darted around, searching for any possible escape route, but there were too many guards... too many eyeballs on her.

As they approached an imposing iron gate, two armed gate-keepers stepped aside, allowing them entry through a high stone wall that enclosed the extravagant estate. The Briggans escorted her up an expansive cobblestone drive, Rax's rough hand still gripping her arm. She gazed up at the towering white marble pillars and the grand portico above.

"Welcome to your new home," Rax sneered, shoving her forward through the grand entrance, sending her stumbling inside the foyer of the impressive estate.

Sonya's eyes widened at the ostentation within the mansion. Crystal chandeliers hung from the ceiling, casting a deceptive warmth over the marble floors. She took in the luxurious tapestries that adorned the walls, depicting pirate conquests; the giant, solid, gold-framed mirror; and the dark wood foyer table with mother-of-pearl inlays and brass finishings. Yet, beneath the opulence, there was an unmistakable aura of brutality—weapons strategically placed and guards patrolling every conceivable exit.

Sonya was ushered up a grand staircase. As she ascended, she looked below, trying to memorize the layout of the mansion. At the top, Rax led her down a corridor lined with heavy, rein-forced doors. He stopped, rapped his knuckles twice, opened the door, and shoved her inside.

The room was nothing short of spectacular. She stood for a moment, awestruck by the opulence—the four-poster bed with intricately carved wood, decorated with a satiny, bone-colored comforter with beige piping, matching pillows, and a headboard made of curtains that fell ceiling to floor... they floated like swaths of silk caught in a light breeze.

Overhead was a New Orleans-style chandelier made of antique, patinated brass. With curvaceous arms extending outward like delicate vines, they supported a cascade of shim-mering crystals, casting a warm glow over the room. Every detail spoke of 19th-century luxury, a far cry from the dingy, bug-infested pirates' vessels.

As she took in the gilded splendor around her, her eyes widened. "What is this... why am I here?"

Rax looked incredulous. "You think you're going to meet your betrothed looking and smelling like a street whore? You need a bath, and clothes that don't reek."

She didn't know what to say, so she said nothing.

"This is where you and I say goodbye, Princess, although I'm hoping we meet again someday, perhaps under different circum-stances." He waggled his eyebrows suggestively, prompting her to take a step backward.

He and his men left, closing the door behind them. Thinking she was alone, Sonya was startled by a woman's voice from behind. She turned to see a petite woman dressed as a housemaid, holding a stack of folded towels.

"My name is Elara. I'll be looking after you while you're here. Please, come this way, my lady," the maid said softly. "Let us get you cleaned up, yes?"

Scrubbed clean and wrapped in a plush bathrobe, Sonya collapsed onto the bed, the events of the past few hours crashing down on her like a tidal wave. Viggo's lifeless eyes flashed in her mind, his blood pooling around his head. She could almost hear the echo of her own voice, gasping in horror at what she'd done.

"You did what you had to do." she whispered to herself, staring at the coffered ceiling. "But this nightmare is far from over."

Exhaustion was taking its toll. Biting her lip, she forced herself to think clearly. There was no way she was going to stay here, just waiting to be handed off to Bastion Thunderballs like some twisted prize. Escape was her only option. A crooked smile tugged at her lips. At least I'm clean and away from Rax and his asshole miscreants.

A rap sounded and the door swung open. The young woman from earlier stepped in, balancing a tray laden with a steaming hot breakfast—a small vase cradled a single, flawless red rose. Elara was dressed in a simple, button-down dress, floppy cotton hat, and a maid's apron. Was that pity she saw in the housemaid's eyes?

"I brought you some food and drink," Elara said softly.

Sonya nodded, her throat too tight to form words. Her head was a whirl of conflicting emotions.

The maid placed the tray on a small table in the corner. "You must be thrilled," she said, her smile warm. "It's like a dream come true for you, isn't it? Such a fortunate moment." She curtseyed, adding, "If you need anything, don't hesitate to ask."

Sonya watched Elara leave, the door closing with a soft click. The air was heavy with the scent of the awaiting meal—a tantalizing counterpoint to the knot of fear twisting in her stomach. Taking a seat, a plate of scrambled eggs, bacon, and blueberry pancakes lay in front of her. How long had it been since she'd had a real meal? The aroma was enough to make her mouth water, but the fear constricting her chest gave her pause.

Sonya finally started to eat, each bite a desperate attempt to stave off the emptiness gnawing at her insides. As her hunger began to curb, she started to feel a little better, stronger. A flicker of hope swept over her, as fragile as a candle flame in a hurricane, whispered that her uncle was searching for her at this very moment.

Later that evening, Sonya lay on the bed, back staring at the ceiling. Sleep eluded her, her mind too full of worries and fears.

The hours dragged, each one more suffocating than the last. What are they waiting for? She'd tried the door, multiple times. It was locked every time. Desperation clawed at her insides, whispering that *things were only going to get worse.*

Sonya bolted up as the door to her room swung open.

"A simple knock would be nice before barging in like that," she barked, catching her breath.

An elderly, stooped man in a dark suit filled the threshold, the quintessential butler, sans the erect posture.

"Apologies... rise and shine, my lady. My name is Rupal," the butler said in an old man's voice. "Up, up... Elara will be here momentarily to help you get dressed. It's time to meet your groom."

She sat up and blinked. Muted sunshine was coming in through the sheer curtains. She replayed old Rupal's words through her still sleep-muddled mind— *It's time to meet your groom.*

Panic seized Sonya, as she threw off the covers, leaping out of bed.

Rupal was already leaving, and Elara was now bustling in, clutching the kind of long, zippered garment bag Sonya had only seen in photos. Another maid followed, balancing a tower of boxes so high it, no doubt, obscured her vision. Sonya blinked at the spotless white boxes, each one adorned with a pale, pink ribbon and bow.

"What is all this?" She stared, her breath catching, unexpected interest getting the best of her. With curiosity, she eyed the ornate packages, their presentation promising hidden gifts. She had to remind herself, she had been kidnapped, abducted, and nearly molested on multiple occasions. She wasn't *Pretty Fucking Woman*—she was a hostage.

There again, there's no way I'm spending the day in this

nightgown. Might as well take a peek at what they've brought me.

ONE HOUR LATER SONYA WAS STARING BACK at herself in the room's full-length mirror.

Chapter 31

Sonya felt like she was in a dream as she descended the grand staircase. Draped in a stunning gown of emerald-green silk that set off her dark hair and made her eyes sparkle, she could almost forget the terror of the past few days. Lace gloves covered her arms, just past the elbows, and a delicate, gold pendant hung around her neck, catching the light of the chandeliers. Her hair had been styled in soft waves and pinned back with jeweled combs for a truly regal effect.

Rax was gone, hopefully never to return. It was nice to have old Rupal, the reliably dutiful butler, now by her side. He walked with her slowly, his gentleness almost unsettling given her recent traumas.

"Everyone will be so delighted to see you," Rupal said, smiling kindly as they approached the courtyard. "You have quite the admirable heritage, Miss Winters."

She had to clench her jaw tight to remind herself that none of this was real. These people treated her like a princess, but she knew what awaited her. She fought to keep that reality in the forefront of her mind as she stepped into the courtyard.

A large crowd had gathered, their eyes full of curiosity and admiration, the judgment from earlier now somewhat muted. She felt their gaze on her like the weight of an anchor, dragging her resolve into the depths, compelling her to muster every shred of willpower to stay afloat.

At the far end of the courtyard stood a tall, dark-haired figure with chiseled features. His expression, instead of being menacing as she had feared, projected a curious politeness. Bastion Thunderballs was, much to her astonishment, more than handsome—he was mesmerizing. Standing tall, he exuded authority, a sleek data tablet tucked beneath one arm. His presence, so different from the brutish pirate she had pictured, left her momentarily speechless. She watched as he periodically checked his tablet as if he was engaged in an ongoing conversation.

Seeing her approach, Bastion met her with a smile, his eyes warm and sincere. "Good morning, Sonya. I hope you had a comfortable night's sleep."

The contrast between his courteous manner and her expectations caught her off guard. She had expected cruelty, not chivalry. She quickly masked her surprise with her usual snarky insolence. "It was okay, I guess. The blankets didn't feel like sandpaper, so there's that."

Bastion's smile widened, but he didn't rise to her bait.

"You're Briggan by blood, Sonya. With that, you are no wilting flower."

A wilting flower, what does that even mean?

"And that's something to be proud of," he said, holding her gaze with an unnerving intensity.

"Proud?" Sonya repeated, eyes blazing as she struggled to hold back her anger. "Proud of what? My father's betrayal? Being kidnapped and shoved into a marriage I want no part of?"

Bastion kept his face unreadable. "Our clans may differ,

Sonya. But strength and endurance define our heritage. Over time, you'll see this pact will benefit us both."

Even as she listened, Sonya felt the need to remind herself of her true circumstances. Everything here was designed to lull her into compliance. She couldn't afford to forget that. She bit her tongue, saving her retort, choosing instead to observe him.

Bastion gestured kindly to the path in front of them, and the crowd parted as he led her through the mansion once more, his grip gentle yet firm on her arm. As they continued down the hallway, Sonya found herself fascinated by the honey-colored walls; they appeared to have a leather texture, tempting her to stop and touch them—each detail a reminder of the gilded, but all too real cage she was occupying here.

As they walked side-by-side, they found themselves trailing behind Rupal, the hobbling, hunch-backed butler, who moved with a painstakingly slow gait. Bastion made an exasperated expression, rolling his eyes. Behind Rupal's back, he gave exaggerated two-handed shooing motions, silently urging the butler to pick up the pace. Sonya found the antics only slightly amusing but kept her expression neutral, not wanting to encourage him.

In a burst of playfulness, Bastion began to exaggerate his walking, mimicking Rupal's stooped posture and slow shuffling. He hunched his back and took tiny, deliberate steps, keeping his face comically serious. Sonya tried to suppress a grin as she watched him.

Eventually, Rupal detoured left down another corridor, and Bastion straightened up, resuming a normal walk, still straight-faced. He quickly stole a look at his device, his fingers tapping a ten-digit security code before slipping it back under his arm.

Sonya's eyes narrowed, her mind cataloging the code with the speed and precision of a seasoned hacker. *So, is that where you keep all your secrets, Bastion Thunderballs?*

When they reached a small, elegant room, Sonya was thankful for the moment's respite. She sank onto a velvet sofa, trying to pull herself together while Bastion stood by, watching her with those disarming eyes.

Sonya's gaze wandered, seeking an escape from the unease curling through her. She took in the French doors that led to a Juliet balcony, the giant family portraits in gold leaf frames, and a meticulously polished grand piano off in one corner. The aesthetic screamed luxury—a luxury that suffocated her. The mansion's extravagant splendor, though captivating, wrapped tighter around her, deepening the prison-like grip on her psyche.

"May I sit next to you?" Bastion asked, his voice soft.

Sonya shrugged, trying to appear indifferent. "Not my house, do what you want." Bastion took a seat beside her, the proximity both comforting and unnerving.

He studied her for a moment before speaking. "I know this is all very strange for you. But I want to get to know you, Sonya."

She rolled her eyes, unable to stop herself. "What's there to know? I'm a pirate's daughter forced into a fancy dress."

Bastion chuckled, a warm sound that made her insides twist. "There's more to you than that, I'm sure."

She crossed her arms, feeling defensive. "Why do you care? This is all just some political move, right?"

"Maybe it started that way," he admitted, his gaze never leaving her. "But I'm genuinely curious about you. You're different from anyone I've ever met."

"Different how?" she challenged, unable to hide her skepticism.

"You're strong, independent, and incredibly resilient," he said without hesitation. "You've been through so much, yet you're still standing."

Sonya felt a pang of something she couldn't quite identify—pride, perhaps? She quickly masked it with more snark. "Yeah, well, you try growing up with rogue pirates and U.S. Space Navy geeks, see how you turn out."

"Well, you're home now. Back with the people you're meant to be with."

"Home?" She scoffed. "This is just another cage, Bastion. A pretty one, but a cage nonetheless."

He looked at her with such intensity that she almost believed he cared. "I don't want you to feel like a prisoner, Sonya. I want you to have a choice in all of this."

She laughed bitterly. "Choice? What choice do I have?"

"You have more power than you think," he said quietly. "You just have to see it."

Sonya felt her resolve wavering, her snarky exterior cracking. She hated that he was getting to her, hated that she was starting to believe him. "Why are you doing this?"

"Because I believe we can build something better together," he replied, his sincerity shining through. "I know it's hard to trust me, but I want to earn that trust."

She shook her head, feeling overwhelmed. "That's all bullshit and you know it."

"No... it's not," he said gently.

She locked eyes with him, probing for deceit. Instead, she found concern and warmth. Her yearning to believe him frightened her. Seated this close, their faces nearly touching, she noticed the freckles dusting his cheeks, the slight gap between his front teeth, and the adorable dimples that surfaced when he smiled. His youthful appearance seemed at odds with his confidence.

Sonya struggled for words, her mind racing. She needed to stall, though she had no idea why. "Just... give me some time," she murmured, barely audibly.

"Of course," Bastion agreed, a soft smile on his lips. "Take all the time you need."

As he stood to leave, he said, "I have some... um... unexpected loose ends to deal with right now. Please wait for me. There's so much to discuss. Learn about one another."

Sonya felt a pang of loneliness. She didn't want to be alone with her thoughts, didn't want to face the conflicting emotions swirling inside her. "Wait," she called out, surprising herself.

Bastion turned back, his expression hopeful. "Yes?"

She hesitated, unsure of what to say. "Can you... stay a little longer?"

His smile widened, and he returned to sit beside her. "Of course."

They sat in silence for a while, the tension slowly easing. Sonya hated that she felt a sense of peace with him there, hated that she was starting to let her guard down. But for now, she allowed herself to enjoy the moment, knowing that she would have to face her inner turmoil eventually.

Bastion's presence was a double-edged sword—both comforting and threatening. But as she sat there, feeling his warmth beside her, Sonya realized that maybe, just maybe, she didn't have to face everything alone. And that thought, as terrifying as it was, gave her a small glimmer of hope.

FOR THE NEXT HALF HOUR, HE PROBED about her experiences aboard U.S. Space Navy warships, curious about life without a stable, stationary home. She fired back, asking about life in the shadow of one of history's most infamous pirates. Was he the heir apparent, primed to take over the plundering of the cosmos? Their conversation flowed naturally, candid and unfiltered, neither holding back.

Listening to Bastion's calm ramblings, she found herself

questioning whether he could be different from the monster she had imagined. No. She couldn't afford to be deceived. She needed to stay wary of the reality. Yet, despite her resolve, she was drawn into his words, captivated by his voice.

She suddenly sat up straight, "Wait. What did you just say? Say that again."

Looking perplexed, he said, "The buried treasure of the Desolate Blue star system—"

"How do you even know about that!" she said, her voice rising in volume to the point others nearby glanced their way.

Her thoughts spiraled. After all these years, her father's story had resurfaced twice—first with Pristy, and now again. A childhood story, a fable she never completely believed, one her father would tell her night after night. This was only his and her legacy, he'd tell her: a hidden alien treasure of unfathomable riches, buried within a star system with a dying sun and four cold and lifeless worlds. A star system her father had laid claim to—a star system nobody in their right mind would ever desire. Desolate Blue was a name only two people knew about, her and her father. She shook her head, grappling with disbelief. She'd thought that had been little more than an old pirate's bedtime story. But now...

And then, a dark, indistinguishable figure appeared, interrupting their moment. It happened in the blink of an eye. Sonya opened her mouth to ask another question, but Bastion was already being whisked away. She needed answers, her thoughts racing as she watched him disappear down the long hallway.

Her eyes fell to the spot where just moments before Bastion had sat, in his place now lay the data tablet he'd inadvertently left behind.

Without a second thought, she snatched it up and punched in the memorized security code, her heart pounding in anticipation.

The tablet's display flickered to life, granting her access to a trove of documents and files. Sonya's eyes scanned the information with the rapid voracity of a speed reader.

The first document that caught her eye was an Intergalactic Property Deed—her father, Land Quintos, Galvin's half-brother, had filed an official claim for ownership of an entire star system, labeled only as **Desolate Blue**.

Alongside the property deed, Sonya found a separate document—the purchase of a highly specialized *Extraction Crawler*, a massive mining vehicle designed specifically for extracting one very specific gemstone—a gemstone that wasn't listed.

She accessed another file, revealing what looked like a secret correspondence, a letter. It was from an administrator, Rutledge Primwell, at the Frontier Registry.

What the hell is that?

She read on. Apparently, her father's submitted official records had caught Primwell's attention—subsequently, this correspondence had been sent to someone high up within the Pylor pirate clan. The records were dated ten years ago when she had been just seven. The administrator had dug deeper into Land's property and equipment claims within the Desolate Blue Star System—the possibility for hidden riches, quickly came to light.

Sonya opened another file and then another. This document provided more insight into that Extraction Crawler thing —apparently, it was designed specifically for harvesting the valuable chrysoberyl gemstone, also known as Alexandrite.

Sonya's mind raced, putting the pieces together. *If my father purchased this vehicle, then there must be a hefty deposit of Alexandrite on one of those desolate planets. Yeah, this would have been more than enough to pique the interest of the pirate clans, particularly the ambitious Cardinal Thunderballs of the Pylor clan, who was very much alive at that time.*

Sonya's grip tightened on the tablet as she scrolled through more files, her father's name appearing again and again. Landers Winters. She shook her head, struggling to reconcile this information with the stories she'd been told.

Further down, she discovered the details of the arranged marriage: *As per the arrangement, Sonya Winters will marry Bastion Thunderballs*. But why? She felt her stomach twist as she read the terms.

Land Winters—his secret treasure now no longer a secret—had made a desperate deal with Cardinal Thunderballs. The truth was here, staring her in the face... just before his death, Land had agreed to an arranged marriage between Sonya and Bastion.

But there was one crucial condition—Land would only hand over the specific coordinates and the location of the Alexandrite-rich planet within the four-world Desolate Blue system—information that no one else knew yet—if his daughter Sonya was made an equal beneficiary of the riches. This agreement had been formally entered into the official pirate records, binding Sonya's fate to the Pylor clan.

I was just a child. Why would he do this?

"My father might as well have sold me," Sonya muttered, vision blurring as tears threatened to spill down her cheeks. She'd dismissed the tales of Desolate Blue as mere fables—or at least doubted them—that is... until now.

In that moment, as the pieces had begun to fall into place, Sonya felt an overwhelming need to get away from all these people. She bolted to her feet, her legs moving before her mind caught up. She sprinted blindly, eyes scanning for the way out. Every few paces, the silk gown tangled around her legs. "Shit!" she cursed. High heels—torturous instruments, not elegant footwear—had to go. She kicked off one, then the other, and then grabbed the hem of her gown. She glanced back. Two security guards closed in, their steps steady and resolute, an odd contrast to her frantic dash.

Panicked thoughts tumbled over each other as she charged forward, every pair of eyes in the room seemingly fixed on her. Navigating this opulent maze felt impossible. The countless chambers and hallways outnumbered those on any dreadnought she knew. Her dress tangled at her ankles again, slowing her down. *This world isn't mine. These people aren't my own.*

Navigating through a sea of shimmering gowns and tailored suits, Sonya's gaze fell upon a knight's polished armor standing lifeless and empty, within an alcove. A metal gauntlet, fingers wrapped tight around a ginormous broadsword's hilt. No time to think, only act, she lunged, pulled, and yanked at the weapon, but it wouldn't budge. Struggling now, she was frantic; it was wedged into the knight's grasp. Sonya fought as if defying its ghost.

"Let go, you overgrown fuckhead!" And with a final grunt, she wrenched the blade free. Cumbersome and beyond heavy, it was a far cry from her favored tagger pistol. Her arms trembled under its weight, the mighty sword reduced to an unwieldy burden in her unsteady grip. Her mind raced. *They want to take what was my father's—what's ours!*

The guests recoiled in shock as she strode forward, flailing the menacing blade, the edge of the steel wavering in the air. Whispers and shouts mingled, painting Sonya as a madwoman, a spectacle to be feared and pitied all at once.

"Move!" she barked at the wide-eyed elderly woman obstructing her escape route. A burst of nervous laughter erupted from her—a wild, almost manic sound, matching the absurdity of the situation. The imminent threat of the security goons loomed, closing in fast.

Then, Sonya found herself right where she needed to be—

staring at the mansion's imposing front door, her escape route to freedom.

Despite her trembling stance, with the sword now poised as much for offense as for her own balancing act, the door swung open smoothly at Bastion's relaxed turn of the knob. He stepped aside, revealing the yawning expanse beyond. "But before you go... know that the shuttle you arrived in is long gone. There is nowhere to run off to, especially without shoes."

Bastion smiled.

The revelations hit her with a cold clarity. *No place for me to go... the shuttle is gone...* the thoughts danced cruelly around her.

She lowered the precarious sword just an inch as confusion clouded her mind, arm muscles screaming in protest. Bastion watched her with an air of bemusement, gauging her next move.

The sword, guided more by Sonya's hesitation than intent, drifted until its point met Bastion's chest.

He leaned in, steel whispering against his shirt. "If it's my end you seek, Sonya, so be it... your choice." His words were gentle yet charged with a dark edge... disarming calm and unmistakable Pylor brutality. For the first time, she caught a glimpse of the man behind the mask.

Chapter 32

Nylor-5 Upper Atmosphere
Arrow Fighter

Captain Galvin Quintos

I was on a straight vector toward the shipyard. Listening to the open channel, the battle chatter between Strickland and the Marines, it was more than apparent that I might be arriving a day late and a dollar short.

The 100 Symbio 4.0s were being obliterated at an astounding rate, and Derrota, with his new-fangled Quansporter, was unable to replace the fallen fast enough. The same went for Max and his Marines, with their NEOGENE genetic enhancements. Sure, they were warriors elevated to astounding levels of battle competencies, but they were being taken out almost as fast as the Symbios. One more thing struck me as I made my way through the Krygian atmosphere. Each quansport regeneration seemed to exacerbate personality shifts, hinting at what? Psychological disorders? I knew these people, had worked alongside them for years. This wasn't normal. My thoughts flashed to Pristy, her internal psychological struggles with being brought back to life from some quantum-stored echo, that should have been enough of a warning. I forced myself back to the present.

The open comms echoed with unsettling anger and viciousness. I was instantly on edge.

Commander Strickland: We can't hold this position—fallback, fallback!

Derrota: I'm attempting to bring more Symbios back online... but the Quansporter buffer is bottlenecking! The system is overwhelmed, simple as that.

Dr. Tangerie: We wouldn't be in this mess if you'd stabilized the goddamn neural interfaces, Stephan! This isn't on me!

Then Wanda's voice pierced through the mix, ragged and angry.

Wanda: Come on, bugs. You want a piece of me? You think you... fucking insects, are up to it, huh? Die, motherfuckers, die! die! die!"

What followed was gibberish, incomprehensible. She wasn't making sense, her words blending into growls as she battled what I assumed were several Krygians, simultaneously.

Then came Grip, sounding utterly worn out, yet disturbingly relentless.

Grip: Kill, kill, kill... kill, kill, kill...

He continued the chant, his words mechanical, an eerie mantra as he battled his own attackers.

I grimaced, adjusting my course. Their voices carried a mix of viciousness and downright madness. Realizing the razor-thin line between survival and catastrophe, I pushed my Arrow harder, desperate to reach them before everything unraveled at the shipyard.

One question haunted me: would these psychological repercussions be permanent, even after they returned to their human forms? And why hadn't Tangerie foreseen this? The Marines had been treated like lab rats who might be paying with lifelong disabilities. The Doctor's overconfidence and arrogance were a problem, one more thing I'd be dealing with.

On the horizon of Nylor-5, I saw rising, billowing black smoke. Distant explosions—flashes of yellow and amber light flickering like tiny fireflies within the haze-covered shipyard.

> **Captain Quintos:** I'll be making a pass overhead in ten seconds, Commander. Any highest priority targets you want me dealing with first? Over.
>
> **Commander Strickland:** Shipyard's power station. The adjacent military base... after that, take your pick. Over.
>
> **Captain Quintos:** Understood. Any intel on potential Krygian reinforcements from their homeworld, Tavor? Over.
>
> **Commander Strickland:** Negative, but we can't rule it out. Tavor is only about 4 light-hours away. We need to move fast. Over."

The Arrow's aft thruster roared as I propelled the fighter toward the Nylor-5 shipyard. I kept my gaze locked on the target data streaming across my HUD. A sea of columns and scaffolding unfurled below, an expanse of twisted, alien architecture. Smoke and fire bled upward from the battleground, the thick haze a makeshift curtain between my Arrow and a sky keeping secrets below.

Captain Quintos: Making the pass now, Strickland. Power station first.

I gripped the control stick, feeling every vibration and shudder of the ship echoing through my bones. Arrows are sleek, nimble birds of war, bristling with weaponry, right now I favored the rail cannon. It wasn't unlimited, but it had the kind of punch you needed to break a Nylor-5 power station into a molten heap of regrets.

The Marines' desperate voices still echoed in my helmet, unnatural growls of determination and adrenaline.

Captain Quintos: Ten seconds to target. Over.
Commander Strickland: Understood. Light 'em up. Over.

I began my descent, eyes narrowing, pulse quickening. In the back of my mind, I knew we were racing against time, with the impending threat of Krygian reinforcements from Tavor looming over us. My hands felt steady, practiced. The power station's phosphorescent glow grew incrementally brighter until I could almost smell the superheated air peeling away from the facility's energy shields.

Suddenly, crimson bolts of energy erupted from the ground, filling the sky with trails of searing light.

Captain Quintos: No one mentioned there'd be incoming fire!

The controls were wrenched from my grasp. The Arrow

dipped and swiveled as if possessed. NELLA's cold voice chimed in, calm and disinterested...

Engaging evasive maneuvers, Captain.

The evasive pattern sent us barrel-rolling to avoid the plasma bolts, my stomach twisting with every spiraling turn. Within another blink, I took back the controls, fingers itching along the weapon triggers.

Captain Quintos: Maybe next time you give me a heads-up.

NELLA replied with an acknowledging *ping*.

Captain Quintos: Taking the shot. Over.

The Arrow lined up with the power station. *Come on, make this count.* The rail cannon hummed as it pivoted for target lock. I fired and with a heart-stopping jolt, violent vibrations coursing through my hands. White-hot rail spikes rocketed through the air, striking the power plant right on target—a perfect shot. The power station erupted into an explosive display of fire and debris.

Commander Strickland: Good shot, but don't get cocky, Captain. Over.
Captain Quintos: Copy that. Putting eyes on the next target. Over.

Adjusting my trajectory, I zeroed in on the adjacent military base. Krygian forces swarmed like ants at a picnic, undeterred by the unfolding chaos.

A barrage of plasma fire greeted me as I made my approach. "Damn!" I veered off once, then a second time, swearing again under my breath. Gritting my teeth, I prepared for another run. Their defenses were formidable, but so was my resolve.

The Arrow's rail cannon fired again, straight into the heart of the base. Another brilliant explosion followed, a blast so powerful it swallowed every other sound.

Hardy: Oh, now you're just showing off.

I chuckled, the ChronoBot's jab, a reminder I wasn't alone. Then NELLA chimed in...

Captain, rail spike munitions
have been depleted.

Captain Quintos: No problem. Switching to Phazon Pulsar fire. I'll need the accuracy anyway.

The Phazon cannon was less spectacular, more surgical. Fine by me; I needed precision for these close-quarter runs. I saw them down there—the Krygians... like scattering cockroaches. I gasped seeing the disparity in numbers between friend and foe. It was time to go to work.

Back and forth, I made one strafing run after another, my trigger finger working overtime. My Arrow was being hit—and hit often—but her shields were somehow holding. In the process, I was effectively punching holes into their ground forces, ensuring none of those bugs had a free pass to maneuver. Even as I focused on the immediate threats, the specter of

Krygian reinforcements from Tavor loomed large. We had to finish this before they arrived.

OVER THE COURSE OF AN HOUR, THE systematic strikes started showing results. The lack of enemy reinforcements from the obliterated military base became increasingly obvious.

> **Derrota:** Quansport regenerations stabilized. Excellent work, Galvin.

It wasn't long before I heard the cheers, the whoops of an imminent conquest filtering through from ground comms— Marines reveling in their triumph in their efforts toward victory. And then—

> **Grimes:** Captain, I've been trying to reach you. Have you been following what's happening on the far east quadrant of the shipyard? Over.
> **Captain Quintos:** Been a bit distracted. How about a SitRep, Mr. Grimes?
> **Grimes:** Uh, it's about *Oblivion*, Sir. Over.

My stomach dropped. *Now what's going on?*

> **Grimes:** Her drives are powering up. She's on the verge of heading into space! Over.

Blood surged through my veins like molten lava. *Shit-shit-shit! Oblivion* couldn't be allowed to escape, not after everything we'd fought for here. Sure, Strickland and the Marines had their battle to fight, but the bigger fight, hell, the whole fucking point of us being here, was that damn ship! My grip tightened on the controls; the Arrow bucked like a horse raring for another race.

Captain Quintos: Roger that, Mr. Grimes. Be ready to pursue. Stephan, I need you to quansport me out of this Arrow and onto *Ike's* bridge. And bring the team up from the surface. Like right now. Over.

Chapter 33

I materialized within the Captain's Mount, the air crackling with energy from the precision quansport that delivered me there. Derrota, or more likely NELLA, had outdone themselves, my hands instinctively finding the controls on the armrests.

The bridgecrew didn't seem phased by my sudden appearance. The familiar faces glanced my way, awaiting orders. Except one. Akari was conspicuously absent—I panicked, my mind flashing to her Arrow being struck by multiple Krygian plasma bolts... then I remembered she was now safe and snug within a regrow pod in HealthBay.

"*Oblivion* is just now leaving Nylor-5's atmosphere and picking up speed, Captain," Grimes said.

"Stay on her!" I barked, eyes flicking over readouts and the primary halo display. *Oblivion* loomed large at the center of it all, the extinction-class titan growing smaller by the second as it picked up speed.

Ensign Blair Paxton looked frazzled, her fingers darting nervously over Tactical's controls. "There's a couple of Krygian fighters coming up from Nylor-5. They don't see us."

Experience lent me a quick judgment—the young Ensign wouldn't be ready to handle what was coming.

"*Oblivion* still accelerating," she reported, her voice almost trembling. "God, she's fast."

I shouted over the din. "NELLA, I want Hardy quansported here within five seconds!"

The ChronoBot materialized—blocky sections forming a cohesive whole. Metallic hands raised mid-task, he glanced around. "Well, this is awkward. I meant to hit the button for Men's Wear," he commented, his voice oozing with insufferable nonchalance.

"Relieve Paxton at Tactical. Chop-chop, Hardy," I ordered, then turned to the overwhelmed Ensign. "Paxton, I'm sorry, but this is no time for on-the-job training."

Paxton vacated her post with visible relief, walking over to the vacant Science Station... where she settled in.

Hardy stiffly slid into the Tactical seat—I held my breath, hoping it would support his girth.

"Nice view from here," he remarked, eyes scanning the diamond glass canopy.

Grimes cast a worried glance my way. "*Ike* won't be able to keep up once the dreadnought brings her big drives fully online. We're barely keeping pace as it is."

Hardy cut in, "Just wait till they manufacture a wormhole, then we'll really be up a creek without a paddle."

No doubt that was exactly what *Oblivion's* Captain intended to do. "Does anyone know how to stop that dread from manufacturing a wormhole?" I asked, scanning the tense faces around me. "No suggestion's too ridiculous. I'm looking for ideas, people!"

Silence filled the compartment, the only sound the hum of *Ike's* drives laboring to keep pace with the dreadnought. Seconds felt like minutes, the tension building with each passing moment while *Oblivion* gained distance. Then came a voice from my TAC-Band. "I may have an idea, Galvin," came Derrota's tinny-sounding voice.

"Get up here then, Stephan! Better yet, NELLA—"

Before I could complete the sentence, Derrota was already quansporting onto the bridge.

NELLA was on her game.

Derrota, looking startled, looked about the compartment.

"Your idea?" I said, no time for niceties.

"In the moments before a wormhole materializes, there will be a localized region of intense, spacetime, curvature forms, characterized by a significant increase in energy density composed of virtual particles and negative energy states."

"Get to the point, Stephan!"

"These components, derived from quantum fluctuations and vacuum energy, create a Casimir-like effect, stabilizing the wormhole throat and allowing for the manipulation of space-time to connect distant points in the galaxy."

"Stephan!"

"Yes, sorry, NELLA should be able to quansport those initial virtual particles and the negative energy state, as they are just beginning to form."

I looked to Hardy, knowing that he'd be fact-checking that with his inner LuMan. The ChronoBot shrugged. "It's never been done, but yeah, it could work."

Derrota, with a sympathetic smile, gestured to Ensign Blair Paxton. "May I?"

Paxton scrambled from her seat at the Science Station and stood, nervously crossing her arms over her chest, looking like the last one standing in a game of musical chairs.

"We... might have a somewhat bigger problem to deal with," Hardy said.

My eyes went to the halo display. Momentarily speechless, I

managed to order, "Battle stations! NELLA, have crewmembers to their posts!"

Derrota, his concentration with his tapping on his control board, said, "Picking up energy spikes from *Oblivion*..."

But all my attention was on what was quickly approaching Nylor-5, more specifically, approaching *us*.

"I count five warships, Cap," Hardy said, holding up a hand, and then one by one, raising four metal digits, and then a thumb. "Yup, five."

"Is he always like this?" Paxton asked, looking at the robot, a slight tilt to her head.

Derrota nodded but kept doing what he was doing. "*Oblivion* has just initiated the creation of a wormhole!" He sat back and looked at the halo display.

"So... what do we do?" I asked, incredulous.

"It's up to NELLA. We'll just need to wait to see if what I proposed earlier is feasible."

Lieutenant Earl Gray spoke up for the first time since I'd arrived on the bridge. Pointing to the halo display, he said, "What are those?"

Hardy said, "More."

"More?" I repeated. Then I saw them. Two more warships just showed up on the halo display. Hardy had changed the view to *Logistical Mode* whereby all the players were now glowing icons upon a black background. Metadata accompanied each of the red, Krygian assets, and the lone, smaller, green icon which was *USS Ike*.

"We're cloaked, tell me they don't know we're here, Hardy?"

He wobbled his oversized noggin. "They wouldn't have, but someone here on the bridge, and I'm not naming names, has been scanning for quantum energy readings ten kilometers out in front of *Oblivion's* bow. Those scans aren't passive, and they've been noticed. We've been found."

Derrota looked, perplexed... an expression that quickly turned into realization. "Oh my... I'm so sorry."

"Mr. Grimes, be ready to take evasive action."

NELLA, with a cool-as-a-cucumber voice, announced...

Quanslock established. Energy profile disrupted. Initiation of *Oblivion's* wormhole manufacture has been obverted.

"I'm sure they'll try again," I said. "Stay with it, NELLA."

Hardy spun around to face me but said nothing.

"Is there a reason you're looking at me, Hardy?" I asked.

"Captain, this predicament we are in..."

I waited. "Yes?"

"It's a Schrödinger's cat with no box."

Derrota looked up from what he was doing—now interested in what the ChronoBot was saying. "Galvin, he's basically saying that no matter what we try, we have no chance of succeeding."

"I don't believe that," I said, irritated that the robot might be right.

"Oh, I see what he's saying," Ensign Paxton said with a subtle charge of adrenaline... on par with a Jeopardy game contestant. "Not only do we have those seven fast-approaching Krygian warships to deal with, but also that extinction-class dreadnought we've deterred from leaving. And that Schrödinger's cat with no box reference—"

I cut her off before she went off on another tangent. "Yes, I get the reference, Ms. Paxton."

I fixed my gaze on the halo display, aware that every moment of hesitation further eroded our chances of survival. I chewed the inside of my lip.

"Who's on that dreadnought?" I asked.

"Oblivion?" Hardy asked, spinning back to tap at Tactical's console.

I waited.

"Huh... not many. Not many at all. My sensors tell me there are less than two hundred bugs. NELLA says one hundred seventy-five." He did one of his clumsy shrug gestures. "Tomayto tomahto."

My eyes locked onto the crewman seated at Helm.

Grimes squirmed in his seat. "Uh, Captain?" he said.

I kept my gaze fixed on Grimes, my mind racing. "Even when I captained *Oblivion*, it outclassed most vessels from the Pleidian and Thine shipyards—the very architects behind our fleet. If the Krygians have their hands on it now, I'd wager that Gorvian dreadnought's been pushed beyond anything we've encountered."

"Undoubtedly," Hardy commented.

Derrota said, "What's your point, Galvin?"

"My point is... what is my point? My point is, that ship has Zero Entropy Deterrence Shields... ZEDS."

"Yes, uses Spidites, spider-quantum-nanites, to maintain shield integrity," Derrota added. "Self-repairing shields that are second to none."

"Shields that won't allow us to simply quansport an assault team onto that ship," I said.

"You're only making my earlier point," Hardy said. "We're not getting onto that ship. No quansporting and no pulling into *Oblivion's* flight bay without being vaporized by *Oblivion's* Dual Pion Pulsar Beams."

"The point that I am making is this... we have to act and act now. Like this minute."

All eyes were on me now.

"Listen up, I won't be here to repeat myself," I said. "Ensign Paxton, you have one job and that is to ensure that Commander

Strickland has his Ops team ready to deploy within ten minutes."

"Ten minutes... they've only just arrived. They're probably exhausted, battered from combat—"

"No, Ensign they're not. Those versions of themselves were left behind when they quansported back onto *Ike*."

Confusion transitioned to an *Ah-ha* realization. She nodded but thankfully kept her mouth zipped.

"Mr. Grimes, you'll stay at Helm, and your only job will be staying clear of the enemy while keeping relatively close to *Oblivion*. Keep the enemy assets busy, cloak when you have to, dodge and weave, keep those Krygian warships off guard and totally preoccupied. Can you do that?"

"You bet I can, Cap," he said with a crooked smile. "Ready for the challenge."

"Stephan?"

"Yes, Galvin..."

"You will be working with NELLA to do the impossible."

Derrota's smile faltered.

I glanced to the halo display and found what I was looking for. Two red icons that were smaller than all the others. "Pick one of those Krygian fighter craft, your choice, and quansport the two pilots into deep space."

His smile returned, "I think I can do that. You know, NELLA's accuracy has gotten—"

"I'm not done, Stephan. What you'll also be doing, as simultaneously as possible, or as the technology permits, is to quansport two new pilots onboard that same fighter... two out, two in."

The Science Officer looked back at me blank-faced.

"You can do that, right?" I asked.

"I suppose it is possible, but considering the fighter is moving at an incredible rate of speed, and there are a number of variables—"

I looked up and cut him off, "NELLA, can you do what I'm requesting or not?"

Affirmative Captain.

Lieutenant Earl Gray shifted in his seat, "Who is it that's trading places with the bug pilots?"

I stood. "Hardy, up and at 'em; we're taking a little road trip."

"Can we stop at 7-11 for snacks? Red Vines, a couple of Big Gulps—oh, and three-day-old hot dogs spinning on metal rollers!"

"What's 7-11?" Paxton asked.

"Long before your time," Hardy said.

"*Oblivion* is picking up speed," Grimes warned.

It occurred to me that I had no weapon, no combat suit, and no clue as to what I was getting us into.

Derrota must have been reading my mind because he said, "The Krygian pilots... they don't wear helmets, I'm assuming their cockpits are pressurized with a breathable atmosphere."

I looked to Hardy. Whatever weaponry I was lacking, he'd more than make up for.

I turned back to my Science Officer. "Stephan, can you do this? Can you and NELLA get us onto one of those fighters and do it, like right now, this instant?"

Without hesitation, he nodded.

"NELLA, you know what to do."

Her calm, perhaps too calm, voice filled the bridge...

Two Krygian pilots have been quansported into the void. If you are ready, Captain, Hardy, I will—

"Just do it, NELLA!" I commanded.

Chapter 34

Haven
Admiral Arlington McMasters' Mansion

Sonya Winters

S onya tossed and turned in her plush bed, the luxurious sheets tangling around her legs. She stared up at the decorative leaves etched into the ridges of the coffered ceiling, feeling the weight of the opulent room pressing down on her. As much as she tried to clear her mind, thoughts of Bastion Thunderballs swirled relentlessly.

He certainly didn't seem to be the tyrant pirate his father had been. When she first met him, his courteous manner and warm smile had taken her by surprise, leaving her conflicted and uncertain.

But, the truth was, she was still reeling from his comments just hours earlier... *the shuttle you arrived in is long gone. There is nowhere to run.* Her initial instincts in that moment told her that Bastion was no different than his father, but what if she was wrong? She was in a heightened state of anxiety, after all.

The teenager squeezed her eyes shut, trying to banish his image from her thoughts. But the harder she tried, the more vivid the memories became—his disarming compliments, the way he spoke of her Briggan heritage, and the genuine way he seemed to listen to her. Her heart pounded in her chest, betraying her resolve to remain indifferent. She had grown up quickly on one warship or another, facing dangers and challenges that made her strong and resilient. Yet, in matters of the heart, she felt a nagging naïveté that left her off-balance.

A gentle knock at her door interrupted her turmoil. She sat up, heart racing. "Who's there?" she called softly, her voice barely above a whisper.

"It's me, Bastion," came the reply, equally hushed.

Curiosity piqued, she slipped out of bed and padded across the room, her nightgown brushing against her legs. She cracked open the door, spotting Bastion in jeans and a t-shirt, an older model TAC-Band strapped to his wrist. He appeared younger, more approachable than the figure she had encountered earlier. He pressed a finger to his lips, signaling silence.

"Do you want to see something amazing?" he whispered.

Sonya hesitated, her mind racing. This was a man she barely knew, yet she couldn't deny the pull of intrigue. Nodding slowly, she consented. She knew she was barefoot and only in her nightgown, but something about his demeanor made her throw caution to the wind.

Without another word, Bastion grabbed her hand and pulled her from the room. She stifled a laugh as they tiptoed down the corridor, the excitement of the moment bubbling up inside her. The mansion was eerily quiet, the opulence around them now cloaked in shadows. They navigated through hallways and down staircases with practiced ease, Bastion leading her with confident, swift movements.

Before she knew it, they were out of the mansion and

sprinting across the back lawn. The cool grass tickled Sonya's feet, and she found herself laughing freely, the sound of her voice mingling with the night air. Bastion's grip on her hand was firm, his warmth comforting against the night's chill.

As they ran, Sonya's thoughts swirled. She couldn't deny the rush of exhilaration she felt, the sense of adventure that Bastion was awakening in her. For so long, her life had been about survival and resilience, but now, in this moment, she allowed herself to embrace a different kind of thrill.

The journey across the lawn seemed endless, yet she wished it would never end. For now, she focused on the feeling of Bastion's hand in hers, the joy of running barefoot under the stars, and the relishing in the unadulterated freedom of it all.

The shadowy outline of a stable came into view as they neared the edge of the lawn. Sonya's breath quickened, exhilaration and anticipation coursing through her body.

Bastion led her inside the wooden structure, shoving the large barn doors apart, his stride confident and sure. The faint, welcoming scent of hay, horses, and leather enveloped them.

Sonya could see the dim glow of lanterns illuminating parts of the stable. Several men stood quietly, their attention fixated on one particular stall. There, a beautiful mare lay on her side, clearly in labor.

Sonya's breath caught in her throat, and she instinctively moved closer, her gaze riveted on the scene. She was mesmerized. The mare's majestic form quivered with effort, her eyes wide but calm. The men around her remained hushed, silent witnesses to the miracle of birth. A sense of awe and a feeling of strange serenity washed over her.

The tension in the stall seemed to break as the newborn colt emerged, trembling and wet, its fragile form a testament to the strength and resilience of life. Without realizing it, Sonya squeezed Bastion's hand, her heart swelling with the beauty of the moment. She glanced at Bastion, only to find him already watching her, a soft smile playing on his lips.

"Beautiful, isn't it?" he whispered, his voice barely audible over the soft murmurs of the men.

Sonya could only nod, her emotions too tangled to form words. In that instant, she felt an unexpected kinship with the young colt—thrust into a world it didn't fully understand.

Sonya couldn't help but notice the way Bastion's eyes had moistened looking at the mare. "Why is this colt's birth so important to you?" she whispered, her curiosity piqued.

Bastion glanced at her, a subtle smile playing on his lips. "Bella, the mare, has a special story. She wasn't always in a place where she was cared for."

Sonya tilted her head slightly, intrigued. "What do you mean?"

"Bella belonged to a breeder in the Darvan quadrant—a truly unscrupulous man," Bastion began, his voice barely audible above the soft sounds of the stable. "She tore her suspensory ligament during a race she shouldn't have been running in. Her owner was furious and planned to send her to the local butcher. Can you believe that? He wanted to make horse steak out of her."

Sonya's eyes widened in disbelief. "That's horrible. How did she end up here?"

Bastion's expression grew serious. "This was several years back, I was younger than you at the time. My crew and I were visiting Selton-Prime, where the breeder's estate was. We watched the whole fiasco. The horse falling, the owner's tirade. We knew we had to act. That night, we donned bandannas and smuggled Bella away. It wasn't just about saving a horse—it was a stand against their abhorrent cruelty."

"You took a huge risk," Sonya whispered, feeling a pang of admiration she hadn't expected.

"We had no choice," Bastion responded, his voice filled with conviction. "We brought her here to the McMasters Estate, where I knew she'd get the care she needed. She healed, and now she's giving birth. This colt is a symbol of strength and new beginnings."

Sonya looked at him, quiet and misty-eyed.

Bastion's eyes met hers, and she could see the depth of emotion within them. "In a strange way, I feel this colt has become part of my family. Bella and her foal deserve my care and protection for as long as they're alive. It's a promise I made when we rescued her."

Sonya's heart wavered, what remained of her defenses, slowly crumbling. "Thank you for sharing that," she said softly, a newfound respect for Bastion blossoming within her.

"I wanted you to know the truth. There's more to me, and to my clan, than you might think," Bastion replied earnestly. "I hope this gives you some insight into who I really am."

Sonya watched the colt struggle to its feet, captivated by the raw energy of life bursting into the world. Her heart pounded, each beat echoing in the silent stable. Bastion stood close, his face bathed in the soft glow from the overhead lighting, illuminating his features and casting gentle shadows across his handsome face. The intensity of the moment pressed them closer, their faces just inches apart.

She met his gaze, her breath catching as she saw something deep within his eyes—vulnerability and warmth. Without warning, he leaned in and kissed her, a gentle, uncertain touch of lips that took her breath away. Time seemed to stretch, the world around them disappearing into a haze of emotion. Sonya felt a passion she had never known, caught up in a moment so pure and unexpected it sent shivers down her spine.

But then, the dim light of Bastion's TAC-Band blinked to life, casting an unsettling glow in the shadowed stable. Sonya's eyes flickered toward it, catching a glimpse of a message flashing on its screen. In an instant, her chest turned to ice, a chill racing down her spine. Her breath caught, previous feelings of tenderness, gone in a heartbeat.

Bastion's grip tightened around her wrist before she could fully grasp the situation. The sweet connection between them snapped, replaced by an unyielding roughness as he yanked her away from their view of the newborn colt. The spellbinding moment they had shared moments ago vanished, leaving her breathless. Panic surged through her as he pulled her forward, her feet struggling to keep pace.

"Stop! Where are you taking me?" she demanded, her voice rising with fear as she resisted, trying to pull her hand free.

But he was stronger, his grip unyielding. The mischievous, kind expression she had found so disarming was gone, replaced by what... anger, hatred? The sudden shift in the situation left her reeling. She fought back tears, her bare feet slipping and sliding on the wet grass as he dragged her along. Each step felt like a betrayal, every tug on her arm a reminder of the cold distance now between them.

That TAC-band message replayed in her mind, an unending loop of dread and uncertainty.

Terminate the girl. Found the father.
Terminate the girl. Found the father.
Terminate the girl. Found the father.
Terminate the girl. Found the father...

Chapter 35

XO Gail Pristy

Pristy paced the narrow confines of the Briggan shuttle, her breaths coming out in frustrated huffs. Filton, the bruised and bloodied pirate, sat defiant and glowering beside the comms board. His split lip and the crimson trickle from his nose told the story of his initial capture and her subsequent persuasive methods. But here, with a tagger pointed squarely at his temple, he continued to hold his ground.

"Do it, asshole!" Pristy said, her voice low and deadly, "and tell them everything is fine."

Filton spat blood on the deck, his eyes full of hate. "Go to hell," he snarled. The two other pirates, bound and gagged near the bulkhead, squirmed but remained silent in their restraints.

Ryder fumbled with the shuttle's comms system, his expression marked by frustration and doubt. "This isn't working," he muttered, shaking his head. He glanced at Pristy, irritation in his eyes. "Look at him, he's made up his mind."

Pristy's patience was also worn thin. They had no other options, and time was running out. She pressed the tagger harder against Filton's skull, her finger itching to pull the trigger. "I'm only going to ask you one more time. Tell your Captain everything is fine and that we need to take the shuttle down to the surface to get a replacement part."

Filton barked a laugh, despite the painful wince it cost him. "You think I'm scared of you?" He shifted his gaze to Ryder. "Or him? I'm not afraid to die."

Pristy's jaw tightened. "That can be arranged."

Ryder stepped forward, sighing heavily. "Let me handle this, Gail." Without warning, he pulled his tagger and fired at one of the bound pirates. The blast reverberated through the compartment as the pirate's face was suddenly eviscerated, turning into a charred and smoldering crater. His bound body now lay lifeless against the bulkhead.

"Oh, hell," Ryder muttered, realizing he'd forgotten to set the tagger back to stun. "Well, that escalated quickly."

Filton's eyes widened in fear, his defiance crumbling in an instant. "Wait! Wait, don't shoot me! I'll do whatever you want," he stammered, his bravado gone. "Just don't do that to me!"

Pristy swallowed back her revulsion, her grip on the tagger tightening. Ryder's rash action had worked, but the cost left a bitter taste in her mouth. She forced herself to focus. They had come too far to falter now.

Filton glanced nervously at Ryder, then at Pristy. "Did you hear me for fuck's sake? I'll say whatever you want," he babbled, eyes pleading. "I'll tell them everything is okay, that we need to take the shuttle down for a goddamned part!"

Pristy nodded, lowering her tagger slightly but keeping it aimed at him. "Go on then... Do it."

Filton turned to the comms board, his hands trembling as he keyed in the frequency for the Briggan destroyer. His voice, though quavering, carried the message they needed.

Filton: Tranquilo. Here with the Hub Gunther folks, yeah, the piece of shit Gunther's drive has crapped out.

Briggan Captain: Not our problem, hurry up and get back here.

Filton bit his lip, clearly exasperated.
Pristy raised her tagger.

Filton: They've offered us 5,000 credits to fix their drive.

Thirty seconds elapsed...

Briggan Captain: Tell them to make it 10,000 and they have a deal.

Pristy rolled her eyes, it didn't matter it wasn't as if they were going to actually pay anything. Annoyed, she nodded to the idiot Filton.

Filton: They've agreed on the price. We'll finish it up in three, maybe four hours. We'll need to take the shuttle down to the surface for a replacement part.

A slight pause, then...

Briggan Captain: What a clusterfuck. Fine. Just get it done.

Ryder cut the connection.

Pristy seized the moment, locking eyes with Filton. "You're going to tell me everything you know about Sonya's situation down there," she demanded, her voice unwavering. "Everything!"

Filton's resolve had crumbled long ago, a torrent of words spilling out... "Once her marriage is complete, her life is ... well it's pretty much over," he confessed, eyes darting nervously between Pristy and Ryder. "They'll toss her aside like garbage, probably send her to one of the whore camps off-world. That's all she'd good for. Uh, to them. I don't think that. God no." He continued to shake his head.

Pristy's stomach churned with rage. She raised the tagger, tempted to end Filton right there. But Ryder's hand on her shoulder stopped her.

"We need him alive for now," Ryder reminded her, his voice steady. "We're not done yet."

Filton sat, looking relieved with the reprieve.

Pristy took a deep breath to steady herself, casting one last look at the bruised and bloodied pirate. "If you try anything, attempt to warn any of your foul friends, you'll end up like him," she warned, gesturing to the dead pirate.

Filton nodded. "I understand. I'll cooperate."

Ryder said, "Give me a few minutes to get the Hub Gunther locked down."

Pristy's voice cut through the tension, "Hurry. Every second matters. We need to reach the surface before anything happens to Sonya, if it hasn't already."

With Ryder at the shuttle's helm, Pristy and the two surviving Briggan pirates made their final descent into New Petite Goave.

Filton, back on comms, reassured ground control and provided the codes for a landing permit.

Ryder glanced to Pristy and pursed his lips.

"What?" she asked

"We're not going to get very far dressed like this. Me, like a U.S. Space Navy officer, and you... still dressed like a harlot."

She looked down at herself and then to Ryder. He was right. "This is all we have. It's not like we have a suitcase full of wardrobe changes."

His eyes flicked to the two bound pirates. Both of which were awake and looking back at them.

"No. No way," she said with a definitive shake of her head.

Ignoring her, Ryder said. "Sorry boys, we need to borrow your clothes."

Chapter 36

Deep Space, Near Nylor-5
Krygian Fighter

Captain Galvin Quintos

NELLA executed my quansport command faster than I'd anticipated. It took a moment for the nausea and vertigo to subside. When I looked out through the Krygian fighter's canopy, I gasped. Just ten feet in front of me, a Krygian pilot thrashed and flailed in the -450 F void. Guilt gnawed at me for abruptly taking his place in the cockpit.

Glancing to my right, I saw Hardy's oversized form sitting comfortably in the parallel cockpit. The ChronoBot looked right at home. At nearly seven feet tall, he fit the Krygian design perfectly. Me, on the other hand... I could barely see over the dashboard.

With a Parisian lilt replacing his usual Boston accent, Hardy said, "Garçon, a booster seat for my tiny friend here, please?"

"Ha ha, very funny," I muttered, tucking my legs beneath me to gain a bit more height.

Off in the distance, I caught sight of *USS Ike*. The Corvette-class warship looked fast and nimble, even stationary in space. I scanned the controls in front of me, but nothing made much sense.

Hardy's voice, back to normal, filled the confined space. "I got this, Cap. Like riding a bicycle—once you piloted one alien insect's spacecraft, you've piloted them all."

I waited.

The subsequent grunts, hemmings, and hawings, were almost funny.

"You have no idea what you're doing over there, do you?"

"Not a clue," Hardy said. "But how complicated can it be?"

I watched as the robot began tapping buttons, flipping levers, and then started futzing with the odd-looking controls array.

"How about I take a swing at the ball," I said.

It took a full ten minutes before I was minimally competent enough to get the fighter moving. It took another few minutes to figure out the equivalent basics of Roll, Pitch, and Yaw.

"We've got company, Cap," Hardy said.

I glanced up in time to see the other Krygian fighter making a B-Line in our direction. *Shit!*

"Please tell me you can speak Krygian, Hardy."

I heard his transmitted voice coming over an open channel: "Breaker one nine, breaker one nine, I've got a smokey on my tail, gumball machine's flashing, the siren's a blaring, over."

"Knock off the jokes, Hardy. Tell that pilot to back off, make something up, use your imagination!"

His voice was now spewing gibberish with a mix of clicks and clucks. The Krygian pilot answered back—the language impossibly complicated—what Hardy had lacked in fighter controls expertise, he'd just made up for with his linguistic skills. The other fighter suddenly veered away, with seconds to spare before the two of us would have been visible to the alien pilots. The alien craft was rocketing back toward the planet's surface.

"What did you tell him?" I asked.

"With some input from LuMan and NELLA, I went through past comms chatter from that fighter. Turns out the senior pilot's dealing with marital issues. I mentioned that word on the street was his wife was, at this very minute, doing the wild thing with his best friend, Glornick."

"Glornick?" I said, glancing at Hardy with a dubious expression. I had no idea how much of what the ChronoBot had just told me was true, but he'd managed to do what I'd asked, which was all that mattered.

"How you doing establishing communications with *Ike*?" I asked.

"Working on it. Two very different comms tech... Ah, okay, that should do it."

I heard Chen's voice...

Chen: Yes, Hardy we read you loud and clear and you don't have to yell. Over.

I cut in...

Quintos: You're now talking to the Captain, Mr. Chen. Tell me our Science Officer, Doctor Tangerie, Commander Strickland, and his team are ready for the next phase of this Operation. Over.

Chen: A little resistance having to go back into action so soon after the Nylor-5 shipyard battle... but yes, Sir, they're all ready. Over.

It occurred to me that if I could see *Ike,* the fast-approaching Krygian warships could also see her.

Quintos: Tell Mr. Grimes it's time *Ike* goes invisible, dampen drive signatures, and cut all comms transmission. Over.

I heard a double-click of an acknowledgment. *USS Ike* suddenly disappeared from view.

A little clumsily, I got the Krygian fighter on a direct trajectory toward *Oblivion,* which seemed to be picking up speed again.

"Hardy, use your linguistics prowess to let that extinction-class dreadnought know we're experiencing engine trouble and need permission to land in its flight bay."

I listened to Hardy and the alien voice from *Oblivion.* Their Krygian exchange grew more heated with each incomprehensible click and cluck.

Hardy looked my way from his cockpit. "All's good, Cap."

"Didn't sound that way to me," I said, accelerating toward the dreadnought.

"Nah, he just wanted to get the skinny on Glornick and Planklon's wife."

I rolled my eyes. *Idiot.*

I flashed back to *Oblivion's* flight bay, recalling its unique layout from when I'd skippered her. There'd been a good many ships in between. Each bay had its quirks, with different entry sequences and landing protocols. I needed to pilot this fighter as if I'd made this same approach many times before.

I honed in on the glowing blue energy barrier of *Oblivion's* flight bay.

Hardy said, "We have final approach clearance, Cap."

I counted on *Oblivion* functioning well below peak capacity, given its bare-bones staff of just under two hundred. A vessel of such scale and intricacy normally demanded several hundred, if not a thousand-plus crew. The hangar likely had minimal personnel.

Damn! Oblivion's artificial intelligence would certainly trigger an alert upon sensing a human and a ChronoBot attempting to slip aboard undetected. I was almost certain her sensors had already identified our existence within this fighter craft. Who... what kind of ship's AI was I dealing with?

Then it hit me, it had been MORROW. I now remembered the AI, and its unique personality—once described as an *abomination* by an earlier commander, a Varapin, Captain Shout Coke. He'd suggested the AI had been significantly modified from its original Gorvian design. I wondered if MORROW was indeed still the artificial intelligence running things behind the scenes of the colossal ship. What I did remember was, MORROW was probably the most unique ship's AI I had ever interacted with. A real smart-ass, opinionated, and difficult to work with.

I slowed our approach, did my best to fly normal... whatever that meant.

"Hardy, have you reached out to the ship's AI?"

"Sure, MORROW and I are old friends."

"I'm serious, Hardy. A lot depends on that ship's computer not spilling the beans as to who we are."

"I dealt with that the nano-second we arrived in this fighter. I may not enjoy an AI with such blatant sarcasm, but I think we've come to an understanding."

"What? Are you saying MORROW may be exhibiting some loyalty to us, over the Krygians?"

"Loyalty would not be the word I go with... I would say MORROW is far more entertained with you playing Captain than the previous inhabitant of your seat. The AI has chosen not to interfere with what we have planned. But he won't be overtly helping us either. In other words, MORROW will be loyal to whoever comes out on top."

"I can live with that," I said. "Okay, here we go, try to make yourself look more bug-like."

I slowed to a mere crawl, coaxing the fighter in through the energy barrier. The bright lights had me blinking as my eyes adjusted. What I saw before me was a ghost town of a flight bay. There were a myriad of different craft, Varapin shuttle craft and several Cyclone Death Fighters, a few Krygian fighters identical to the one I was piloting now, and no less than twenty U.S. Space Navy Arrow fighters. The same Arrows I'd been pressured to leave behind while simultaneously being forced to hand over this one-of-a-kind dreadnought—*Oblivion*—to the Varapin.

What I didn't see was movement. Not even the typically present bay-bot scurrying around or conducting maintenance. I found an open spot between two larger vessels... troop carriers would be my guess.

Hovering, I performed a 180-degree yaw maneuver around our center of mass, fired up the landing thrusters, and set us down on the deck.

I glanced to my right. "Hardy, it's go time. We've got one main objective: take down this ship's shields so Strickland's team can quansport in and seize control. Any chance MORROW will play nice and handle that for us?"

"Nope, MORROW is sticking to his *watch-and-see* stance. With that said, I have scanned the ship's nooks and crannies, and I can tell you, very little about his ship has changed since we called it home. I know precisely where we need to go to bring down the shields while meeting the least amount of resistance."

"Where's that?"

"Second level of Engineering and Propulsion."

Scanning the dash for the canopy release, a loud and recognizable klaxon echoed from above.

"Terrific. So much for going unnoticed," I said.

Chapter 37

The klaxon's wail echoed through *Oblivion's* cavernous flight bay. I cursed under my breath as Hardy and I sprinted from our commandeered Krygian fighter towards the nearest bulkhead. My heart pounded in my chest, adrenaline swelling through my veins.

"So much for the element of surprise," I muttered, pressing my back against the cool metal wall.

Hardy's hulking frame dwarfed mine as he took his position beside me. "Don't worry, Cap. I've got enough firepower for both of us."

As if on cue, his five integrated plasma cannons snapped into place with a series of metallic clicks. The familiar sound sent a chill down my spine—a reminder of the lethal armory of Phazon Pulsars the ChronoBot held at the ready. This wasn't the first time I thanked the powers that be that this battle bot was playing for our side. "You sure there's nowhere closer than the second level of Engineering and Propulsion to take down the shields?"

Hardy nodded. "I'm sure."

His face display flickered with an animated schematic of

Oblivion's layout, our intended course through her passageways and corridors, highlighted in glowing green. "Oh, and we'll need to take the StreamLine lift to save time."

"Lead the way, big guy."

We moved swiftly through the deserted corridors, our footsteps echoing off the metal deck plates. The ship felt eerily familiar yet alien at the same time. Gone were the bustling crewmembers and the hum of human activity. In their place was an unsettling silence, broken only by the persistent blare of the alarm.

As we rounded a corner, we came face-to-face with our first group of Krygian defenders. Five insectoid aliens, each easily seven feet tall, their chitinous exoskeletons gleaming under the harsh overhead lights.

"Get back!" Hardy shouted, shoving me behind him with one massive arm.

His plasma cannons roared to life, filling the corridor with blinding, blue light. The air crackled with energy as super-heated plasma tore through the Krygians' bodies. They fell in a heap of twitching limbs and smoking carapaces.

The acrid smell of burnt chitin filled my nostrils as I surveyed the carnage. "Nice shooting, Tex," I quipped, trying to mask my unease.

I knelt beside one of the fallen aliens, reaching for its weapon—a strange, organic-looking gun that seemed to pulse with an inner light. As I wrapped my fingers around it, I realized with a sinking feeling that the trigger mechanism was completely incompatible with human anatomy.

"Damn it," I growled, tossing the useless gun aside. My eyes fell on one of the Krygian's severed arms, its razor-sharp edge glinting in the light. "Well, beggars can't be choosers."

I hefted the alien limb, surprised by its weight and balance. It felt not unlike a sword in my hand.

"Cap, we've got company!"

Hardy's warning snapped me back to attention.

More Krygians were pouring in from both ends of the corridor, their chittering battle cries filling the air. Hardy's weapons blazed again, cutting down the ones in front of us.

"The StreamLine is just ahead," he shouted over the din of battle. "We need to move!"

I gripped my makeshift weapon tighter and followed Hardy as he plowed through the Krygian ranks. His massive frame provided the perfect cover as we sprinted toward the lift. A stray energy bolt sizzled past my ear, close enough that I could feel the heat on my skin.

We reached the StreamLine doors, and I punched the call button repeatedly. "Come on, come on," I muttered, glancing nervously over my shoulder at the approaching horde.

The doors finally slid open with a soft hiss, and we tumbled inside. Hardy worked the control panel, selecting our destination. As the doors closed, I caught a glimpse of the enraged Krygians, their mandibles clicking furiously.

The lift surged into motion, and I leaned against the wall, catching my breath. "That was too close," I panted.

Hardy's face display flickered with what looked like a grin. "Admit it, Cap. You miss this."

I couldn't help but chuckle. "Like a hole in the head."

The momentary respite was short-lived. As soon as the lift doors opened on the engineering deck, we were met with another wave of resistance. The corridor ahead was a labyrinth of pipes, conduits, and humming machinery—the very heart of *Oblivion's* power systems.

Hardy took point once again, his massive frame filling the narrow passageway. I stayed close behind him, my alien-arm-sword at the ready. The air was thick with the smell of ozone and machine oil, bringing back memories of countless hours spent in this very section of the ship.

WE ENCOUNTERED POCKETS OF KRYGIAN defenders at nearly every junction. Hardy's plasma cannons made short work of most, but their sheer numbers were becoming overwhelming. My arms ached from swinging my improvised weapon, its razor edge slicing through alien exoskeletons with surprising efficiency. Each impact sent shockwaves of pain through my torso, reminding me of the possible broken rib I'd sustained earlier in the fight.

Hardy's once-pristine chrome surface was now a patchwork of craters and scorch marks, confirmation of the ferocity of our battle.

As we fought our way deeper into the engineering section, I couldn't help but marvel at how little had changed. The layout was exactly as I remembered it, each turn and corridor etched into my muscle memory. It was like coming home after a long absence, only to find squatters had taken over.

I winced as a stray plasma bolt sizzled past, searing the side of my head. The acrid smell of burnt hair filled my nostrils, and I could feel the heat radiating from the wound. Shaking off the disorientation, I pressed on, knowing we couldn't afford to slow down.

"We're close," Hardy called out over his shoulder, his friendly Bostonian lilt an odd contrast to this killing machine's devastating capabilities. "The main shield control should be just ahead."

No sooner had the words left his vocal processor than a massive explosion rocked the ship. The deck plates beneath our feet buckled, and I was thrown against a nearby console. Alarms blared, and emergency lights bathed the corridor in an eerie red glow.

"What the hell was that?" I shouted, struggling to regain my footing. Fury coursed through my veins as a terrible thought struck me. "Hardy, tell me *Ike* hasn't started firing on *Oblivion*. They know that would be suicide, right? Even David versus Goliath would be a fairer fight!"

Hardy's sensors whirred as he conducted a quick scan of our surroundings. "Cool your jets, Cap. It's not *Ike*. They're still cloaked and hidden, just like you ordered."

"Then who—"

"It's the Krygians," Hardy cut me off, his voice tinged with surprise. "Several dreadnoughts and battle cruisers, by the looks of it. They must have realized *Oblivion's* been boarded."

I cursed under my breath.

Hardy continued, "They think we've already taken control of the ship. Little do they know... it's just two of us bumbling around in here."

The irony of the situation wasn't lost on me. We'd gone from trying to avoid detection to suddenly appearing far more competent and dangerous than we actually were.

"We need to move faster," I urged, ignoring the pain in my side and the searing pain at the side of my head. "If the Krygians are willing to fire on their own ship, our window of opportunity is rapidly closing."

Chapter 38

Haven
On Approach to New Petite Goave

XO Gail Pristy

Pristy grimaced as she pulled on the smaller pirate's grimy shirt, the stench of body odor, stale tobacco, and cheap alcohol assaulting her nostrils. She fought back a gag reflex, her face contorting in disgust.

"This is revolting," she muttered, adjusting the ill-fitting garment.

Ryder, already dressed in the other pirate's clothes, chuckled from the shuttle's controls. "Come on, Gail. It's not that bad. Adds to our cover, doesn't it?"

Pristy shot him a withering glare. "Easy for you to say. You probably can't even smell yourself."

She pushed and pulled at the oversized clothes, trying to make herself look less like a walking tent. Every movement wafted another wave of the nauseating odor towards her face.

Pristy's mind raced, torn between her revulsion and the urgency of their mission.

"Focus," she told herself sternly. "Sonya needs us."

She replayed the information they'd extracted from their captives. Admiral McMasters' mansion. Well-guarded. Around-the-clock sentries. The enormity of what they were about to attempt was almost enough to forget about her stench.

"We'll be completely outgunned," Pristy muttered, more to herself than to Ryder. "This is insane."

Ryder's voice cut through her spiraling thoughts. "Approaching the town's shitty little landing port. Time to put on our game faces."

Pristy nodded, steeling herself. She moved to stand behind Filton, pressing her confiscated weapon against his back. "Remember, one wrong word and you're dead," she hissed in his ear.

Filton swiped at beads of sweat on his forehead as he swallowed hard. He keyed the comm system with shaking hands.

"Port Control... uh... this is Briggan shuttle two-three-four-four requesting landing clearance," Filton said, his voice surprisingly steady.

There was a moment of crackling silence before a gruff voice responded. "Two-three-four-four, state your business, Briggan."

Pristy dug the barrel of her weapon deeper into Filton's back. He winced but kept his voice level. "Returning with... uh, clothes and stuff, you know, for the Winter's kid."

Ryder spun around, looking incredulous, and mouthed, *clothes and stuff?*

Pristy's returned expression said it all, *what do you expect?*

The seconds stretched like hours as they waited for a response. Pristy's heart hammered in her chest, her finger tense on the trigger.

"Yeah, okay... clearance granted, Briggan shuttle. Proceed to landing pad seven."

Pristy let out a breath she hadn't realized she'd been holding. As Ryder guided the shuttle toward the designated landing pad, she moved to check on their bound and gagged prisoners. Both men, naked except for their dingy undies, glared at her with hatred and fear.

"Sorry, boys," Pristy said, not feeling sorry at all. "Can't have you raising a commotion."

The shuttle touched down with a gentle thud. Pristy exchanged a look with Ryder, seeing the determination she felt mirrored in his eyes.

"Ready?" he asked.

Pristy nodded, her jaw set. "Let's go get our girl."

They exited the shuttle, ensuring the aft hatch was secured. It was late, more like early morning, maybe 2:00 AM local time. The spaceport was quiet, not a soul out and about. That is, except for the armed pirate-looking dude heading their way.

"Oh for fuck's sake," Pristy hissed under her breath.

Ryder gave her a sideways glance. "The Gail Pristy I know doesn't typically swear like a pirate."

"Yeah, well it's called method acting. Also, that Gail Pristy you once knew... she died onboard USS *Washington* over a month ago."

She put on her game face as the guard approached—hyperaware of how out of place she must look.

"Just act like you belong," Ryder muttered under his breath, raising a 'howdy-there' hand and taking a step forward.

The pirate guard stepped into their path, his eyes narrowing as he took in their appearances. "What are you Briggans doing skulking around New Petite Goave at this hour?" His gaze lingered on Pristy, trailing over her from head to toe in a way that made her skin crawl.

Ryder gave a disarming smile. "Just dropping off some essentials for the new bride-to-be. We got caught up in other duties and couldn't make it earlier." He held up a beat-to-shit-looking satchel for the guard to see.

The Pylor pirate snorted in disdain. "Essentials, huh? Funny time of night to be running errands. You Briggans sure know how to pick your hours."

Under the guard's lecherous gaze, Pristy felt a wave of nausea. Before the Pylor could react, she whipped out Filton's knife and pressed it against his throat. "You look me up and down like that one more time and I'll cut off your nuts and feed them back to you," she hissed.

The guard raised his hands, smirking. "Well now, ain't you a feisty one?" He inhaled deeply as if filling his lungs with her scent. "God, I like the way you smell. I'm off shift at 6:00 AM. We should... get to know each other. I gotta tell you, I like my bitches with a little crazy."

Ryder stepped forward, his expression smooth, his voice full of charm, "I can assure you, Genevive here will be waiting. Just do us a solid and call up the sentry manning McMasters' gate to let us in with the girl's stuff."

"Genevive, huh?" he said eyes drifting south to her chest.

Pristy cocked a suggestive eyebrow. "You just better hope what you've got hidden in those trousers can handle my kind of crazy..."

The guard chuckled, eyeing Pristy with a predatory leer as he adjusted his pants provocatively. "One thing. You sure this is cleared with Thunderballs? Bastion's not big on drop-ins. A good way to get yourselves shot."

Pristy and Ryder exchanged a quick look. They now knew for sure the son of Cardinal Thunderballs was, in fact, at the mansion. That was welcome intel.

Captain Ryder turned back to the guard, giving him a hard

look. There was still a whiff of charm in Ryder's voice but now it carried an edge of urgency, "It's all cleared. But if you want, we can make sure Bastion hears you tried to delay his new bride's delivery. Your choice."

The guard's smirk widened, eyes gleaming with amusement. "Alright, alright. I'll make the call. But remember, Genevive..." His eyes bore into Pristy. "... 6:00 AM, don't keep me waiting."

Pristy lowered the knife and forced a confident smile. "You might want to scrounge up a toothbrush, I'm sure someone around here has one."

The guard chuckled, pulling out a comms device. "Gotcha. I'll clear you with the gate. Just don't go wandering off."

As they moved past him, Pristy's stomach twisted with tension. They had gotten one step closer, but the path ahead promised many more obstacles.

They navigated the empty main street, guided by the rough signs leading to Town Center. The gas lanterns' sputtering flames painted New Petite Goave in a nostalgic glow. She thought of Galvin, curious what it would be like to visit a place like this not for a mission, but simply to be together. Could it ever just be a romantic destination for the two of them? She shrugged at the thought, unsure if romance was possible for the woman she had become—this Gail Pristy.

Continuing at a quick pace, the town loomed before them, a bizarre blend of old-world architecture and high-tech add-ons. The Admiral's mansion wasn't hard to spot—towering, it loomed like a monument of lavish excess and ill-gotten wealth.

As they drew closer, Pristy's unease grew. The mansion was indeed heavily guarded, with armed sentries patrolling within the gated exterior, and advanced security systems were clearly visible.

"This is impossible," Pristy whispered, her earlier bravado faltering. "This is never going to work."

Ryder's eyes scanned the perimeter, his expression grim. "We take it one step at a time. Our first step... let's see if your boyfriend back at the landing pad got us the clearance we need."

Pristy nodded, trying to quell the rising panic in her chest. They had come too far to give up now. She'd already let Sonya down once by not protecting her, she'd be counting on her to rectify that. But as she looked at the fortress-like mansion, a cold dread settled in the pit of her stomach.

Chapter 39

Deep Space, Near Nylor-5
Oblivion

Captain Galvin Quintos

T he sound of the alarm klaxon pierced through the cacophony of battle, a constant companion to the chaos erupting around us. Every few moments, *Oblivion* shook, rocked by the incoming Krygian fire. Flashing red lights cast eerie shadows on the bulkheads, creating a surreal, hellish battlefield within these damn corridors. My heart pounded in my chest, each beat reverberating with the weight of the mission ahead and the lives depending on us.

"Cap, sensors detecting multiple combatants up ahead," Hardy announced, his voice blending seamlessly into the din of blaring alarms and distant explosions.

I tightened my hold on the Krygian limb sword, eyes narrowing. "Let's hope they're not rolling out a Sherman tank to greet us."

Turning the corner, the sight that greeted us brought me to an abrupt halt. "You've got to be kidding me."

I breathed hard, staring at the spectacle before us. Instead of the Krygian bugs I'd expected, we faced a swarm of squat, three-foot-tall, three-legged droids. Each clutched an array of primitive weapons—mop handles, metal wrenches... I even spotted a toilet plunger in the mix.

"Stay focused!" I muttered to myself, silencing the creeping dread gnawing at the edges of my mind. "Just what we need, the stink of swampy buckets and toxic cleaning supplies."

Beside me, Hardy was grumbling under his breath, one snide remark after another. The ChronoBot chuckled, a dry, robotic sound that seemed almost human. "Looks like we're off to see the Wizard, Captain," he quipped. "Uppity Munchkins, anyone?"

I laughed despite the tension, the absurdity of the situation momentarily breaking through the grimness. "They're maintenance droids," I shouted over the din, dodging the first swings aimed at my head.

"What was your first clue?" Hardy retorted, his mechanical limbs moving with impressive speed and precision as he engaged the droids.

The corridor became a battlefield, filled with the metallic clang of weapons striking Hardy's chrome exterior and the ring of my blade slicing through droid after droid. Each successful strike brought a brief moment of satisfaction, quickly replaced by the urgency to move forward.

"What's going on with your Phazons?" I asked, noticing Hardy had significantly lessened the use of his energy cannons.

"LuMan's restricting access."

LuMan was Hardy's core factory-embedded operating construct... usually quite reliable. So, this wasn't good. This was unprecedented. This was a fucking disaster in the making.

"Why?" I yelled, just as something hard hit the small of my back—nearly bringing me to my knees.

"I think it's Morrow... jamming up LuMan with a barrage of I/O signaling. Overloading processors, weapons not responding..."

I yelled out, "MORROW! Knock it off! I'm the last person you want to fuck with!"

Hardy grunted, kicking out a 24-shoe-sized foot at a nearby droid. "Think what you said helped... but it's going to be a while before LuMan resets."

"Get back! "I yelled, parrying a mop handle aimed at my ribs.

Oblivion seemed to audibly groan—a grim reminder that time was slipping through our fingers. I needed to get Strickland and his team on board. I needed to retake the ship's bridge. The reverberations of incoming fire felt like an ominous ticking time bomb.

"Hardy!" I called out, slicing through another droid. "You need to get to E&P. I'll hold them off here."

Hardy paused, his faceplate displaying the middle-aged, balding John Hardy, an expression of sheer disbelief that nearly made me laugh again.

"No time to argue. Go!" I yelled, swinging and cutting through another droid, sending its legs skittering across the deck.

"Roger that, Cap," Hardy said reluctantly.

I watched as the ChronoBot headed toward Engineering and Propulsion, several droids fast on his heels. Hardy turned and fired his shoulder cannon—the three droids dropped, hitting the deck, metal upon metal. "Huh, looks like that one's working again."

As he strode away, I felt the weight of our mission settled even more heavily on my shoulders. I knew the only reason I was still standing was because of the Gorvian cocktail Doc Viv had injected me with years earlier. Yeah, it gave me somewhat superhuman strength and stamina, but right now, it felt like it was waning fast.

"Owww!" I yelled as a mop handle cracked against my left kneecap.

I swung my sword with renewed vigor, determined to buy Hardy the time he needed. Lopping the heads off droids in one swift motion had become second nature now, each new strike an act of desperate survival. But despite my best efforts, the swarm seemed endless. For every droid I dismantled, two more took its place. *How many damn mop bots does this ship have?*

I told myself for every second I hold out here, I'm giving Hardy time to do what he needs to do.

A long-handled socket wrench came down on my left shoulder, the pain reverberating all through my arm. I gritted my teeth and continued fighting, my energy draining with each passing moment. The image of maniac kids with sticks whacking a piñata flashed in my mind, and I was the damn piñata.

My Krygian limb blade cut through the metal droids with the ferocity of a storm. Another head *clanked* onto the deck and another droid stepped forward. The onslaught was showing no sign of stopping. My movements were beginning to slow, each strike less effective than the last. Pain, fatigue, dread, while being greatly outnumbered—it was all coming for me like my own Four Horsemen of the Apocalypse.

"Come on, Hardy!" I yelled.

Then there was a lightning bolt of pain, and everything went black.

∼

I awoke in a puddle of my own blood. Well, more of a mixture of drool and blood.

The deck was cold, wet, and sticky on my right cheek. The metallic taste in my mouth confirmed what my tongue had discovered—my upper lip was split wide open. I tried to move, but every muscle in my body screamed in protest. It felt as if I were one massive bruise, an overripe banana left out too long and turned to mush.

With a jolt, I remembered the countless three-legged mop bots. They'd gotten the best of me. Wincing, I felt the back of my head, throbbing as if someone had taken a jackhammer to it. I tensed, expecting another strike from a pipe or a broomstick. But there was nothing. All was quiet. Even the overhead klaxon was silent.

With tremendous effort, I raised my head just enough to look around... dozens of maintenance droids lay scattered in pieces across the deck. Yet, others—miraculously unscathed—harmlessly moved about.

"What the... are they... cleaning?" I muttered, my voice cracking, barely audible.

Deckplates jittered beneath me, as if King Kong himself were striding toward me. I looked to my left and saw Hardy, the ChronoBot, making his way closer. He came to a stop several feet away, his towering frame casting a shadow over me.

"Have a nice nappy?" Hardy's tone was sarcastic, as always. "Looks like the brigade of the Molly Maids got the best of you?"

"What's a Molly Maid?" I slurred, shaking my head and instantly regretting it. "Just tell me you took down *Oblivion's* nullifier shields," my strained voice rasped.

"Just a single section of the shields," Hardy answered, the blue glow of his faceplate thankfully free of any annoying animations. "We're still taking fire from those seven Krygian warships. But it's an opening—enough for Commander Strickland and the Marines to quansport onboard."

"Help... help me up," I groaned, reaching up with a trembling hand. Hardy complied, lifting me to my feet with ease, his metal hands surprisingly gentle.

"They're clearing the ship, starting with the aft quadrant," he said, his voice void of any tension—today was just an ordinary walk in the park.

"I need to get to the bridge," I managed to say. My legs felt like rubber and dizziness threatened to overwhelm me.

Hardy held me upright, his grip firm and steady. "What you need is a few days in HealthBay, Cap," he said, his tone conveying real concern, devoid of mockery.

Ignoring his advice, I steadied myself and began to walk toward the nearest bank of lifts, the dizziness ebbing with each determined step. "We don't have that kind of time, Hardy. Let's move."

Together, we made our way across the wreckage-strewn deck. Maintenance droids continued to clean, their mundane, mechanical whirring a stark contrast to the carnage around them. Every step sent jolts of pain through my body, but I pushed on. The mission wasn't over, and as long as I could stand, I'd see it through.

The auto-hatch parted with a soft hiss, and we entered the lift. My pained breaths were coming in ragged huffs. The bridge awaited, along with a battle I knew was going to be like none other before it.

Chapter 40

Making my way through the gutted corridors of *Oblivion* was a study in shifting tactical priorities. Every new section presented some fresh hell— from small skirmishes with mop bots swinging their makeshift weapons, to full-blown ambushes where the Krygian forces threw everything at us but the spatulas and tongs in their goddamn mess hall. Hardy kept pace at my side, his hulking form serving as both guardian and cannon fodder, soaking up whatever heat came our way.

"Cap, most of the Krygian bugs have moved aft, likely being funneled towards Commander Strickland's Ops team," Hardy said.

Finally, we reached Deck 23—now remembering the sheer size of this major artery within the ship. It felt like stepping into the ribcage of a massive whale, the vaulted overhead arching in massive support struts. Up ahead, no less than fifty Krygian bugs were arranging themselves behind makeshift barricades, energy weapons gleaming. I swore under my breath. Dread settled in, a tangible weight. Not from fear, but from realizing the firepower that would be needed to clear this corridor.

"Hardy, your Phazon Pulsars operational?" My voice was clipped, tense.

The ChronoBot lifted his massive metallic hand halfway up and wobbled it. "Comes and goes."

"Terrific," I muttered, assessing our slim odds. Spurred by desperation, I tapped my TAC-Band and hailed Strickland.

"Go for Strick."

"Can you spare a couple of Marines? I have a bridge to take."

Strickland's reply was a blunt "No," but he continued, "I'll send two anyway. Send to your coordinates?"

"Affirmative," I said and cut the connection.

Within moments, mere feet away from us, two genetically altered beasts quansported in. Their appearances took me by surprise, only now did I recognize them as Ham and Aubrey.

The on-loan-to-the-Marines Petty Officer, now *Sharpshooter,* sashayed toward me. Her transformation had preserved her lithe, sensual figure but augmented her strength markedly. Her eyes glowed with an intense blizzard-blue hue, antennae-like tendrils extending from her temples. Her hands and forearms were threaded with neuronal fibers, endowing them with incredible precision and accuracy. Retractable claws glinted at her fingertips, ready to slice through enemies with surgical precision. She looked at me, a bemused smile pulling at her lips.

"You called, Captain?" she said with an inflection that I wasn't sure I wanted to decipher at this moment. She tossed him a Shredder rifle. "Strickland said you might need this."

I dropped my Krygian limb and caught the big gun.

Ham, next to Aubrey, took the form of *Behemoth*. He, in a much different way, was also a sight to behold. His skin sported zebra-like stripes that gave him an exotic, surreal appearance. However, it was the sheer size and density of his muscle mass that made him terrifying. He looked like a walking sledgehammer, his oversized, bony fists resembling war hammers ready to bring down walls. His cognitive processing had been enhanced, making him a strategic powerhouse, not just a brute.

I locked eyes with Ham, and he gave me a nod, his expression betraying a fierce determination.

Aubrey had fixed her steely, focused gaze toward the bugs at the far end of the corridor. She raised her Shredder and put an eye to the scope. "Yeah, I can take out three, maybe four of them right now." Disconcertingly, she kept one eye on her scope while her other eye swiveled toward me. "Just give the word, Captain."

When I looked to Ham, he returned a nod—he was ready.

Hardy said, "It's time we exterminate these creepy-crawlies once and for all."

"Go ahead, take your shots, Ms. Laramie," I commanded.

Aubrey didn't need to be told twice. She squeezed the trigger, and three rapid-fire energy bolts tore through the stale air. Each bolt found its mark with deadly precision, reducing three Krygian bugs to smoldering heaps in the blink of an eye.

"Nice shot," I managed to mutter before Hardy and Ham surged forward.

They moved like two hulking linebackers tearing through a defensive line—each footfall echoing like the thrum of a broadside cannon. There was no finesse, just raw power and relentless aggression.

I fell in behind them, dragging the heavy Shredder into firing position as Aubrey and I brought up the rear. The weapon felt solid in my hands, the kind of reassuring heft that promises swift justice. Still, I couldn't shake the strange attachment I felt to my Krygian sword, now lying on the deck somewhere behind me.

Within seconds, the corridor erupted into chaos. Green and red plasma bolts crisscrossed through the dense haze, each scorching through the air with a crackling hiss. The smell of ozone burned my nostrils, and the heat was intense, my skin prickling from encompassing white-hot plasma fire.

Hardy bulldozed through the makeshift barricades, his metallic fists punching through steel and flesh with equal ease. Ham wasn't far behind, his bony fists smashing enemies into unrecognizable piles of gore. The sound of their assault was a brutal dose of reality—each punch, each swing, an offering of utter destruction.

Aubrey's shots continued to pierce through the turmoil, her movements fluid and graceful, even amidst the pandemonium. One moment she was in front of me, taking out a Krygian with surgical precision, the next she had my back, diverting a plasma bolt intended for my head. Her antennae tendrils swirled, giving her an otherworldly awareness of the battlefield.

I tried to stay close to Hardy, knowing his massive frame would provide at least some semblance of protection. The chaotic melee and blinding plasma fire made it nearly impossible to stay clear of danger.

And then the unthinkable, at least for me, happened. A blinding light and searing pain exploded in my chest. My eyes widened in shock—time seemed to stretch infinitely. My legs buckled, and the taste of copper filled my mouth as I gasped for air. In that instant, I knew without a doubt—my life had reached its end. I was finished—time to close the curtain.

Chapter 41

Haven
McMasters' Estate

Sonya Winters

Sonya's bare feet slipped and sunk into the clammy, mucky slop, each step like dragging her legs through quicksand. Bastion gripped her arm tighter, his fingers digging into her flesh as he hurried her along through the swampy grounds. Beneath the drooping branches of weeping willows, she struggled to keep up, her thin nightgown plastered against her skin by the oppressive humidity. The stench of decay and rot filled her nostrils, making it hard to breathe.

"Move!" Bastion hissed, his voice barely more than a harsh whisper.

Sonya caught snippets of his conversations with the pirates tromping along in their heavy boots beside them. Words like *treasure, alien*, and then, *Desolate Blue* reached her ears, putting her on heightened alert.

"Why the mad rush?" she taunted, trying to glean some information. "Seems like your little plan's hit a snag, eh?"

Bastion's eyes darted, and the tension in his grip tightened. "Just shut the fuck up, Sonya."

Sweat mingled with the swamp's moisture, trickling down her face and neck. Mosquitos buzzed in her ears; the biting bugs had obviously found her exposed skin irresistibly alluring. But the stings of the little bloodsuckers were the least of her problems right now.

She compelled herself to focus. "The boy pirate not up to playing with the real men?" she needled further.

A sudden cry escaped her lips as a sharp pain bit into her ankle. She stumbled, looking down to see a small, dark shape scurrying away. A gator, an unnaturally large rat, maybe? The swamp no doubt harbored countless threats.

"Shut up!" one of the other pirates hissed, pulling her roughly back on track.

The ground sucked at her feet, the mud thick and unyielding. Her nightgown was a sodden mess, clinging to her body in a way that made her feel exposed and naked under the pirates' leering gazes. Her mind reeled, trying to piece together what this sudden shift in plans meant. Bastion seemed more than just angry; he was scared.

"Your stupid plan... it's crumbling all around you, isn't it?" she pressed, her voice tinged with defiance... and taunting. She narrowed her eyes, studying Bastion's reaction for any flicker of doubt. Dim light from the swamp cast shadows across his face, accentuating the tension in his jaw and the darting of his eyes. His breath came fast and heavy. Sonya's heart pounded in her chest; she needed information, and clearly, she was infuriating the boy pirate—good. Maybe she can coax more from him.

Bastion's face twisted with fear and fury, his eyes darting

around the shadows of the swamp as if the darkness itself threatened him.

The sounds of the marsh grew louder—the croaks of frogs, the buzzing of insects, the rustling of unseen creatures. Sonya gasped, trying to pull away from a long, slithering reptile gliding through the water nearby, a meaty tail swishing and splashing through the muck. "Oh God... I just saw a fucking alligator!"

Bastion glared back at her, "I'm not going to tell you again, keep quiet!"

He growled an order to one of his men, who acknowledged the command with a terse nod. Their continuing conversation was muted, she only picked up the odd word or phrase. Her ears perked up when she caught *Trent*—a name that aroused warning alarms in her mind. *What does he have to do with all this?*

She stumbled, her legs giving out under the strain, sinking to her knees. The thick, black muck enveloped her up to her hips. Thrashing, desperate, she couldn't free herself—escape the clutches of the swamp. Bastion yanked her arm upward. A scream tore from her throat, searing pain shooting through her as her arm nearly dislocated from her shoulder. He pulled her roughly to her feet. Hands gripping her shoulders, he spun her around to face him.

His eyes bore into her like a pair of hot pokers. "Slow us down again, and I'll leave you here for the gators," he threatened, his voice hoarse with panic.

Sonya's anger had already been brewing, her breaths were coming fast now, her nostrils flaring, a volcanic eruption building, the very fires of hell ready to burst open. She had had enough. She was dizzy with rage.

This fucking stops now! Channeling all of her anger—all of her strength—she unleashed the haymaker punch of all haymaker punches, resulting in a clobbering hammer blow to

Bastion's face. She felt her knuckles meet cartilage—his nose shattering with a sickening crunch. He screamed, the loud anguished cry echoing into the darkness. He staggered backward, clasping his nose, blood flowing in a torrent.

"You bitch!" he yelled, no longer worried about being quiet.

His face was a mask of unhinged wrath, wild-eyed and crazed. He grabbed a fistful of her hair, turned, and dragged her along behind him. Unable to stay on her feet, she fell into the bog getting a mouthful of putrid swamp water. Gagging and coughing, she couldn't breathe—when she tried to take in air, her mouth filled with putrid sludge. She gasped, struggling to wipe the muck from her face as he continued pulling her along.

Suddenly, another pirate took hold of her free wrist. Bastion, clutching his bloodied nose, released his grip on her, handing her off like a too-hot-to-handle baton in a relay race.

Desperation clawed at her as she used her free hand to wipe at her eyes. Her fingers brushed against something puffy and worm-like on her cheek—a leech. She shrieked, prying the thing off with clawed, desperate fingers.

Oh God... they were all over her body. The realization made her gasp for breath. Do leeches move like that? Her skin crawled with the sensation of the slimy creatures, their squirming, embedding themselves into her flesh, adding to her horror. This was an alien planet. Who knows what leeches do here?

She willed herself to shift her focus. *Just get through this, Sonya. You can do this.* The muddy bog sloshed beneath her bare feet, each step feeling like she was sinking deeper into this nightmarish reality.

Up ahead, through the hanging branches and trunks of tall trees, she spotted a distant light. The sight gave her a momentary glimmer of hope amid the overwhelming dread. Maybe there, she could get some answers... find a way to escape.

"Keep moving," barked the pirate who was now dragging

her. She could sense a desperation in his voice. It wasn't just Bastion, even his underling pirates seemed on edge... who were now arguing amongst themselves.

Sonya needed to exploit their disarray. Bastion was terrified of something or someone. She needed to find out why and use it to her advantage.

"What's wrong, Bastion? Just figuring out that Trent's an even bigger, lying, deceitful scoundrel than you?"

He didn't answer but she could see the shadow of him, slogging through the brackish water. He stiffened; Sonya had hit a nerve.

"Just admit it, the real men have come for that precious treasure... they're taking it right from under your nose," she sneered, her voice ragged, pushing through the fear and exhaustion.

He abruptly turned to face her. She watched Bastion's eyes widen with a fusion of shock, anger, and hatred. "Shut up, Sonya. You know nothing," he spat, but his fear was palpable.

They continued through the swampy terrain, the stench of rot and decay growing stronger with each step. The humidity clung to her like an oppressive pall. And to add insult to injury, her wet nightgown, now tattered and drenched in filth, left nothing to the imagination. The pirates' leering eyes fixed on her hungrily, but she didn't care. She focused on Bastion, who was practically quaking with terror.

All around, the sounds of the swamp grew louder, an orchestra of menace. The buzzing of insects, the croaks of frogs, and the distant calls of nocturnal predators created a cacophony that heightened her sense of dread. The silhouettes of the willows, their hanging branches like skeletal fingers, swayed in the humid night air.

Sonya's senses were on overload. The ground squelched beneath her feet, every step a struggle. Her skin stung with bites, the muck seeped under her toenails, and the leeches clung to her, drawing blood. She could barely hear Bastion's orders through the din, but the urgency in his voice cut through the noise like a knife.

"Move it!" Bastion snapped.

Up ahead, through the maze of swamp water and trees, the light grew closer. What awaited her there was unknown, but anything was better than the suffocating darkness of the swamp. The pirates continued to bark insults at each other, their agitation rising. She had to keep pushing Bastion, had to figure out why he was so frightened.

"You were so cocky before, Bastion. What changed?" she taunted. "Scared you're in over your head? That you're not living up to your dead daddy's legacy?"

Bastion spun around, eyes wild with anger. "Shut up! Don't you ever mention my father again, not ever!" Out of nowhere came his back-handed strike—her head wrenched sideways as if being twisted from her neck.

Sonya, held upright by another pirate, saw spots dance across her vision. She fought to stay conscious, refusing to give him the satisfaction of seeing her crumble. Smirking, she pushed the pain aside with sheer determination. She needed to exploit his fear, keep him off balance.

"Is that all you got? Oh, right, you're just a little boy. Better leave the real beatings to your men."

Another pirate grumbled, "I still think we should've waited for Trent's signal."

"Shut it!" Bastion roared, but his voice had lost some of its venom.

Sonya's heart raced. There was his name again. Trent. It was impossible, but hope flickered in the back of her mind. But how could this be connected to her father? Her thoughts scattered as she once more was jerked along to move faster.

"I'm not liking this," another pirate muttered. "Something stinks about this."

"Yeah, it's you, dickwad," she spat.

As they edged nearer to the light, Sonya's pulse pounded in her ears. She hated being so clueless as to what was happening. Trent, the Desolate Blue treasure, and Bastion's growing fear—how was it all connected? Was it even remotely possible her father could still be alive? And if so, why hadn't he contacted her? Why had he abandoned her so many years prior?

It wouldn't be long now, one way or another, it looked as if she would be getting answers.

Chapter 42

Deep Space, Near Nylor-5
Oblivion

Captain Galvin Quintos

I awoke with a start, a frantic gasping intake of air. I tried to sit up—then a white-hot pain in my chest had me gasping again.

A hand came to rest on my shoulder, a woman's voice, calm yet firm, "Lean back, Captain. Breathe... slow, deep breaths."

My eyes focused on the woman now leaning in close, her gaze intense, perhaps checking the responsiveness of my eyes.

"Doctor Tangerie," I managed to croak out.

"Good," she said. "No apparent brain impairment. Time will tell though..."

"I was shot. I... died."

"Maybe. For a few moments. It was a ricochet, a glancing plasma bolt off the robot's back."

Confused, I took in my surroundings, my mind still cloudy. "I'm in HealthBay."

"Very good, sharp as a tack," she said.

Was she being funny? I couldn't tell. Then her deadpan expression gave way to a bemused smile.

"You're onboard *Oblivion,* Captain."

"I understand that... but how are you here?" I asked, then noticing others were milling about, a nurse wearing scrubs, another doctor, and several MediBots.

"You were out cold for two hours. Commander Strickland took over in your absence."

"'That doesn't answer my question."

"USS *Ike* was having a difficult time evading the arrival of the Krygian warships. Something to do with *Ike's* cloaking algorithms no longer being effective against the enemy's sensors. You'd have to ask Stephan for the technical reasoning. Leave it to say, *Ike* is now safely stowed within *Oblivion's* flight bay. Pockets of Krygian forces are still onboard, both organic and those menacing droids of theirs."

"Help me up, Doctor," I said, wincing from the pain in my chest.

"Absolutely not. You're still recovering—"

Her mouth snapped shut under my stony gaze. Swinging my legs out from under the covers, she took my hand, steadying me as I rose to my feet.

I glanced down at myself. A hospital gown with playful puppy dog prints, each tiny canine prancing across the fabric. "'This won't do," I said, still trying to get my sea legs.

TEN MINUTES LATER, I ARRIVED AT THE BRIDGE entrance, moving gingerly, but at least moving. The remains of Krygian combatants lay scattered across the deck, marking where they had made their last stand.

The auto-hatch slid open at my approach and MORROW's voice boomed down from above...

Captain Quintos on the bridge.

Heads turned in my direction, Commander Strickland extricated himself from the Captain's Mount. With one glance toward the halo display I could see that everything was relatively quiet here, no plasma bolts crisscrossing out in local space, no incoming missile icons heading our way. The bridge was devoid of loud klaxon alarms, or PA directives for *Battle Stations*.

USS Ike's bridgecrew was now here, taking up their respective posts: Crewmember John Chen situated at the Communications Station, Crewmember Thom Grimes, at the Helm Station, Lieutenant Earl Gray at Ship Operations, and Ensign Blair Paxton was manning the Engineering Station. Undoubtedly, they were all doing double duty—*Oblivion* was a massive ship that required a bridgecrew of twice, no, more like three times the size that currently manned her.

But it was the woman seated at the Tactical Station who had me doing a double take.

"Lieutenant Akari James, status on your recovery!" I said, heading for the Captain's Mount.

She offered up a reluctant smile. "Besides having to learn to walk like a normal person again, I'm doing okay... considering." She glanced down at her newly regrown lower appendages. "I'll have to replace the ink that had taken me years to acquire, though."

I nodded. She did love her tattoos. "In any case, welcome back to active service, Lieutenant."

Commander Strickland was now standing to one side of the Captain's Mount.

"SitRep, Commander. Tell me why there are no Krygian warships breathing down our necks at this moment?" I slumped into my seat, waves of relief washing over me. The pain in my chest had been boring into me like a relentless power drill.

Strickland narrowed his gaze, "You up for this, Captain? Heard you took quite the shot to the chest."

I waved away his comment, "Just a ricochet. I'm fine." I raised my brows, waiting.

"I would like to tell you we've jumped away from Krygian space, but that is not the case."

I shrugged, regretting the movement with a wince. "There shouldn't be any reason we can't manufacture a wormhole and do just that."

Before Strickland could answer, Ensign Blair Paxton, freckle-faced and perky, piped up instead, "You would think so, Captain. But it seems the Krygians have taken advantage of Tachyon wave tech. One of the few particles that can move faster than light, they've been dousing local space pretty much non-stop. Science Officer Derrota explained to me how the—"

I held up a palm. "That is more than enough, Ms. Paxton, thank you." I knew the over-achiever Chatty-Cathy could go on and on for an hour if I let her.

Akari toggled the halo display to a logistical view of the star systems. The seven Krygian warships appeared as red icons off our port side, all stationary, showing no signs of aggression.

Strickland let out a slow breath. "Before you ask, we don't know why they've paused their attack. Lieutenant James is busy trying to determine that now via *Oblivion's* sensor arrays."

"Okay, that explains one aspect... so why are we just sitting here and not taking the battle to them? This dreadnought should be up to the challenge."

Paxton looked to be chomping at the bit to answer, the smart kid in grade school, the one who sat in the front row, and had to be the first to raise her hand to answer the teacher's questions.

Without turning away from her board, Akari said, "*Oblivion* was sitting there at that shipyard for a reason. The Krygians were in the process of installing their own ship's AI. For one thing, MORROW does not speak the bug's language. Not a small issue when trying to make a warship operational."

"MORROW is still operational, I heard his voice over the PA—"

Akari now looked at me. "*Oblivion's* AI is no longer state-of-the-art cutting-edge technology. The ship's artificial intelligence, MORROW, has four layers of outdated quantum processors and archaic neural networks. The bugs were in the process of methodically deactivating the AI. What we have left is only the most simplistic layer still intact, that does basic ship functionality... like announcing the captain's entered the bridge or ensuring the ship's environmental filters are operational."

"So, *Oblivion* couldn't have manufactured that attempted wormhole earlier."

"Probably not," she said with a shrug.

I looked to Strickland, a cold sobering chill running down my spine. "Without a fully operational AI, we're totally screwed."

I purposely avoided looking at smarty pants Paxton.

"Stephan may have a solution," the Commander said. "One... you may not be all that thrilled to hear about."

As if on cue, Science Officer Stephan Derrota was now hurrying onto the bridge. His lab coat was even more rumpled than usual, his dark hair tousled. His eyes, looking bloodshot, locked onto mine before his face lit up with a wide grin.

"Ah, Galvin! So glad you're not dead."

"Me too," I said, exchanging a quick glance with Strickland.

"Um, when was the last time you got some sleep, Stephan?" I asked, concerned.

He stopped momentarily befuddled as if the question itself was one of science's most complex dilemmas. "I'll get some sleep when NELLA's fully operational."

"When NELLA's fully operational?" I repeated.

Akari chuckled.

Strickland cleared his throat. "Our choices were nil. We needed a ship's AI, and not just any ordinary AI. With what we're up against here, we needed the latest and greatest."

"He's right, Galvin," Derrota motioned toward the display. "While pulling NELLA from *Ike* would be impossible with our time restraints, we now have hardwired cable runs snaking throughout *Oblivion,* terminating into the flight bay and connecting to *Ike's* core. NELLA's been integrated into *Oblivion's* primary systems for almost an hour now."

"And you did all that in just two hours?" I asked.

Both Derrota and Strickland nodded. And it was then that I noticed the Commander's left hand—there was a slight, but unmistakable, tremor. He immediately flexed his fingers and shoved his hand in his pants pocket.

Cutting the man some slack seemed only fair—he'd just returned from brutal hand-to-hand combat with the enemy. Still, looking into Strickland's eyes, another battle seemed to be raging in his head. I'd need to watch the Commander closely.

Chapter 43

Sonya Winters

Each step—hers and the pirates'—made a squelching sound in the mud. Sonya's heart pounded as they *finally* approached the clearing. The humid air was thick with the scent of damp vegetation, and her eyes strained against the gloom. Blue lights glowed softly ahead, illuminating the silhouettes of two parked spacecraft.

Bastion hurried toward a cluster of shadowy figures standing in a tight circle. They greeted him with what looked like disinterest and vague hostility, making it clear he was a minor player among the group.

Coming to a standstill beneath a tree there in the muck, the mud still covered her bare feet like a hungry beast, threatening to drag her under. She needed to move, to keep walking before *something* decided to nibble at her toes. She took a step and then another, willing herself to stay unnoticed, even as the presence of silhouetted pirate forms loomed all around her.

As Sonya moved closer to the group, her breath caught in her throat. Someone mentioned *Land*.

She looked to see a tall, shadowy figure being addressed. Her heart nearly leaped out of her chest. "Dad! Dad! It's me! It's Sonya! I'm here... help me!" Sonya cried out, desperation tearing at her voice.

But her father barely acknowledged her—hadn't even turned to look at her, the neon blue running lights casting a faint illumination across his features. He raised a halting palm in her direction, his voice gruff and distant. "Stay where you are, Sonya. It'll all be okay."

Something felt off, dread gnawing at her thoughts. She inched closer under the cover of shadows, straining to pick up pieces of their conversation. Pirates around her paid more attention to the men in the circle, their interest in her waning. Bits of words floated her way, and the essence of their discussion began to crystallize.

"Land Winters, the man who has risen from the dead!"

She recognized that voice—*Chaplain Halman fricken Trent*. Excitement laced his words, as though he relished each second of their confrontation.

"Your reputation precedes you," Trent continued. "Now, let's dispense with the pleasantries and get down to business. The treasure within the Desolate Blue system—you have the coordinates, and we have the means to retrieve it. A mutually beneficial arrangement, wouldn't you say?"

The man she initially believed to be her father spoke, but his voice was all wrong. It lacked the warmth and depth she remembered.

"I've spent years keeping this secret, Trent. What makes you think I'd hand it over to the likes of you and your fanatical cult?

You were never a part of this arrangement. This is Clan business between us Briggans and Pylors, represented by the Thunderballs boy. There's no room for you here, Chaplain."

Her eyes brimmed with tears. This was not her father. The voice, the mannerisms—nothing added up. She focused on his features, now clear in the dim light, and her stomach churned. *What the hell is going on here?*

Bastion stepped forward, his assertive tone infused with desperation. "Please, let's all just calm down. There's more than enough for everyone." He seemed almost earnest, or maybe just hopeful. "Look, Trent is little more than a silent partner in all this. Do you have any clue how expensive a mining operation would be on that frigid, desolate planet? And why do you care how we bankroll it anyway?"

Bastion turned to Trent. "For shit's sake, Trent! You just show up here? You and I agreed that I would handle this. Can't you see that all you're doing is screwing things up?" He couldn't conceal his frustration. "This is our chance to reclaim what is rightfully *pirate bounty*—a chance for Briggan and Pylor clans to mend our ways and build something together. With this treasure, we can restore our power and influence across the galaxy."

Trent feigned a look of total boredom.

Sonya continued to listen, her mind racing. The imposter hesitated when Bastion addressed him as "Land." It became clear Bastion truly believed this was her father and saw this alliance as a means to further his goals. She was the only one here who knew the truth. Or, part of the truth.

The tension between the Briggans and Pylors grew, their murmurs rising. One of the Pylors stepped forward, clearly impatient. "Enough talk. We've upheld our end of the bargain, Winters. It's time for you to deliver on your promises. Give us the coordinates, and we'll make sure you get your fair share of the spoils."

The imposter's voice carried a note of annoyance. "You'll get what's coming to you, Pylor. But let's not forget who holds the key to this particular kingdom. Without me, you're all just fumbling in the dark."

Sonya weighed each word, piecing together motives and alliances. Trent, blinded by his obsession, believed in the imposter as a vital player in uncovering the treasure—unaware of the deception behind the man. Didn't he know Pirates, driven by greed and power, would side with whoever promised the biggest bounty—*Idiot*. While Bastion, eager to claim his birthright, had thrown himself in with Trent for backing. They were all scoundrels and deserved each other.

The conversation grew increasingly heated, factions vying for control and leverage. Sonya noted the fidgety pirates placing their hands on weapons, ready to take action. When it seemed like everything was about to boil over, a flash of movement drew her eyes.

Trent whipped out a knife in a blur, pressing its point under the imposter's chin. The Chaplain's voice was soft, almost friendly, but laden with menace. "You have five seconds to give me the exact coordinates of the chrysoberyl deposits."

Alarm shot through Sonya. Trent knew about her father's Alexandrite but not the location. The imposter's composure faltered, bluster evaporating under the knife's threat. No, this absolutely wasn't her father. The man looked almost fragile now, terrified, as blood trickled down his neck, stammering and sputtering.

"Please! I'm not Land Winters!" he admitted, eyes wide with terror.

"Then you are of no use to anyone," Trent said, pressing the blade farther into the folds of the man's chin.

"Wait! I'm the only one who can get you that treasure!" The imposter cried out.

Bastion's eyes widened with a mix of confusion and fury. "I'll kill him myself!" His voice trembled with rage as he lunged at the imposter. Trent's men intercepted him, locking his arms and dragging him back. Bastion struggled, thrashing and kicking, trying to break free.

The fraudster—still being held at knifepoint by Trent—tore his gaze away from Bastion who was still flailing in front of him. He strained, trying—impossibly—to make eye contact with the Chaplain. Then he lowered his voice, pleading for his life, "Listen to me. Nobody knew Land Winters like I did. We were close. Closer than brothers!"

"Yeah, right," Sonya muttered, shaking her head in disbelief. "He never mentioned you to me."

The imposter raised an arm and pointed a finger directly at her. "She knows where it is... she's always known. Her father told her. He made her memorize the coordinates. I swear. She knows exactly where the trove of Alexandrite is located!"

Sonya's blood ran cold. All eyes turned to her, and the night was pierced by the sharpened blades of silence. She crossed her arms over her chest, feeling suddenly naked within her clinging wet nightgown. The pirates advanced with predatory intent. She felt the weight of their gaze and the burden of her father's secrets pressing down on her. The game had changed, and what —now she was the linchpin?

Every muscle screamed at her to run, but there was nowhere to go. She steeled herself, locking eyes with the imposter. A mix of fear and defiance churned in her chest. She couldn't let them see her break.

Pylor and Briggan pirates began circling closer, their hunger for the treasure barely contained in their eyes. She had no idea what the imposter was eluding to. If she knew the coordinates of that fabled treasure, she'd remember.

Bastion's expression was one of bewildered betrayal, realizing the scope of the truth he'd been kept from.

But before anyone could act, Trent's knife thrust upward into the imposter's chin. He let out a strangled cry. The Chaplain pulled his knife free, letting the man slump to the ground as his life bled into the damp bog.

"Time's up." Trent bent over and casually wiped the blood from the blade on the man's jacket. He rose and took several steps toward the girl, a grim satisfaction tugging his lips upward.

All eyes leveled on Sonya.

Bastion's voice cut through the night, tremulous with desperation. "You've memorized the coordinates? Is that true?"

Sonya took a steadying breath, feeling the press of danger all around. She weighed her options, knowing the wrong move here could be her last. No, she had no clue what the coordinates were, but they didn't know that.

They looked at her, the sounds of the swamp becoming deafeningly loud around her.

She forced herself to stay calm, to think not so much as her father would have, but how Galvin Quintos would—no one could be as sneaky and deceptive as that man... She needed a way to keep these thieves at bay long enough for... for what? A rescue? Unlikely. But maybe an escape—however slim the odds.

She took a breath, "You know... Chaplain Trent, you've been duped." She glared at Bastion. "You should have learned by now, never... never, take what a pirate says at face value."

Trent, now suspicious, eyed the younger man. "Tell me more, girl."

She huffed, "There was never just one mining deposit. There were three. Two smaller ones on one of the system's worlds, and a much, much larger one on another world farther out within that Desolate Blue Star System."

"What?" Bastion barked, his voice cracking like an adolescent hitting puberty.

"Fine," Trent said, "then you will be giving us the coordinates to all three. And you'll do it now." He glanced toward the dead imposter, half submerged in the mud as if the bog was already claiming the remains as its own.

"You want the coordinates? I have them, but they're not... like in my head. That's hundreds of numbers."

Memorizing hundreds of numbers was well within her capacity, but she wasn't going to tell him that. She made a slack-faced expression that hopefully made her look dumb.

"They're stored within my personal cloud account."

Trent raised an eyebrow, skepticism evident. "And how do you propose we access this 'personal cloud'?"

Sonya fixed her gaze on Bastion, eying the tablet sticking out of his oversized pocket. "I'll need access to my NebulonCloud account. That tablet Bastion totes around should be fine."

Bastion frowned, reluctant. "No way. You're not getting a chance to call for help."

Trent nodded, agreeing, "Absolutely not."

Sonya remained calm, calculating. "You can watch my every move, every tap of my fingers. But there's no other way to get the information. First, I'll need to access the local Haven comms network, then my cloud."

After a tense silence, they grudgingly agreed. Bastion handed her the tablet. Both he and Trent stood behind her, eyes glued to the display, ready to intervene at the slightest hint of subterfuge.

Sonya's fingers moved slowly, deliberately. She pretended to struggle with the interface, grunting and mistyping repeatedly, each keystroke filled with visible frustration. She hoped it looked like the bumbling efforts of a total moron.

"For crying out loud, you're typing like a third grader,"

Bastion lamented with impatience. "Give it to me, I'll gain you access to the Haven network!"

Trent, however, remained vigilant. His eyes narrowed suspiciously. "Just hurry up and get it right. We're keeping an eye on you."

Unbeknownst to them, Sonya was imperceptibly writing self-executing QuansCode commands, utilizing her advanced hacking skills to insert lines of code that looked like gobbledygook to the untrained eye. She knew she had to act fast and under the radar, or her time would run out.

She gritted her teeth, feigning frustration. "There. I got it this time."

She spun around, "I'm not going to let you see me entering in my account password."

"What are you—" Bastion put his hand on her shoulder but she jerked it away with a bemused smile.

After some quick—deliberately fumbled—attempts, she nodded, turned back to them, and said, "Done!"

She had created a dummy NebulonCloud account within ten seconds flat. Ten more seconds and the display showed three encrypted files—each containing precise coordinates of distant, actual celestial bodies. She showed them the screen.

"Chaplain, you'll get the encryption codes to one location file. Bastion, you'll get the code for the other. But I can give you a quick peek."

Trent's eyes flickered with suspicion but, seeing no immediate threat, he relented. "And the Alexandrite motherload?"

Sonya paused, looking both of them in the eye. "The motherload stays with me until I see an upfront payment. Two smaller deposits first, then we'll talk about the final one."

She tapped at the display and the two encrypted files opened. Two distinct sets of spatial coordinates filled the screen. She looked at Bastion and pointed to the top set. "Your set of coordinates leads to a deposit of Star Emeralds near the southern pole of the currently *un-named* world." She looked at Trent, "The second set of coordinates is for a hidden cache of Silvano rubies some three thousand kilometers, northeast of Bastion's emeralds."

Both men leaned over her shoulder, scrutinizing the nonsensical numbers. Bastion seemed eager but skeptical. Trent's suspicions hadn't waned.

"Let's verify this," Trent ordered, reaching for the tablet. He was quick, but she was quicker.

"Not so fast," she said, keeping the device out of his reach. She made a few more taps to the tablet, then held it out to the Chaplain.

Trent immediately called over one of his minions, who snatched the tablet from her hand.

Fortunately, she had already cleared all her QuansCode subterfuge, while leaving behind one file with its one set of spatial coordinates—coordinates she was fairly certain were real for a small moon located within the Parolox 9 constellation.

The minion said, "There's only one set of coordinates here, boss."

She shrugged and looked to Bastion. "You want me to give Trent the coordinates to your hidden cache of Silvano rubies? It's up to you."

He glared at Trent, "Absolutely not!"

SONYA CHEWED AT THE INSIDE OF HER LIP—Trent's man had left, apparently continuing to cross-check the data within the confines of the closest spacecraft. Once again the swamp came alive with menacing sounds—sounds that filled her with an unsettling sense of paranoia. Had she successfully written the QuansCode commands? No time to double-check her work.

One wrong keystroke... she did her best to shove the doubts aside.

The teenager looked to the others and inwardly smiled. Subtly, there'd been a shifting of the power dynamic. While Trent's man would inevitably verify the authenticity of the coordinates, it would be the motherload—one that didn't actually exist—that would remain her bargaining chip.

She had only had time to program just one self-executing deep space call for help. One desperate plea to the one person she knew, at this very moment, was risking everything, even her own life, to save her.

Chapter 44

Deep Space, Near Nylor-5
Oblivion

Captain Galvin Quintos

I'd been wondering where Hardy was, how he'd fared battling the Krygian bugs out in the corridor. I expected he was making sure his extermination efforts were far-reaching.

What I hadn't expected was to see Hardy appear directly on the bridge, materializing right before my eyes. Quansporting onto the bridge was strictly forbidden, reserved for emergencies, due to both protocol and technological limits. Yet here he was, defying both.

Hardy's faceplate was a moving jumble of strange icons and geometric shapes. As if the 300-year-old robot built by the Sheentah had blown some crucial circuit that we'd never find a replacement for out here in the middle of nowhere.

Hardy said, "I've figured it out."

"How to fix your face?" Blair Paxton said with a deadpan expression.

I glanced her way, *not bad*—okay, my opinion of her just went up a notch.

Hardy's faceplate flickered and returned to his 3D John Hardy face. "I know why they're holding back from attacking us."

"How would you know that?" Derrota asked, looking a tad irritated—perhaps that someone else had uncovered a truth that he hadn't.

"I speak their bug tongue, remember? With Chen's help, we've been tracking their lightning-fast, ever-changing, multi-channel comms back to their homeworld."

I looked over to Chen, who hitched one shoulder. "A little side project... guess it worked."

"Damn good job, Mr. Chen," I said. "Excellent initiative."

"You too, Hardy," Akari said, seeing that the ChronoBot was being left out of the *at-a-boys*.

"So what's going on?" I asked, my patience waning.

"Seems we've arrived here at a most inopportune time... for the Krygians, that is. Every year, they enter what they refer to as, *the Birthing*. It takes place on the fifth planet—"

"Uh-uh, robot, this system only has four worlds," Paxton corrected.

"It's definitely not on any updated star charts," Hardy continued, "and there's a good reason for that. The Krygians would, and have, kept the location of this world that's a quarter light-year away, from the other four worlds, a heavily guarded secret."

"That's all fine and good Hardy, but why do I care they're celebrating some kind of alien holiday? This *Birthing* thing..."

"As we speak," Hardy said, "thousands of Krygians on those seven warships are glued to their displays, hoping and praying to get a first glimpse of their offspring. Eggs are hatching, and those little bundles of joy—those creepy crawlies—are emerging into the light of day for the very first time. Right now, they're watching with rapt intensity, like a stadium full of football fans packed shoulder-to-shoulder, awaiting the kickoff at the Superbowl."

Looking dubious, I said, "You have to be kidding. We're not being attacked so they can watch TV?"

Hardy nodded. "Seems their eggs only hatch during the light of day. Once the sun, well, Hekaton in this case, sets, they'll be ready for battle once more. That's in a few hours from now."

I set my gaze upon Derrota. "And... can we expect NELLA to be operational prior to the setting of that Hekaton sun?"

My Science Officer got to his feet looking unsure. "I best get back to my lab. Hardy, if you'd be so kind, I could use your help."

I called after him, "You didn't answer my question, Stephan!"

As it turned out, the unanswered question was mute—NELLA became operational just in time, but barely. But my doubts about the AI continued to persist; I hadn't trusted it aboard *Ike*, and I trusted it even less here.

Oblivion's bridge was a hubbub of tension and activity, a whirlwind of coordinated chaos. My eyes darted from the halo display to my bridgecrew, my mind racing with calculations and contingencies. I needed to keep NELLA's operational quirks from gnawing at the back of my mind; she was all we had.

Thanks to Derrota, and under Hardy's watchful eye, Z9 had been cobbled back together—generous strips of duct tape evident. The droid was now back keeping vigil, scrutinizing NELLA's every action.

"Captain, I'm seeing movement from the Krygian ships. Their propulsion drives are winding up," Akari announced from Tactical.

"Which of the *Oblivion's* weapon systems have come fully online and have properly interfaced with NELLA?" I asked, trying to keep my voice steady.

Akari's fingers tapped over her board, bringing up a small projected display. "We've got the Dual Pion Pulsar Beams, a few low-yield hydro-missiles, Phazon Pulsar Turrets, and the Nullifier Missiles. Those weapons are operational and synced with NELLA," she reported.

"Good," I said, somewhat relieved.

"As for shields, *Oblivion* has those Zero Entropy Deterrence Shields or ZEDS."

I nodded, "I recall... shields employing spider-quantum-nanites to continuously repair and enhance themselves."

I knew the tech had been cutting-edge several years back, almost too good to be true.

"The ZEDS are designed to disperse energy attacks," Paxton rattled on eagerly, "across a multi-dimensional lattice, effectively nullifying the impact—"

Akari cut in, "That and the shield's strength doubles during peak absorption, but there's a catch—NELLA is still stabilizing the quantum lattice. If I'm reading this right, we might get an hour, maybe two of full-shield functionality."

I nodded, absorbing the information. "Understood. Notify me immediately if there's any change. So, we'll need to take full advantage of that time."

I looked to Lieutenant Gray, eyebrows raised.

"Um, well... primary ship systems are all online, Captain. Engineering and Propulsion systems are green, life support is stable, HealthBay, as you well know, is functioning, Helm and Navigation are also green, while communication channels are operational and open."

"All right people, prepare for engagement. Helm, bring us about."

Strickland glanced at me, his eyes filled with skepticism and something else... maybe concern?

He leaned in, lowering his voice, "Captain, I suggest we give it another hour. Put some distance between us and those enemy warships. *Oblivion's* fast. Outrun the bugs until we better integrate NELLA into this Gorvian-designed dreadnought. You know, taking a bit more time to cross some T's and dot some I's. It could be the difference between success and failure."

I squared my shoulders, meeting his gaze. "Thank you for the speech, Commander. But it'll have to be now or never. We strike fast, catch them unprepared, or take the chance of being crushed by seven battle-ready Krygian warships."

He opened his mouth to argue but seemed to think better of it. His jaw clenched as he nodded in reluctant agreement. "Understood."

Again, I witness the man's inner turmoil. *Hold it together, Commander—we need everyone at their best right now.*

"NELLA, initiate battle protocols. All hands, *Battle Stations*," I commanded, feeling the adrenaline coursing through my veins.

Battle Stations...
Battle Stations...
Battle Stations...

Console displays throughout the bridge flickered with a myriad of colorful data readings, status updates, telemetry coordinates—everything necessary for this bridgecrew to do their jobs.

"Uh-oh, they know we're coming for them!" Akari announced.

The halo display was locked onto the Krygian warships, which indeed were readying for battle, undoubtedly powering up their own weaponry.

It happened within the blink of an eye. Crimson plasma bolts and rail cannon munitions began to fill the dark void of space as the Krygian warships made it clear that they were coming at us with everything they had. The deck beneath my boots shuddered as the first wave of enemy attacks struck *Oblivion's* shields.

"Return fire!" I barked, my eyes fixed on Akari's tactical display. Her hands moved with practiced precision, targeting the Krygian ships with the Dual Pion Pulsar Beams. The beams blazed, slicing through the darkness and cutting into the hull of the nearest Krygian ship.

"Take that you motherfu—" Akari cut herself off while glancing back at me with a sheepish grin. "Sorry Cap."

I stood up, needing to pace. Eyes on the halo display, the Krygian ships moved with chilling precision, their efficiency a testament to countless battles won. This insectile race, I mused, was undoubtedly accustomed to prevailing over their enemies.

I steadied myself, placing a hand on the back of the Captain's Mount, as plasma bolts hammered *Oblivion's* shields, overhead lights flickered and dimmed with each impact.

NELLA's calm voice cut through the chaos. "

Shields at 70% and falling.

"Damn it," I muttered under my breath. "Gray, give me a status report on why our shields are already shitting the bed."

Gray's fingers maneuvered his controls. "Captain, ZEDS are indeed degrading faster than expected. The self-repair function... Spidites, spider-quantum-nanites... they're operating too slowly to counter the onslaught. And now we're down to 60%."

"I need help on Tactical 2!" Akari barked.

"Hardy!" I yelled, not sure he was even within earshot.

A blur of towering metal moved past me. The ChronoBot took the seat next to Akari.

I looked to Grimes. "Helm! Bring us about, let's minimize our profile, put our bow to the enemy, not our damn flank!"

The ship trembled again as another volley of Krygian fire made contact. I could almost taste the metallic tang of fear mingling with the recycled air on the bridge.

From Gray's station, came an update, "Mid-ship shield breaches detected, power fluctuating across several decks."

NELLA's voice remained eerily calm, announcing each new failure with clinical precision...

Deck 23 breached. Atmosphere venting. Decks 15 through 18 showing signs of major hull damage. Engineering reports a partial containment loss.

A fiery explosion caught my eye on the halo display. The first Krygian ship had met its end, thanks to Akari and Hardy at Tactical. Finally some good news.

The ChronoBot was saying something, his big head, slightly turned my way. "By the way Cap... earlier today, I'd managed to track down a stockpile of Gravity Cores within a hold on Deck 5, let me tell you, those things are heavy... got several loaded onto HoverCarts. Then realized there were Armory droids just standing around with their thumbs up their respective keisters— well... leave it to say, I put them to work."

Only half-listening, I now gave Hardy my full attention. "Wait, what are you talking about? Some kind of munitions?"

His head bobbed as he worked Tactical 2's board. "That's what I've been trying to tell you, Cap. The bugs were in the process of installing their own home-grown brute-force cannons... think U.S. Space Navy's Broadsides but with a twist."

Hull breeches—
Decks 56 through Deck 58—
Atmosphere venting.

Oblivion was methodically being torn apart. Hopefully, none of my limited crew had been up on those decks.

My TAC-Band vibrated. I saw it was Dr. Pippa Tangerie. "Go for Captain."

"Yes, Captain... I know you have your hands full..."

"Just get to it, Doctor," I barked.

"It's the Marines... they're..."

"What about the Marines?"

"They're here. Max, Ham, Hock—"

"I know who the Marines are, what about them?" I barked, getting more annoyed by the moment.

"They're all here in HealthBay. I'm not sure if it's strictly neurological issues... but it's also, I don't know... maybe psychological too. And with Grip attempting suicide—"

"Wait, what! Grip committed suicide? Is he—"

"Not committed, attempted. He's alive and stable," she said from the projection on my TAC-Band, but concern filled her eyes.

My mind spun, unable to process everything amidst a raging battle that threatened to be our last.

I yelled over to Grimes, "Get us out of here, Helm! Hard to port, pedal to the metal!"

Pippa Tangerie's projected image looked back at me from my TAC-Band.

"I'm not sure what you want me to do, Doctor. Maybe they caught a bug down on the surface. You'll have to figure it out—Captain out." I cut the connection.

Grimes was doing a masterful job, weaving *Oblivion* in between two enemy ships, while Akari let loose with port and starboard rail spikes. But it clearly wasn't nearly enough. We were taking far more damage than we were handing out.

"Go on Hardy... tell me more about those Krygian cannons."

"Graviton Siege Batteries are a nasty piece of work. Imagine medieval catapults, but instead of hurling rocks, they're launching concentrated glowing balls of gravitational energy."

I raised an eyebrow, intrigued. "Gravitational energy, huh..."

Hardy continued, "These babies compress gravity into dense spheres, like fireballs of pure gravitational force. When they hit a target, they don't just impact—they warp the very fabric of space-time around the point of contact."

The implications were staggering. "So, it's not just about physical damage..."

"No, no, no," Hardy said. "It's about tearing apart the target at a fundamental level. Ships, shields, even the space in between—nothing's safe from these gravity bombs. They're new to the bugs. So new, they've yet to integrate them into their fleet."

I wasn't sure why I was wasting valuable time on something that wasn't operational yet.

"And they're yet to be fully functional, right?" I asked anyway.

"No, they should be fully functional, they're just not integrated with NELLA."

"Hold on... " I said, "Can they be activated, deployed, whatever... here from the bridge?"

Hardy tapped at his board.

Akari was also now more than a little interested.

"Only two of *Oblivion's* Graviton Siege Batteries are loaded with Gravity Cores, one on each side of the ship. And yeah, both are bridge accessible, but, again, NELLA isn't configured to calculate trajectories, provide targeting locks—"

Impatiently, Akari chimed in, her eyes alight with enthusiasm. She looked to the Helm Station, "Hey Grimes, can you turn us 33 degrees to port so I can get a rough firing solution on that all-too-fast-approaching dreadnought?"

Realizing she'd overstepped—it's the Captain who dictates course changes. She cringed, glancing up at me. "Sorry, Sir."

Grimes looked at me for confirmation. I nodded, "Do it. Make the course change, Helm."

The ship convulsed under another barrage—rail cannon munitions tearing at *Oblivion's* bow.

Sparks erupted from a console to my right, followed by a violent explosion. Shrapnel-like shards flew through the air, forcing everyone, myself included, to dive for cover.

A smoky haze filled the air making it hard to see and breathe. Lifting my head and looking about the bridge, I was relieved to see no one was seriously hurt.

"Back to your stations people," I said, totally unnecessarily since that was exactly what my bridgecrew was already doing.

The klaxon continued to blare incessantly, a hellish underscore to a rapidly unraveling battle. If things didn't get turned around soon...

Battle stations...
Battle stations...
Battle stations...

I yelled, "Dammit, NELLA, we're already at battle stations, shut the fuck up!"

Thankfully, nobody reacted to my inappropriate outburst. I needed to get a grip. The hovering dark cloud of smoke was like a grim harbinger of our fast-approaching fate—we'd been outgunned and outmaneuvered. Hell, we'd been outmatched from the start, and I'd been too pigheaded to notice.

As if reading my thoughts, Strickland said, "Permission to ready *Ike*, for possible evac, Captain?"

Multiple shield failures detected.
Decks 12 and 13, critical breaches.

"Go, Commander," I said.

Oblivion shook, the overhead lights blinked out—several moments later, the emergency lights flickered on.

Direct strike to *Oblivion's* reactor core—Drive
propulsion no longer feasible.

I clenched my fists, feeling the weight of every hit to the ship pressing down on me. We were losing ground fast, and those six remaining Krygian warships were closing in for the final kill. Then, as if mocking our desperation, NELLA's voice—still infuriatingly calm —announced...

Environmental systems have gone offline.

My heart skipped a beat. With everything else happening, soon we would be gasping for air.

Akari's head spun around to look at me. "I think I've got a shot, with those..." she looked to Hardy questioningly.

"Graviton Siege Batteries," he said.

"Fire at will, Lieutenant," I said, eyes glued to the halo display. "Just make every shot count."

The ship rumbled as the portside GSB cannon suddenly roared to life.

Boom! Boom! Boom! Boom! ...

Each thunderous blast propelled a colossal, glowing sphere into the void, resembling molten meteorites streaking through space.

Akari was now directly barking off course changes to Grimes—guesstimating all those intricate and complex calculations NELLA, or MORROW, would normally have been tasked with.

I watched, heart up in my throat, as now the other, starboard-side, GSB cannon suddenly came alive.

Boom! Boom! Boom! Boom!

More meteor-like fireballs streaked into the void. One enemy warship took a direct hit, then the other—Akari's aim proved devastatingly precise. Both Krygian ships erupted into brilliant white flashes—all-consuming torrents of destruction.

"Looks like the rest of their ships are bugging off!" Akari exclaimed, punching the air in triumph.

I let out a weary sigh, feeling the weight of the battle lift, if only slightly. There was no time to revel in our hard-won victory. With the Krygian threat temporarily neutralized, our focus had to shift to assessing our ship's damage and ensuring the safety of those still aboard.

"All right, people," I called out, rallying the crew. "I want comprehensive damage reports for every department. I need to know what's still operational, if anything."

I suspected *Oblivion* had sustained irreparable damage—

holding together just long enough for us to have secured this marginal victory.

Would Krygian reinforcements arrive soon, perhaps with a fleet or armada of warships? Almost certainly. The pressing question was whether we had enough time to set *Oblivion* on a delayed self-destruct, evacuate, and escape this hellish star system onboard *Ike* before they showed up.

Chapter 45

XO Gail Pristy

Pristy's TAC-Band vibrated as they neared the outer gate of the McMasters mansion. She glanced at the display and frowned, seeing a jumbled string of words.

"Something up?" Ryder asked as he noticed her frowning.

Pristy shook her head slowly, staring hard at the nonsense message. "It's just... odd. Here, look at this."

Ryder leaned over, eyebrows furrowing as he read. "Looks like TAC-Band spam to me. I get those... ignore it, just a bunch of gibberish."

She shook her head vehemently. "No—wait, look here."

Ryder sighed but leaned in closer as she began reading the words aloud, "Imposter. Trent. Alexandrite. Desolate Blue. Tablet. Erase. Betrayed. Danger. Help. Hurry. Ha—"

Ryder shrugged, a wry smile on his lips. "It's still garbage, Gail. Some random code of words. Means nothing."

Pristy huffed. "Are you purposely being this stupid? How many other Trents do you know? It has to be Chaplain Trent. And... I've heard that Desolate Blue reference before." She placed a palm onto her forehead, frustrated. "Where the hell did I hear that?"

Ryder lifted his gaze to meet hers. "Who cares? Let's just do what we came here to do."

Pristy took a deep breath. "Sonya had mentioned Desolate Blue, something about it being a pirate's tale of treasure—I don't remember the details." She locked eyes with Ryder, "This has to be from Sonya."

Ryder didn't look convinced, but at least he wasn't refuting what she was saying.

"I think Sonya managed to send a message. I don't know how, but this is too specific to be random. And this last word, that's cut off, Haven... that's got to be Haven."

"Okay," Ryder said, his tone shifting to seriousness. "How does that change things? What's the plan now?"

Pristy nodded toward the gate. "I guess it doesn't. We flag down a guard and get ourselves inside."

Ryder looked at her, dubious of that suggestion.

"What?" she asked.

"Earlier... on the way here," Ryder began. "Did you notice a ship of some sort pass overhead? Then a few minutes later, another one?"

"Not really," she said. "Why?"

He pursed his lips. "The first ship I thought nothing about, but the second, I noticed it had slowed, then engaged landing thrusters." He took several steps backward and looked up with narrowed eyes.

"What!" Pristy said, loud enough that a patrolling guard on the other side of the gate glanced their way.

They both ducked behind a manicured bush, just barely

avoiding being spotted.

"How about we *not attempt* to get inside that heavily guarded and fortified estate, and instead check out why one or two spacecraft had landed somewhere off behind it?"

"Now's not the time to run off on a wild goose chase, Wallace. A girl's life is on the line."

Tilting his head, he held up a forefinger. "Did you hear that?"

"No. And you're really starting to annoy me..."

"Shut up and listen!" he hissed.

Letting out a breath, she did as told but heard nothing.

Then she did. But it was faint. Someone's talking... maybe a few people talking. "So? There's a conversation going on."

"I heard Sonya's voice," he said. "You know how she speaks, that petulant, snarky tone she has. I heard it... I think."

Ryder spun around and headed down the street, stopping beyond the far outer wall of the estate. He motioned for Pristy to follow.

She joined him and tried to see what had so captivated Ryder's attention. "What am I looking for? All I see is a lot of trees and maybe some water."

"Keep looking."

Then she saw it too. It was far away, maybe a-quarter-mile's distance. Tiny blue lights. "You're thinking those are what, a ship's running lights?"

He shrugged, "Could be."

Pristy's nostrils flared, getting a whiff of something bad. Something foul. "You're not suggesting we march into that bug-infested, stinky, hellhole of a swamp are you?"

About an hour later, Pristy crouched low in the swamp, her eyes fixed on the eerie blue glow of the ship's running lights. Beside her, Ryder exhaled softly, rubbing his leg, and scanning the surroundings for any danger.

Pristy nervously took in the scene. Sonya was there—apparently the object of everyone's attention—in her clinging nightgown, damp and bedraggled, still somehow managing to exude defiance. Nearby stood several others—Trent, the unmistakable arrogant prick, and a handsome young man. Could this be the man Sonya was meant to marry? What was his name?

The name came to her—Bastion. There were others, too... a group of menacing figures, pirates no doubt, their presence looming over her like a den of mangy dogs, leering and hungry.

The sight of the dead man lying on the muddy ground sent a shiver through Pristy. She reached for her tagger. Every muscle in her body tensed, ready to spring into action and take down the threats surrounding Sonya. But Ryder's grip on her arm pulled her back.

"Stop," Ryder whispered, his eyes meeting hers, his expression cautious. He gestured toward the shadows cast by the dim lights. There, barely visible, stood numerous men, more pirates, lurking in the nearby woods. Weapons at the ready, they presented an insurmountable force against any attempt at daring heroics.

A mosquito buzzed near Pristy's ear, landing on her neck. Without thinking, she slapped at it, killing the bug. The sharp smack echoed slightly louder than she intended. Ryder's glare cut through the shadows, signaling her to stay absolutely still. His Are you *crazy?* expression left no room for argument.

Pristy wondered who the dead man was. Was Sonya next? If only they had arrived earlier.

. . .

A little over an hour ago...

Not long after they'd entered the bog, Ryder was striding out ahead of her in his borrowed boots, squelching in the wet mud. Pristy followed, trying to keep up while making an effort to keep to the drier patches. Suddenly, Ryder stopped in his tracks, a low hiss escaping from the marshland's depths.

Before she could react, a hideous, mutant-looking alligator thing lunged from the murky water, its jaws clamping around Ryder's left calf. Blood instantly spurted from the wound, while Ryder stifled a scream, his face contorted in agony as he tried to pry open the reptile's jaws.

"Oh God... Ryder!" Pristy hissed urgently, her heart pounding. She dared not make a sound that could attract further attention. "What can I do to help?"

Ryder's eyes were wide with pain and terror as he continued trying to pry open the seemingly locked-in-place jaws. Pristy, acting on instinct, grabbed a thick branch from the ground and jabbed it into the creature's side. The alligator shrieked, loosening its grip just enough for Ryder to wrench free. He stumbled back, clutching his bleeding leg, while the alligator slithered off into the swamp, leaving a trail of disrupted mud.

She rushed to Ryder's side, ripping her sleeve to fashion a makeshift tourniquet.

"Hold still," she ordered, cinching it above the wound while Ryder winced but managed a silent nod.

"We have to keep moving," Ryder muttered through clenched teeth, using Pristy's shoulder to haul himself up. But even the slightest amount of weight on the leg had Ryder writhing in pain. Every slight noise made Pristy fear the beast's return. It had taken a full hour for Ryder to be able to put his weight on the injured leg—hobbling along in relative silence they'd made slow progress.

. . .

THEY HAD FINALLY REACHED THEIR CURRENT vantage point after an hour of painstaking progress. Pristy adjusted her crouch slightly, glancing down at Ryder's leg. The tourniquet held, but blood still oozed, painting a dark stain in the moonlight. Their patience bore fruit as they observed the scene unfold before them.

Chapter 46

Haven
McMasters' Estate

Sonya Winters

Sonya shifted uncomfortably, her sodden nightgown clinging to her skin like an unwelcome, second layer. The oppressive humidity of the swamp seemed to intensify with each passing minute, amplifying the stench of decay and stagnant water. A half-hour had crawled by since Trent's man had retreated to the ship to verify the coordinates she'd provided, and the wait was becoming unbearable.

She could feel the hungry eyes of the pirates roving over her body, their lewd whispers mixing with the ambient chorus of crickets and frogs. A shiver ran down her spine, not from the damp chill of the night, but from the palpable tension in the air.

"Bet she's real sweet under that wet silk," one pirate muttered, just loud enough for her to hear.

Another chuckled, a low, menacing sound. "Maybe the boss'll let us have a taste when this is all over."

Sonya clenched her jaw, forcing herself to stare straight ahead, refusing to give them the satisfaction of a reaction. Instead, she focused on the delicate balance she'd managed to strike between the competing interests surrounding her.

Trent, the zealous Chaplain-turned-cult-leader, stood a few paces away, his eyes never leaving her. She knew what he wanted—power, pure and simple. The Alexandrite deposits weren't just a treasure to him; they were the key to expanding his influence, to spreading his twisted ideology across the stars. He needed those coordinates, and he needed them to be real.

Then there was Bastion, the boy who would be King. Sonya's gaze flicked to him momentarily. He was pacing, his nervous energy radiating off of him. The failed marriage arrangement still hung between them, an unspoken tension. For Bastion, this was about more than just wealth. It was about proving himself, about living up to the legacy of his father, and securing his place as the future leader of the Pylor clan. He needed to unite the Briggan and Pylor clans, which meant leapfrogging over Admiral Arlington McMasters—a bold risk, if not outright foolishness.

The coordinates she'd provided were real, yes, but they led to nothing more than a barren moon, undoubtedly light-years away from any valuable deposits. It was a desperate gamble, but it was all she had.

Her eyes drifted to the corpse of the imposter, still lying where he'd fallen. A grim reminder of the stakes at play. She suppressed a shudder, remembering the cold efficiency with which Trent had ended the man's life. That could be her, if this charade fell apart.

"How much longer?" Bastion's impatient voice cut through her thoughts.

Trent's lips curled into a sneer. "Patience, boy. Verifying

interstellar coordinates isn't like checking your comms messages."

Sonya watched the interaction carefully. The rivalry between them was a tool, she realized. A wedge she could potentially use to her advantage.

"I'm sure it won't be much longer," she said, injecting a note of confidence into her voice that she didn't feel. "The coordinates are good. Your man will confirm that soon enough."

Trent's eyes narrowed, studying her. "For your sake, I hope you're right. I'd hate for you to meet the same fate as our friend there." He nodded toward the dead imposter.

Sonya swallowed hard but met his gaze steadily. "I told you the truth. Two smaller deposits, and the motherload. That's what my father left me."

"And why should we believe you?" Bastion interjected, stepping closer. "You've lied to us before."

Sonya turned to him, seeing the conflict in his eyes. There was anger there, yes, but also something else. A lingering attachment, perhaps? She decided to play on it.

"I lied about a lot of things, Bastion," she admitted, her voice softening. "But not about this. This treasure... it's my legacy. My father's legacy. I wouldn't lie about that."

She saw doubt flicker across his face and pressed him to her advantage. "Remember why our families wanted us to marry in the first place? To unite the clans, to share in this wealth. That plan might have failed, not what you'd wanted... but the treasure is still real."

She'd baited the hook, now all he had to do was bite.

Bastion's expression wavered, and for a moment, Sonya thought she saw a glimpse of the boy she might have known under different circumstances.

"You don't know what I wanted," he said.

Trent scoffed, breaking the moment. "Touching. But sentiment won't get us those Alexandrite deposits. Only cold, hard facts will do that."

As if on cue, the hatch of the nearby ship opened with a hiss. Trent's man emerged, datapad in hand, his expression unreadable.

Sonya's heart pounded in her chest. This was it. The moment of truth. She silently prayed that her hastily concocted plan would hold up under scrutiny.

"Well?" Trent demanded.

The man nodded slowly. "The coordinates check out, boss. They're real. Lead to a small moon in the Parolox system."

Sonya allowed herself a small breath of relief, even as she maintained her outward composure. Of course, they were real coordinates. She'd made damn sure of that. But they were utterly worthless, leading to nothing but an empty chunk of rock floating in space.

Trent's eyes gleamed with triumph. "Excellent. It seems our young friend here hasn't been entirely dishonest with us after all."

Bastion stepped forward eagerly. "Then we can move forward with the extraction? Finally, claim what's ours?"

"Not so fast," Sonya interjected, her mind racing. She needed to buy more time, to ensure her safety before they discovered the truth. "That's just one set of coordinates. There are still two more deposits to consider."

Trent's triumphant smile faded slightly. "You said you'd give us all the coordinates once we verified the first set."

Sonya shook her head, forcing herself to maintain eye contact despite the fear churning in her gut. "I said I'd cooperate. But I'm not stupid. Those coordinates I gave you? They're for the smallest deposit. A taste of what's to come. You want the motherload? You need to guarantee my safety first."

She could see the anger building in Trent's eyes, the tightening of his jaw. But she pressed on, knowing her life depended on it.

"Think about it. You kill me, and you lose any chance of finding the other deposits. The information dies with me."

Bastion looked between Sonya and Trent, clearly torn. "She has a point. We need her."

Trent's hand twitched towards his weapon, and for a heart-stopping moment, Sonya thought he might simply decide to torture the information out of her. But then he relaxed, a cold smile spreading across his face.

"Clever girl," he said, his voice dripping with false admiration. "Very well. Let's discuss terms. What exactly do you want in exchange for the remaining coordinates?"

Sonya took a deep breath, steeling herself. This was the moment she'd been working toward, the knife's edge between survival and disaster.

"First, my immediate release. No more threats, no more captivity. I walk away from here free and clear."

Trent's eyes narrowed. "And how do we know you won't simply disappear with the information?"

"Because I'm not stupid," Sonya retorted. "I know I can't run forever. But I want my freedom and a guaranteed share of the profits from all three deposits."

She glanced at Bastion, seeing the calculations running behind his eyes. "Think about it. With my share, we could still unite the clans. Not through marriage, but through a mutually beneficial partnership. Isn't that what you've always wanted? To bring the Pylors back to their former glory?"

Bastion nodded slowly, clearly warming to the idea. "It could work. We'd have the resources to challenge any rival in the sector."

Trent, however, remained skeptical. "A pretty picture you

paint. But I'm not in the habit of letting valuable assets walk away so easily."

Sonya felt a chill run down her spine at his words, but she forced herself to stand her ground. "I'm not asking to walk away entirely. I'm offering a partnership. You get the coordinates for the two larger deposits, verified and ready for extraction. In return, I get my freedom and a fair share of the profits."

She could see the wheels turning in Trent's mind, weighing the potential rewards against the risks. The pirates around them shifted restlessly, clearly eager for a resolution.

"And what's to stop us from simply taking the information by force?" Trent asked, his voice dangerously soft.

Sonya swallowed hard but met his gaze steadily. "Because you're smarter than that. Torture me, and you risk getting false information. Kill me, and you lose everything. This way, everyone wins."

The silence stretched out, broken only by the ambient sounds of the swamp and the occasional mutter from the assembled pirates. Sonya could feel sweat beading on her forehead, not just from the oppressive humidity, but from the sheer tension of the moment.

Finally, Trent spoke. "You drive a hard bargain, girl. But I'm inclined to accept, with one condition."

Sonya's heart leapt but she kept her expression neutral. "And that is?"

"You stay with us until we've verified all three deposits. Once we've confirmed the Alexandrite motherload, then you'll get your freedom and your share."

It wasn't ideal, but it was better than she'd hoped for. More importantly, it bought her time. Time for her distress signal to be answered, time to figure out a way out of this mess. Sonya knew freedom wouldn't come that easy. Nothing good ever did.

"Deal," she said, extending her hand.

Trent grasped it, his grip painfully tight. "Understand this, Sonya Winters. If you're lying to us, if these coordinates lead nowhere, your death will make our friend here," he nodded toward the imposter's corpse, "seem merciful by comparison."

Sonya nodded, suppressing a shudder. "I understand."

As Trent released her hand, Bastion stepped forward. "What about the Pylor claim? Our arrangement?"

Trent waved a dismissive hand. "Your clan will get its share, boy. Assuming, of course, that our young friend here is telling the truth."

Sonya looked between them, seeing the delicate balance of power, the competing interests at play. She'd bought herself some time, but she was far from safe. Every moment from now on would be a dangerous game of deception and survival.

As the group began to disperse, making preparations to return to the mansion and begin the verification process for the remaining coordinates, Sonya allowed herself a small, hidden smile. She'd done it. She'd survived, for now. But the real challenge was just beginning.

Sonya took a deep breath, steeling herself. She knew she had to be more assertive, to make them see her not just as a means to an end, but as an essential partner in this venture.

"Listen," she said, her voice carrying a newfound strength. "I'm not just some girl with information. I'm the rightful heir to this treasure. My father intended it as my birthright. This isn't just about coordinates; it's about fulfilling his legacy."

Trent's eyes narrowed, but she pressed on before he could interject.

"You need me as a partner in this. Not just for the coordinates, but for my knowledge, my understanding of what we're dealing with. Killing me or torturing me isn't just risky—it's stupid. You'd be throwing away your best asset."

Bastion stepped forward, his expression a mix of hope and

calculation. "She's right. This was always meant to be a partnership between our clans. Maybe... maybe we could still make that happen."

Sonya caught the implication in his words, the lingering hope of their arranged marriage. She didn't share that hope, but she knew she could use it.

"Bastion's right," she said, softening her tone slightly. "Our families had a vision. Maybe it doesn't have to be exactly as they planned, but we could still unite our interests. Make something greater than either of us could alone."

She turned back to Trent, her gaze unflinching. "And you, Chaplain. You bring resources, manpower. Together, the three of us could do what none of us could manage alone."

Trent's face remained impassive, but she could see the calculations running behind his eyes. "A pretty speech," he said finally. "But words are wind. I need guarantees."

"The coordinates are your guarantee," Sonya countered. "I've already proven I'm willing to share the information. But I won't be a prisoner or a tool. I'm a partner, or this doesn't happen at all."

The tension in the air was palpable as Trent considered her words. Sonya knew he would never truly let her walk away - she was too valuable, too central to his plans. But she needed him to see her as more than just a means to an end.

"Very well," Trent said at last. "You'll be a 'partner' in this venture. But you'll remain under our... let's call it, protection, until we've verified all the deposits. For your own safety, of course."

Sonya nodded, knowing it was the best she could hope for at the moment. "Agreed. But I want it understood - I have a say in how this plays out. No decisions about the extraction or the distribution of the treasure without my input."

Bastion nodded eagerly. "Of course. We'll work together, just as our families always intended."

Sonya gave him a small smile, hating herself for the deception but knowing it was necessary. "Yes, Bastion. We'll figure it all out together."

As the details were hammered out, Sonya felt a mix of relief and growing dread. She'd pulled it off, for now. The fake coordinates had been verified, buying her precious time. But she knew she was far from safe.

Trent motioned to one of his men. "Escort Ms. Winters to my ship. We'll make preparations to verify the remaining coordinates."

As she was led away, Sonya caught sight of Bastion—hope and sadness converged across his face; it pulled at her heart. She knew she had nothing to feel guilty about, still... she pushed the feelings aside. Survival was all that mattered now.

With each step towards Trent's ship, Sonya's fear grew. She'd seen the way Trent looked at her, the barely concealed lust in his eyes. It wouldn't be long before he came for her, she was sure of it.

Suddenly, the night erupted into chaos. A plasma bolt sizzled through the air, missing her by inches. Shouts and screams filled the swamp as an all-out battle exploded around them.

Sonya dropped to the ground, her heart pounding. Plasma fire crisscrossed overhead as Bastion and his pirates returned fire, trying to retreat to the safety of the trees. Trent and his men had taken cover, their weapons blazing in the darkness.

In the chaos, Sonya felt hands grabbing her arms. She struggled for a moment before realizing it was Ryder, limping but determined, with Pristy on her other side.

"Come on!" Pristy shouted over the din. "We've got to get out of here!"

They half-ran, half-stumbled towards a ship in the distance, plasma bolts whizzing past them. Ryder turned, returning fire, while Pristy covered their retreat.

As they neared the clearing, Sonya's eyes widened in shock. There, amidst the chaos, stood Admiral Arlington McMasters, flanked by a small army of pirates. They were making short work of both Trent's and Bastion's forces.

Through the mayhem, Sonya caught sight of Trent, bloodied but alive, scrambling up the gangway of his ship. Her eyes then fell on Bastion, held by two of McMasters' men. Time seemed to slow as she watched McMasters raise his weapon, pointing it at Bastion's chest.

The shot rang out, and Bastion crumpled to the ground. Sonya gasped, a wave of horror and unexpected grief washing over her.

"Keep moving!" Ryder urged, pulling her along.

They reached the ship—whose, Sonya didn't know or care—and scrambled inside. Ryder threw himself into the pilot's seat, his fingers flying over the controls. The engines roared to life as plasma fire peppered the hull.

As they lifted off, Sonya found herself drawn to a porthole. Her eyes locked onto Bastion's motionless form, growing smaller as they ascended. A lump formed in her throat. A feeling of relief swept over her... and something else... a strange, unexpected sorrow for the boy who might have been something more.

The swamp, the battle, and all its horrors fell away beneath them as they soared into the night sky. Sonya slumped against the bulkhead, exhaustion finally overtaking her. Now they needed to get as far away from this pirate's den as quickly as possible.

Chapter 47

Deep Space, Near Nylor-5
Oblivion

Captain Galvin Quintos

NELLA's voice echoed throughout the corridors and passageways of *Oblivion*.

ABANDON SHIP... ABANDON SHIP...

I felt my stomach drop as she repeated the alarm, feet pounding through the metal deck towards HealthBay. Inside, the entire Ops team struggled to get out of their beds. Commander Strickland, as haggard-looking as the others, was in the process of helping Aubrey—who seemed barely responsive, her face twisted with pain, eyes darting wildly in mania. The scene gripped with horror as the Marines, though returned to their human forms, exhibited severe distress. Tremors shook their bodies, pain etched deeply into their manic expressions.

I caught up to Dr. Pippa Tangerie, shaking with fury. "What the hell has happened to them!?" I yelled, barely able to contain my outrage. "What did you do?"

Ignoring my anger, she turned on her heel. "If you can't talk civilly, I'm not going to answer you." Her tone was icy, uncaring.

My rage exploded. I wanted to throw her out an airlock, launch her into the void for what she had done. Before I could act, Derrota burst into HealthBay, face red with emotion.

"Galvin, it's the NEOGENE technology," he said, his voice tremulous. "The same technology that had had such a detrimental effect on Pristy. While DeckPort tech and quansporting have been proven reliable, this genetic tampering aspect... well, it should never have been approved."

His words landed like a sledgehammer. Gail Pristy had been pulled back from some unknown quantum realm. She'd come back a different, genetically altered, version of herself— one that lingered on the brink of despair amid a whirlwind of physical and emotional chaos. So, what does the EUNF go and do? They harnessed that same deviant science to forge super-human, genetically modified, monstrosities! Now, these Marines, just like Pristy, have returned as damaged goods.

My anger crystallized, constricting around my throat like a steel wire. "When we get through this," I said to Tangerie, my voice a sharp whisper, "you'll be brought up on charges. Count on it."

Without waiting for her response, I hauled Ham up, getting beneath one of his thick, tree-trunk-like, arms; we headed for the exit. Chaos reigned and it seemed to take forever as Ham and I navigated *Oblivion's* long passageways.

Hardy's voice crackled through my TAC-Band from his location somewhere within Engineering. "Setting the ship, with what's left of MORROW, to start the self-destruct countdown."

Entering flight bay, *Oblivion* groaned. We raced for the

awaiting *USS Ike*. Cables that were snaked into the smaller ship were hastily being disconnected by panicked crewmembers.

We were on the gangway now but our progress slowed; I focused on putting on foot in front of another, straining under the weight of Ham. The pounding of boots drowned out everything else, as I trudged forward.

I spotted several of my bridgecrew hurrying past—I shouted over the din, "Get to the bridge! *Ike's* drives should already be winding up!"

I stumbled, straining to keep Ham upright. I saw that Strickland was being carried by Hock.

It was MORROW's voice now coming from the PA...

SELF-DESTRUCT SEQUENCE UNDERWAY— MINUS TWO MINUTES AND COUNTING...

Once inside *Ike*, I eased Ham down to the deck where several crewmembers rushed over to collect him. Looking back, I saw Hardy, the indomitable ChronoBot... the last of the crew to hurry up the gangway, Z9 close on his heels.

One minute later, as I entered the bridge, I glimpsed Grimes in the process of getting *Ike* lifted off the deck.

MORROW's muffled voice filtered in through the diamond glass canopy.

SELF-DESTRUCT SEQUENCE UNDERWAY— MINUS ONE MINUTE AND COUNTING...

The sleek Corvette was now picking up speed within the flight bay and heading towards the open bay doors. Holding my breath, I went perfectly still not tempting fate—and then, we were rocketing out into space, getting as far away from *Oblivion* as quickly as possible. Ten seconds later that one-of-a-kind, incredible, Gorvian-designed dreadnought... exploded. The resulting brilliant white flash may have been enough to burn retinas—fortunately, we were moving away from the explosion, not toward it.

Ike was suddenly being tossed about—a dingy navigating an angry sea—a wave of sub-space turbulence that had all of us desperately reaching for something, anything, to grab hold of.

I sagged into the Captain's Mount, the weight of the mission's cost settling upon my shoulders like leaden chains. Silence fell, broken only by Akari's restrained voice. "If you're interested... we're approaching the Krygian true homeworld."

"Careful, let's not tempt fate," I said.

"We should be safe at this distance, especially combined with the speed we're traveling."

Akari switched the view on the halo display—we were fast-approaching a distant, rust-colored sphere.

I leaned forward in my seat. How far can you zoom in, Lieutenant?

"Let's see," she said.

The feed zoomed in once, twice, three times... I was now looking at large, rustic-looking land masses—perhaps not so different from the rocky deserts of the western United States.

"Wait, I have one more zoom level..." she said.

As the greatly enhanced, zoomed-in view of the surface now filled the halo display, the bridge went eerily quiet. I stared in horror, my blood running cold. Before us lay an endless sea of moving jittering Krygian insects. Not millions or even billions of them—but trillions. They clambered over one another, a churning mass of insectile limbs and torsos. I had to turn away, the sight twisting my gut with revulsion.

"Oh my..." Paxton's voice quivered. "Someone please tell me they won't be heading to Earth in search of new territory..."

I closed my eyes wondering how many other worlds had already been infested by the Krygian. In truth, I didn't want to think about it.

Chen interrupted, saving me from contemplating that nightmare any further.

"Captain! Just received a deep-space transmission. It's from the XO. She has your niece, Sonya. She's safe. XO Pristy, Captain Ryder, and Sonya are currently making their way back to Earth."

We hope you have enjoyed **USS Ike - Quansport Ops** *from the* **USS Hamilton Series** *by Mark Wayne McGinnis. If you enjoyed this book, PLEASE leave a review on Amazon.com—it really helps! And to be notified the moment all future books are released, please join my mailing list. I hate spam and will never ever share your information. Jump to this link to sign up: http://eepurl.com/bs7M9r*

Discover more of Mark's exciting novels on Amazon.com

And stay tuned! The next book in the USS Hamilton series in in the works.

SHIP'S DIRECTORY
USS IKE

Top Deck (8): Command & Observation

• **Bridge (fore):** Command center with panoramic views of space.
  • **Captain's and Senior Officers' Quarters (mid-ship):** Strategically placed near the bridge.
  • **Weapons Turrets:** 2 Phazon Pulsar cannons positioned for optimal coverage (aft).

Deck 7: Administration and Strategy

• **Command and Control Hub (fore):** Centralized ship systems oversight.
  • **Meeting and Briefing Rooms (mid-ship):** Equipped for tactical and strategic meetings.
  • **NELLA's Core (Nano-cognitive Entity Logical Luminary AI):** Securely housed within a hardened ship's bunker. This command and control hub is dedicated to adminis-

tration and ship management, carrying out critical strategic and administrative decisions.

• **Weapons Turrets:** 2 Phazon Pulsar cannons with control access (mid-ship).

Deck 6: Medical and Science

• **HealthBay (fore):** Emergency and routine medical care, next to the science department.

• **Science & Research Department (mid-ship):** For exploratory, analytical, and experimental scientific work.

Deck 5: Recreation and Lifestyle

• **Galley/Mess Hall (mid-ship):** Central eating area for crew members.

• **Crew Lounge and Recreation Areas (aft):** For relaxation and crew morale maintenance.

Deck 4: Logistics and Armament

• **Environmental Systems (fore):** Critical life support controls.

• **Weapons Turrets:** 2 Rail Gun cannons placed strategically for defense (mid-aft).

Deck 3: Special Operations and Robotics

• **Quansporter Compartment (fore):** For specialized personnel and equipment transportation.

• **Ship Service Bots Hold (mid-ship):** Storage and maintenance area for service bots.

• **Symbio 4.0's Hold (aft):** Docking stations and control hub for battle-ready Symbio units.

Deck 2: Secondary Flight Operations

• **Flight Bay (top-mid-ship):** Flight Control and Maintenance (mid-ship): Support for flight bay operations, including refueling and repairs.

• **Weapons Turrets:** 2 Rail Gun cannons for ship defense during flight operations (aft).

Deck 1: Main Operational Deck

• **Flight Bay (bottom-mid-ship):** Core area dedicated to Arrow Fighter operations.

• **Barracks and Armory (mid-aft):** Accessible to the flight bay for rapid combatant deployment.

• **Main Engineering and Propulsion (E&P) (far aft):** Engineering hub and drivetrain of the ship.

• **Sponson Decks (Port and Starboard, Decks 1-3)**

• **Drive/Engine Rooms (Deck 1 aft, sponsons):** Contain the ship's two main engines for movement.

• **Maintenance and Repair Shops (Deck 2, sponsons):** Facilities for in-depth technical repairs.

• **Auxiliary Control Rooms and Backup Systems (Deck 3, sponsons):** Secondary control rooms and emergency systems.

General arrangements throughout the vessel

• **DeckPorts:** Consisting of four per deck, placed for optimal internal movement.

• **Escape Pod Bays:** (10) Evenly placed for access in emergencies.

—END OF DIRECTORY—

Acknowledgments

First and foremost, I am grateful to the fans of my writing and their ongoing support for all my books. I'd like to thank my wife, Kim—she's my rock and is a crucial, loving component of my publishing business. I'd like to thank my mother, Lura Genz, for being a tireless cheerleader of my writing. Others who provided fantastic support include Lura & James Fischer, Sue Parr, Charles Duell, and Stuart Church.

Check out my other available titles on the page that follows About the Author.

About the Author

Mark grew up on both coasts, first in Westchester County, New York, and then in Westlake Village, California. Mark and his wife, Kim, now live in Castle Rock, Colorado, with their two dogs, Sammi, and Lilly.

Mark started as a corporate marketing manager and then fell into indie-filmmaking—Producing/Directing the popular Gaia docudrama, *Openings — The Search For Harry*.

For the last nine years, he's been writing full-time, and with over 40 top-selling novels under his belt, he has no plans on slowing down. Thanks for being part of his community!

Also by
Mark Wayne McGinnis

Scrapyard Ship Series

Scrapyard Ship (Book 1)

HAB 12 (Book 2)

Space Vengeance (Book 3)

Realms of Time (Book 4)

Craing Dominion (Book 5

The Great Space (Book 6)

Call To Battle (Book 7)

Scrapyard Ship – Uprising

Mad Powers Series

Mad Powers (Book 1)

Deadly Powers (Book 2)

Lone Star Renegades

Star Watch Series

Star Watch (Book 1)

Ricket (Book 2)

Boomer (Book 3)

HOVER

-

Heroes and Zombies

-

The Test Pilot's Wife

-

The Fallen Ship

The Fallen Ship: Rise of the Gia Rebellion (Book 1)

The Fallen Ship II (Book 2)

-

USS Hamilton Series

USS Hamilton: Ironhold Station (Book 1)

USS Hamilton: Miasma Burn (Book 2)

USS Hamilton: Broadsides (Book 3)

USS Hamilton: USS Jefferson –

Charge of the Symbios (Book 4)

USS Hamilton: Starship Oblivion –

Sanctuary Outpost (Book 5)

USS Hamilton: USS Adams – No Escape (Book 6)

USS Hamilton: USS Lincoln – Mercy Kill (Book 7)

USS Hamilton: USS Franklin - When Worlds Collide (Book 8)

USS Hamilton: USS Washington - The Black Ship (Book 9)

USS Hamilton: USS IKE – Quansport Ops (Book 10)

ChronoBot Chronicles

Printed in Great Britain
by Amazon